Wild Animals

Also by Robert Sims Reid

The Red Corvette

Wild Animals

ROBERT SIMS REID

Carroll & Graf Publishers, Inc.
New York

First edition 1996

Carroll & Graf Publishers, Inc.
260 Fifth Avenue
New York, NY 10001

Library of Congress Cataloging-In-Publication Data is available.

ISBN 0-7867-0257-5

Manufactured in the United States of America.

98 97 96   5 4 3 2 1

This is for Lynette,
a real pal when the chips are down.

ACKNOWLEDGMENTS

Sometimes, it's fun to think that you manage to do everything completely on your own resources, but of course that's a lie. So once in a while, it's not a bad idea to thank people. First of all, Lee Scott, for taking me backstage, and not getting me into a mess like the one that happens to the people in this novel. And Al Baker, for some tips on bombs, as well as for advice in the past on Airborne. Jim Crumley and Rich Ochsner are both good friends from my two different lives, and both know how to administer a proper dose of attitude. Jim and Liz Trupin came through with great patience, and help on the manuscript. Karen Townsend was an excellent legal and spiritual adviser, and my late-night pal, Dominic, always seems to know just when to give me a call and a boost. I owe Scott and Gretchin Hibbard more than they can imagine their friendship, and for sharing Adel.

And finally, as always, my wife Gayle, the one person in the world who makes all this worthwhile, and gets a considerable amount of grief for her trouble.

"The most dangerous subversive is the one who never tells anybody what he thinks about anything . . . the one nobody guessed was there the whole time."

> *Thomas Cassidy,*
> *police detective, pulp novelist*

April

Chapter 1

The cramped road sparkles in the moonlight, a bright ribbon of decomposed granite winding through the trees. Along the creek bottom, a flat, narrow strip between mountains, the road bends to the left, then disappears altogether under the thick canopy of alder and cottonwood, which are just turning green in late April. Higher up, along the flanks of the mountains, that same green repeats itself in new tamarack needles.

After dark, you would not know at first that there was anything out there. Anything but forest, that is, forest and the creek, and rounded granite boulders. And animals. Big animals, like deer and elk, bears, lions. Perhaps sheep. A rare renegade wolf. Moose. Porcupines and weasels too. Wolverines. And birds. More animals than you can imagine, their eyes caught now and then in the headlights of a pickup truck, that swing from side to side as the truck grinds its way up the twisting road.

Abruptly, the lights flick out and the truck glides to a stop. A bright cigarette stub arcs through the darkness outside the driver's window, then lands on the road amid a tiny shower of sparks. Moments later, the noise of engine and tires is replaced by the soft crackle of boots moving over crushed rock past the smoldering cigarette, the rhythmic huff of a man who is maybe out of shape, maybe nervous. Maybe both. The sounds of a man going someplace.

It has rained earlier, a light shower at dusk, leaving the air alive with that perfect blend of trees, early flowers, rain, fern, and rot. The light of the half moon filters through the clouds and forest.

Follow the man, and it soon becomes clear that there is some-

3

thing more out here than forest and animals, something waiting up ahead in the shadows. You can't miss it, there, behind a grove of shaggy ancient cedars. At first it would be the shape that caught your eye, a dark, thick box, angular and at odds with the texture of the woods. A geometric figure slashed among lumpy shadows. Then the glint of moonlight off wet metal.

And what do you make of it, that something else, the thing out of place? The helicopter. Long, thick fuselage crowned at each end by drooping rotors, which give the machine an attitude of exaggerated repose, as though the thing were asleep, and you could sneak up and touch it, then get away into the underbrush before green light begins to shine behind the cockpit glass, before the rotors begin their first tentative strokes through the damp, fecund air, and the thing comes to life.

Now the man stops, slips a heavy duffel bag from his shoulder to the ground, and pauses to catch his breath before getting down to business. Standing there in the moonlight, the man drains the tension out of his shoulders, first by letting his arms dangle heavily at his sides, ignoring the bulge of metal and leather that rubs heavily against the left side of his ribs as he breathes in . . . out . . . in, a deliberate act of composition, designed not just for relaxation, but for attention, as though if he tunes his body properly, he will be able simply to absorb the presence of any risks waiting out there in the shadows.

After several moments of meditation the man slowly lifts his hands and, gently, gently now, touches the palms together just below the point of his chin, all the while maintaining an attitude of exquisite concentration. Seeing the man standing just so that night in the forest, you might think that he had now lapsed into prayer. If you knew him, though, knew him to the depths that perhaps only three or four people still living had ever known him, you would sooner believe that the earth had gone flat than offer even the slightest speculation that he has come to this dark place to pray.

It was the groan of an engine from the lower canyon that awakened Henry Skelton, and the pain in his right hip that kept him awake. Squirming inside the sleeping bag, Skelton rolled onto his back and looked up at the sky, where a veil of stratus clouds rippled across the moon. It was still too early for any of the logging crew to be showing up, so when the engine went still, Skelton didn't think too much about it. A man and woman out knocking off a piece. Or a solitary drinker sleeping off last night's binge. Well, more power to them.

Skelton's right hand and forearm had gone numb as a club, and as he flexed the circulation back into his fingers, his hand at first tingled, then burned. At least the spring rains seemed to have broken for a while, so maybe he could pass the entire night in the open air on the narrow ledge outside the cave. Air that had never circulated through a ventilation system.

Quiet. Not silence, because the forest is full of sound, sound that is not noise. Wind drawing through the canyon. The rustle of serviceberry, mock orange, and chokecherry. The small spring nearby. Nocturnal animals nicking through the brush. Not like prison at all, which is nothing but noise, pure round the clock noise.

No doubt about it, open air was best. The cave worked fine in bad weather, but sometimes Skelton would start awake in the middle of the night, as though mashed down into himself by the damp stone walls curling around him, and he would feel in those moments like he was back in the joint.

Skelton closed his eyes again and tried to stretch away the pain in his lower back. He tucked his hands flat behind the elastic waistband of his polypropylene long johns. He breathed in and out deliberately, and watched the steam of his breath fade off into the sky. He closed his eyes.

In a few hours the loggers would roll into the bulldozed clearing below, less than a quarter of a mile away. That meant the start of Skelton's workday, too, because he had come to consider himself one of the crew. Everybody's got a job, the way Skelton saw it. There was the helicopter pilot. And truckers. Sawyers. Guys who set cable. Those were the official crew, the people who got paid. And then there was Henry Skelton. Skelton worked for free. He was the witness. The person whose job it was to see the whole calamity, and make sure somebody remembered.

The witness.

The wind was a little gusty, now and then swirling ashes out of the small fire pit, drawing them across Skelton and on into the shallow cave. By morning, Skelton thought, the ashes would be settled over him like dry frost.

There were several small caves scattered through out this part

of the canyon, all of them scooped into the seam between beds
of heavily folded limestone and the weathered granite intrusion
spilling up from the heart of the mountain. Skelton's cave was
maybe fifteen feet wide, ten feet deep. All of the caves contained
animal beds, but at the deepest recess of this particular cave,
Skelton had made the discovery that settled him here: tufts of
bear fur.

Stop here and listen.

He hadn't heard those words, hadn't actually heard anything
at all. It was more as though, upon finding the bear fur, some
kind of inexplicable new rhythm had shot through him.

It's here.

Gibberish, Skelton believed at first. Yet, when he shouldered
his pack that first day and moved on out, intent on climbing
higher, toward the tree line, that odd flutter struck him again.

Be still.

That was three weeks ago. At first Skelton resisted the prospect
of spending his time in the forest at a location overlooking an
industrial site. But as his visits to the cave continued, lengthen-
ing from stretches of several hours to several days, he'd gradually
become ensnared in something he could describe only as the
life of the mountain. He refused to call it mysticism—that was
too pat. It was though a cadence pulsed through all that rock,
and with that cadence came a sense of possibility that Skelton
hadn't known for years.

A week after Skelton's discovery of the cave, some guy from
the Forest Service trooped up the mountain to check him out.
Sent up by the crew boss on the logging job, because loggers
these days were always worried about terrorists. After that, both
Skelton's presence and his status as an ex-con were no secret.
He was encouraged to move on. He told the Forest Service guy
to go fuck himself. He was on public land, so there was nothing
anybody could do but bitch. That was one thing they taught you
in prison. How to learn the rules, and cut to the chase.

Nearly asleep again, Skelton was once more awakened by
noise from the lower canyon. A truck door opening, closing.
Skelton peeled himself out of the bag and padded quickly into
the cave to get his binoculars.

The business that followed was quick. There wasn't much
light, but through the treetops Skelton could make out shapes.
The helicopter. A rubber-tired skidder. Fuel tanks. A pickup.

Voices now, but he couldn't make out the words. He saw

movement in front of the pickup. Then the pickup's lights flashed on, catching a man in the cone of light. More voices, then the first man was joined by another, who stepped out of the shadows, apparently the man who'd just gotten out of the truck. Skelton recognized this second man as one of the loggers he'd seen on the job.

The first man carried a large, dark duffel bag in his left hand. Even from this distance Skelton could tell through the binoculars that he was big, with a barrel chest that seemed barely contained inside a dark windbreaker. For several seconds, the man stood absolutely still. When a gust of wind riffled the man's dark hair, the detail seemed oddly delicate on such a man as that. Though there was nothing really distinct about this man, Skelton knew that he could pick him out of a crowd.

Seconds later, the wind reached Skelton, himself a man of considerable size, and he gave up an involuntary shiver.

The voices became shouts, and when the logger made an excited gesture with his arms, the first man reached inside his jacket with his free hand, pulled out a gun. He motioned with the gun toward the helicopter, then followed the logger off into the darkness.

The voices stopped now, though Skelton continued to squint through the binoculars, trying to detect movement. When the first man next appeared, he was backing into the light, moving quickly as he brushed out his tracks with a pine branch. He still carried the duffel bag, but it flapped emptily against his leg. When the man got to the front of the pickup, he made a quick survey, then stepped to the driver's door, and the lights went dark. That was the last Skelton saw of any movement in the clearing.

Skelton shifted his attention to the road, figuring that the man had walked in from the vehicle he'd heard earlier. For just an instant, he saw the man run along one of the intermittent sections of road that showed through the trees.

And that was it.

Back to the clearing, where the helicopter gleamed dully in the moonlight. What the hell was going on? The intruder. The voices. All of it. And where was the guy from the pickup?

Skelton scarcely had time to formulate these questions, when his eyes seemed to erupt in a ball of flame. Immediately, he dropped the binoculars and squeezed his eyes tight against the flash just as the noise and concussion from the blast hit him.

"Jesus Christ," he muttered in spite of himself. "Christ almighty."

The fireball rippled into the sky like an expanding globe, but quickly burned itself out, and in the ringing silence that followed the last echo of the blast, Skelton could hear bits of debris settle back to earth. The clearing was speckled with a few small fires, but these, too, soon burned themselves out.

Skelton took a short step ahead, which brought his bare toes to the very edge of the escarpment. In a way that forever after would leave him quite amazed, he felt himself crammed full of the night. Abruptly, with only the flimsiest thought of what he was doing, he threw back his head and began to howl.

October

Chapter 2

Election time was coming around in about a month, and as far as anyone could tell, Merle Puhl's bid for the United States Senate was in the tank. Although Montana took up a huge geographical area, its population could still be considered rather cozy when compared with grittier parts of the country, where lobbyists, investigative reporters, and crack dealers prowled the streets with frequency, enthusiasm, and dazzling success. Even so, running for the Senate in Montana was no small undertaking, and Puhl had lashed out against every evil known to mankind. Nothing, though, had been able to disturb the current electoral snooze.

And why not? Football season was in full swing, and in just two weeks it would be time for elk hunting. Not that electing a senator wasn't important. The Constitution said you had to do it every six years, and people in Montana believe in nothing if not the Constitution. But Puhl was running against an incumbent so entrenched that people now called him simply "the senator." It made more sense to bet on the Buffalo Bills actually winning a Super Bowl than to bank on Puhl in the Senate. Even if you didn't get your elk, just trying at least got you a few days in the woods with your cronies, where you could get dirty and stink, talk about your boss and your wife—or your husband—with impunity.

But when Merle Puhl announced that the former president of the United States was coming to Rozette to help him get democracy back on track, more than a few people looked up momentarily from their box scores and hunting maps, and thought, well, maybe it's about time.

"You just wait till I get within earshot of that sonofabitch," Detective Ike Skinner was saying. As he spoke, Skinner fiddled with the strip of white adhesive tape that served as padding on the bridge of his heavy black glasses. "Far as I'm concerned, he's just another swingin' dick." Skinner, who everyone knew had recently been transferred into detectives because he was considered to be a hazard on the street, was talking about the former president. His tone conveyed a conviction that calling the former president a sonofabitch and a swinging dick indicated a degree of political savvy that commanded respect.

"You're right, Skinner," Thomas Cassidy said, "you tell him." Cassidy looked at Ray Bartell, then at Linda Westhammer, baring his teeth in a friendly manner before turning back to Skinner. "Play your cards right, Ike, you might even land yourself a job. Making license plates, maybe. Or do they make license plates in the federal pen?"

The four detectives were having coffee that Monday morning at the Green Parrot, a new restaurant along the Holt River about half a mile upstream from downtown Rozette. The Green Parrot was mostly a supper club that hadn't yet caught on with the breakfast crowd. That meant there weren't many other customers to be offended when the detectives started talking in loud voices as Skinner had just done. The loud-voices part wasn't so bad, but the subject matter only rarely achieved such a high plane as national politics. More often than not, the subject was sex crimes. Or crude stories about the job that gave a peculiar slant—sometimes sexual, sometimes scatological, often both—to almost every other aspect of life on the planet Earth.

In the past, the detectives' conversational habits had caused restaurant managers to ask them, in a very deferential sort of way, to take their morning trade elsewhere. Indeed, the list of restaurants from which they had not at one time or another been barred was fairly exclusive. The Green Parrot, on the other hand, still wasn't established enough that the management could do without the detectives' steady, if meager, business. If nothing else, the manager of the Green Parrot reasoned, the sight of a few cars in the parking lot could only help the morning trade. Despite this apprehensive hospitality, though, the cops weren't completely sold on the place, since the tables all had white tablecloths and flowers, and the coffee was overpriced, too. Bartell and his buddies compensated for the overpriced coffee by refusing to tip—not that they would have tipped even if the coffee were dirt cheap. But the sense of being out-classed by floral displays and starched linen was harder to resolve.

"This is a democracy, ain't that right?" Skinner said. "I can say anything I want to the guy. And believe me, I got plenty to say."

The former president was scheduled to speak at a Puhl rally this coming Friday. It was Skinner's fondest desire that he land a slot on the security detail, and from there finesse a private audience with the visiting eminence. Kiss the great man's ring, so to speak, then deliver up the gospel according to Ike Skinner.

"More guns," Skinner said. "More guns and less government."

"Christ, Skinner," Cassidy said, *"we're* the government. You want to put us all out of work?"

"We're not the government," Skinner said. "We're the cops. That's different."

Linda Westhammer looked at her fingernails, which were very long, and very red. "Hell, Skinner, you probably don't even vote." Like many women in the police trade, Linda had learned how to talk like she heard men talk. Men cops, at any rate. She came from a large family with many brothers, and had required few lessons in this regard. Linda was a compact, muscular woman, but not at all unfeminine. A stick of dynamite, some of the men called her, though never to her face, for fear she would detonate.

Skinner hoisted his eyebrows. "What's that supposed to mean?" He replaced his glasses, which made his small, beady eyes look large and round. "Huh?" He had black, oily hair, and hairy hands.

"Sure," Cassidy said, not wasting a beat. "They keep a list of everybody that votes, who they vote for. You're not on the list, you don't get to talk to the guy." Cassidy spread a glob of peach jam on an English muffin that was oozing butter. He had a round, boyish face, graying sandy hair, and the remnants of freckles under his eyes, which gave him the look of Howdy Doody with a hangover. Because Cassidy had been lucky enough to publish several sensational detective novels, he had a habit of trying to convince some people—people like Skinner— that he was smarter than they were. Just last week Cassidy was boasting about a fan letter he'd received from a humanities professor in Alabama about his latest book, *God on the Lamb, Satan in Chains.*

"That's right," Linda Westhammer said. This month her hair was auburn. To match the autumn leaves, she liked to say. "A list." She reached under the collar of her black silk blouse and discreetly adjusted the shoulder strap of her brassiere. "I even heard the IRS gets the names of all the unpatriotic slobs don't vote at all."

Skinner glanced at Bartell. "These guys hosin' me, or what?"

"No, Ike. No, they're on the level." Bartell really didn't care what Skinner might say if he came face-to-face with the former president. And he especially didn't care that Skinner was getting hosed by Cassidy and Westhammer. It was Ike Skinner's destiny to get hosed all the time by somebody. On his good days it was another cop, and not a criminal.

Skinner thought for a moment. "I mean, goddamn, I'm a life member of the NRA, that ought to count for something." Skinner jerked his necktie loose and unbuttoned his collar. "Politicians. Nothing but a bunch of maggots, you ask me." No doubt about it, his political acumen was completely irrepressible. He should be writing a syndicated column, perhaps even have a slot on talk radio.

Bartell smiled. There was a TV show he liked to watch, a show called *Hunter*. In reruns now. During the opening, after a bunch of shooting and car chases, the credits end with Hunter standing alone on a road high above Los Angeles. Mulholland Drive, Bartell liked to think. He'd never been on Mulholland Drive, but Bartell always had it in his head that if you wanted a vista overlooking the City of Angels, the kind of place where you could spend a few minutes thinking about life, then a storied street like Mulholland Drive would be just the ticket. Anyhow, this guy Hunter stares out at the smoggy, teeming city. He surveys the indescribable grime and sprawl, and a hard look settles over his already-hard face. A real cop face.

What, the viewer must wonder, is Hunter thinking at such a moment? What depravity is he trying to purge from his blood-stained soul?

Well, Ray Bartell had been a policeman now for over ten years, and he knew damn good and well what Hunter, the urban warrior, was thinking. *Somewhere down there,* Hunter grouses under his breath, *somewhere in all that horror of crime and bureaucracy, somewhere in this godforsaken city of millions, there's a decent place to have coffee.*

"What I'll do," Skinner went on, tugging at the hair on the

back of his left hand, "I'll just kinda badge my way past all the bodyguards, tell 'em it's police business, his mother died, something like that, and I gotta deliver the message—"

"His mother's already dead," Cassidy cut in.

"The hell," Skinner said.

Cassidy shrugged. "Last year. It was in the paper."

Skinner looked at Westhammer. "He hosin' me again?"

Westhammer lit a cigarette, one of those long, skinny kind made especially for women.

"Never mind," Skinner said. "But trust me, I'll tell the scumbag just what's what."

"Never happen," Westhammer said through a cloud of smoke. Her green eyes were like damp jade.

There were all kinds of special security requirements, of course, presented by the former president's two-day stay in Rozette. The Secret Service crew would be at the heart of things, but the local cops and sheriff's deputies could look forward to a variety of special assignments. Still, of the fifteen city police detectives, Ray Bartell was the only one so far to land a job that attached him directly to the Secret Service. Bartell's task, he'd been told, was to assist his Secret Service counterpart in identifying people who might pose some special threat. Proactive evaluation of potential sources of security breach. That's what Vic Fanning, the captain of detectives, called Bartell's assignment. Bartell called it the lunatic patrol. What the detail amounted to was doing local record checks, pointing out known head cases in the crowd, that sort of thing. Giving the feds a leg up on ferreting out the next Lee Harvey Oswald or John Hinckley before the shithead had the chance to get his rocks off. Bartell thought about expanding the scope of his duties to include morons, but that would mean he'd have to round up Fanning too. Not a bad idea, but administratively ticklish. He could take it up with the chief, except that there was a better than even chance that the chief was a moron too, you got right down to it. Christ, there was no end in sight.

Personal views aside, Bartell wasn't about to voice anything truly disparaging about his job with the Secret Service. Promotions on the Rozette Police Department were done strictly by seniority, and came about as fast as death from old age. So like most of the other cops, Bartell had trained himself not to waste any mental energy contemplating the impossible. Being a detective, though, was only a lateral transfer, often based on nothing more than administrative whim. Detectives had the chance to get inside the skin of things, and Bartell's desire to keep that assignment was just about the only leverage anybody on the department had with him.

Not that getting the transfer had been easy. During his early days on the department, Bartell was tagged as something of a golden boy. Then, one winter night seven, eight years ago, when he was still a new cop, and already angling for a slot in detectives, Bartell had been held at gunpoint by a fugitive killer named George Rather. After several fast moments of urgent negotiation, Bartell believed he'd talked Rather into surrendering. But at the last instant, Bartell's partner, Paul Culp, had ridden to the rescue and shot Rather dead.

In the days and weeks after the Rather shooting, Culp had been subjected to an exercise in departmental hero worship, while Bartell ended up being shunned as a goat, the one-time golden boy now an eternal rookie. His transfer to detectives, by all accounts a lock until that night, was shitcanned. For his own good, his bosses said. So the other cops wouldn't think he was running away from the street. Instead, they'd transferred Billy Stokes, hiding him out from yet another excessive-force beef.

In the aftermath of that winter night, Bartell soon learned that there was no course open to him but to remain silent and to persevere, no remedy for his condition save time and work. Several months later, though, when Paul Culp was killed on the job too, it felt as though time had run out. That left only work.

Despite his transfer to detectives two years later, Bartell still carried a bitter and risky secret from that earlier experience. How good, truly, was his ability to shape a dangerous situation by simple force of will? Tucked away in the attic of his memory, he maintained those few terrifying, frigid moments, when he'd faced a man who was certain to kill him, and brought that man to the brink of surrender. That night, however it might be interpreted by others, had infused Bartell with a sense of purpose that managed to be both defiant and restrained, an overall effect that sometimes left him feeling so earnest, he could puke.

Enough. Bartell studied Skinner's long, drooping face and tried to decide just how much territory the term *lunatic* covered. Finally, he said, "I was you, Ike, I wouldn't push this idea of democracy too far." Bartell was scheduled to meet Arnold Zillion, his Secret Service contact, later that morning. Maybe he could start right in by pointing out Skinner.

"No shit," Skinner said. "The goddamn liberals took care of democracy."

"Oh, Christ," Cassidy moaned, "here it comes."

"It's true," Skinner said. "When's the last time they executed somebody in this state? Huh? The last time you ever heard of somebody in the joint going all the way to discharge?"

"What do you care?" Cassidy said. "It's not like you ever actually sent somebody to prison. Right, Linda? Ray? Am I right?"

"Eat shit, Cassidy," Skinner said.

"Boys, boys . . ." said Linda Westhammer.

Again, Bartell's attention wandered from the conversation of his three partners. He was tired. He and Helen, his wife, had been late getting back last night from a weekend visit with his father on the Hillegoss ranch, a big outfit along the east slope, over in the Big Belts south of Cascade. Cash Bartell had been with Hillegoss for almost a decade, and a weekend of elk hunting with the old man had become the closest thing to a family tradition that Bartell had ever known. If, that is, you didn't count Cash's bouts of bottle flu as a family tradition.

Recently, though, the Hillegoss family had sold out to Brandon McWilliams, the tough-guy actor, and the big news was that McWilliams had divined that he would save the West by selling off all his newly purchased cattle and sheep. Buffalo, that's what Montana needed. Just get those buffalo roaming again, and everything would be all right. Cash was indignant as spit about the whole thing.

It also turned out that McWilliams's vision of the New West included making sure that none of the wild animals on his spread died from gunshot wounds. Bartell had decided to make the trip anyway, and compensated for the lack of hunting by going in early October, before hunting season opened, while the weather was still fairly warm and reliable. Luckily, he'd been able to choke down the warm glow he felt whenever he thought about all the enlightened rich people, people such as Brandon McWilliams, swarming into the state these days. All of them, praise God, with a plan to make God's country wonderful.

Cash was something of a jack-of-all-trades on the ranch, but mostly his job was handling the horses. He'd moved recently into a one-room cabin that belonged to the ranch company. Ray and Helen had slept in a big wall tent.

Bartell shook his head and sighed, remembering the look on his daughter Jess's face when he'd asked her if she wanted to go along on the trip. Jess was in high school, and sleeping in tents, she told her parents bluntly, sucked. Even with the possibility of glimpsing Brandon McWilliams thrown into the deal. Sleeping in tents with parents, she probably meant. And with your clothes on. He didn't want to think about that.

"So what's your problem?" Linda Westhammer said.

Bartell realized that she was looking at him. He sat up straighter and blinked once. "Just mulling over this Secret Service deal," he said. "It's an awesome responsibility, you know." Although he routinely made light of the situation, he was quietly excited as hell, hoping that the assignment might be a chance to eat in the dining room, so to speak, rather than with the rest of the help out in the kitchen. There, Bartell thought, he'd admitted the truth to himself. And the flash of heat that followed was a reminder that the lies you tell yourself are the easiest, and most dangerous, to believe.

Westhammer, making an arch expression, looked slowly at Skinner, then at Cassidy. Then she licked the tip of her index finger and touched Bartell's shoulder. "Tssssst!" she hissed. "I was right, boys. Definitely hot shit."

The waitress, an attractive, muscular young woman named Shawna, approached the table with a coffeepot.

"Not for me, thanks," Westhammer said.

Shawna smoothed a tuft of thick black hair away from her face and looked at the other three detectives, who also declined.

"I thought you were quitting this place," Westhammer said, smiling. Last week, Shawna told them she'd landed a new job as an aerobics instructor.

"Decided to keep two jobs for a while," she said. "Pay off some bills." Then, as she walked away, Skinner and Cassidy followed her with their eyes. Muscles rippled up the backs of her legs and disappeared under her skirt. Morning sunlight from the window to her right glistened in her thick, kinky hair.

"Whew!" Skinner breathed softly. "So tell me, Linda, what do you think of that stuff?" Since announcing plans for his most recent divorce, Skinner had been trying unsuccessfully to date Linda Westhammer. On good days, he managed not to drool. "Maybe you like that, huh?" Panting remained beyond his control.

"Fuck you, Skinner," Westhammer said.

"Promises, promises," Skinner said.

Maybe, Bartell decided, they'd been talking about sex crimes after all.

All in all, it was a hell of a deal. Here was a man, the former leader of the free world, who would soon be standing behind the podium at the Rozette Civic Arena, singing the praises of Merle Puhl, an old standby in the legislature who could be counted on to oppose just about everything that had transpired in government since the closing of the frontier. In private life Puhl had made a pile of money developing real estate and selling Chevrolets. Now Puhl was semiretired on a gentleman's ranch outside Rozette, where he had defied his frontier heritage and gone into the ostrich-raising business, an enterprise that turned the spread into something of a local attraction, the target of many weekend drives with Mom and the kids. People were used to seeing Puhl's ruddy face on TV selling used cars, so he must have decided it would be a comfortable jump for them to listen to him hawk the dual virtues of free enterprise in the heartland, and Merle Puhl in the nation's capital.

Puhl . . . the Chosen Man from God's Country. That was the campaign's tag line. You had to admit, it had all the resonance of *Tastes Great . . . Less Filling,* all the substance of *You Got the Right One, Baby.*

But the former president of the United States—that was something else again. Chances were, though, it would take more than a Dutch rub by a former president to transform Puhl into something more than his party's winner of the human sacrifice lotto.

Ray Bartell stared at his feet, which were propped on the edge of his desk in the basement of City Hall. He shook his head, trying to remember if he owned any shoe polish. He could use a haircut too. With all these high rollers coming into town, perhaps he should have invested more effort in making Vic Fanning's sartorial A list. He looked at his watch. Five minutes till his meeting with Arnold Zillion, who was driving over that morning from the Secret Service office in Great Falls. Zillion was new in Montana, and this was his first visit to Rozette.

Last week, Vic Fanning had briefed Bartell on the former president's complete itinerary. First, you had your arrival at the airport, followed by your motorcade into town to the Civic Arena. Then, after the speech that afternoon, the traveling road show moved out to Merle Puhl's ranch, where the former president would spend Friday night, maybe get in a photo opportunity with some of Puhl's great big birds before leaving at noon on Saturday.

Transportation and crowd control. That was the name of the game. Archie Phegan, the new captain of uniform patrol, was in charge of transportation. Puhl's ranch was out in the county, which made security there the problem of Sheriff Riley Saulk and his band of deputies. And Vic Fanning would see to it that the arena was well covered by detectives dragging down overtime.

But always, there was the potential for shitheads, and shitheads, whether the city or the county variety, were Ray Bartell's personal turf. While this was of obvious importance, Bartell was given to understand that among all the array of brass and juice, he was a grunt. Fine. A grunt on the lookout for shitheads. Perfect.

Across the office, Billy Stokes, another of the detectives, and Linda Westhammer, were both muttering into telephones. Ike Skinner was using his index fingers on a computer keyboard, mauling keys with all the finesse he would use to poke a drunk in the chest.

Bartell was thinking about phoning his wife, when Red Hanrahan walked in, carrying a thick file in one hand and a cup of coffee in the other. Hanrahan had been a detective longer than anyone in the division. He was getting ready for the start of a homicide trial. A nineteen-year-old kid named Trevor Kidwell was charged with putting a .357 Magnum against his estranged girlfriend's forehead and turning her into a cyclops. The girl's name was Julie. She was sixteen.

Hanrahan dropped the file on his desk. "This guy ought to hang himself in the jail," he said. Hanrahan was a loosely constructed man with wild red hair and a soup-strainer mustache. His green pants were baggy, and his shirttail wagged over his hips. His green-and-yellow necktie was crooked. Hanrahan slipped out of his shoulder holster, then hung the rig from a hook behind his desk.

Bartell was Hanrahan's partner on that case. The two often partnered, and Bartell suspected that it was Hanrahan who had successfully pressured Vic Fanning into accepting him finally into the division.

Bartell thought now about the sobs that had torn through

Trevor Kidwell when they interviewed him the first time. Julie, oh, Christ, Julie, how was he going to live without his Julie? Who would do this to sweet, pure Julie? From the autopsy, though, they learned that Julie had slept with somebody recently, and that somebody turned out not to be Trevor Kidwell. When confronted several days later with this nice morsel, Trevor Kidwell decided that perhaps sweet Julie might be a bitch. He also decided he needed a lawyer. His lawyer decided that Julie really was a bitch, and that this constituted a mitigating factor and entitled Trevor Kidwell to leniency.

"Guys like that," Bartell said, meaning murderers who whine and take you to trial, "they never do the stand-up thing." Even though he'd been Hanrahan's partner, they had worked together the entire time, so it was likely that Hanrahan would do most, if not all, of the testimony. And since Hanrahan was also the lead investigator, the trial was his to work.

Hanrahan swatted at his shirttail, then sat down. "Justice," he said, thumbing through the file. "It sure takes us a lot of moves."

"No shit," Ike Skinner said from across the room. "So many assholes, so few bullets."

Trial or not, the case was in front of Judge Randall Roper, Randy the Rope, and the smart money said that Trevor Kidwell shouldn't be making any career plans.

Bartell lowered his feet to the floor, sat up, and surveyed his desk. Paper. Nothing but paper, scattered all across his desk like the residue of a typhoon. Mostly burglaries, forgeries, and car break-ins. There were a couple of child-molesting cases too, but those had been around for nearly a month, and no matter which way Bartell tried to steer them, they were turning up inconclusive. The best thing about this detail with the Secret Service was that he could use it as an excuse to slough off the pile of trash on his desk.

Overhead, the plumbing from the upstairs men's room belched and strained above the low ceiling, and one of the long fluorescent lights flickered. Bartell gritted his teeth and waited. Someday, unspeakable ugliness awaited the detectives.

A moment later, Bartell's phone rang, and Vic Fanning summoned him into the inner sanctum.

As he sat in Vic Fanning's office, Arnold Zillion, a large, fit man in his late forties, clasped his hands behind his head and leaned back in the straight metal chair. Fanning, trim and brittle in his starched white shirt with French cuffs, sat behind his desk, while Lieutenant Frank Woodruff and Sergeant Sam Blieker, Fanning's two immediate subordinates in the division, stood on either side, like bookends. Woodruff, tall and aristocratic, with a pleasant, unlined face, adjusted the lapels of his camel jacket and stared straight ahead. Blieker, on the other hand, shoved his glasses up onto his high, wrinkled forehead, then began a series of shrugs and rumples, as though trying to rearrange his body inside his baggy brown suit.

Fanning introduced Bartell to Zillion, who leaned forward slightly and offered his large, soft hand, which Bartell shook briefly. Zillion had a crisp big-city air about him, a friendly, business-as-usual manner, which said he knew some things but wouldn't bore you with them unless it became necessary.

"I've been doing this job since the early seventies," Zillion said to Fanning, apparently resuming a conversation that Bartell had interrupted. "And I've always been lucky." Zillion laughed self-consciously. "Lucky enough to be somewhere else whenever there was bad trouble. No need to change the pattern now." Zillion wore a blue blazer, a pale blue button-down shirt, floral tie, gray slacks, and cordovan Bass loafers. His full brown hair, graying at the edges, was sprayed in place. "I'm sure Detective Bartell—Ray, is it?—I'm sure Ray and I will get along fine."

Despite the cynicism that Bartell felt toward federal law enforcement in general—an attitude shared by most local cops all across the country—he was struck again by that same flutter of excitement he'd felt when first informed of the assignment. Whatever grandiose designs Zillion, Fanning, and the other honchos might cook up, snooping around backstage at the big show promised to be fun.

"By the way," Zillion said, pointing to a large sterling-silver loving cup that sat prominently on a bookcase shelf behind Fanning. "That's quite a memento."

Fanning's pasty face flickered with a sign of life. "Competition shooting," he said, reaching back for the cup, which he handed across the desk to Zillion. On the computer stand to Fanning's left, the monitor displayed the vivid colors of a solitaire game in progress.

Zillion accepted the cup and eyed the inscription. "Combat courses?"

Fanning nodded. "Nothing but combat courses. That's the only true test. State champion three years running." Then, when he saw Bartell eyeing the computer screen, Fanning reached quickly for the keyboard and punched *Escape*. The screen went blank.

Woodruff looked over Fanning's head at Blieker and rolled his eyes. Blieker lifted a hand to the side of his face and violently scratched away a grin.

"I've got a cup similar to that," Zillion said, giving Bartell a sly, eloquently hasty glance. "From a tennis tournament in Palm Springs." Now he looked over at Fanning and smiled. "Almost the same size as yours." His expression was tight with false modesty, but it was clear from Zillion's tone that *almost the same size meant bigger*.

Testing the waters, Bartell said, "You play polo too?"

Fanning made a throaty noise that could have been a cough or a snarl.

But Zillion didn't mind playing straight man. "Not anymore." He passed the cup back to Fanning.

Bartell nodded sympathetically. "So hard to find a decent horse."

Ignoring the exchange, Fanning set the cup back on the shelf, then shot his French cuffs. Blieker lowered his glasses back down onto his nose, as though adjusting a pair of goggles for the work ahead. Bartell knew from experience, though, that neither Woodruff nor Blieker, both first-class detectives, would waste many words in Fanning's presence.

"Well," Fanning said, "down to business. Ray Bartell here is the best we've got," he said with too much conviction. "He spent a lot of years on the street, and now he's a top-flight investigator. Believe me, nobody knows crazy people like Ray Bartell."

Zillion peered up at Bartell. "Just by looking at him," he said, "I can see that if I ever needed a crazy person, Detective Bartell is the man I'd come to see." With this, everyone in the room—even Fanning—had a short laugh.

Bartell knew, of course, that there was bound to be a command post in place when the former president arrived. Fanning, Woodruff, and Blieker, along with anybody else in the department with any weight, planned to be there, and not out fingering asswipes in the crowd. Beyond that, Bartell's selection was surely nothing more than the luck of the draw. If taken to task, even Fanning would admit this. Like all bureaucrats, Fanning went to great pains to avoid singling out any of his subordinates as being more worthy than the rest to draw a choice detail. Not that work-ing social mutants could be considered choice. But the way Bar-tell saw it, being singled out for a particular job did amount to something better than just showing up Friday afternoon to stand around in the crowd and gather dust.

"We've talked this over several times," Woodruff said, "here in the office. To be honest, none of us came up with anybody we believe might really be a threat."

Zillion's voice was a model of patience. "I'm glad to hear that."

Fanning made a matter-of-fact gesture with his hands. "Of course, there're all these militia people who've been in the news lately. Freemen, some of them call themselves. Or constitutional-ists. One-world-government paranoia, black helicopters, all that nonsense. But they've never really caused us any confrontations. Not here in Rozette."

Blieker cleared his throat. "Since Oklahoma City, they don't really have time to act up. They're all too busy doing talk shows."

"The FBI works those guys pretty hard," Woodruff said. "If I were you, I'd check with the Bureau on those guys."

Zillion scowled thoughtfully. "Already done."

"Just the same," Fanning said, hustling to reclaim his city's place in the pantheon of mean streets, "anything can happen."

"That's right," Zillion said, smiling again.

"For some reason," Fanning went on, "this town attracts a lot of wing nuts. You know the type. Your bleeding hearts and com-plainers that don't really understand or care about what this country really means. Years ago, we kept files on all those peo-ple. Not anymore though. The sonsofbitches catch you at that these days, they'll sue your ass off. That's how far this country's slid. This is a free country, goddammit, and the one thing I can't abide is a bunch of malcontents who don't want to do anything but rock the boat."

Fanning's views on social dissidents were well known around the department, and to a large extent shared. A few years back, he'd advanced a plan that would have required all the detectives to be screened on their views regarding capital punishment as a matter of establishing their qualifications to work homicides. How else, Fanning reasoned, could the department be sure that a cop wouldn't shade his work, maybe even let some killer skate, just because he felt squeamish about the sentence that may lay in store? It was only after one of the guys in the shop, Bill Gaines, filed a grievance through the union, that Fanning's plan was shelved. A few months later, Fanning quietly shipped Gaines back to uniform patrol, telling everybody off the record that Gaines's work had been substandard for years.

"The way these punks operate," Fanning stressed to Zillion, "anything can happen, like I said. *Anything.*"

"But *not,*" Zillion said, "until after I retire. The trouble is that there are always nut cases in these crowds. And Ramrod always attracts his share."

"Ramrod?" Sam Blicker said

Zillion explained. "Presidents are assigned code names. The former president, he's called Ramrod And you're probably right, Frank. Most of the wackos are harmless. Still, local officers are always helpful in sorting those folks out. On the other hand, Captain"—Zillion crossed his legs and smoothed his tie— "there's something here in Rozette that has us a little more concerned than usual."

Fanning scowled, and fiddled with his cuff links, which were miniature gold replicas of bullets. "Yes?"

"Taxpayers," Bartell said. He felt the weight of four pairs of eyes slam into him.

Fanning opened his mouth to say something, but Zillion waved him off. "I like a man with a sense of humor," Zillion said. "Makes the interface that much smoother."

Interface. God, Bartell thought, I love it when they talk federal.

"Especially an upgraded interface like this," Zillion added.

"And just what is it," Bartell wondered, "that's put the upgrade on this interface?"

"Not a what," Zillion said, "a who." He covered his mouth with his right hand as he coughed lightly, clearing his throat. "A man named Henry Skelton. A terrorist."

"Good God, that's right," Fanning said. "Henry Skelton. The fucking bomber."

For a moment, the five men in Fanning's office eyed one another. Recent history told them all that bombs in America now amounted to more, much more, than lunatic aberrations or con-tract hits. The World Trade Center. Oklahoma City. The Unabomber. Today, bombs in America were a form of communication. And for those in officialdom who had the inside track on a celebrity bomber, there was almost certainly a warm chair waiting on Larry King.

Henry Skelton, Bartell thought dreamily. Why hadn't he realized on his own that Skelton would be on Zillion's mind? If Skelton didn't exist, somebody would have to invent him.

Chapter 3

When the helicopter was sabotaged back in April, the story was front-page news for several weeks all over western Montana. The entire Pacific Northwest, actually. Television crews turned up from as far away as Seattle, and print journalists flogged their stories right and left over the wire services. *Emblematic of environmental tensions through out the region.* That was the phrase, penned by some now-forgotten scribbler, that best summed up the event.

Law enforcement agencies of every stripe, always sensitive to political winds—though always declaiming that they were simple finders of facts—jockeyed for position out of the gate. Since the business went down on the National Forest, which was federal property, the FBI, Forest Service, Bureau of Alcohol, Tobacco and Firearms, all had a piece of the action. For all anyone in Montana knew, even the CIA had found a line item tucked away in its budget to finance a little Rocky Mountain travel. Bombs equal terrorists, isn't that right? And in the murky world of terrorists, who could say to what dusty or muddy foreign stronghold the trail of bread crumbs might lead? Who knew what questions some musky congressman or senator might ask one day in the oaken bowels of yet another Washington hearing? At latest count, according to one of the whatever-happened-to stories appearing recently in Rozette's local newspaper, *The Free Independent,* the federals had larded on three million dollars and change in their efforts to bring the affair to a satisfactory conclusion. And in this case, *satisfactory conclusion* seemed to amount to saddling Henry Skelton with the deed and riding him off into the sunset. So far, though, Skelton had managed to avoid even being herded into the corral.

Henry Skelton himself squatted on his heels that Monday morning in October and listened to the small, unnamed creek that was fed by a spring farther up the mountain at his back. He poured a last cup of coffee, then set the pot on a flat rock next to the small pack stove.

In the bulldozed clearing below, a red pickup truck pulled to a stop near the large twin-rotored helicopter that had replaced the one destroyed in the explosion last spring. Work on the job had come to a halt for a couple of weeks after the bombing, but now, with the exception of a security man at night, things looked pretty much back to normal. Well, not normal exactly, since the twisted wreckage of the first chopper still sat on that patch of bare dirt, where it had come back to earth after its last flight. Rather than clear away the remains, the crew had simply enlarged the clearing to accommodate the new aircraft. For all Skelton knew, the Forest Service had decided to leave the scorched hulk there forever, like some kind of ultra-avant-garde sculpture. But then, the Forest Service was about as far from an avant-garde outfit as you could get.

Skelton, while something of an interested bystander, to say the least, in all of this investigative meandering on his behalf, had nonetheless managed to maintain a sort of emotional equilibrium. If asked to describe his attitude toward the whole business, he would have settled on bemused. A man with less, shall we say, legal experience, might have been angry. Or frightened. Or both. Skelton, though, had constantly relied on the simple fact of his innocence, and it was only in this reliance, he supposed, that he could be considered truly reckless. So reckless that despite all the interviews and surveillance, all the hounding and warnings, he continued through the summer and fall to return to his canyon, his mountain. His cave. He'd left his smell on it all.

Across the way, the morning sun continued to inch deeper and deeper into the canyon, warming frost from the mountaintop and lighting the broad, ragged expanse of a clear-cut, an area of maybe eight hundred acres from which all the trees had been logged years before. Even from miles away you could see the gullies cut into the bare ground by rain and snow runoff. You could also make out the scorched remains of five large slash piles, where brush, branches, smaller trees, and treetops, all the residue from the old logging job, had been burned.

Below, Cradle Creek flashed intermittently through the cotton-woods. The cottonwoods followed the canyon floor until they gave way to cedars as the canyon narrowed and the elevation increased. The white road followed the creek. Farther up the canyon, the higher elevations were checkered with more clear-cuts, and countless roads zigzagged back and forth like sutures across the mountainsides. And finally, at the head of the Cradle Creek, loomed the huge, barren expanse of Red Wolf Peak, which rose to nearly eleven thousand feet, and separated Cradle Creek from Red Wolf Canyon, the next drainage north.

But it was the clear-cuts that kept grabbing at your attention. The clear-cuts always reminded Skelton of his bit at Lompoc. Or was it the other way around? Was doing time like a clear-cut slashed across the heart of your life?

Skelton took a sip of coffee, let it sit on the back of his tongue. Gone cold. He began to swallow, then spit the coffee onto the rocky stoop.

Once in a while lately there had been light snow instead of frost in the high country at Skelton's back. One night soon it would begin to snow for keeps. His sojourn ended, he would make the last hike of the season out to his pickup, which he kept hidden off an abandoned logging road about three miles to the east. Then he'd be able to spend more time back in town with Gina. Gina, who had waited through those months in prison, and now continued to wait out Skelton's obsession with this damned mountain. Waiting for Skelton. You thought about it, Gina had made it practically a career.

With aching nimbleness Skelton got to his feet and ducked into the cave. When he came out a moment later, he held a 7mm Sako rifle cradled in his left arm. He moved up the hill, then circled back onto the top of the limestone overhang above the cave, where he had a cleaner view of the clearing. There, he dropped to his belly and crawled ahead to the edge of the over-hang.

Shouldering the rifle, Skelton focused his right eye through the nine-power scope. He could just make out the contours of the right seat inside the cockpit of the new helicopter. As he watched, a man appeared from back inside the helicopter and fitted himself into the seat.

Moments after the explosion back in April, Skelton understood that he would undoubtedly be among what you might call your usual suspects. And sure enough, bright and early that next morning, as Skelton watched through binoculars, the crew boss pointed his finger straight up the mountainside toward the cave. Skelton knew what was coming, so he took time to stash the rifle and ammunition under some rocks well away from camp. With the felony conviction on his sheet, simply having a firearm was enough to buy him some more time. They made certain you understood that before they kicked you.

By mid-morning his camp was surrounded by half a dozen federal investigators, and when they finally came in, they took him down hard. No simple roust like the time a couple of weeks before. On his belly at gunpoint. Cuffed him up first, then started talking. Talked and talked and talked. Talked that morning on the mountain, talked for hours inside gray offices back down in town. Talked for days on end. Surprise visits to the house, teams of gray men in gray suits working the neighbors up and down the street, while he and Gina, mostly Gina, watched from inside their tiny house.

It was bad enough, he knew, the helicopter getting blasted. Even worse, though, was when the investigators found a charred body inside the smoldering hulk, and Skelton realized what had happened to the guy who'd stepped out of the pickup the night before. Rather than make the long drive back into town, one of the sawyers had decided to stay over, and now he was toast. So, while the bomb itself might have been more than enough cause for the federal cops to give him a good pounding, now they had a homicide on their hands, and they'd come after him with a real sledgehammer.

What were you doing, spending all your time on that mountain?
Camping. Hiking. Watching. Waiting. Nothing.
Nothing. Just nothing at all.
Do you want a lawyer?
Do I need a lawyer?
Guilty guys get lawyers. Assholes get lawyers.
Fuck a bunch of lawyers.
What group are you with? Earth First! . . . Sierra Club?
The humans, he guessed. He was a card-carrying human.

When he was finally named as a suspect in the news media, an "unnamed federal source" mentioned his prison record. Skelton was not pleased about this, but his anger was more for Gina's sake than his own. He knew what she'd gone through with friends in California, when his troubles started down there. Everybody was polite, Gina said, and oh, so supportive. Friendly enough, it made you want to toss your lunch. Why would things be any different here in Montana? She had a job as a registered nurse. She worked with doctors, other nurses, investing her hours in tending the sick and dying.

Skelton could have helped himself, he supposed, if he'd just told everybody what he'd seen. Told them about watching the lights snake up the canyon. Told them about the voices, the gun, the figure he saw standing in the headlights.

Sure, he could have told them everything. Dumped his guts right out there on somebody's desk.

But why should he? Although he was sorry about the dead man, he wasn't exactly displeased that somebody had the stones to just drive right in and take that helicopter off. Wasn't there a difference between murder victims and casualties of war? You bet there was, there had to be.

And who said they would believe him anyway? There was no evidence to say that what he saw was true, just as there was no evidence to say that he was guilty. He was simply *there*, that was all, a witness now in an unexpected bitter context. Why expose himself by saying anything at all? They'd just claim he was lying, then turn around and use that to jam him too.

We're taking this to the grand jury.

Fine, take it. Take it to the moon.

This isn't over.

No, it wasn't anywhere close to over.

Stay off of that goddamn mountain, you know what's good for you.

A warning that Skelton steadfastly ignored. The logging company took on their security guard, and Skelton entertained himself by skulking through the woods at night, spying on the old boy as he read *Penthouse* in the cab of his pickup.

Six hundred yards, Skelton thought now as he peered through the scope. What would happen if he lobbed a few rounds through that big Chinook helicopter down there? How would the steep downhill trajectory effect a shot? Hard to say until you tried it.

Maybe that's what he should do. Try it. Some morning just like this, while the logging crew was going about what they thought would be a perfectly ordinary day. Just for fun. He could pick a spot on the broad, smooth fuselage between the two drooping rotors, then start busting caps. See how the shots grouped.

But if he got too crazy . . . got *that* crazy . . .

Skelton continued to scan the clearing through the scope. There were maybe half a dozen pickup trucks now gathered, all parked between a silver-colored fuel tank and a large yellow machine, like a backhoe, but with a claw on the end of its long, jointed arm. This was the machine they used to load logs onto the trucks that hauled them off to a mill somewhere. Probably a mill in Japan. It was illegal to export raw logs off federal timberlands, but since when did the law have anything to do with it?

At last, Skelton took the rifle back into the cave, slid it inside his sleeping bag, and got ready to head out.

About fifty yards below the ridge top, Henry Skelton paused to catch his breath. Just ahead, the trees fell away, and the country opened into a broad, grassy park that saddled the divide. For the past half hour he had been climbing through dense timber, detouring several times to avoid being exposed to view from the air. Twice now, the Chinook had passed overhead into Red Wolf, then returned with a log dangling from a long cable. As always, Skelton had left his rifle behind in the cave.

Leaning against a thick larch tree, Skelton thought about his burning thighs. The day would come when his legs would no longer carry him up and down these mountains. If he were a primitive man—a concept he had come to feel uneasy about applying to Indians—he would walk these hills until his legs no longer served him sufficiently, and then he would die. Simple as that. Sure, others might provide food for him when he got old. And for a time he could substitute stealth for fading speed. Even so, there would always be a minimum pace demanded to sustain life, your own life, and sooner or later, if you were lucky enough to survive into old age, sooner or later you would be unable to keep up and you would perish.

Coyote bait. That's what Gina called it. Coyote bait. Crow food. Magpie meat. Gina had a lot of epithets for being dead.

Skelton had discovered Cradle Creek early the previous summer, when, after studying a geological guide, he'd driven up to spend the afternoon digging for quartz crystals, sapphires if he got very lucky. The surrounding canyon was on the edge of a batholith, and it was there that millions of years ago, when the batholith was still molten, water seeped into the mass, forming gas pockets. Then the trapped gases crystallized as the mass cooled into granite. Skelton wasn't under any illusion that crystals had mystical powers, as some people believed. But he did think of crystals as the mountain's teeth.

"I saw this other spot marked on the map," he'd told Gina that night. "So I checked it out too."

Indian burial ground. That was the notation Skelton had seen, and he had made a point of seeking out the spot. What he found was a small meadow, maybe ten acres. Just another meadow. It was about a mile upstream from where that gypo logging outfit later carved out the landing site.

Cradle Creek, Skelton came to learn, was one of the traditional routes used for centuries by the Nez Perce hunters, when they ventured east from what became Washington and Idaho into the valleys of western Montana, in search of buffalo.

Indian burial ground. That was all the map said. But what Indians? Nez Perce hunters? Or members of Joseph's band, who broke from reservation into Montana, in 1877? And if those dead were white, would the map read *White people burial ground?* Or *Cemetery?*

"Thick with grass," Skelton said to Gina. They were in bed. She lay on her belly beside him, her head turned away, near sleep. He played the tips of his sun-darkened fingers slowly up and down the small of her back, over her hips. "And ringed with lupine." The flowers were a perfect blue, like the sky directly overhead just after dawn. Skelton closed his eyes and thought about the lupine. He felt the sweat cooling on his shoulders, and he pulled Gina close again. "You'll see," he said.

Gina turned onto her side, and threw her leg over his thigh. "I can imagine," she said. She was a compact woman, with dense black hair, and eyes that were improbably blue. Lupine eyes, now you thought about it.

But Gina couldn't, it turned out. Couldn't imagine the strange way that Skelton felt drawn to Cradle Creek. The next afternoon, he drove her to the meadow. She said it gave her the willies. "A bone farm," Gina said. "Doesn't matter what race they are. Just a damned bone farm."

Maybe she was right. It was all pretty mush-headed, you thought about it too hard. Pretty California. And if there was one thing Henry Skelton had given up, it was thinking California. Nowadays Skelton was content to let his legs do his thinking for him. He pushed away from the tree and started uphill, reminding himself that he was still alive.

The Red Wolf site was still about a two-hour hike away. But within an hour he'd be able to hear the whine of the chain saws. If not for the Chinook, though, the site would remain concealed and unknown in the backcountry. As logging jobs went, this kind of selective, isolated cutting was considerably less damaging to the forest than more conventional methods, which seemed like search-and-destroy missions instead of what the timber industry delicately called a harvest. But the logging business, Skelton figured, was like cancer, most damaging of all when it worked its hidden way through the body. At least with exposed clear-cuts, you could take one look at the patient and tell she was pretty sick.

As Skelton neared the ridge top, the trees grew more stunted and windblown, the canopy overhead more sparse. For the last couple of hours, the helicopter had been crossing regularly into Red Wolf and back, so he stopped frequently and listened, making sure that he had time before moving across open ground.

"Idiots," Skelton huffed. He was thinking about those people who claimed it was a waste of money to use a helicopter, since the Red Wolf sale was in a remote area you couldn't even see from a highway. If there isn't a highway past a place, some seemed to think, and people couldn't drive by on their way to work, or on vacation, and see that the forest is gone—just fucking *gone,* then it's okay. A Forest Service bigshot even had the brains to suggest that this whole timber-harvest crisis could have been avoided if his predecessors had just been smart enough to eradicate forests without ruining the view.

And anyway, Skelton reminded himself, it wasn't the degree of cutting that had sent him into such cold fury. It was the—what? —the *invasion* it signified, the mechanical insult to something so important that he couldn't describe it without sounding ridiculous. Hell, go ahead, call it something sacred.

Skelton's legs were on fire, but he refused to let up his pace. Above his breathing, and the blast of wind drawing over the saddle, he heard the first rising wail of the chopper. Caught in the open, he forced his legs to run the last fifty or sixty steps to the crest, at the eastern margin of the saddle.

Skelton fell to the ground near a group of granite boulders. When he looked back down into Cradle Creek, the chopper was just rising into view. He scrambled for cover behind the rocks and wedged himself under a clump of juniper.

As the helicopter climbed toward him, Skelton caught some movement at the tree line along the lower end of the park, the area through which he had just passed. He looked closely at the patch of brown and realized that it was a bear. A moment later, the bear stepped completely clear of the trees and stood broadside to Skelton just over a hundred yards away. Even from that distance Skelton could see the hump at the base of the bear's neck, and he knew it was a grizzly. A big, nasty goddamn grizzly bear, and it was between Skelton and his camp.

His camp. Shit. Like that cheesy cave was going to be some kind of shelter from a bear.

But the rifle. That was something else.

No. He wouldn't kill the bear. He didn't want to kill the bear. That was the whole point.

If the bear now had Henry Skelton's full attention, the same appeared to be true for the pilot of the helicopter. As Skelton watched the bear, he noticed that the trees and grass around it were beginning to whip under a powerful, unnatural wind as the chopper descended to within forty or fifty feet of the ground and hovered over the bear.

Rather than run, the bear looked up, studied the machine, then all at once he stood on his hind legs, extending himself to his full height. The bear reached his forelegs above his head, swatting at the end of the cable that hung from the chopper. The grizzly's mouth was open. Skelton knew that the bear was roaring, but he couldn't hear it, not above the *thumpa-thumpa-thump* of the rotors.

A few moments later, the helicopter gained altitude as the pilot pulled away and dropped on over the ridge, heading for a load.

That left the bear. The bear and Henry Skelton.

After being distracted briefly by the helicopter, Skelton realized that while the machine might be an irritation and his ultimate enemy, an enraged grizzly bear was an immediate jolt of heaving life on the hunt.

When Skelton looked back down the slope, he saw the bear running uphill with sickening speed, chasing after the chopper. And heading right into Henry Skelton's lap. The bear's brown fur was thick for winter, and tipped with silver, which gave the bear a liquid shimmer in the sunlight as he moved.

Skelton took a very deep breath and began drawing farther back into the junipers, hoping for the best, which in this case might come down to being killed quickly rather than maimed.

But the grizzly pulled up short, lifted its snout to test the air. Then he shook his huge shoulders and ambled back down toward the trees, looking harmless now, like an oversized brown dog. Sure, a big brown dog with claws large as a man's fingers, jaws powerful enough to munch a Buick, and an attitude that was just that, a real fucking attitude.

Henry Skelton had to take a piss. He reminded himself to start breathing again. He closed his eyes. He tried not to think about how badly he had to take a piss.

Throughout the summer he hadn't seen any bears at all, to say nothing of a grizzly, and he had begun to have doubts about the meaning of the tufts of fur he'd found inside the cave. Some old scat, he'd come across that. But no living, breathing bears. Now maybe he'd been right after all. Maybe it was those caves, and the need for a place to settle in and sleep out the winter, that had drawn this bear into Cradle Creek.

Skelton was nowhere near an expert on grizzly bears, but it struck him as odd that one would venture into such proximity to the logging job. Still, he knew that it wasn't uncommon in the country north of Helena and Missoula for grizzlies to roam out of the Bob Marshall Wilderness onto nearby ranches. That happened, too, west of the Mission Mountains on the Salish-Kootenai Reservation south of Flathead Lake. It was a lot easier to treat *Ursus horribilis* like some sort of fragile icon when one wasn't charging up the hill toward you, maybe on the verge of ripping your guts out. Especially when you had to take a piss.

Had to take a piss while you're huddled in a clump of brush, scared to death of a giant man-eating beast that's between you and anyplace you need to go. Between you and your camp, you and your truck, your camp and your truck.

Skelton's teeth started to chatter from needing to take a piss.

Finally, the bear passed out of sight, his movements through the forest now completely unpredictable. Skelton eased out of the junipers. After relieving himself, he decided that his best bet was to cross the saddle, then get back into the sparse trees along the upper flank of Red Wolf Peak. From there he could make his way farther up into the canyon and loop down to his camp from above. At the camp, perhaps the lingering stench of the fire, along with the activity in the clearing below, would divert the bear to some distant part of the canyon. And if not, there was the rifle. Skelton didn't like to think about that, but he was getting closer by the second to seeing the rifle as not a bad alternative. He wasn't ready to be magpie meat. Not hardly.

The chopper would return soon, this time with a log dangling from the cable. All day the chopper would be crossing back and forth. With luck the chopper would keep the grizzly from noticing Skelton. Who knew, maybe the bear would even keep Skelton from noticing the chopper.

No, there wasn't that much luck to go around.

Chapter 4

Ray Bartell's daughter Jess, his only child, was going to be a senior in high school. *A senior in high school.* Bartell felt crushed by the weight of those words. Not long, and she'd be getting married. Married. God, who could imagine it?

As he drove toward home through the late-afternoon traffic, Bartell finally got sick of the cop chatter and turned down—but not completely off—the volume on the police radio. He remembered once reading the results of a study that said police work was one of the most behavior-modifying activities people could engage in. Whatever that meant.

Married. Married and moved out.

Married, moved out, and knocked up. In that order, he hoped. Grandpa Bartell. Now, there was something really behavior-modifying.

Behavior-modifying. From a study on policemen. Seemed like people studied cops about like they studied disease. What did it all mean? If it meant being a cop messed you up, well, there were days when Bartell could buy into that in a flash. In the abstract, people seemed to want their cops to entertain with vengeance and bloodshed, all manner of chemical, ballistic, automotive, romantic, and always violent mayhem and self-destruction. Sometimes, he thought, people deserved the kind of cops they so deeply fantasized about. Bartell was a rules guy himself. You don't break rules, you learn how to milk them for every drop of advantage.

Moved out, knocked up, divorced.

Divorced and moved back home.

Bartell pressed his hand against the thick file on the seat beside him. The Henry Skelton file. It was generally accepted among all the cops in town that Skelton had the lucky number in the great helicopter-bombing sweepstakes last spring, so it only made sense that he would be a Secret Service headliner too. Bartell knew from shop talk that Skelton fell into that group of suspects whose guilt was presumed because of the circumstances surrounding a case. On the other hand, Skelton couldn't be charged because the evidence didn't contain enough nails to hold the coffin shut. So, although it was nominally Bartell's job to work up the background on Skelton, everyone on the job understood that the real goal was somehow to neutralize Skelton until Ramrod had safely blown through town. The preferred solution would be to come up with some hook to get him into custody. But if months of investigation by the federal luminaries hadn't accomplished that, there seemed little chance that Bartell and Zillion could do the trick in a couple of days. Not if they wanted to stay legal themselves.

Yet, from the moment Arnold Zillion brought up Skelton's name, Bartell's excitement had begun a slow dissolve into anxiety. Over the last several years, Helen Bartell had taken up causes and committees. One of those causes was wilderness preservation, a topic that was guaranteed to send Helen scurrying for the nearest, tallest soapbox on the horizon.

Why not, Helen had once wondered, sponsor a great chain saw surrender? You know, like big cities were doing with guns.

Then what? Bartell asked. Melt all those chain saws down, cast them into some kind of New Age altar? And how might the opposition respond? What about drowning a sack of wolf pups in a vat of *latte?*

Helen was not amused.

While Bartell was actually proud of his wife's convictions, and even shared some of them, he also was not naive enough to advertise them around the police department. Vic Fanning aside, all police departments are by nature reactionary, and any social activism is viewed from inside the guts of those departments as profoundly subversive. Mother Teresa could save all the poor, sick people she wanted, collect all the humanitarian awards in creation—hell, she could even get herself made a saint—as long as she did it in somebody else's jurisdiction. After all the institutional camouflage that Bartell had donned to survive in the police department, the last thing in the world he needed was any institutional mistrust of Helen spilling over onto him.

When word of the helicopter bombing—and Skelton's role as the designated suspect—hit the news, Bartell's wife told him in short order that Skelton was being railroaded.

How did she know?

She knew because Skelton's girlfriend told her so.

Skelton's girlfriend? Helen was hanging out with the girlfriend of a puke?

Helen wasn't *hanging out* with Skelton's girlfriend. She simply knew her from some ad hoc antisubdivision committee. So did that make the girlfriend a puke too?

No, it didn't.

Sure it didn't. Cops thought everybody who wasn't a cop or related to a cop was a puke. It was a proven fact. You could look it up. But Henry Skelton wasn't a puke. Or a criminal either, for that matter.

Maybe. At least, maybe not since he got out of the joint, Bartell reminded his wife. After all the newspaper treatment, Skelton's record was no secret.

Helen always hated it whenever Bartell applied his cop logic to situations and people for whom she held sympathy. He didn't have any inside line to convince her that she was wrong about Skelton, and even if he did, he wouldn't have pursued it. The goods on Skelton were none of her business. And really, for all Bartell knew, Helen may have been right.

Over the police radio, a couple of uniforms were dispatched to remove an intoxicated Native American male from the Bismarck, one of the uptown bars.

"We've had him before," one of the uniforms said after the dispatcher broadcasted the man's name.

"Oughta hold this call for the animal warden," another patrolman said.

The comment made Bartell's whole body sag, and he shut the radio off completely.

Divorced, and moved back home with a kid. There he was, thinking blunt cop thoughts about his own daughter.

When he got home ten minutes later, Bartell found a pot of lentil soup on the stove and a note on the kitchen counter: *Gone to the mall with Jess. Home later. Love and kisses, Helen.*

The mall. Bartell felt the Visa card smoldering like boiling gold in his wallet, eating a hole in his ass. At the stove he twirled a wooden spoon through the simmering soup, brown sludge with chips of red carrots and green celery. Three or four years ago, Helen had changed jobs, left her position as office manager for a physician and surgeon and gone to work for Gabriella Fosdick, a woman who billed herself as an herbal healer, holistic-inner-child therapist, and counselor in general assertiveness strategies. The first time Bartell met Gabriella Fosdick, he introduced himself as a carnivore. He had seen barely a single steak or pork chop since, but the whole experience had taught him tolerance.

Bartell turned off the burner. Then he went to the phone and ordered a pizza. A big pizza with pepperoni, onions, olives, garlic, and extra cheese. And a pint of chocolate mocha almond ice cream.

Tolerance. Holistic assertive herbal inner childishness. Married, knocked up, and divorced. A behavior-modifying career to go with a behavior-modifying marriage. Last winter, Helen had even gone so far as to get him to quit cursing. To Bartell's surprise, he'd gone along, even around the other cops.

Fuck it.

Well, at least he'd gone along as far as what he *said*. What he *thought* was something else. Quit cursing inside your head, he believed, and before long you lost track of your perspective on life. Your edge. Your humility. The whole goddamned thing.

Bartell went to the refrigerator and got a beer, then sat down at the breakfast counter and turned on the little TV set next to the blender. He found *The Terminator* on one of the premium cable channels. Schwarzenegger. Now, there was a guy knew how to modify fucking behavior.

By the time Helen and Jess got home, it was dark, and Bartell was nodding his way through the Skelton file. An old Allman Brothers album was finishing up on the stereo. After eating, he had built a small fire in the fireplace and burned the pizza box and ice cream tub. Then, to further the deception, he flushed a bowl of lentil soup down the garbage disposal and left the dirty bowl and spoon in the sink. Helen hadn't learned tolerance quite as well as he had, and she seemed to have this notion that you could live forever *and* be well adjusted if you just ate good food and thought good thoughts.

When Jess came into the living room, she carried a plastic sack full of panty hose and cosmetics.

"What's with the fire?" Helen said, standing next to the mantel, which was festooned with small abstract clay figures, candlesticks, and potted plants, trophies attesting to the household's sensitivity. "You call the air quality number first?"

"No."

"It looks pretty grim out tonight." Smog was a big item in Rozette, where temperature inversions, traffic, and wood smoke could turn the air into soup in the blink of a stinging eye. "You should have called."

Sure. And left behind the evidence of his felonious meal.

"How was school?" Bartell asked his daughter.

"Boring," Jess said. She was about an inch taller than Helen now, and styled her light brown hair these days in tight moussed curls. She wore baggy jeans full of ragged holes, black basketball sneakers, and a baggy brown leather flight jacket. "School sucks," she said.

"That's why they call it preparation for life," Bartell said.

"Ray," his wife said. The echoing scold in her voice when she said his name filled the gap that followed.

"She knows I'm kidding," Bartell said.

"Layne Collier got busted last weekend," Jess said. "For ripping the stereo out of some dude's car. Layne and his chick both, they got busted. Her name's Mandy." Jess fished around in the bag and pulled out a packet of panty hose. "She's a sleaze," she said. Then, to Helen: "You're sure these'll match that new skirt?"

Before Helen could answer, Jess had returned the packet to the bag and left the room.

Bartell already knew that Layne Collier and his sleazy chick Mandy had been busted. He knew it because he'd come across the report that day at work. Layne Collier and Jess had gone to school together since the first grade. Now the kid was car hopping. Boosting stereos and radar detectors to trade for cocaine. And to sell too, because Mandy was knocked up and she was after him for the money to do something. That's what Collier told the cops who talked to him the night he got busted. Christ, the whole world was either knocked up, or soon going to be. Knocked up, blowing coke, and getting busted. Where had Jess been all that weekend while he and Helen were out of town and Layne Collier was out scoring cars?

"What's all this?" Helen pointed to the Skelton file.

Bartell hastily scooped the file aside, hoping that she hadn't spotted Skelton's name. "Just boring cop stuff."

"You mean secret cop stuff."

Bartell took her hand, which was cold. She leaned over and kissed him. Her soft, cold hair brushed his face. She sat back and straightened the sweatshirt that she wore. The sweatshirt was gray, with a large sprig of broccoli silkscreened in dark green on the front.

Bartell shrugged. "Part of my job on the Ramrod detail." Bartell had told his wife last week about his assignment to the Secret Service detail, but it wasn't until that day that he'd been issued his secret decoder ring.

"Ramrod?"

"The former president." Bartell said, "That's what they call him, their code word. Ramrod."

"*Ramrod,*" she huffed. "You ask me, he's nothing but a wrinkled up old Fascist."

I don't recall asking you, Bartell thought. Off and on during their visit to Cash over at the ranch, Helen had needled him about becoming part of the power elite. Tonight, it sounded like she'd traded in her needle for a lead pipe. Even though he might share many of his wife's political views, things were complicated enough without having to factor in how *he* felt about Ramrod. Let that conversation get started, and then next thing he knew, Helen would be off plunging into the depths of Merle Puhl's political philosophy, a choking, gasping journey at best. More than once Helen had expressed the belief that if Puhl were ever to devise a coat of arms, it would consist of crossed chain saws.

"So what's the big secret?" Helen said, making a show of eyeballing the file. "Kickbacks? Illegal campaign contributions? Criminal stupidity?"

Desperate that she not spot the words *Henry Skelton,* Bartell made a more obvious attempt to shield the file from view. "You were right the first time. Secret police stuff." He wasn't used to such deliberate attempts at keeping her nose out of his work, but it also was not Helen's habit to make this big a production out of prying. Helen's normal attitude toward his work was good humor, which now and then bordered on condescension. Her persistence tonight made him uneasy.

"Well," she said, "isn't this special. The lonely detective, shouldering society's burden all by his manly old self."

Bartell lowered his head and closed his eyes. "Give it a rest, okay?" Why had he ever believed that bringing work home—even paperwork—could be easy? When he and Helen first met, both were students at the University of Montana in Missoula, Helen in sociology and Bartell in a grab bag of courses that an optimist would call eclectic, a realist a waste of time. In their third year, both had majored in producing Jess.

"Sure, honey," she mocked. "We all know there are some things in life only the police can really understand." Helen loved making fun of what Bartell himself often derided as macho cop bullshit. That's what he'd called it anyway, back in the days before he'd stopped saying *bullshit* out loud. Christ, even agreeing with Helen could be a chore and a half. Bartell stifled a belch and swallowed a blast of heartburn, trying to pretend nothing had happened.

"Pepperoni." Helen made a pinched face and got up from the couch. "You know what they put in that stuff?"

"Pork," Bartell said.

"Dead hogs," Helen said. "That's what they put in it. You know what kind of karma those hogs pick up in a slaughterhouse? My God." She started out of the room, shaking.

Thank you, Jesus, Bartell thought. Saved by the pepperoni. "Maybe so," he said after his wife. "But it's the spices really make it special."

Henry Skelton was forty-six years old, five years older than Bartell. In San Francisco a little over four years ago, he had assaulted a federal officer. That was the polite term for giving one of the FBI's finest an ass whipping. Like cops everywhere, when it came to violence against one of their own, the Bureau had a notoriously bad sense of humor. In the blink of an eye, Skelton was counting off twenty months at Lompoc. After leaving Lompoc, he'd done twenty-four months on parole. Well, not parole really, since the politicians had done away with federal parole as part of their unstinting war on crime. Now, instead of parole, they had supervised release. Four months into his parole that was not parole, Skelton transferred to Rozette. He'd discharged his time last April, with no record of violations.

According to the file, Skelton had grown up in a series of small towns on the Olympic Peninsula in western Washington, and there was nothing special in his background there. He moved to the Bay Area in 1969, and started a sketchy career as a student at Berkeley. By the late seventies, Skelton was out of school, working as a draftsman, and living with Gina Lozano. It was during this period that he began to associate with people who had some pretty radical environmental views. Schemes to bomb power substations, sabotage nuclear reactors. Sink tuna boats. Drive heavy spikes into trees destined for a sawmill. The basic eco-terrorist mantra. There was some speculation in the file about Gina Lozano too. In the end, though, the only thing suspicious about her seemed to be her attachment to a man like Skelton.

As Bartell interpreted the documents, Henry Skelton's genesis as a living, breathing threat to the republic had started out as not much more than a twitch on somebody's computerized cross-reference spread sheet. But an intelligence file is worthless if it doesn't generate intelligence targets, so it wasn't long before a couple of Bureau agents started bird-dogging Skelton in their spare time. Not long after that, Henry Skelton began publishing pamphlets, and lengthy, ranting letters to newspapers.

Gutshoot the Bastards! That was the title of one of the pamphlets in the file, an engaging little document that had been especially damaging to Skelton in his later criminal case, since among the bastards he had advocated gutshooting were special agents of the Federal Bureau of Investigation.

In another pamphlet, *Nuke the White House!*, the title pretty much said it all.

The latest additions to the file dealt with the bombing at Cradle Creek. There were copies of the official reports of the summary variety, along with a sampling of journalistic accounts, some of which included sidebars recounting background on the Red Wolf Canyon timber sale, which was being run from the site in Cradle Creek. The Red Wolf Canyon sale was controversial, but when applied to any timber sale in recent memory, that term was more or less meaningless. Scarcely a tree was cut down in the National Forest these days without the benefit of a gaggle of court decisions. The timber business might be a dying way of life for loggers, but it had become the lifeblood of consultants and lawyers. In that sense, the timber industry mirrored all civic life in late twentieth-century America. Why actually *do* anything, when there was so much money and PR to be made talking and fighting about it?

The helicopter had been blown to hell with a crude pipe bomb. PVC pipe, filled with black powder, and touched off by an electronic squib, a kind of glow plug commonly used to launch model rockets. You could buy the pipe in any hardware store, the black powder at your nearest friendly sporting goods shop, and the squibs from dozens of hobbyist catalogues. The timer was a simple mechanical alarm clock, the power source a common six-volt battery. Crude, basic, effective. Nothing sophisticated at all, which, of course, did not mean that the perpetrator was unsophisticated, since such generic materials left nothing to trace back to point of origin. The investigators had done a search warrant on Skelton's house and truck, but found nothing resembling any of the bomb's components.

Even though none of the hardware could be tied to Skelton, it was hard to get around the fact that except for the poor bastard who was blown up with the chopper, he seemed to be the only human being within miles of the blast.

And Skelton's defense? It was the most common defense of all: *Who, me?*

Bartell set the file aside and massaged his temples. The Red Wolf Canyon timber sale. He'd heard all about it from his wife, and now here he was, seeing it in a federal investigative file.

When the sale was first proposed and publicized, the job would have resulted in the construction of a network of roads through some of Montana's last remaining undeveloped National Forest. Needless to say, this touched off a huge spasm of protest, appeals, and counterprotests. Every place you turned, there was a tree hugger, and in every tree hugger's face was a guy with a chain saw. Word processors melted down all over western Montana as people on both sides started hiring lawyers, writing letters, circulating petitions, and courting celebrity activists. Too much ancient forest lost, too many roads. Not enough jobs. Ghost towns, global warming. The death of civilization as we know it. You name it, everybody with a set of lungs had a bitch. If Bartell remembered correctly, good old Candidate Puhl had done his share of finger pointing and flag waving during the Red Wolf controversy too. So the sale was greatly modified, with the road system and clear-cuts replaced by a helicopter and selective cutting. And still, nobody was happy.

Henry Skelton. Right. One of *those* people. Granted, there seemed to be no shortage of activist cranks more than willing to vaporize anything having to do with the Red Wolf sale, but when you thought about it, their sheer number had the effect of camouflaging any alternative suspects. Put a man with Skelton's history in the Cradle Creek scenario, and it made perfect sense to anoint him the guilty party.

And always, there was Helen, bless her heart, who believed that Henry Skelton, a man she did not even know, had been wronged.

The fire was nearly out now, the house quiet. Bartell looked around the room. It was a large room, with a cathedral ceiling, new carpet, a sliding door opening out onto a deck. It was a great room, light-years removed from the tough ranch cabins in which he'd grown up. Somehow, he'd come to find himself living in the sort of house a man might be afraid to lose. For nearly eighteen years, he and Helen had strolled along one step after another, one day at a time. He had enough seniority in the police department that layoffs were no longer a concern. He waltzed with misfits all day, every day, at work. On his own time, he wanted nothing more than a little peace and quiet, a drive in the woods now and then, without somebody yacking at his conscience about acid rain. A little fishing that sometimes ended with fresh fish on a plate. A paycheck from the city that was printed with ink instead of the blood of tax protesters, more and more of whom seemed these days to be retired civil servants from out of state.

Weary at last of his own trials, but still restless, Bartell went downstairs to the small, paneled rec room, where he turned on the TV. News. Sports. Bad movies. Worse talk shows. Paid programs about weight loss, hair loss, getting rich quick, and phone sex. Finally, his channel surfing created on one of the many documentaries about the Nazis, this one about Goebbels and his propaganda machine.

Goebbels. His face drawn and skeletal, a prophecy in itself. Grainy, black-and-white film of some invasion or another, with the sounds of battle clearly overdubbed after the fact. No screams. Blood simply the color of a shadow. Goebbels speaking with Hitler, giving him that crisp Nazi salute like a giant hardon. And Hitler's return salute, languid, oddly effeminate. Hitler inspecting a battalion of boys, accepting flowers from a platoon of sparkling blond girls. Their faces smug, supremely confident, all of them. Utterly correct.

And those other faces, etched every bit as sharply as Goebbels's, yet all of them punctuated by their eyes. An entire text of

Semitic and Slavic eyes, sunken, it seemed, clear through to the backs of their skulls. Home of enough sorrow and fear to shame the entire world for generations. Maybe.

We were just following orders. Of all the words uttered during that catastrophe, it was those that haunted Bartell the most. Followed orders. Followed the law. And here he was, an agent of the law. A country moves through time, he thought, and every step of the way there's that chance of making a wrong turn, one that leads into a tunnel of murder. It made Bartell feel melodramatic to think like this, as though doing so from his own position of relative security and luxury somehow degraded that other suffering. On the other hand, abandoning such thoughts made him scared. Better that kind of fear, though, than the fear that seemed to be driving the country these days. Jobs, politics, AIDS, immigrants, religion, race. Everybody was scared to death of something, looking for somebody to blame. And too many gutbags like Merle Puhl to help them make the *right* choice.

So here he was, Ray Bartell the policeman, dispatched out into the community to get the goods on Henry Skelton, a man who may have broken no law but left others feeling all tingly because they thought he might have. Or might be right now. Or might later in the week. Maybe. Who could say? Who could take the chance? Would they break out the brown shirts tomorrow, or wait until Wednesday?

Bartell heard a noise to his left and looked over to see Helen coming into the gray, flickering light from the TV. A long blue nightgown nicked at her ankles, shimmered around her breasts, belly, hips.

"Getting pretty late," she said, sliding back onto the sofa beside him. She and Jess had turned in over an hour before.

"I'm done working," Bartell said. "I was just sitting here thinking. You can't know too much about Nazis."

"Nazis were an aberration," she said.

"You think so?"

"I hope so."

Hope was better than nothing, Bartell decided. Helen leaned over and kissed him. She tasted of toothpaste.

"Jess's asleep," she said, raising her brows in a question.

"Thinking, too, about how tired I am," he said, smiling, almost unbearably pleased that their fights never ran deep. "Now that I'm getting to be an old guy."

She laughed. "Not that old." She squirmed around on the

sofa, hoisting the gown over her hips, then swung one leg over him so that she now straddled his lap.

"You could hurt my back," he said, flirting with her.

She gave him a long kiss, then leaned back and unfastened his belt buckle, all the while holding his eyes with hers. "I could give you a heart attack."

Bartell ran his hands up her strong back under the gown. "Go ahead. Take your best shot."

He found the remote control and punched off the TV. It seemed cruel, forcing all those electronic ghosts to witness his joy.

Chapter 5

Sprawled on the granite ledge near the fire, Skelton watched the firelight flicker on the walls of the cave at his back.

The bear. Huge goddamn beast, a rippling nightmare of teeth and claws.

Out of the corner of his eye he glanced at the rifle, which was propped against the rocks at the mouth of the cave, not much more than an arm's length away. A sane man would probably be long gone back to town by now. But as far as Skelton was concerned, that was no way to respond to answered prayers. Instead, he kept brooding on that bear, on the way it had lashed out at the machine.

Well, maybe he was crazy. But was he any crazier than that grizzly somewhere out there in the dark woods? Suppose the cave where he'd chosen to trespass was this bear's winter home? What if the tufts of fur in the dust had come from this bear, along with the rank, musty stench you could still detect under the odor of damp rock and moss? *This bear,* drawn right down on top of Skelton by some incomprehensible command of blood?

Somewhere in the woods around him, the great beast was sleeping. Stalked through his dreams, perhaps, by Nez Perce ghosts. Those ghosts stalked Skelton, so why not the bear too? The fire was dying down, and there was no wind. Skelton listened to the nearby creek. The sound of cold water over rocks was always the same, but not really the same, when you listened closely. The pitch and rhythm constantly shifted, but always within a certain range. It would be a deviation from that range that would bring your head—the bear's head—up, instantly awake, your long snout testing the air.

Stupid, romantic bullshit. That's what it was. Imagining yourself as the bear. The bear was a hunter and a killer, a wild thing. Not a man given to abstract diatribes. Henry Skelton had never for an instant confused himself with anything truly wild. Really, it was the difference between himself and the bear, rather than some idiocy about similarities, that made the diatribes worthwhile.

The half moon was just now nudging the sky above the ridge top across the way, and the heavy spray of stars seemed startled, as though abruptly frozen in place by Skelton's glance. He stood up and dusted himself off. After feeding more wood into the fire, he waved the smoke away from his face. A tricky breeze now shifted through the treetops, then caught the smoke, carrying it out across the canyon, a long wisp tangled in moonlight and the breeze. He listened to the trees and the water, breaking each sound down into its elements. He listened for the bear in a way he thought the bear might listen.

Chapter 6

From his perch on the limestone escarpment overlooking the shallow ravine, Bartell watched as Arnold Zillion picked his way down toward the patch of grass on a dangerously narrow island of level ground. When Zillion's foot faltered once on the scree, he glanced up at Bartell and grinned. A tight, nervous grin. Then, steadying himself with his hands against the rocks, Zillion edged his way out of sight under the escarpment.

Bartell, squatting in the shade of a gnarled cedar near a large clump of cactus, used the back of his thumb to hook a bead of sweat from above his right eye. Hot. Too goddamned hot for October. Not even mid-morning, and already the distant mountains rippled with heat. It was the kind of freaky autumn day when rattlesnakes straggled out from under rocks to loll in the sun. Bartell peered uneasily into the tall brown grass off to his right, and tried to swallow the dusty knot in the back of his throat.

Zillion was in big trouble all right. Dire straits. And he had realized it, Bartell knew, from the moment he decided to crawl down into that ravine. Only a reckless and driven man would venture down there. Zillion, without an instant's hesitation, had said there was no choice. No choice at all.

With great care Bartell leaned ahead on all fours, peering over the escarpment after Zillion, who at least was back in sight, safe on the grassy ledge maybe fifteen feet below, less than halfway to the bottom of the ravine. Sickeningly, Bartell's hand skidded toward the edge, sending a small shower of gravel down onto

Zillion. Bartell caught himself. Zillion ducked, then looked up, his teeth clenched.

"Sorry," Bartell said.

Zillion appeared to relax. "That happens." Zillion collected himself and looked around, studying the situation.

"What do you think?" Bartell said, trying to sound casual and manly.

Zillion looked up at him again, his pale eyes determined. "I was right. Toss me a three iron."

A three iron. Amazing. Anybody but a federal cop would blow off a lousy drive and take a drop. But this guy Zillion persisted in believing that he could get back in play by making a long, flat shot along the shortening escarpment, play the three iron with a radical slice that would bring it back onto the fairway. Anybody with more brains than testosterone knew that if you were determined to save a penalty stroke, the only play was a sand wedge, and all the loft you could muster. But Zillion was not the kind of guy who would sacrifice distance for anything. Bartell got to his feet and walked back to the cart, completely satisfied now that Zillion was a fool.

Playing golf while on the payroll was, Bartell decided, the epitome of government work. But it was Zillion's idea, if that made any difference. Beginning tomorrow, both men would be pulling down long hours on the presidential detail, so today they had started out at the golf course, without even going to the office first. All work and no play, Zillion explained, was strictly for the private sector. And anyway, it was a crime to waste such perfect autumn weather in Montana. Snow, tons of it, lay somewhere out there on the horizon, and both Palm Springs and April were a long way off.

Vic Fanning was also a graduate of the FBI's National Academy, so he understood all about the intricacies of federal law enforcement, and late the previous afternoon he'd pulled some strings to get Zillion and Bartell on the country club course under his membership. Actually, the favor was for Zillion, and as far as Fanning was concerned, Bartell's presence on those treasured private links was nothing more than a necessary evil. Fanning would have come along with them, except he was afraid the chief might need some care and feeding that morning. He had, however, insisted that Bartell carry a beeper.

"If you're going to be working with the big boys," Zillion had said on the first tee, "you've got to learn the ropes."

Then Arnold Zillion absolutely mashed a drive, and Bartell followed by topping his. Three strokes on, he'd managed to reach Zillion's first lie. Forty-five minutes later, Zillion, with utter arrogance, decided he could cut the dogleg on number three. But this time his drive fell short, and now he had descended into his current despair in the ravine, frantic to save par. Not par for the hole, mind you, but par for the round. Zillion didn't want just the dogleg, he wanted the whole goddamn dog.

Bartell slipped the three iron from among Zillion's set of Pings. For all he cared, Zillion could fall and break his miserable neck down there in the rocks. Let the coyotes and crows have him.

As the round had progressed, Zillion told Bartell that he'd blocked off an hour and a half early in the afternoon, when the two of them would start to work on the Skelton situation. The best approach, Zillion thought, was to pay Skelton a visit, meet him head-on, get a sense of him. That was important, because Bartell and Zillion also had a meeting tomorrow out at Puhl's ranch, and Skelton was sure to be on the table.

Meeting Skelton, especially with Arnold Zillion along, was not Bartell's idea of a walk in the park. What if Skelton started off by saying something like, hey, aren't you the guy who's married to Helen, that gal who helps my old lady carry petitions? From that moment on, Bartell would be an object of suspicion. Zillion would mull over this development with Fanning, and Fanning would start up a round of nauseating discussions with his bene-factor, the chief. Within a week, the word would be out at coffee: You hear the latest on Bartell, how he compromised the job? Always knew there was something not quite right about that guy.

Bartell eased his way back to the edge of the escarpment. "Here you go." Zillion looked up, and deftly caught the club when Bartell dropped it.

As the Secret Service agent went through his endless preamble of practice swings, settling into a radically open stance for the shot, Bartell studied the small, monkish bald spot on the top of his head, which the hot wind had exposed.

Then, with Zillion poised at the top of his backswing, the beeper on Bartell's belt went off in a series of nerve-shredding squeals. Too late to pull back, Zillion dubbed the shot, sending the tiny white ball bouncing hopelessly into the rocky wasteland below.

"Je-sus Christ!" Zillion glared at the offending three iron, then threw the club high into the air and watched as it spun end over end—a beautiful sight, really—after the ball. This, Bartell decided, must be why smart policemen always leave their guns locked in the car when they go to the golf course.

Bartell knew that pagers were Vic Fanning's lifeblood, so he knew before looking that it would be Fanning's number displayed on that vile little box. By the time Zillion had resurrected himself from the ravine, Bartell had already returned to the cart, and he headed off as Zillion swung into the seat beside him.

"I played a foursome with Norman once," Zillion said finally. "Saw him make a shot just like that. A brazen, deliberate slice out of trouble. I've tried my whole life since to make a shot like that." His assured tone made it clear that he wasn't talking about just any old Norman from Boise or Peoria.

"Life," Bartell said sadly as the cart bounced along over the fairway. "Just one long string of disappointments."

Gazing off at the horizon, Zillion thought for a moment, then said, "I'll tell you what life is. For guys like you and me anyway. I met this fellow once, an archeologist. He'd just come back from a dig down in Central America."

Every night, Zillion explained, this man would walk barefoot from his tent across an open field to the latrine, heeding the call of nature. As the weeks passed, the archeologist came to look forward to these carefree strolls, anticipating the sense of peace that came over him there in the center of those perfect tropical nights.

"So one night," Zillion went on, "this guy takes along a flashlight. No particular reason. He just does it. Then, when he's out in the middle of that nice grassy area, he switches the flashlight on. Turns out the ground all around is covered with coral snakes. Has been all along. And him out there every night, barefoot in the dark."

As the cart skirted a long bunker behind the green on number one, Zillion folded his arms across his chest and settled deeper into the seat. "That's the best description I know of my job," he said. "Yours too."

And don't forget, Bartell thought, slowing the cart outside the clubhouse, that sometimes a snake can crawl inside under the tent.

It turned out that the page was really for Zillion. Some cheesy detail about traffic control, that Fanning—who didn't even have anything to do with traffic matters—decided couldn't wait. When Bartell and Zillion got back to the station, Fanning snagged Zillion into the patrol captain's office, leaving Bartell to trudge off alone to the basement.

Downstairs, Beth McCoy, the secretary in detectives, collared him to collect scores and his two dollars for the weekly National Football League pool. Beth kept a Pittsburgh Steelers banner hanging from the ceiling above her desk, and a large poster of Terry Bradshaw tacked to the brown paneling behind. Bradshaw held his arm extended to make a pass, and somebody had drawn a spiderweb in his armpit. When Beth McCoy offered a ten-dollar reward for the name of the culprit, Billy Stokes confessed, and tried to collect the ten bucks for himself.

"Who won last week?" Bartell asked.

Beth McCoy made a sour face. "The chief." The earpieces of her dictaphone hung like a stethoscope from the sides of her face. "Again."

"That scum," Bartell said. "I think he cheats. I know he does. I hear he always uses the money to take the mayor to lunch."

Beth McCoy held out her palm. "Pay up, or shut up."

Bartell made a zipping motion across his lips.

"Suit yourself," Beth McCoy said. She adjusted the earpieces and returned to the statement she was transcribing.

Except for Beth McCoy, the office was empty, and by the time Bartell got to his desk, the phone was ringing. Some guy said his name was Duckworth. Said he was Merle Puhl's campaign manager.

"I was referred to you by the chief of police," Duckworth said.

Excuse me, Bartell thought, while I do a couple of handsprings and a back flip, go fetch some hoops to jump through. He said, "Is that so."

"Yes. He told me you were part of the department's special liaison with the Secret Service. For the presidential visit."

Bartell thought the voice sounded both crisp and casual, East Coast. Well heeled. "I don't know about the special part," he said, "but I'm tagging along."

"I'm sure you're just being self-effacing, Detective," Duckworth said. "I've been in contact with Agent Zillion, of course. Your Secret Service counterpart?"

"Right."

"And I understand he's briefed you on Henry Skelton."

"We had a conversation, that's right."

"Well, I wanted to reach out to you now . . . Detective . . . Ray. Do you mind if I call you Ray?"

Would it have mattered? "That's fine. You can call me anything you want, Mr. Duckworth."

"As I said, Ray, I wanted to reach out to you and make sure you understand how much importance we all attach to the Skelton situation."

Upstairs, someone flushed the toilet in the men's room. Dismayed, Bartell watched a droplet of tan water grow from the corner of the light fixture overhead. The ceiling tile bore a brown half-moon stain where it bordered the fixture. The droplet fluttered with a tiny splat onto the green linoleum about three feet from the end of Bartell's desk.

"Have you been vaccinated for typhus?" Bartell said into the phone.

"I beg your pardon?"

"Cholera?"

"I'm afraid I don't understand, Detective."

"Nothing," Bartell said. "Just a passing thought. Anyway, yes, we recognize that Skelton could be a problem. We'll do everything we can to head off trouble."

"That's good," Duckworth said. "Because I have to tell you, we at the campaign think that right now Skelton is arguably the most dangerous man in the state. So with the president—"

"Former president," Bartell said.

"I beg your pardon?"

"He's not president anymore. That makes him the former president." Bartell thought about calling him the ex-president, but decided that was a special title, reserved just for Nixon. *Ex*-President. Like President X.

"Fine," Duckworth said stiffly. "Have it your way."

In the pause that followed, Bartell could sense Duckworth gathering himself. Given the balancing act that this Skelton business might force upon him, Bartell knew it made no sense at all to antagonize the main push on Puhl's campaign. Yet, Duckworth's voice oozed such self-importance that Bartell couldn't think of a single honorable reason to lay off him. Another drop of water, a long one, sailed clear of the light fixture and hit the floor. Just what the world needs, Bartell thought. Electrified sewage.

"I'm sure, Detective," Duckworth said, chilly now, "you deal with people like Henry Skelton every day. Check forgers, petty thieves . . . *really bad men.* But you'll pardon us if we on the campaign take him just a little bit more seriously."

"Oh, we take him seriously too, Mr. Duckworth. Arnold Zillion and I had a task force meeting on him just this morning."

"That's good to hear," Duckworth said. "Maybe you'll have something constructive to add after all. I'll see you in the morning."

Before Bartell could respond, Duckworth rang off.

Bartell didn't know much about political campaigns, but it didn't take a political genius to recognize when you had an asshole on the other end of the phone, and this Duckworth sounded like a sphincter with legs.

Since early morning on the first tee, Bartell had toyed with the idea of simply coming clean with Fanning about Helen and Gina Lozano and asking off the detail. Yet, even if Fanning quietly let him off the hook, Bartell knew the ins and outs of the police department well enough to understand that the thing he wanted to avoid most—suspicion among his peers—would still result.

Suspicion among his peers. There you had it, the whole ball of wax. Try as he might, Bartell couldn't avoid that shriveling sensation behind his belt buckle, a sure sign that the spirits of George Rather and Paul Culp were alive and well. Detectives who were lazy or inept could be easily tolerated. But detectives at odds with the soul of police culture, those detectives were trouble. They were also doomed.

Doomed or not, though, there was also the matter of Bartell's own ego. Given what he knew about Skelton, there was a chance—remote, but still a chance—that the situation could get seriously out of hand. If Bartell kept close tabs on things, and had anything resembling good luck, then maybe he was the one cop on the landscape who was in a position to defuse trouble. Fatal logic, yes. Complete hubris. But what else do you do? Hang on tight and ride things out. And don't kid yourself that you're riding in any other condition than alone.

And finally, there was the simple fact that Bartell was flattered to find himself in the rule of inside man. He thought the whole business would be fun. A lot of fun.

Bartell's reverie was interrupted by the noise of steadily dripping water. He studied again the source of the contamination, then got up and went into Captain Vic Fanning's office. He pulled Fanning's sterling-silver cup from the bookcase, returned with it to the open bay, and set it on the floor under the slobbering ceiling.

Once Bartell had the division's immediate health crisis under control, he decided to take advantage of Arnold Zillion's absence and start working Skelton on his own. He phoned the 911 center and asked for an A-B-C check on motor vehicles. A '76 Ford pickup, green, was registered to Skelton. Sounded like one of those old rigs periodically auctioned off by the Forest Service. Minutes after getting this information, Bartell signed himself out until noon.

Outside the dungeon of the City Hall basement, a black limo was parked across the street under the carriage entrance on the side of Rickenbacker's, one of the town's funeral parlors. A handful of transients straggled toward the noon feed at the Blind Faith Mission in the next block north. Government, homeless people, and mortuaries. You didn't see any of that in the glut of glossy picture books about Montana. Shining mountains and glittering streams, that was the order of the day, and those books weighted down coffee tables like ballast on a ghost ship.

Hell, Bartell thought, getting into his car, when I was a kid . . .

No. Just stop it right there. Life inches ahead in its own way, and trying to ratchet back the past is like picking up the phone to reserve space at Rickenbacker's.

According to the background material from Zillion, Skelton's last known address was a small house out on River Flats, a neighborhood raw as a boil on the western edge of town. That address was the same as the one appearing on the registration for Skelton's truck.

At mid-morning, the day continued to warm as the sun burned away small pockets of fog that hung in the tight valleys in the surrounding mountains. Traffic was light, and Bartell made good time through downtown on Defoe Street, then across the river and on out toward Fort Kittredge. There were shorter ways to River Flats, but an extra twenty minutes in the car were twenty minutes he wouldn't have to put in around the office, posing, as he sometimes saw himself, in the role of policeman. Pretend long enough, and you become real thing, the authentic item.

Was that it? Carry a gun until you no longer notice the weight. Get burned too many times by people who lie just for practice. That's easy. Just streamline trust out of your program. And most damaging of all, you end up believing your own sentimentality, until you finally get soft and lazy.

A knock and talk. That's what he would do with Gina Lozano. A knock and talk was what you did with players. Players were people you had intel on but who weren't yet the subject of any particular crime except taking up memory space in a cop's daydreams. So you go knock on their doors and talk to them. A knock and talk. Or a tap and rap, if you were feeling frisky. Knock and talk, tap and rap. That's what you did with players.

On the other hand, once a player committed an honest-to-God crime, he ceased being a player and became a perp, and once he graduated from player to perp he also moved on up from knock and talk, or tap and rap, to hook and book. As in "Hook him and book him," slap on the cuffs, and off to jail. Unless the perp decided to go hard. Then a hook and book wasn't enough, and you had to step things up to a slam and jam.

So police work was really pretty exciting if you just kept everything organized under the proper vocabulary.

Payday. That was the most important concept. Cashing paychecks meant that, no matter what else, in the end you were still just another kind of hired man. And hired men always had the option of moving on when the terms went sour. Crusaders, on the other hand, were stuck for the duration.

Chapter 7

Skelton started walking out to his truck at first light, bumping along at a steady pace across the sidehill above the loggers. He kept a cautious eye out for the bear, but there was no sign of the animal.

It was mid-morning when Skelton pulled his truck to a stop back down at the main road. He was about to turn out, when another pickup, a beat-up tan Ford, swung around the curve to his left, heading for the logging site. A couple of guys inside the truck. Green hard hats. The passenger eyed Skelton idly, then got an excited look on his face, pointed Skelton's way.

Just past the turnoff, the truck stopped in a spray of gravel. Both men got out, walked back toward Skelton. Skelton got out to meet them.

"You were told to keep your ass away from here," the passenger shouted. He parked his hands menacingly on his hips. He was the older of the two. Burly, a full head shorter than the driver, who was thin, not as tall or broad as Skelton. The burly man's belly punched out between his wide red suspenders and draped over the top of his black jeans, which were flecked with wood chips.

Skelton bore down on him.

"You hard of hearing?" burly man said, not giving an inch.

Skelton felt his legs pounding, felt something welling up inside his gut. Something like noise.

Not slowing, he walked squarely into the passenger, chesting him, knocking him back a couple of paces.

"Goddamn you," the man said, regaining his balance.

"You sonsofbitches," Skelton said. "Respect. That's the trouble. You sonsofbitches've got no respect."

Over the man's shoulder Skelton saw the driver lunge toward him. Skelton batted him aside with a forearm.

In back of the loggers' pickup, Skelton saw an ax. Once he had the ax in hand, everything came to a standstill.

"I watch guys like you on TV," Skelton said, "listen to you crying about losing your way of life." He eyed the pair. Nobody likes to go up against an ax. "Some way of life. Shit."

Burly man looked like he was about to blow an artery. "We shoulda come up to that cave one morning and buried you."

"No guts either," Skelton said. "No respect and no guts. There's the story. I guess you'll call the cops again."

"I'm not calling nobody," the man said. "I'm not wasting my time. I'll tell you this, though—"

"Yeah?"

"I'll tell you this, you show your face around here again, there won't be any talk. No more talk, you got that? We'll just take care of business."

"Suits me," Skelton said. He eyed them again, then began slowly backing away to his truck. The men stood frozen, not coming after him, but not easing off either.

When he got to the truck, Skelton hefted the ax lightly. He regarded the ax curiously before tossing it haphazardly into the brush. With that, he stepped back into the truck and got the hell out of there. When he looked back, he saw that the loggers weren't following.

Chapter 8

The man rummaged through the black cordura bag on the ground beside his right leg and brought out a thermos of coffee. He poured coffee into the lid, then replaced the bottle in the bag before setting the coffee aside to light a cigarette. Using a short stick, he gouged out a small hole in the ground to accommodate the ashes and the butts that he knew would accumulate while he waited. Then he dangled the cigarette from his lips while he went through the bag again, pushing aside the thermos, the sandwiches, the camo Gore-Tex parka, the CAR-15 and extra magazines, until he found the binoculars.

Now the man thumbed the smoke from his eyes, took a long draw on the cigarette, then set it aside with the coffee. He straightened on his knees and looked over the brush toward the small house at the end of the cul-de-sac. The house was about two hundred yards away across a ragged, trampled horse pasture. Finally, he raised the binoculars to his eyes and studied.

No sign of the green pickup at the house. Just the blue Toyota junker. But that didn't count for much. The part about the pickup not being at the house. Weeks ago, when he first came on the job, the man learned early on that Skelton never left the truck at the house. Instead, he would pull in, unload his gear, then within less than an hour he would move the truck about a third of a mile from the house and stash it in a grove of trees along the river. Not far, it turned out, from where the man parked his own pickup while surveilling the house. Then, after hiding the truck, Skelton would follow a game trail back through the cottonwoods to the house, sometimes passing no more than twenty, thirty yards, from where

*the man lay drawn back into the brush, an exercise that tended to
make the job mildly interesting.*

*No movement either outside the house or at the windows. No
movement anywhere except for the black-and-white magpies that
now and then swooped down to light on the pasture, where they
swaggered from one pile of horse shit to the next.*

*Now the man swung the binoculars to his left, where the cul-de-
sac joined the main road. Here there was movement. A small gray
car, heading toward the house at the dead end.*

The roads on River Flats were all unpaved afterthoughts of
rutted gravel, which wound near a stand of enormous cottonwoods along the Holt River. Most of the residences were set up
on two-acre tracts, and many were flanked by stacks of firewood
big as boxcars. The firewood was destined to be burned in wood
stoves that frequently ignited creosote deposits clogging the insides of triple-wall stovepipes or cinder-block chimneys, sometimes torching off a whole house, incinerating entire families in
the middle of bitter nights. The musty smell of dry cottonwood
leaves made the neighborhood smell like a fire waiting to happen.

Near many of the houses, bonehead horses milled around on
dusty hardpack. Bartell figured that every horse owner on River
Flats believed his particular horses were the smartest, best-
trained horses in creation. How the hell else could you tolerate
horses? But horses like these never got any real use, and as far as
Bartell was concerned, that was the ticket to ruin. Even the
smartest horse in the world is still nothing more than a big, stupid beast, and unless you work its ass off—and keep it worked
off—it's not good for much more than vet bills and scenery. And
processing hay into shit. Horses didn't need any schooling to do
that.

There were a lot of dogs on River Flats too. Rangy dogs, with a
jumpy, starved look, like they were just waiting for one of those
fat, shaggy horses to look the other way.

Only rarely did the mailboxes in River Flats have names or
numbers. That didn't matter, Bartell figured, since most of the
people who lived out here got through life as Occupant.

So there you had it, your basic late-twentieth-century Montana
homestead. A trailer house with a wood stove and a couple of

barren acres. Sluggish, underused horses and opportunistic dogs. You'd never see a rich dandy like Brandon McWilliams scouting locations in this neck of the woods. Bartell doubted, too, that the former president and Merle Puhl would be stopping by either, to shake hands, kiss babies, and get their picture taken. It was a smarter bet to put a clock on the second coming of Christ.

Not seeing the green Ford pickup, Bartell raised a dispatcher on the radio and began checking license plates. On the fourth try, an old blue Toyota Celica with a terminal case of rust, the plate came back to Gina Lozano. The Celica was parked outside a small green clapboard house. End of the street. No number showing. The roofline had a shallow pitch, and as he parked beside the Toyota, Bartell noticed moss growing along the edges of the shingles. In the window beside the door, a yellow curtain fluttered back into place.

Bartell didn't have to knock. By the time he got to the door, a trim, attractive woman with black hair was waiting for him.

"Yes?" the woman said. She was about thirty-five. Her eyes were dark and bright. She wore blue jeans, purple-and-white Nike running shoes, and a blue-and-black rugby shirt with the sleeves pulled up to her elbows. On her right arm, a silver Hopi bracelet shined against her dark skin.

Bartell smiled. His traveling salesman smile. "Are you Gina Lozano?"

"You know I am."

"Excuse me?"

"I watched you talking on the radio. Checking my license plate?"

Bartell decided not to waste a smile on a woman who spent her time looking out the window for the cops. He pulled his ID card from his shirt pocket, held it out to her, and introduced himself. "I need to talk to Henry."

"You got a warrant?"

Bartell laughed in spite of himself. "Lady, you watch too much TV."

"Fuck you," Gina Lozano said. Then she pushed the door closed.

Bartell caught the door with his forearm. "Let's try this again," he said, this time with an edge in his voice. "I'd like to talk to Henry Skelton. I don't have a warrant, and as far as I'm concerned, I don't have any reason to get one. This is not a big deal. Now, please don't jerk me around and make it into one."

Gina Lozano's eyes met his, and she held her own. Her cheeks were drawn, her lips slightly pursed from the tension. Then Bartell felt the pressure of the door ease against his arm.

"Please," he said softly.

"You said your name was Bartell. As in *Helen* Bartell?"

"Her husband."

"Did she know you were coming out here?"

Bartell shook his head. "Helen doesn't have to know the cops have business at your house. Right now that's nobody's business but yours and mine. And Henry's."

"He's not here."

"Maybe you could spare me a few minutes, then."

She thought about this for several seconds, then let out a deep breath, stepped back from the door, and nodded him inside.

The living room was small and crammed with bookshelves. There was a large drafting table in the front window. The table was set in a level position, and stacked with books and papers. A poster made from an Ansel Adams photograph—"Moonrise, Hernandez, New Mexico"—hung on the wall above a narrow library table. Bartell smelled something burning, and noticed a braid of sweetgrass with one end in ashes laying in a small brass bowl on the library table. He didn't see a TV set. All in all, the place had a clean, organized clutter, like the grave markers in the foreground off Adams's photograph. Neither the decor, nor the woman, for that matter, seemed to fit with the wreckage that made up the rest of the neighborhood.

Gina Lozano pointed to a barrel-backed armchair upholstered in dark blue velour. "You might as well sit down," she said. Then she sat down herself on the beige-and-green cushions of a futon.

The chair was narrow, and compressed Bartell's shoulders into a posture that was remarkably uncomfortable. He squirmed slightly, and crossed his legs.

Gina Lozano said, "So what is it this time?"

"Nothing urgent," he said, hoping to minimize the situation. "And nothing about the bombing." What was the point in not being open about Skelton's recent notoriety?

"That's a relief. It took me three days to clean up after the search warrant." Gina frowned, looked away, and shook her head. "Don't you people ever let up?"

Bartell leaned forward, bracing his elbows on his knees. The chair was really killing his back. "Like I said, it's nothing to get excited about," he said. "But something came up, and I decided that ten minutes with Henry now might save us both a misunderstanding later." He went on to explain about the presidential visit, and the reason why the Secret Service had gone to the trouble of making Skelton a project. Ordinarily, Bartell would have been more secretive. But if the idea was to defuse a potential threat, wasn't it best to let Skelton know he could attract attention just by being around? *We know what's on your mind, and it won't work, so don't even try.* That was the message. It seemed remarkably simple.

As she listened, Gina Lozano's face remained blank. She sat erect on the futon, with her arms folded under her breasts, her breathing steady.

"It occurred to me," Bartell said finally, "that if for some reason Henry felt compelled to cause a problem, then something as simple as me showing up at his door might derail a bad idea. At the same time, if he's just a guy putting his life back together, I didn't want him to get all bent out of shape, maybe do something stupid, if he heard that people were checking around about him."

"The direct approach," Gina Lozano said.

Bartell risked his traveling salesman smile again. "Exactly."

Holding her arms tightly in place, Gina shrugged. "I'll give him the message."

"You got any idea when he might be back?"

"No. He spends a lot of time out in the woods."

"Working?" Although there was nothing in the background to indicate that Skelton did something so fundamental as hold a normal job in the woods, Bartell wanted to keep the conversation moving.

"No. I'm the one does the working these days."

Surprised by the sharpness of her comment, Bartell nudged her ahead. "What kind of work do you do?" He knew, of course, that she was a nurse.

Her laugh was bitter. "Don't patronize me, okay? I've lived a long time with a guy who's in the system. That puts me in the system too. And I'm sure Helen has told you about us."

Bartell returned to being matter-of-fact. "Okay, so you're a nurse. There are lots of places somebody can be a nurse. Big brother isn't quite as big as you seem to think. And Helen hasn't really told me that much about you. Other than that she thinks you're good people." But he knew from the file that she worked at St. Francis.

"Maybe," she said, "maybe not. Anyway, you sure couldn't prove it by those FBI shits."

"The ones in Montana?" Bartell said, taking a chance. "Or the ones in San Francisco?"

Gina threw up her hands, then slapped her palms onto her thighs. "See there? I knew it. I knew you'd read his file."

"Of course I read his file. You'd think I was an idiot if I hadn't." Bartell sat back and licked his lips. "Look at it this way. You publish a pamphlet called 'Nuke the White House,' then put the hurt on a federal cop—a *special agent of the FBI*, no less— even if you do your time, every now and then somebody's going to reshuffle all that paper and point a finger at you. May not be right, but it's going to happen. This is one of those times."

Gina Lozano fell silent. Bartell glanced around the room. The selection of books was eclectic, with noticeable groups of American fiction, art and design, and Native American history. Most of the books on the drafting table seemed to be about Indians, with a scattering of Forest Service publications.

"He wanted to be an architect," Gina said at last, perhaps because Bartell kept staring at the drafting table. "When we first met, fifteen, sixteen years ago. He'd worked his way through three years at Berkeley, doing construction in the summer. That's what got him interested in becoming an architect. Because he loved the way things were put together underneath, along with the way they looked on the outside."

"I hear it's a real grind becoming an architect."

"Yeah," she said. "A real grind. Anyway, he got this job as a draftsman for a big contractor. Figured he'd lay out a few years, get himself grubstaked, then go back to school."

"But he never made it," Bartell said.

Gina Lozano's smile was bleak. She worried the Hopi bracelet. "The same sad old story, huh? A job too good to quit, too lousy to keep. Then we both changed jobs, and moved over near Sausalito."

Her observation was well within Bartell's frame of reference. "Like being a policeman."

"You'll excuse me," she said, "if my view of cops isn't quite that generous. Not even for Helen's husband."

Bartell couldn't have cared less what she thought about cops. "I understand you've been living in Rozette for about a year and a half." He remembered Gina's remark about being the one who did the work these days. "Has Henry been able to find any work since you moved here? Montana's a tough place to be out of a job."

She nodded. "Last summer, I mean the summer before this, when we first got in town, he went to work right away with a landscaping contractor. That was steady until he got laid off over the winter. But he went right back as soon as the weather broke last spring. That probably would have lasted all summer again."

"Probably?"

When Gina Lozano smiled, Bartell found himself hoping that such a look might come over Helen's face when she spoke of him. "Henry's a man of obsessions, which I'm sure you've figured out by now. That's what drew us to Montana. He crowds easily."

"I take it, then, he's gotten wrapped up in something." Bartell glanced at the drafting table again, then back at Gina.

"Indians," Gina said. "Last spring he started spending a lot of time by himself out in the woods. On the weekends at first. Then one day he came across this archeological site. Something to do with the Nez Perce. You'd never know it was a site at all if it hadn't been marked on the map."

Skelton soon started collecting books about the Nez Perce, Gina said. Within a few weeks, he was ditching his job, spending even more time on his own out in the woods, sometimes as long as a week at a stretch. Pretty soon there was no job left to ditch. As she spoke, Gina sounded by turns bewildered, angry, and protective. And always somewhat compulsive. She talked about Henry Skelton the way people talk about those they love but do not quite understand.

"Sounds like," Bartell said, "he's made himself into kind of an expert."

"I guess." Gina's frustration sounded through again. "But those books, he buys them and all, but I don't think he reads them much."

"He got friends who are Indian?"

Abruptly, the chill returned to her voice. "No."

"You must've talked to a lot of cops," he said. "Last summer. About the helicopter." He didn't want to use the word *bombing*.

"They came a lot looking for Henry. But they talked to me only once. That was on the day they searched the house."

"And what did you tell them?"

"I told them he wasn't here that night."

"You could have lied. Alibied him."

"I don't do that. I don't tell lies." Her eyes were locked on his.

"Anything else?" he said. "You tell them anything else?"

"No. I don't know anything else." Her eyes flickered away, and Bartell was certain she had more to tell.

Bartell tried another tack. "Seems kind of odd," he said, "a guy would quit his job just because he got curious about something out in the woods."

"He called it a sacred place. It was a big deal for him. I don't know, what can I tell you?"

"A sacred place?"

"That's right. But he never explained exactly what that meant."

Bartell scowled. "Sounds pretty intense."

She relaxed again, gave up a short laugh. "You're being polite. Some people would call it crazy."

Bartell laughed too. "Some people would. Yeah."

"But it wasn't just the Indian stuff. Not completely. With him quitting, I mean. He was working on this big condo development. That one up—what is it they call it?—Bride's Gulch?"

"Canyon. Bride's Canyon." Bartell knew the job she was talking about. Bride's Canyon opened at the east edge of town, and consisted mostly of National Forest. But there was a pocket of several hundred acres of private property between the city limits, and the National Forest boundary. A few years ago, the first bulldozers had moved into that area, and the place had been a battleground ever since. At first the plans allowed for low-density housing with generous areas of open space. But every year or so, the developer came forward with a new plan, and a request for rezoning. Slowly, houses had crept over the mountainsides, getting ever closer together as they approached the Holt River, where people were now busy slapping up condos along the river itself. And the first thing most of the new residents seemed to do was complain loudly about over-development.

"One day," Gina said, "Henry got to ragging on his boss. Told him, I guess, that the whole project was bullshit."

"Fired?"

"Sort of. Depends on who you ask, Henry or his boss."

"So what's the attraction with Cradle Creek?" Bartell said, swinging the conversation back to the subject that seemed to be some sort of key to Skelton. "I mean, we all get hung up on things, but it sounds to me like he's being a little excessive. It's not like he's Indian himself."

Gina began to bounce her right heel on the floor. "Look, Detective Bartell—"

"—Ray."

"Fine. Ray. Look, I love Henry, but one thing I've learned is it's no use denying he can be kind of . . . loony. You have to remember, we're talking about a man who once proposed murder as a means of trimming government bureaucracy." She sounded as though she didn't necessarily disagree with the idea. That was fine with Bartell as long as she—and Skelton—didn't decide to start with him.

"You think he's serious?"

She found the question ridiculous. "I suppose he might believe it when he writes that crazy stuff. But no, he's not some kind of homicidal maniac. Listen, if he was serious, he'd have left the city of San Francisco littered with dead politicians."

Bartell made a mental note of her logic, then went on. "Does he talk about Cradle Creek a lot? What he thinks, what he does when he's out on these trips?"

"No. In fact, that's the part that's not like Henry at all. We always talked a lot. About everything. That's one of the things that's held us together through some pretty tough times." Her eyes met Bartell's again. For the first time, she seemed to be looking past his profession. "This is different," she said.

"Why?"

"I'm not sure." She looked away quickly, then stood. "I'm sorry," she said. "It feels good talking about Henry. But not so good talking about him to you. To you, a cop, it feels disloyal. And you being Helen's husband and all, it makes me feel like maybe I can trust you, when I really shouldn't."

Bartell wanted to tell her that he was different from other policemen, that he understood Henry Skelton and he knew that Skelton wasn't like all the other head cases on the loose in Montana these days. We all want to believe that the people we love are different from the rest of the mouths in the world's breadline, because we want to believe we're different too. Henry Skelton, he could tell her, sounded like the kind of man who would endure winters on a homestead in the Big Belt Mountains, the way Bartell had grown up, and do it for reasons more serious than simply enjoying the view. Where was the truth in that though? And even if it turned out to be true, what were the odds that someday Bartell would write a report about Skelton, and that report would find its way into a hundred photocopies of his federal file? And ten years from now, some other well-meaning policeman, or maybe a not-so-well-meaning policeman, would be smiling like a leopard at Gina Lozano, saying, *Hey, sweetheart, trust me, I'm not like all those other jerks.*

Bartell knew he was making this too complicated. After all, it was Gina Lozano he was responding to here, not Henry Skelton. Likely as not, Skelton was just another shithead with a smart mouth.

Bartell hauled himself out of the chair. He started past Gina for the door, stopped, and offered her his hand. "Thanks," he said. "And I wouldn't worry about being disloyal. At this point, nobody wants anything except to make sure Henry isn't about to get himself in trouble. Like I said, Helen doesn't know I'm here. But from what she's told me, you sound like the kind of woman who wants that for Henry too."

Gina stood and took his hand. Her grip was small and hard, the fingers like warm hooks. She let Bartell's hand slip away, then went quickly to the door.

"I was looking through Henry's books one night," she said over her shoulder. "In one about the Nez Perce I found a place he'd marked. A passage about something called the *Wyakin.* A personal spirit that you can find only by going on a solitary journey through the wilderness."

"A quest," Bartell said.

"I guess. Anyway, if you're lucky, you discover your guardian spirit, and it will help you through life."

"So you think that's what Henry's after?"

"God knows what he's after," Gina said. "Anyway, I'll probably never know. According to that book, part of the whole *Wyakin* thing is, once you discover your guardian spirit, you can't tell anybody. Tell people, it said, and the spirit will turn on you."

Bartell grinned. "Give you the shaft."

"I guess." Gina's face warmed again.

"Sure," Bartell said. "Given the shaft by ghosts. Ruin your whole day."

Gina's eyes brightened as she finally seemed to give up the last of her wariness. "Don't do that. This is supposed to be serious business. You make it sound silly."

Bartell pulled a face and shook his hands beside his head. "Booga-booga!"

And then they were both laughing. Stupid, it was, like a couple of kids. When they stopped, he felt ridiculous. Who could possibly take him seriously as a cop? Certainly not Gina Lozano. Not now. She was quiet now too, standing with her hands in the pockets of her jeans, staring down at the floor. He wondered if she thought he was hitting on her. He wasn't. But he could be if he did things like that. Except he didn't. He wasn't. He did like her though.

Bartell coughed. "Sorry."

"No, that's okay."

He pulled a card from the small stack he carried in his shirt pocket. "This thing with the former president," he said, "has Henry said anything about it? Talked about the visit?"

Gina thought for a moment. "I don't think so." She sounded straightforward. "Since the trouble in California, he doesn't talk much about that stuff. Politics. And he's even more tight-lipped about it since all that mess with the bombing. But I can tell you one thing."

"What's that?"

"If you want Henry to stay out of your business, then you leave him out. He doesn't deal well with being pushed."

Bartell handed her the card. "Nobody's pushing."

"Maybe," she said, "maybe not. But if you could figure out a way . . ."

"A way to what?"

"I don't know. Nothing."

"Are you afraid of him?"

"No. No, I've never been afraid of Henry." Again, her eyes faltered briefly. "Afraid *for* him."

"Just tell Henry to give me a call."

Gina said she would, and closed the door after him.

Outside, the breeze had picked up and the patches of valley fog had all dispersed. Upriver, Bartell caught the approach of maybe a dozen geese, circling low in a shallow V above the cottonwoods. Christ, Bartell thought, the only thing more of a pain in the ass than an eco-terrorist was a mystic eco-terrorist. A mystic, *Californian* eco-terrorist. Or was that redundant? He was halfway to the car, when he heard the door open. A moment later Gina was at his side.

"About the bombing . . ." A worried, uncertain look came over her face.

"Yes?" Bartell suppressed a flutter of anticipation.

"I want to tell you something. Henry made me promise I wouldn't say anything." She stopped again, needing her own time.

Almost involuntarily, Bartell began to think about how he would word the report that would lead to an arrest warrant for Skelton. *During an interview with Gina Lozano, Ms. Lozano told me . . .*

"But this isn't going to go away, I know that."

"What did he tell you, Gina?" . . . *that Skelton had admitted to her he'd done the bombing.*

"He told me he saw the man who did it."

"I beg your pardon?" In Bartell's mind, all those pre-fab phrases in his imaginary report crumpled on the page.

Her large eyes were full of tears now, and she wiped them harshly with her sleeve. "He said he woke up when he heard something on the road. Said he got out his binoculars and saw two men standing in the headlights of a truck. One of them had a gun. A few minutes later the bomb went off."

Now Bartell's anticipation was more than a flutter, lots more. This sure as hell wasn't in the file. "He say what the men looked like?"

"He recognized one of them as one of the loggers."

"The one with the gun?"

"No."

"And did he tell this to the cops?"

"I don't think so. I'm sure he didn't."

"Did you?" Of course, he already knew the answer.

"No. He made me promise."

"Why?"

"Because it was the cops. Because he's Henry Skelton. God-dammit, I don't know. If you had our history with the feds, you probably wouldn't tell them anything either." Her voice was defiant now, and she was a long way past tears.

Bartell wanted to ask her why she was telling him now, but he already knew the answer. Helen. He'd done business on his wife's friendship with this woman, and he couldn't bear hearing Gina tell him this. He hoped what he'd learned was worth it, but he was far from sure.

"What else?" There was always something else.

This time her voice was measured and detached. "Voices. He said he heard voices." Her eyes welled up again. "And I knew one of them," she whispered, "one of them was that poor man who was killed."

"Do you know what they were saying? The two men?"

"No. But it's crazy, I keep imagining that I can hear the voices myself. The way voices will carry on a quiet night? I hear those voices when I'm trying to get to sleep at night, and it makes that man seem real to me . . . alive. Does that make any sense?"

"Yes." It wasn't uncommon to discover that some detail or other managed to keep the dead alive in someone's imagination. "Did Henry tell you anything else? What the second man looked like? Where he came from?"

Again she swiped a forearm across her eyes. "That's all of it. If he knows anything more, he didn't tell me."

"So what is it you expect me to do, Gina?" Bartell's actions could not be governed by her wishes. It would be easier, though, if he knew in advance what she hoped to get from him.

"I don't know. Just leave him alone, I guess. Look, I'm not stupid. I know you're out here because you think he blew up that helicopter, and now you think he's maybe going try something with the president . . . the former president . . . whatever the hell he is. But I know he didn't set off that bomb, and if you could just see that, *believe* it, then maybe you'd just leave him alone. I don't know."

Bartell sensed that she was starting to withdraw, afraid, perhaps, that she should not have trusted him with her secret.

"Because if you don't leave him alone—" She stopped now, turned abruptly, and walked hastily back into the house.

Bartell started to follow her but held back. Gina had already passed through some barrier that she had once believed impenetrable, and right now it was important to keep her on the line. Tug sharply now, and she would be gone.

Overhead, the geese wheeled and disappeared behind the trees. In the neighbor's tiny, ragged pasture, an Appaloosa rolled on his back in the dust, snorting wildly as he thrashed at the air with his black-and-white hooves.

When the man—undoubtedly a cop—finally got into the gray car and left, there were four cigarette butts mashed into the gouged-out hole. The man in the brush sat back on his heels and groaned slightly in response to the kinks in his knees. When he

straightened his legs to ease the pain, his knees crackled deep inside like muted popcorn. Music of middle age, he thought. How far out to his car? Maybe half a mile? He could have parked closer, but he'd deliberately selected a spot on a road that offered no access to the cul-de-sac. It was a longer walk, sure, but it was worth it to lessen the chances of having his car made.

The man looked at his watch. Nearly noon. Where was Skelton? He could leave now, shoulder the tools of his trade, and hike back on out to his car. Find a quiet joint, have a few drinks. Check back later for the green pickup. Who would know?

He would know.

Among other things, the man was paid to wait and watch. Compared with those other things, waiting and watching were easy money. And at some level it made him uncomfortable to explore, it was almost . . . what? . . . pleasant? Voyeurism was for perverts, though, and not at any cost to be confused with surveillance.

The man crouched again, got a sandwich from the bag. Ham and cheese. Mayo. No mustard.

The invisible man, that was it. Fly on the wall. He glanced at the binoculars in his lap, then at the small house across the pasture, where inside the woman went about her private business, her own brand of waiting, as though no one might take notice. Chewing on the sandwich, the man felt unexpectedly as though he had taken root. Taken root through his ass, his arms and legs branches, his hair leaves. His eyes everywhere. Who needed a dark bar and drinks—or even a payday—when he had all this?

As it turned out, the man didn't have all that long to wait.

Chapter 9

"You stink," Gina said, making a face as she waved a hand in front of her nose.

Skelton took a couple of long strides across the kitchen and made a move to embrace her, but she good-naturedly pushed him away. After dumping his gear just inside the kitchen, he'd gone out right away and moved the truck; this was the first Gina had seen—and smelled—of him since his return.

"That creek where you go," she said, "maybe you should try squatting down in it with a bar of soap before you come back to town."

"It's that natural-man aroma," Skelton said. "Wood smoke and hormones. I'm told some women find it quite appealing."

"You were told wrong. BO and dirt, that's more like it."

Now Gina moved toward him, gave him a quick kiss through his beard. Skelton smiled at their coded banter and abbreviated intimacy, the things that made it possible both for him to leave on his forays into the mountains and to return home. Stepping now to the sink, he turned on the tap, ran cold water over his hands and wrists, then splashed several handfuls onto his face.

"Better?" he said, thinking that she had spent too long smelling the insides of hospitals and doctors' offices, where all the stink of corruption and life is masked by antiseptics.

"A good steam cleaning would be better," Gina said. At the stove, she poured two cups of hot water, then got tea bags from the cupboard.

"I think I've about had it for the year," he said. Walking out from his cave to the truck that morning, Skelton had thought he'd probably return to Cradle Creek once more before the snow flew. And butting heads with that pair of loggers at the turnoff hadn't done anything to change his mind. If anything, just the opposite. But coming into the tiny kitchen a few moments ago, catching Gina in the midst of tidying up, triggered a momentary change of heart. For the first time since arriving in Montana, Skelton had thought of himself as coming home rather than simply going back to the house in town. The sensation was fleeting, sure, but nonetheless there, almost visceral. Perhaps that was how the bear felt, loggers or not, when he'd ambled into Cradle Creek with winter in the wind.

"Maybe," Skelton ventured, "you'd like to go back up with me."

She turned away from tending the tea and cocked a hand on her hip. "I have to work. Remember?"

Skelton dusted aside a pang of guilt. "Just for a couple of days?" Gina worked swing shift at St. Francis, and he knew that she was off tonight and tomorrow, and didn't need to be at work until the evening of the third day. "We could be packed up and out of here in three, four hours." It would probably be dark before they reached the cave, but he knew the area so well that darkness wasn't a problem. "What do you say? It's going to be a long winter."

Gina shook her head and went back to their tea. "I think I'll pass."

Given her behavior during the summer, this was the answer Skelton had expected. Even so, he still found it surprising. He knew she shared his views on loggers, and most other kinds of destructive development. If anything, she was even more political on the issue than he was, joining advocacy groups, writing letters, signing countless petitions, where Skelton saw himself as the consummate loner. But when it came down to actual participation in the wilderness she fought to preserve, Gina more often than not seemed to be content to view wild country from afar. Though not offended by this, Skelton was puzzled. As far as Cradle Creek went, Skelton knew that some of Gina's aversion had to do with the bombing last spring, and his refusal to come forward with what he'd seen that night. Now there was a scab he didn't care to pick at any further.

"Suit yourself," Skelton said, accepting a mug of tea.

Gina blew steadily through the steam rising off her tea. "The cops were here a little while ago. Well, not the *cops* exactly, just one cop."

"Yeah?" Skelton thought immediately about those two loggers earlier in the day but gave sign of nothing beyond casual interest. "Another fed?"

Gina shook her head. Her face had that look of combined fear and disappointment which she got whenever the law came sniffing around. A look at which she'd had too much practice. "Local this time." With her free hand she pulled a business card from the hip pocket of her jeans and handed it to Skelton.

Skelton glanced at the card, then tossed it onto the counter next to the sink. "Bartell. Never heard of him. What's a city cop care about something happened out in the boondocks?"

When Gina told him people now had the wild hair that he might have in mind cooling the former president of the United States, Skelton remained so calm, it surprised him. Resignation, he decided. When Gina finally stopped talking, he simply shrugged and gave up a slow smile. "Now," he said at last, "why didn't I think of that?"

"I knew you'd be worried," Gina said sarcastically. She shouldered her way past Skelton and went into the living room.

"Life's a straight-ahead thing for me," he said after her. "I never made any secret of that."

She came up short and looked back at him. "Straight ahead. Right. And look where it's got you. Again."

Skelton followed her into the other room. "I can't help it if people keep getting in my way."

"You could try going around. You could say *excuse me* maybe just once. Like it would kill you to try avoiding trouble?"

Skelton set his tea on the drafting table, then stepped close to Gina and tried to put his arms around her. She wrenched away.

"Not now," Gina said. "You can't just shine things on with me again."

"Listen," he said, his voice rising now. "Listen to me, Gina. I go up in the goddamn woods and I watch these assholes tear it all apart. I mind my own business. *I just watch the wreckage.* I know, in California I went over the edge. But I'm not over the edge now. I'm not even close."

"Then why didn't you tell them about the man you saw? The night of the bombing?"

"Because."

"Because." She started to take a sip of tea, stopped, gestured angrily with the cup, sloshing tea over her fingers. "Because, because, because."

"Because," he persisted, "if you tell them anything, anything at all, they twist it around and use it against you. This sonofabitch must be guilty, right? Why else would he lie? That's what they'd say."

"You tell them, dear," she said as though she were lecturing a child on table manners, "you tell them, Henry, because a man died. Because some poor man got blown to bits and what you saw might help catch whoever did it."

There, she had picked the scab for both of them. "And you think they'd believe me?" Skelton picked up his tea, and took a short sip. "I don't see it that way." Not for the first time, he wondered if he'd have been more willing to tell what he knew if it weren't for those years at Lompoc. The question was purely academic, though, whereas those days and nights inside were now as much a part of his being as chromosomes.

"Well, I told them," Gina said. "Bartell. I told him. Not for you, but for me. Because I couldn't live with it anymore."

Taken aback at last, Skelton simply stared at her. After years of banging up against cops, lawyers, judges, and parole officers, this was the first time Gina had ever stepped out of line—out of *his* line—and started talking on her own. Not that he'd ever asked her to lie for him. He'd never even lied for himself. The man who touched off the bomb? That wasn't a lie. Nobody'd ever *asked* him if he'd seen somebody else that night. They'd only *told* him he was guilty, an asshole and a murderer. Had anyone ever bothered to *ask* what he knew, then maybe he'd have told them. Maybe.

"Sometimes," Gina said softly, "I think you're nothing but a miserable, stubborn sonofabitch."

"What's your point?" he said.

"Just go see this Bartell? Okay?" Her lips were pressed together, hard and straight as a line drawn on the chalkboard by a grade-school English teacher preparing to diagram a sentence.

"I'll think about it."

Skelton went into the bathroom, where he started the water and peeled out of his clothes. In the house—Gina's house—he realized he did stink of wood smoke and sweat. Folding his large frame into the small tub, he slumped low until the steaming water swirled around his groin, then curled up over his chest.

Skelton closed his eyes and slowly inhaled the steam rising off the water. Was Gina making sense? Should he go in and talk to this Bartell? Or had she simply gone over to the other side? God, why did everything have to translate into sides? Even with her. As he lay there, trying to make sense out of it all, he found himself recalling the way he'd felt that morning in San Francisco. The morning he got busted by the feds.

They'd swung in behind Skelton right after he dropped Gina off at the UC Medical Center. He knew they hadn't followed them in from Marin County, because by then he'd been shadowed enough to pay attention to details like that. It made his skin crawl—these guys had him so cold they knew right where and when to find him. He recognized the tan Olds right off. Tan Olds with two guys in suits and sunglasses.

So he doubled back through Haight-Ashbury, then headed cast and turned onto Market, started crawling through the traffic toward the Financial District. Not trying to shake them. Just curious about how hard they would dog him this time.

Dogged him hard enough, it turned out. All the way down to the Embarcadero, where he finally had his fill, and swung the car into an empty space near Greenwich.

Then he started up the Filbert Steps, through the cramped old neighborhood where there were no real streets. There, in the jungle of Grace Marchant garden, he stopped to catch his breath among trendy fishing shacks before climbing on, across Napier Lane and Darrell, before turning north behind the Montgomery Street condos, where rich house cats lounged like the guardians of Egyptian tombs along the tops of privacy fences. Finally, under the dense green canopy, he pounded up a set of worn brick steps and came out abruptly in the parking lot at Coit Tower.

And there they were. Goddamned Oldsmobile, four door boat, parked in the circle near that statue of Christopher Columbus. Laughing.

Half a dozen guys in tight jeans and moussed hair, real tough guys, all started pointing at him. There was a slick man with a load of camera gear draped around his neck. And a Chinese girl who waved a clipboard and screamed that he was messing up the light. The lousy fucking light.

Laughing.

For a long while, it seemed, Skelton just stood there. He looked out across the panorama below. Bay Bridge to Treasure Island. Cold, infinite expanse of the Bay itself. Alcatraz, Golden Gate, Russian Hill. Back to Alcatraz. Alca-fucking-traz.

And then he thought, what the hell, and walked over to that car. Seconds later, nobody was laughing.

To tell the truth, Skelton sometimes still got the shakes when he remembered the smug look on the Bureau guy's face just before he reached inside the car, grabbed him by the necktie, and dragged him out through the window. Through the years since, Skelton had nearly forgotten the rage it had taken to blast him loose that morning.

Forget it, just let it go.

That's what he told himself. Said it several times inside his head.

He was talking to a stranger.

Concentrate. Reassemble all these exploding, unthinking parts into something that could pass for rational.

Skelton lifted his hands from the water and stared at them. He might have been a mechanic considering whether or not he had the right tools. Hands that had tried to beat two men to death.

Gina stepped into the door and stopped. "I know this man's wife."

"Which man?" His voice sounded far away from the fury inside his head.

"Bartell. The cop. I know his wife. Her name's Helen."

"Friend of yours, is she?"

"Not exactly. But we could be. If things worked out."

"That's good. You should have more friends."

"Goddammit, Henry," Gina said wearily. "That's not what I meant, and you know it. I meant I know her, and she wouldn't be married to this guy if he was like the rest of them. The cops."

"Then you're trying to convince me I should go see him."

"I'm not trying to convince you of anything. I wouldn't waste the breath. I'm just telling you what I think."

This, Skelton thought, from the woman who had sold him out.

"Every night," she went on, her voice low, almost a whisper, "every night almost, I think about that man. About the way you told me he was marched off into the darkness. I've worked emergency rooms, Henry. I know what bodies look like when they're burned up and torn to pieces."

Wearily, Skelton raised a hand to her. "If I knew something that would help them find the right man, I would tell them." As he spoke, he wondered if this was a lie, a sentiment cooked up to get square again with Gina. "But it's not like that, I told you. I know I'd recognize the guy, sure. How to find him, though, who he is, I don't have a clue. So what I saw doesn't mean anything. Not a goddamn thing."

She took his hand in both of hers, gripped down tight. "That's not the point, Henry. An innocent man died. When that happens, you do everything you can, tell everything you know. And you don't do it because it will solve the case. You're supposed to do it just because you care enough to try to help."

"Maybe," he said, and the word made him feel as though a fault line had just ripped through a lifetime of certainty. While she still held his hand, before it was too late, he pulled her down closer to him and they kissed. She dropped his hand, and he held her face in both of his huge hands and he kissed her again for a long time.

When Skelton finally stopped kissing her, Gina was crying.

"There aren't many things on earth," he said, "that could make me change directions. But it matters that you might think I'm just a miserable, stubborn sonofabitch."

She pulled away and got to her feet, then stood looking down at him as she sniffled, wiped her eyes with her sleeves, then laughed, trying to make light of things. "Well, that's what you are, you know. And you still stink."

Chapter 10

When Bartell got back to the office at about twelve o'clock, Beth McCoy said that Fanning and Zillion had taken their act across the street at the courthouse, where they were locked up in a meeting with the sheriff, the chief, and other assorted brain trusters. Zillion had left word that they'd have to put Skelton off until tomorrow.

"If it's an emergency," Beth said, "Fanning has his pager. You want me to page him?"

"Go on," said Billy Stokes, who was eavesdropping from his desk. "I dare you. You'll give Fanning an orgasm."

Then Linda Westhammer cruised into the division and picked up immediately on the conversation. "I'd be careful, I was you," she said. "One good orgasm, and Fanning's room temperature."

Bartell wasn't about to pick up on that one. There were probably enough beepers in that meeting across the street to make the room go off like pinball machine. But Bartell despised the thought of stroking Fanning's ego by jingling him out of a meeting with other bigshots. It wasn't like Henry Skelton had actually killed any politicians yet.

There were always reports to catch up, so while the other detectives straggled off to lunch, Bartell chained himself to his computer. He started off with a rape, a case in which he'd coaxed a confession out of some slug by convincing him that his only true wrong may have been a lack of sensitivity. And then there was an internal theft at a convenience store, where the real problem turned out to be that the owner wasn't sensitive enough to the financial needs of the employee who was skimming the till. And finally, Bartell polished off the tale of one drunk who'd smashed another drunk across the nose with a beer bottle. And damned if the problem here wasn't sensitivity too. Nobody, Bartell decided, ever did anything wrong these days. People broke the law, sure, did it all the time. But wrong?

Please.

Yes, sir, it all came down to sensitivity. Either too much or not enough. When Bartell first went into the police business, conventional wisdom held that crimes were committed by people who were incapable of understanding their behavior because they had not, for some unfathomable reason, developed a conscience. But that was way back at the start of the greed-infested eighties, and since then everybody had learned that *conscience* was an outmoded concept based on right and wrong.

My, my, such a quaint notion, right and wrong.

No, the real culprit was sensitivity and its inappropriate applications. Nobody's right, nobody's wrong. You, my good man, are not a worthless piece of shit. It's not your fault that guy in the bar objected to your crude remarks about his wife's large breasts. And it's just your bad luck that smashing his face with a bottle of Bud Lite is against the law, to say nothing of a waste of beer. You just need to be more sensitive. Now, it's off to counseling you go. Not guilty by reason of SD. Sensitivity deficit.

By one o'clock, Bartell had a sensitivity headache and the other detectives still weren't back from lunch. Bartell thought about a hamburger down at Roosa's Cafe. More precisely, he dreamed of a half-pound double-barbecue baconburger. Along with some fries. And maybe a little tossed salad with ranch dressing. Then a slice of Roosa's homemade carrot cake. With a scoop of ice cream. A big scoop.

Bartell tried very hard not to think about the two bran muffins and the apple gathering dust on the corner of his desk.

Bran muffins. Bran muffins might make a halfway decent dessert after you had a worthwhile breakfast. A chili-cheese omelet, say. Or corned beef hash with a couple of poached eggs, and some American cheese melted over the top, all of it spiked with Tabasco sauce.

And apples. Apples were okay as long as you held them to certain limited uses. Like pies, for instance.

But making a whole meal out of bran muffins and apples . . . it was the kind of thing a guy did for only two reasons. One was to please his wife, and the other was to shrink his gut for the dating circuit if trying to please his wife didn't work out. Was a time, Bartell groused, remembering back to when he was a kid on maybe a dozen ranches around central Montana, another time, another life, when he had been an authentic piece of Americana, a regular working cowboy. Now, here he was, reduced to working for wages in a windowless basement that dripped sewage and eating health food to keep a woman happy. It often seemed that the only remnants of that other life—the real one?—were boots and blue jeans. Affectations. How do things get so derailed?

Bartell picked up the apple and gripped it in his right hand, his index and middle fingers spread wide and curving around the red, waxy peel, the way he once saw Tim McCarver or Tom Seaver, one of those baseball guys on TV, saw him demonstrate the grip on a split-finger fastball. Bartell looked across the detectives' bay at Ike Skinner's trash basket, wondering how much break he could get on an apple. Probably not much. No seams.

Beth McCoy stuck her head around the corner. "There's a man out here to see you." She scowled as she stared at the apple in Bartell's hand.

"A man?"

"Kind of a runty little guy," she said. "A cowboy."

"Cowboy?" A runty cowboy? Bartell smacked the apple into the palm of his left hand as though it were the pocket of a fielder's mitt, then set it back on the desk next to the muffins. He could think of only one runty cowboy on earth who might search him out. "He give you a name?"

Beth was exasperated. "Did I tell you his name? Of course he didn't give me a name. If I knew his name, why wouldn't I tell you what it was? Ray, you're acting weird."

Weird? Well, why not? That was easy for Beth McCoy to say. She had no idea of what Bartell feared was about to happen.

"Ray!" a voice cackled from the front desk. "Hey there, Ray, come on out, it's me!"

"Who is that guy?" Beth McCoy hissed.

"A headache, that's who," Bartell said, getting to his feet and following Beth around to her side of the partition, where Cash Bartell waited with his elbows and forearms braced on the Formica counter.

"Howdy, son," Cash said. "Yep, yep, it's me. In the flesh." His stained and battered felt hat was pushed back on his head, and his brown Carhart jacket, ragged and stained, was open down the front.

"*Son?*" Beth hissed to Bartell.

"Hey, Pop," Bartell said, trying to force some enthusiasm into his voice. "I was just thinking about you. Sort of."

"*Pop?*" Beth said, now clearly flustered. "Well, I didn't mean he was, you know—"

"It's okay," Bartell said.

"—*runty,*" Beth whispered.

"Beth, this here's my dad. Cash Bartell." After finishing up the introductions, Bartell lowered his face, closed his eyes, and massaged his temples. He couldn't imagine a single good reason why his father would turn up in Rozette without warning, especially after their visit at the ranch just a few days before. This had all the markings of a tragic development, which, for Cash, usually translated into jail. But the old man was obviously not handcuffed, and he smelled like horses instead of booze.

"So," Bartell ventured, "what's going on?"

Again that cackling laugh. "Got me a job."

But Cash already had a job. He'd been on the Hillegoss outfit for nearly as long as Bartell had been with the police department. "Is that right. Doing what?"

"Movie star."

"Come again?" Maybe Bartell was going deaf, along with crazy.

Now Beth McCoy jumped in. "Movie star?"

Cash nodded. "That's what I said. Movie star."

Bartell took a deep breath, held it, then let it out, bracing himself for a return to the ugly past. Okay, so maybe somebody had one of those crazy humanities grants to do a documentary on derelict cowboys. A grainy black-and-white job, the kind made by earnest people without much money who figured the thing would look real sincere, and people who had never been stomped on by a steer would watch it and think, by *God*, that's what real life really, truly is. "Okay, Pop. How drunk are you? You know what town you're in?" Salient questions from years gone by.

Now Cash sounded wounded. "You cut me to the core, son."

"Ray," Beth McCoy scolded, "be *nice.*"

It turned out that the old man was cold sober, and on the level too. After Ray and Helen left last Sunday, Cash wandered down to the headquarters for a cup of coffee with the cook—a handsome old gal from Harlowtown, made great fry bread—but that was another story.

"Anyway," Cash said, "while we was sippin' and jawin', who walks in but Brandon McWilliams himself. Him and a whole bunch of fancy dudes." And along with an entourage in tow, McWilliams also had a startling idea in his head.

As Cash explained it now, McWilliams was doing preproduction for the sequel to that big movie of his, a western called *Busted Heart. Preproduction.* That was the word Cash used. Bartell didn't know what preproduction meant, and he doubted that Cash did either. But one thing led to another there in the cook house, and before you could get your pants dusted off and say how-do, Brandon McWilliams's very own agent had taken Cash on as a client.

"Brand, he says I'm a perfect type," Cash said.

"Brand?" Beth McCoy said, sounding awestruck.

"Yeah. Brandon McWilliams. That's what his friends call him. Brand. Anyway, Brand, he plays this bounty hunter, and him and his agent and all that crowd they brought along, they all said I'm perfect for this part."

"What part?" Bartell said. What the hell, every western has room for a busted-up used-to-be-drunk cowboy or two.

"The father."

"Can you get me an autograph?" Beth McCoy said.

"Whose father?" Bartell said.

"Can you get me a date?"

"Why, his. Brand's father. Who else?"

"Does he know Eddie Rabbit?" Beth McCoy said breathlessly. She had once camped out in a motel lobby after an Eddie Rabbit concert, hoping to get an autograph. She was undoubtedly the biggest Eddie Rabbit fan west of the Continental Divide. "Could he get me a date with Eddie Rabbit? I'd kill for that."

Bartell stared across the room at the old man. "You're going to be Brandon McWilliams's father. In the movies."

"That's right, you betcha."

Bartell paused a minute, letting it all sink in. At last, he said, "You got any of this in writing?"

"Can I have *your* autograph?" Beth McCoy said. This time, though, she stopped short of asking for a date, proving she hadn't completely lost her mind.

"Faxed me the contracts this morning."

"Faxed?" Bartell said.

"Whatsa matter, you never used a fax machine?"

Bartell found himself both bewildered and giddy. "And you signed?"

"Signed? You're damn right I signed. Hell, I drove all the way over here today just to tell you the good news. Gonna shop around for a new pickup too."

The preproduction for *Busted Heart II: The Innocent,* Cash told Bartell and Beth McCoy with an insider's assurance, had been going on all summer, and his part had turned out to be one of the toughest to cast, since McWilliams was blessed with something he called a high reality standard, and all the good old boy actors around these days suffered mightily from having had their good old boy carcasses picked clean by the movies and TV.

"He don't want no actor," the old man said. "Wants himself a real dad. We start shooting in March. Right there on the ranch. Hell, that cabin I been stayin' in? That's where they got me livin' in the movie. So I get put up in a motel in Great Falls till the shoot's all done. Hell, I might even buy me a trailer house, haul it out after the shoot." He winked at Beth McCoy. "That Brand, he's got a soft spot for me."

Bartell invited Cash back to his desk, but the old man waved him off. "No time for that now, pard. Daylight's wastin', and there's a whole town full of pickups to check out. I thought maybe you'd want to come along. Kind of like one of them father-and-son things. Know what I mean?"

Ignoring the hard fact that he and Cash were at least twenty years past anything remotely resembling father-and-son togetherness, Bartell suggested that maybe this urge to spend big money could wait until later in the afternoon. But Cash was having none of it.

"We gotta get with the program, son. It's either come with me now, or toss me in the bucket to get me out of your hair. What's it gonna be?"

Resigning himself to a lost afternoon, Bartell agreed. "If Fanning asks," he said to Beth McCoy, "tell him I'm out cultivating informants."

"That's the spirit," Cash cackled. "Later on, maybe I'll tell you another surprise." He winked again at Beth McCoy, who blushed.

Cash Bartell in the movies. Wasn't one surprise enough? Lord God, at this crazy rate, Merle Puhl might even win the election.

As Bartell and his old man were about to leave, Thomas Cassidy, the detective-novelist, wandered back in from lunch. Bartell tried to slip past him, but Beth McCoy was having none of it.

"This is Ray's father," Beth said to Cassidy. "His name's Cash, and he's going to be a movie star."

Cassidy stopped so quickly, he could've gotten whiplash. "I beg your pardon."

"A movie star," Beth McCoy said. "He's going to be Brandon McWilliams's father in the new *Busted Heart.*"

"You betcha," Cash said.

Cassidy's eyes went harder than Arnold Zillion's on the golf course. "You know Brandon McWilliams?"

"Hell, son, I break his horses."

"How much they paying you?" Cassidy said.

"A lot," Cash said sheepishly before tightening down to Cassidy's level. "A *whole lot.*"

Bartell felt like hooking the old man's head in the crook of his elbow and dragging him up the steps.

"You getting points?" Cassidy asked.

"Points?" Cash asked, scowling.

"Mr. Bartell," Cassidy said patiently, "Cash, you and I need to have a talk. We need to have lunch."

Chapter 11

It was easier at night. Because you could get closer, and at the same time the people were less careful. More happened at night too. Same reasons. Sneak around. Balance and study it all, like a puddle of water cupped in the palm of your hand, the moisture seeping along all the little creases that might make sense to a Gypsy fortune teller. And that other part too, the moment that sucked your nuts up into your belly and made you want to cry and giggle at the same time, if you let it. The almost, but not quite, getting-caught part.

The man slouched down in the seat of the pickup, fine-tuned the public radio station—only decent blues on the air in this crummy town—and shook another cigarette from the pack, all the while gazing steadily at the house down the street. Lights behind the curtained windows. Shadowed figures now and then. No great shakes. The only vehicle at the house was the woman's Toyota. But Skelton was there. The man knew it. Before turning down the cul-de-sac, he'd checked at the end of the dirt road upriver from the house, and found the green pickup pulled off into the trees, where Skelton always stashed it. You had to love it, a guy with Skelton's paranoia.

The man lit the smoke, checked his watch. Eight-thirty. Dark enough for cover, early enough to make it interesting. End of the twenty minutes he'd given himself parked out in the open just down the street from the house. The giggly part, just to prove he could do it. Like in that movie, The Bridges of Toko-Ri, *where this carrier pilot, William Holden, loses his nerve, so he goes below decks and parks a chair under the catapult system that launches the planes. Measures it off, so when that big hunk of goddamn steel comes slamming at him at—what, ninety, a hundred miles an hour?—it stops just inches before bashing his head into a blob of Vaseline.*

Yeah. Like that.

He drew on the cigarette and gave it another two minutes past deadline. Measures his face a fraction closer to crash.

This was the part you did for free. The part that made those dim fuckers with grocery bags of cash really squirm. The part that convinced them the count better goddamn well not be short.

The man let a bubble of smoke drift out of his mouth and inhaled it through his nose.

Tight enough now.

Fuck it.

He reached for the key in the ignition, and was about to start up the truck, then gave the house down the street one last glance, just as the guy and his old lady came out, climbed into that raggedy-ass Toyota.

No time to think. Just react. Sweat out the plan he'd gone through in his mind a dozen times while contemplating all the contingencies of these twenty, now twenty-two, minutes.

He dropped the cigarette onto the carpeted floor of the truck, ground it under his heel. Tipped over flat on the seat.

Took a deep breath.

Waited.

Skelton told Gina to drive because it felt less like capitulation. Okay, he was being childish. So what? The world was never harmed by children. Should they have had some? Another cliché of the age. Biological clock ticking like your heart winding down. He looked at Gina while she fumbled with her keys. Her jaw had that ground-in look, the kind Skelton used to notice back in California, when they would drive into the city to meet with that tubesteak who was his attorney.

Why, though, bring a child into this world? Douche-bag businessmen, a government without enough shame to be a decent whore.

Skelton, stop it. Another cliché.

How about sparing some poor kid a jailbird freak for a father. No cliché there. Self-pity instead. A perfect trade.

He watched Gina finger her hair behind her ear as she checked the street for traffic.

No. Half a perfect trade. Gina could have made it work. A kid.

"Just remember," Skelton said, "this was your idea."

She threw her head back against the headrest, exasperated. "Then either shut up, Henry, and give it a try. Or get out of the car right now. What's it going to be? No more bullshit."

"Okay. Okay. No more bullshit."

She gunned the car out into the street, and they were off. Down and dirty once again on the latest leg of their journey through life's great adventure.

As he watched the lights sweep by, listened to the Toyota's bad shocks bang over the ruts just inches away, the man's skin began to tingle, and it felt as though he were suspended above the seat, weightless, invisible, his blood wafting like helium through his body. Then the lights passed, the noise faded. Now his blood screamed, hysterical. He allowed a tiny smile to twitch through the muscles of his face. He sat up, watched in the mirror as the Toyota's lights swung onto the main road, then started up his own truck, and followed.

Bonus points, he thought, lighting another cigarette, when you get the chance to go mobile.

Women always claim that men run the show, but that's just a tactic they use when they're trying to pry something more out of you. Isn't that the truth? Everybody knew it. Men did, at least. Most women too, when you could get them to come clean. Henry Skelton sure as hell knew it. Why else was he riding along with Gina that Tuesday night, on this fool's errand, this alleged solution cooked up by Gina and that friend of hers, Helen, the cop's wife? He had been tolerant as they passed through downtown in the old Toyota, but found himself growing sullen again as she turned up into the hills into a part of town he didn't know.

"I got better things to do than this," Skelton said, thinking about the meeting that awaited them.

"No you don't," she snapped.

"My views on nonsense are widely known," he said, trying to blunt his irritation with some semblance of flair. "And this is nonsense."

"No," she said firmly. "It's not."

Right, and she was such an expert. Since when was the law something you could sit down with and explain? The law might get dolled up now and then in herringbone and rep ties, but underneath it was all black leather.

"What kind of people live up here anyway?" he said, watching the neighborhood deteriorate into an endless procession of sterile upper-middle-class tract houses. "Everything looks like some cheeseball knockoff of a cozy farmhouse. Farmers never lived in places like this." Back in the days when he was drafting, he'd walked off better developments than these.

"That's not the point," Gina said, her tone now patronizing.

"Every one of these kitchens," he sneered, "I bet it's got a cutout wooden goose with a gingham bandanna around its fucking neck."

"Geese," she observed, "are sensitive creatures. They migrate enormous distances. They always return home." She reached over and stroked his thigh. "And they mate for life. People could learn a lot from geese."

People *eat* geese, Skelton thought, but he was smart enough not to make the point.

Earlier that afternoon, Gina had gone out for a couple of hours, and ever since returning home, there'd been an air of decisiveness about her. A mood. Not a bad mood, but a definite *mood* nonetheless. Then, about an hour after dinner, she'd told him there was this errand they had to run. Together. There was no stopping it, she'd informed him, and gone on to ask if she needed to bring up all those occasions through the years, when she'd unquestioningly gone along with his whims. When he balked again, she broke down and told him how she and Helen Bartell had taken matters into their own hands.

"You know what kind of people live in neighborhoods like this?" he said. They were passing through a section where all the street names seemed to have the word *cottage* in them. Cottage Grove, Cottage Lane, Cottage Downs. All winding, cozy streets, carefully laid out to look unstructured, haphazard. Neat cedar houses, shake shingles, and trim stained in nice earth tones. Nice. That was it. "It's just so fucking *nice*," he said. Cottage *Cheese*, that's what they should call it.

"Regular people live here," Gina said.

"Petit bourgeois," Skelton said. Maybe she'd been working with doctors too long. Was there a hint of envy in her voice?

"Like I said," Gina told him, "regular people."

"Geese," Skelton sneered. He cranked down the window and let the wind tear through his hair and beard. Soon the car was filled with the odor of barbecued ribs. That was the limit. He closed the window. Wally, Beaver, time for your warm milk and cookies before bed. Now, boys, Mother knows best.

It was a warm, clear night, and off to their right, the moon was just beginning to edge above the ridge line. Gina slowed the car and made a right off the main road, onto a narrow street that traversed a broad pasture. Ahead, the lights of still another subdivision spread across the hillside.

A little farther on the street broke to the right, began to wind up the hillside. Finally, Gina stopped in front of a house. The curtains in the front window were drawn. Lawn framed in low, boxy junipers. Mailbox planted in one of those half whiskey barrels stocked by the hundred in big discount hardware and lawn-care stores. In the driveway sat a nondescript gray Dodge sedan with a stubby radio antenna mounted on the rear fender near the trunk lid. Before Skelton could say anything more, Gina said she would be right back, got out, and walked decisively to the door. Skelton glanced at the ignition. She'd taken the keys with her.

At Cash's insistence, he and his son had stopped off at the video store on the way home from truck shopping and picked up a stack of movies. *True Grit. A Fistful of Dollars.* The original *Busted Heart*, of course. And *The Wizard of Oz.* The titles came from a list given to Cash by Brandon McWilliams, all required viewing, Cash explained, to help him with something called his character's backstory. They started, naturally, with *Busted Heart.* Neither Bartell nor his father had seen it, but Helen was luckier.

"A revisionist western," she said while Bartell tuned up the VCR. "That's what they call it."

Cash tugged at an ear. "Revisionist? What the hell's that?"

"Means the men and women both cuss," Bartell said. "A lot. And there's lots of dust and mud. And when people get killed, which is most of the time, it's real ugly, but graceful too. Like you wouldn't really mind."

"It's a little more than that," Helen said. She was fussy about cultural details. "It means the film tries to take into account the West as it really was, without all the romance."

"Oh," Cash said.

"Like I said," Bartell added, "mud and dust."

McWilliams played a character named Ketchum, the bounty hunter turned sheriff in Busted Heart, a high-country mining camp in Montana. Ketchum was sweet on a reformed whore everybody called China, who refused to tell people—Ketchum included—her real name. China was trying to make a go of it as a seamstress, sewing up dresses for women who weren't quite so reformed. Like all loners worth their salt, though, Ketchum was a man with a mission, and in this case the mission was hunting down the bunch of renegades who'd slaughtered his wife and children years ago down in Texas, when Ketchum and his family were nothing but a bunch of pilgrims on their way west from Missouri. For Ketchum, the sheriffing job in Busted Heart was just a way station on his quest, another grubstake, and China, he assured her, was destined to be left behind.

"Is this what they call 'high concept?' " Bartell asked early on as Ketchum and China, in slow motion, swam naked in a jade-colored pool at the base of a waterfall, while their horses cropped lush grass at the water's edge.

When Helen shushed him, and Cash coughed and squirmed in his seat on the sofa, Bartell decided to keep his mouth shut from there on out through the credits.

As luck would have it—where would the West be without luck?—one day that pack of Texan renegades came riding into Busted Heart.

Of all the half-made ghost towns strung out between Canada and Mexico, Ketchum observed in the voice-over, *they picked this one.*

One of the renegades thought the local sheriff looked familiar —they always do—but couldn't place him—renegades never can. And a hour later, Ketchum was busy making wolf meat out of Texans.

You can't let revenge poison your heart, China said to Ketchum while he was busy poisoning his liver after setting one of the renegades on fire and throwing him over a cliff.

What heart? Ketchum said.

And the doorbell rang.

Helen quickly paused the tape and hurried upstairs to answer the door.

"That's the Jehovah's Witnesses," Cash said after her, "I ain't here."

"Why would the Jehovah's Witnesses come looking for you here?" Bartell said, making a rare stab at small talk with his father. They had terrorized truck salesmen all over Rozette that afternoon, and Bartell was tired, too tired to react any longer to the strain of having his father as an unexpected and uninvited houseguest.

"Those folks can smell me out anywhere, Ray, honest to God." Cash started to laugh, then succumbed to a brief coughing fit.

A moment later, Helen came back into the room and told Bartell that there was somebody upstairs to see him.

"She called me this afternoon," Helen said.

"Hello." Gina Lozano said.

The three stood in the living room near the front door. The room was dim and quiet, with a high ceiling that pitched up to large windows overlooking the city on the side away from the street. The sound of gunfire and hoofbeats echoed up from the rec room downstairs, where Bartell's father was engrossed in the business of learning to be a movie star. And down the hallway at his back, Jess was entombed in her bedroom, doing homework or planning alibis, whatever it was that teenage kids did in their spare time.

Gina offered Bartell her hand. She wore a bright red and blue serape, jeans, and black boots. Her hand was cold, tentative, when Bartell shook it. "I appreciate you letting me stop by tonight," she said to Bartell.

"Is that so," Bartell said, studying Helen for a moment before focusing again on Gina.

Gina engaged in a brief awkward shuffle, then said to Helen, "You didn't tell him, did you?"

Helen ignored her. She'd been employed by Gabriella Fosdick in the self-esteem trade long enough to know when not to give negative thoughts an entrée.

"Gina called me this afternoon," Helen said. "She said you wanted to talk to Henry. Because the Secret Service thinks he may be some kind of assassin." Her voice registered a mix of concern and silliness, as though the whole situation were absurd. "Is that true?" That was the mother's voice. The perfect blend of reproach and ridicule.

Bartell didn't know what to say. He didn't want to talk about Skelton with Helen, didn't want the job in his home like this. But it was Helen who'd brought it there, not him. Right? If that was what she wanted out of him, then maybe that's what she deserved. "That's right," he said. It was no secret anyway. Not from Gina, at any rate.

"Was that the file you were reading last night?" Helen asked. "Or should I say guarding? Henry's?"

Bartell wanted to tell her it was none of her business. He had never told her that before about his work, and until then Helen had always understood their marital code well enough to avoid any questions that might lead to such an answer. "I didn't know you knew Skelton too."

"That's what I thought," Helen said. Not a pounce, exactly. But definitely another mother's scold.

"Do you know him?"

"That's not what this is about," Helen said.

"I knew Gina was a friend of yours," he said. "But if I'd known—"

"If you'd known what?" she demanded. "Known Skelton was my friend too? And what if he was? Then you could have interviewed me too? At the police station?"

Gina tried to stop them. "Helen . . ."

But Helen wasn't having any of it. "You're always secretive, Ray. But last night, it was like you were actually trying to hide all those papers."

"Because," he said, dreading the words that would follow, "it was none of your business."

"But it *is* my business," Helen said sharply. "Because Gina's my friend. That makes it my business."

"And *this,*" Bartell said, gesturing around the room, "this is none of *her* goddamn business."

"I'm her friend, so she thought she could trust you," Helen said.

Well, Bartell thought, she can't. Certainly not if she'd lied to him about Skelton, and maybe not even if she'd told the truth. Sure, Bartell was the point man in the deal with Skelton, but he was, after all, only one man, and pretty low on the food chain at that. Hadn't he gone to great pains that very afternoon to keep Gina from going too far with him? Both Helen and Gina seemed to think that their friendship would offer some kind of payoff in the way Bartell dealt with Skelton, some kind of refuge. But they didn't know their way around enough to recognize that Bartell had already made good on the deal simply by laying off Gina earlier.

Now Gina spoke up. "I called Helen because I didn't know what else to do."

Bartell stared at her, wearing his flat cop's face, a face neither hostile nor satisfied. Keep going, the look said. Show me. The expression he'd caught himself settling into lately when his daughter Jess talked about her friends. "Go ahead," Bartell told her. "You're here. What is it you want?"

"Henry's got to talk to you," Gina said.

"That's right. I told you to have him give me a call. So what?"

"Well, I told him," Gina said. "Just like you asked."

"And?"

Gina seemed about to defer again to Helen, but changed her mind and came straight at Bartell. "He said you could go fuck yourself."

Bartell started to laugh in spite of himself.

Gina looked puzzled. "I don't get it."

"What's to get?" Bartell said. "So your old man's got a mouth on him. So what?"

"So I brought him to you," Gina said.

Now it was Bartell's turn to be puzzled. "What?"

Gina nodded toward the door. "Henry. He's outside in the car."

Bartell stared dumbly at his wife. Women. What was it, they had some kind of secret code, was that it? Meetings at the office, on the street, at a suspect's crib, that was where you did business. *Police* business. But when the asshole comes to your house at night? Because his girlfriend connects up with your old lady, and they decide, what the hell, just bring him on up to the house, whip out some guacamole and chips?

In the police world, context is everything. Bartell tried to imagine himself telling Vic Fanning about this moment. At best, Fanning's mind resembled nothing so much as a torture chamber. *And then what, Bartell?* Fanning might say. *You pour another glass of white wine and you say, So tell me, Henry . . . Hank, you got any plans to stiffen up the president? Any more sawyers you'd like to toast in helicopters? Have you arranged yet, Detective, for the feds to interview your wife? Or would you rather have them call her lawyer?*

Bartell moved past the two women and went into the kitchen, where he drew a glass of water and took a long drink. Context. No doubt about it. Context was the whole works, and Bartell had just been handed more context than he wanted to deal with.

"Ray?" Helen entered the kitchen behind him.

"Just let it go, okay?"

"Let what go? I don't understand."

No, Bartell was sure she didn't. For Helen, appearance and truth were one and the same. It was crazy. While her distrust of government bureaucracies as abstract entities was probably at least as great as Henry Skelton's, she seemed to have a blind spot for the fact Bartell also worked at the pleasure of just that kind of outfit. For instance, Vic Fanning could arbitrarily can Bartell over this little escapade tonight, pack him up and ship his ass back to uniform patrol, take away the only thing he'd ever wanted from the police department—his assignment to detectives—and Helen would never comprehend how or why that could happen. Never acknowledge the fact that she, the good citizen, had left him swirling around the bowl, all primed for the big flush. We all had our doubts from the start, Fanning might say, alluding to that night so many years ago, when Bartell had been cast as the goat, and his partner doomed as a hero. *We all had our doubts.* Sorry it didn't work out, Ray, but it's off you go, back to the great blue manpower pool, where *real* cops get the job done. Think of it as an opportunity to prove you can get the job done too, to prove you're *one of us.* Not that being a street cop was bad. Bartell liked street cops, and he'd enjoyed doing that work, could enjoy it again. It was the terms, which amounted to failure and derision, that he found intolerable.

"That's right," Bartell said, his jaw so tight he could barely speak. "You don't understand anything at all." He was instantly sorry, but what was there to do for it now? If he tried to explain why he'd spent ten years keeping his working life secret from Helen, then he'd also have to explain to her why he'd held his— and by extension, her—personal life secret from his keepers.

"I'm sorry," Helen said. "She's my friend, and she was afraid. I didn't—"

"I know." Bartell set the glass down and put his hand on Helen's shoulder as he stepped around her. "I know." It didn't help matters at all to know that Helen was right.

Chapter 12

When the porch light flashed on and a man came out of the house, Skelton straightened in the seat. The man walked toward the car. He wore a baggy blue sweater, black jeans, black sneakers. Mid-thirties. Six feet, medium build. Loose-jointed, but with an air of purpose. One thing sure, the guy wasn't coming outside to offer Skelton a beer. Skelton got out of the car to meet him.

"I'm Bartell," the guy said. He had lively eyes. But lively eyes or not, there was a brittleness in his voice that said *cop*.

Skelton shook his head and folded his arms. "I don't fuckin' believe this."

"Join the club," Bartell said.

Skelton glanced down at Bartell's ankles, then scanned his waist, his sides under his arms.

"I'm not packing," Bartell said. While it was possible that Skelton was checking him out with an attack in mind, this possibility seemed remote. More likely, Skelton simply found himself every bit as bewildered as Bartell did, and was looking for some way to put himself at ease. "I don't usually carry a gun around the house."

Skelton was sure enough a big guy, with three, maybe four inches on Bartell, and probably fifty pounds. But not fat. You could tell that even through the bulky red-and-black-plaid mackinaw he wore over a green chamois-cloth shirt. And the hair. Kinky and long, with streaks of gray, all pulled back into a tight ponytail. It was the beard that really caught your attention, though, full and black, but with two streaks of silver along the sides of his mouth like froth. From the Charles Manson school of hairstyle, Bartell thought.

"I hear you're looking for me," Skelton said, fighting off his apprehension over talking to this man. Maybe Gina was right about Bartell. Still, Skelton wasn't about to trust her completely, not when it came to cops.

Bartell stared for a moment at Skelton, then said, "And I hear you said I could go fuck myself."

Skelton shrugged. "You must think I'm a dangerous man. Going to all this trouble just to tell me to mind my manners."

"Don't flatter yourself," Bartell said.

"You busting me?"

Bartell looked Skelton up and down. He was glad that so far as he knew, Skelton hadn't committed any new crimes. And he profoundly hoped that Skelton wouldn't commit any while the two men talked there in the street outside Bartell's house. Skelton might belong back in the joint, just like every other cop who'd passed his way seemed to believe, but Bartell wasn't firm enough in that conviction to go offering himself up as a human sacrifice just to get that little job done. Not under these particular circumstances, at any rate.

"Not hardly," Bartell said.

And Skelton thought, There's that brittle edge again.

It may have been a warm night for October, but still, it was October, and it didn't take long for a chill to settle into the two men. Soon they were seated inside Gina's car, Bartell in the passenger seat and Skelton crammed behind the wheel. The house would have been better, but Bartell found himself unable to take the step of inviting Skelton into his home. No more than stubbornness for its own sake, sure, but there you had it.

And so the two men talked. Despite all the resources at a detective's disposal, all the forensic science and computerized gizmos that bureaucrats could dream up and get funded, despite all the laws that politicians might pass, and judges invent, it was still within the voices of people that a real detective made his living.

"I don't like cops," Skelton said.

Bartell remained impassive. "No reason you should."

"My first inclination," Skelton said, "when Gina told me you'd been out to the house, my first thought, it was to head on down to the cop shop and tear off a piece of somebody." Skelton drummed his thick fingers on the steering wheel.

Bartell knew that *somebody* meant *you*. He clasped his hands over his belt buckle. "I've read your file," he said, implying that he already understood all Skelton's inclinations.

"Gina says you think I'm a dangerous man," Skelton said.

Without wasting any more words, Bartell went into his routine about the Secret Service, and the pending exercise in democracy. Skelton sat without moving, not so much as a twitch. When Bartell finished, the car was silent for several moments. In the street outside, a large calico cat, the neighbor's, ambled across the pavement.

And then Skelton started to laugh, a short, harsh burst. "Maybe the government's right. Maybe I rate a whole fucking task force."

"The government right," Bartell said, detached. "Now, there's a novel concept. I wouldn't want to vouch for the whole government, but I can tell you that the Secret Service fellow I'm working with doesn't strike me as a man who likes to take chances."

"Then how come he wasn't with you out at my house? How come he sends some local dick out to do his chores for him?"

"I don't do chores," Bartell said. "The way I see it, you're living in my town, you're my business. I figure, you've got any smart ideas, you and I might as well understand from the start what the score is. If you were still on parole, I'd talk to your PO, cook up some way to just flop you in jail till this whole thing's over." If nothing else, a solution along those lines had the virtue of being easy. It was the kind of out Vic Fanning would have jumped at.

"Unfortunately," Skelton said dryly, "I'm what they call a free man."

"That's right." Free enough to come moping around my house at night.

"And sometimes a free man is the most dangerous kind of all."

"Sometimes," Bartell said.

Skelton leaned forward, bracing his forearms on the wheel. "I used to believe all you had to do was think carefully about things, pay attention to the world, and vote." What was it about Bartell that made him want to start talking?

Bartell shrugged. "That's generally the way it works."

"My old man's a commercial fisherman over on the Olympic Peninsula," Skelton said. "A regular working-class guy. Folks like that, they tend to believe that civics bullshit."

"At least they do when they win," Bartell said.

Now Skelton laughed again. "Sounds like you might think about as much of the FBI as I do."

"The Bureau has its moments." Bartell stared straight ahead through the windshield, appearing to be detached. "Look, I grew up with working people too. You've got no monopoly on that."

"Right. Land of the free, home of the brave, all that shit."

Here, for an instant inside the cramped car, it was as though the arc of the two men's lives passed through a common core. While Skelton sensed this, he wasn't about to go poking around much further in his childhood with any cop. And for his part, Bartell was more interested in noting an area of shared history, a kind of emotional geography to which he might later return and exploit.

"You want to tell me about that FBI agent you clocked?" Bartell asked. "The one made you a genuine desperado?"

Skelton sucked in his upper lip, then stroked his mustache with an index finger, thinking, Cops, just fucking cops. Can't ever let a thing rest until they know it all. Or believe they know it. This one, Bartell, his face was unlined and flat, as though he weren't going to waste any energy on expressions until he knew just what expression would be required to keep somebody on the hook. Still, there was this unexplainable compulsion to go on.

"I never went to meetings, demonstrations. Never carried petitions or got mixed up in any kind of political organization. Never." Skelton thought about this for a moment, trying to figure out an answer. Not simply a factual answer, but a proper answer. "You ever seen young osprey in a nest?"

"Couple of times," Bartell said, still no movement in his face. "So?"

"Young raptors, not yet flying, you see them in the nest, they hoist themselves up, spread their wings out in the wind. Like they know those big wings are there for something, and the wind feels right on them, but they can't quite figure it out. Then one day the wind gusts strong enough, and at that same moment the wings are pitched just right—"

"And he's flying," Bartell cut in, his eyes brightening slightly.

"Sort of," Skelton said. "Not really flying, more like gliding, hanging there in the wind—"

"Okay," Bartell said, nodding.

"—because the bird still doesn't know exactly what he's doing—"

"—okay—"

"—and he doesn't know how to get back to the nest either."

"So?"

"Well," Skelton went on, "one day ten, twelve years ago, I was listening to a bunch of politicians on TV. Let's say those gasbags are the wind blowing—"

"—okay—"

"—I'm a young osprey, and when I say to myself, 'You cunning, greedy bastards—' "

"—okay—that's when you spread your wings."

"Right," Skelton said. "That's right. And a few days later, when I *wrote* 'you cunning, greedy bastards' in a letter and mailed it to the *San Francisco Chronicle,* that's when the wind lifted me out of the nest."

"And this special agent of the FBI?"

"What about him?" Skelton said. "Like you said, I clocked him."

Bartell's smile was matter-of-fact. "And it's like *you* said too. Sooner or later the wind lifts a young osprey out of the nest. But I've got to wonder, see, that assault at Coit Tower, what stage was that in the osprey's life?"

Bartell twisted sideways and studied this jumbo-sized wild man. Everybody wants something. That much, Bartell knew. With most people the obvious hot buttons are some combination of family, money, sex, power. Sometimes drugs, which often as not is just a riff on sex, power, and money. Usually, though, the real reasons why people act are much deeper than a desire for any obvious gain. The same kind of deeply buried reasons that drive a young osprey, as Skelton had described, to stretch his ignorant wings in the wind. With most people that Bartell talked to, he might try to decipher them through a series of precise questions and answers. The basic who, what, where, and when of police work. Then you factor out the answers and see if they lead you to a plausible why. Skelton, on the other hand, had started out—or seemed to have started out—by exposing himself to the core. And it was a core, Bartell feared, that didn't offer much hope that Skelton could be deflected from any course of action that he might have in mind.

Bartell looked evenly at Skelton and said: "Okay?"

And Skelton said: "So it was farther back to the nest than I thought. And the wind was trickier."

"And your wings weren't all that good," Bartell said.

"Not then," Skelton said.

"And now?"

"Who knows."

"What about your father?"

"What about him?"

"How'd he take it when you got busted? Did time?" Funny, Bartell thought, the way his and Skelton's lives were apparently reversed on this point. How many times had he bailed Cash out of jail?

Skelton fingered his mustache again. "Let's say it cut down on the long distance phone bill, and the postage."

"And you really think you can do anything to change things? Change the way of the world?" To Bartell, the question sounded like a TV journalist in a hurry to catch the next plane. Back to you, Tom-Peter-Dan.

Skelton's voice, when he answered, sounded as bored as the question was boring. "Change what? Oh, yeah, I get it. We're talking motive here. Everybody's got to have a motive, right? You got a form someplace, a computer program, maybe, where you have to fill in the blank marked *motive?* That it, Bartell?"

"Everybody wants something," Bartell said, echoing his thoughts from a moment before.

Skelton yawned. "I get up in the morning, and I do what I do. Something gets on my nerves, I tell people about it."

"Am I getting on your nerves?"

"Not particularly. I figure you're the kind of guy, he hauls his ass out of bed, reads the paper, showers, takes a shit. Shows up for work more or less on time. Pours himself a cup of coffee."

"Okay."

"Goes home, watches a little sports on TV. Nothing wrong with any of that." Now Skelton took a closer look at Bartell's house. Just like ten or twenty others he and Gina had passed on the way up. "Where you keep the barbecue?"

Bartell ignored Skelton's comments. "Let's assume for a moment that somebody might decide it's necessary to do an act of political violence." What the hell did a barbecue have to do with anything?

Now Skelton tensed again. "There you are, accusing me—"

"No, no." Bartell threw out a hand, blocking Skelton's words.

"I'm just talking hypothetical here. I want to know if you think there are times when a reasonable man might decide that political violence is the correct thing to do."

"I'm not a hypothetical kind of guy," Skelton said.

"But let's say—"

This time it was Skelton who threw out a hand. "Sorry."

"Okay. Then let's say it happens. The political violence. Do you think a guy who does it deserves a second chance?"

Skelton laid his palms flat along the top of the wheel. "I guess you could say I'm a walking, breathing second chance."

"Yeah, but you earned yours the hard way."

"That's right."

"You figure it was worth it?"

Skelton pulled his hands back and once again crossed his arms across his chest. "Like I said, I get up in the morning, I do what I do."

"And what do you think will happen if this guy Puhl gets elected?"

"What's happening now? People want a lot, and they want it easy. They vote for somebody says he can give it to them. Give them the most, and cost them the least, and screw everybody else in the deal. Then they want his head when he can't deliver."

Bartell leaned slightly toward Skelton. "We're not talking *people* here. We're talking *you*. We're talking Henry Skelton. What're *you* gonna do? That's my problem here. A lot of people think you blew up that helicopter in Cradle Creek. Killed that poor bastard."

Abruptly, Skelton threw up his hands inside the small car, brushing Bartell back. "It's a gift I have," he said lightly. "A true calling. I inspire suspicion. Some people make you feel all warm and cuddly, others, I guess, make you want to carry a gun."

"And you've never made anybody feel warm and cuddly."

"Not as far as I can tell."

"Not even Gina?"

"That's another story." Skelton turned his head toward the window at his left. "That's none of your fucking business. Even if she is friends with your old lady."

"My wife doesn't have anything to do with this," Bartell said, eager to keep Helen as far as possible from his working life.

"Yeah?" A smirk showed through the beard.

Bartell could tell that Skelton sensed his discomfort. He patted his hands lightly on the tops of his thighs and thought about what he would say next. There was one confidence that Gina had shared with him, and he was unsure whether he should use it now. Not unsure for Skelton's sake. That part was easy. No question. But what about Gina, who had shared something with him, then wordlessly enlisted his trust. Gina, who had then gone on to call Helen, and together with her cooked up this harebrained scheme to make everything okay.

"Gina tells me," Bartell went on, "you were a witness to the bombing."

Skelton was still staring out the side window. "So?" It felt as though Bartell's words had just ricocheted off the back of his head.

"But you refused to tell anybody." Bartell could feel the tension ripple through Skelton's huge shoulders.

"And that's a crime?" Skelton said.

"Probably. Obstructing justice, some weenie charge like that."

"If it's true. If you could prove I really did see something." Now he turned, faced Bartell squarely. "Why don't you bust me, and we'll both find out."

Bartell cleared his throat, hoping that Skelton would fall for his pitch. "Let's say I believe you. Let's say you're just scared—"

"That would be a mistake," Skelton said deliberately, his body appearing to bear down harder into the seat. "To think I'm scared."

"Okay, fine. You're not scared, then. Let's say you're just being a jerk. One reason or another, you see something, but you decide to keep your mouth shut about it. Some poor bastard gets vaporized for no particular reason . . . his wife's got nothing left but a bunch of bills and a coffin she doesn't dare open . . . his kids . . . you get the picture. But let's say it's all true, and for some mysterious reason you're the only one can understand, you decide, hey, screw it, it ain't any of my lookout. Set all that aside, Henry. If you really did see something, it could go a long way toward convincing people you're not going to try something stupid later this week."

"But that's your job, isn't it?" Skelton said. "You're the front, right? The beard. You may believe me, but what you believe doesn't count. Not if you can't convince everybody else around here. Far as I'm concerned, I saw what I saw. The rest of it, I can't say as I really give a rat's ass."

Bartell forced himself to remain plodding in the face of Skelton's barely contained energy. He leaned into Skelton again.

"Try to remember," Bartell said, "that *right* doesn't include grabbing some politician's necktie and jerking him out the window of a limo." For Skelton was correct. In the short run, it didn't make a damned bit of difference what Bartell thought about the bombing. "You try that," he went on, "somebody's gonna put you down."

Skelton's voice dropped a notch. "You?"

Bartell didn't give any ground with his eyes. "Whoever's closest."

Now Skelton smiled, and Bartell became aware of the odor of wood smoke trapped among the fibers of the wool mackinaw.

"You tell me something, Bartell." This time Skelton's voice was nearly a whisper. "When was the last time you shook off all the bullshit, stood up like a man, and told somebody what you really believed in? Hell, when was the last time you even knew what you believed in? Huh? Tell me."

At that instant Bartell was reminded of something from his schooldays. What was it Thoreau had said when a friend asked him what he was doing in jail? *What are you doing out there?* But this was a dangerous, romantic notion. And stupid. He had been to enough emergency rooms and autopsies to know the answer. The last thing in the world he had to do was justify himself to the likes of Skelton.

Bartell did not back away. "I'm telling you right now what I believe in, Henry, and I don't care if you buy it or not. The thing I believe is, whatever it is you want, you can't get it done inside a jail cell. All you get inside—at least in this country—is old. Fifteen minutes of prime time, max. Then nothing but a calendar."

Abruptly, by way of dismissing Skelton, Bartell popped open the door. Skelton slumped back and thought. Angry as he might get, he knew that Bartell was on the mark about jail in America, a culture that preferred its martyrs deceased rather than X'ing off the days in the joint. God knows there had never been a committee to free Henry Skelton. So it wasn't jail that Skelton wanted. What he did want, when you got right down to it, was that sense he'd had one afternoon on a meadow along Cradle Creek in the presence of ghosts. That sense of the wind blowing through him. Why was it that something so simple could lead to the threat of jail? Because even if this cop Bartell possessed a degree of good-will—a fact that Skelton had grudgingly begun to acknowledge —the machine still had more than enough gears to grind you up.

It would be no more than an afterthought for somebody with a badge and a gun and a vested pension.

By now Bartell was outside the car, and Skelton got out after him.

Bartell was thinking about another comment that Gina Lozano had made. For an instant, it occurred to him that he was betraying another confidence. And again he decided that Gina had forfeited the right to any such expectation. She did that when she pulled up outside Bartell's house with Skelton.

"Gina tells me you're on a quest. For your *Wyakin.*"

Skelton felt himself caught short, as though Bartell had thrown a rope over him. "Come again?"

Bartell stuck his hands in his hip pockets, cocked his head, and surveyed Skelton across the roof of the car. "*Wyakin,*" he said lightly, as though everyone you met on the street indulged in Native American mysticism. "Some kind of personal talisman or spirit. Something you might find in sacred places."

If Skelton concentrated very hard, he could see the bear rise up on its hind legs, slashing at the helicopter. He could hear the *thumpa-thumpa-thumpa* of the rotor blades. Feel the downdraft tearing through his hair and beard. Understand the bear's indignation, the outrage that came from being toyed with for no good reason.

"Tell Gina," Skelton said, "it's time to go."

Before Bartell could answer, the front door opened and the two women came outside. They studied the men for a moment from the front step, then walked tentatively toward them. When they stopped near Bartell, Helen's smile was thin, tight.

"So," Helen said, "Everything okay now?" Enough forced buoyancy to keep a shipload of evangelists afloat.

Gina shuffled nervously at Helen's side, then started around the car toward Skelton. "Henry, this is my friend. Helen."

"Toss me the keys," Skelton said, his voice not much more than a coarse whisper.

"Henry—"

"The keys."

"It's okay, I can drive." The cheerfulness in Gina's voice was beyond forced.

"I said toss me the goddamn keys. Let's get the fuck out of here." Skelton was staring at Helen, who edged closer to Bartell.

Now Gina looked at Helen and gave her head a tiny shake. Then, to Bartell: "How did it go?"

"I think you'd better give him the keys," Helen said nervously.

Bartell felt his wife tighten all up and down his side, like a guitar string rising in pitch when you screw up the tension. He rested his hand reassuringly in the small of her back. If Helen was going to make a habit of talking to assholes, she really did need some practice.

Gina tossed Skelton the keys.

Now Skelton turned expansive. "Nice to meet you, Helen. Any friend of Gina's is a friend of mine. Next time it's our turn, okay?"

"Good night," Bartell said firmly.

"Sure," Skelton said, waving. "You two kids can come on out to our place, maybe we'll play some cards. Ray knows the way, right, Ray?"

Bartell let it pass, and a moment later Skelton and Gina were in the car and on their way.

"My God," Helen breathed. "Maybe he really is an assassin."

"No," Bartell said. Helen's trouble was that she didn't know enough assholes, so she was handicapped when it came to sorting them out.

"God, I'm sorry, Ray. Sorry I brought him here."

"Forget it," Bartell said curtly. "He's just another mope."

"It's funny," Helen said. "Some women, you think you know them. Then you meet the man they've gotten hooked up with and it's like you're also meeting a completely different woman. Some men, why is it women stay with them at all?"

Bartell was startled by how little patience he could muster this time for his wife's philosophizing. "Love hurts. How's that?"

Helen scowled and edged away. "I said I was sorry. What do you want?"

"Nothing," he said, more impatience drilling through him. "Just nothing. You've done plenty."

"I don't see—"

"No. No, you don't."

"But, Ray, I was just—"

"Just what? Just trying to help? Right. So you cook up a deal and invite some hairball to our home, and then you'll just stand back and get to glowing all over while the two of us big, stupid *guys* work everything out. What is it they call that, Helen? Facilitating? That it? *Facilitating.*"

"I said I was sorry."

"And now you've facilitated yourself into thinking Skelton's a psycho."

"But he is. Didn't you see the way he treated Gina?"

"Yeah. I saw it." Bartell jammed his hands into his hip pockets and gazed off down the street after the Celica. "You ever think he might've felt humiliated? Like a kid being dragged off by the ear by his mother. 'Come on with me, junior, tell the policeman you'll be a good boy.' "

"No," she said. "I guess I never thought of it like that. You men—"

"Just let it go, okay?" He softened now. Not because he'd stopped being angry, but because Skelton wasn't worth any more grief in the Bartell family. "This isn't a battle-of-the-sexes thing. It's just business. Let's leave it at that."

Helen seemed to relax too, but only slightly. "That's fine with me. But I still say he's dangerous."

Bartell gave his wife a short kiss. "Maybe. But I don't think he really wants to do anybody." As long, Bartell thought, as we manage to give him plenty of room. Play Skelton wrong, and all bets were off.

When Bartell and Helen turned and headed back inside, Cash was watching from the front step. The old man stood with his hands in his hip pockets, rocking back and forth slowly on the balls of his feet.

"Say, who was that?" Cash said. "That big hairy fella?"

"Nobody," Bartell said. "Business."

"A killer," Helen said shortly, pushing past Cash into the house.

"Ah, yes," Cash said, arching his grizzled brows. "But *why* is he a killer? What's his *motivation?* Brand says I've got to start studying people that way, I'm gonna be in the movies."

"Because he likes it," Helen said.

Jesus Christ, Bartell thought. He could hardly wait to start tiptoeing through all this with Vic Fanning, Arnold Zillion, and the Puhl bunch.

The man touched up the focus on the binoculars as the Toyota passed from view down the hill. There were more cars parked up and down the street here than had been at the other house back near the river, which decreased the chances of being made. Plus,

he'd been able to find a spot with a good view between the houses on the next street up the hill. He thought about picking up the Toyota again. But what was the point? Skelton and his old lady would go back home, or they would not go back home. The terms were well set by now, and from here on out it didn't really matter much what Skelton did.

At the house down below, the door squeezed closed behind the man and woman and the outside light flicked off. The man in the truck shifted his gaze back to the gray car in the driveway. Same car he'd seen that morning out at Skelton's. Same guy too.

The man lowered the binoculars to his lap and felt for the smokes in his shirt pocket. Empty. He crumpled the pack, dropped it into the neat bag of trash in the foot well across the cab. Found a fresh pack in the black bag on the seat beside him. Opened it, enjoying that little flush of self-congratulation that always came from knowing he never went out on a job unprepared. Perfect.

No. Not perfect.

Perfect was not wanting a cigarette at all. Not needing to eat. Need a drink. Sleep. None of it.

Perfect was leaving no tracks, just a mystery.

Perfect was a globe of fire in the night sky that you didn't need to wait around to see because you already knew exactly how it would look.

The man tapped out a cigarette, got the Zippo from the pocket of his jacket. Nobody used Zippos anymore. He'd known guys who'd move heaven and earth because they'd gone off and left their goddamn Zippo lying on a bar, on some chick's nightstand, any of the dozens of places where a guy settled in for a while and smoked cigarettes.

He thumbed the side of his own Zippo, which he had carried for over thirty years, and smiled at the smoothness of the metal. No engraving. No dates, places, unit numbers. No crest.

No clues. And even then he'd never left it behind for some snoop to come across.

One, two steps, at least, toward perfection.

He popped open the lighter, got the cigarette burning with a quick, practiced flourish. Snapped the cap closed over the flame, returned the Zippo to his jacket pocket.

"Hold up there, pard, what's going on?"

That's what that guy up in the woods had said when he climbed out of the pickup, half asleep. Pard. They called everybody pard in the rural West. Bunch of hicks.

"Howdy," the man had said back, mimicking the local lexicon. *"What kind of business you got out here, middle of the night?"*

"Some papers. Court papers." Just enough of an excuse to give him the moment it would take to reach inside his coat, where the .45 was tucked under his arm. After that it was business as usual. Or close to it anyhow.

So you're not perfect. So what? Who gives a fuck, really? Huh? Nobody alive, that's for goddamn sure.

Bash the guy good, a couple three times, that's the best you could do sometimes. Act of kindness, really. Put him out solid so he wouldn't realize the ugliness later, when the blast ripped through him.

Okay, okay, and so he won't wander off either. Go telling stories. Who said perfection was a one-dimensional kind of thing? And who would have figured there'd be anybody hanging around out there? Middle of nowhere, middle of the goddamn night.

Skelton, he was out there, sure. But that was all part of the deal.

The man drew long on the cigarette, listening to the muted crackle and hiss of the igniting tobacco there inside the truck. Perfect, he believed, was dealing with a bad surprise, and still managing to leave behind nothing but smoke.

No, first smoke, and then nothing but the memory of smoke.

Idly, he looked back down at the house below, where Henry Skelton had come calling. What did that mean? And who was this other guy, the same one he'd seen earlier at Skelton's house? Undoubtedly a cop of some kind. What was his stake in things? What was the perfect solution to this latest imperfection? The man's employers would certainly have some views on this development. If he chose to tell them. Sometimes, you have to be careful what you report, how you report it. In a life where spin is everything, playing straight is not exactly a valued element when it comes to survival.

Fuck his employers. Really, just fuck them. Their asses were at risk, sure, but who, you got right down to it, who was first in line? Didn't really matter anyway. As things stood now, he already had a big enough hook into them he could do anything he pleased. And that, the man decided as he started the truck, that was the high ground, the place you always wanted to end up when all the smoke faded off into thin air.

Chapter 13

The next morning, Cash Bartell, his biological clock permanently locked on *early* as a consequence of a lifetime of ranch work, was up before dawn and already out of the house. The night before, Helen had made it clear that her definition of a good breakfast included only fruit and fiber. Cash, concluding rightly that there was no way to successfully fry either low-fat granola or pears, wasted no time leaving the house to go prowling for the best plate of corned beef hash in Rozette. Once adequately fueled, he'd be back on the hunt for a new pickup.

Following at least part of Skelton's prediction from the night before, Ray Bartell hauled himself out of bed and fixed a cup of coffee. Read the paper. Tried to read it anyway. He found himself, though, distracted by Skelton. Not Skelton, really, but the Cradle Creek bombing. And not the accounts of the bombing, but the bombing itself, the rip of flame and fist of noise pummeling metal and man alike, filling the forest with the stench of burned fuel, rubber, and meat. These were the details, Bartell knew from his own cases, that never made their way into the recorded accounts—both official and journalistic—of any violent event.

Bartell glanced across the room at Helen, who was plowing her own way through part of the paper. He thought about photographs he'd taken, or watched others take. Nice, sharp eight-by-ten color glossies showing the configuration of bone fragmentation inside bullet-riddled skulls. How else to document entrance and exit wounds? Lacerations inside the vagina of a woman who'd been sexually mutilated before she was murdered so you

116

could prove the horror really happened. The face of a child gassed inside a car by his mother. All the photographs, the images, the stories that never made it into print, onto the evening news, or even into trial testimony, because they were inflammatory. Because they were upsetting. Because they were in bad taste, as though murder and butchery were some sort of virus and you had to tidy up the truth to protect the sensibilities of decent citizens from infection. Well, Bartell had been vaccinated years ago, and in weak moments it was difficult to maintain respect for people who demanded the truth but wanted to down it with a handful of aspirin to take the edge off.

Bartell finished his coffee and took his part of the paper over to Helen. He bent over and gave her a kiss. She crumpled the paper in her lap and stared up at him.

"I think he did it," Helen said. "God help me, I think he did. That bombing."

Bartell shrugged and started toward the bathroom. "Maybe he did, maybe he didn't. So what?"

"My God, Ray. He knows who we are, where we live. He knows you're investigating him."

"I told you," Bartell said. "He's nothing. Just another mope." He refrained from reminding his wife that it was she who had opened their door to Skelton.

Helen was about to go on, when Jess came into the room, all ready for school. She looked at her father, still not dressed, and punctuated her disapproval with a dramatic sigh. "I told you—"

"I won't need a minute," Bartell said, cutting her off. He was supposed to give her a ride to school, and that day she needed to be early. Something about a conference with her French teacher.

In the bathroom, Bartell brushed his teeth and shaved. He remembered the statement he'd taken once from a woman who told him about how her boyfriend had walked deliberately toward her across a barroom after being shot, how the bullet wound in his chest gurgled every time he tried to take a deep breath and ask her for help. How he'd collapsed, and later when the ambulance crew got there, they had to pry her off his body because if she moved, made the slimmest movement at all, her hand would slip aside and all the blood would come pouring out of him and he would die and it would be her fault. But he was already dead.

Bartell stared at himself in the mirror and felt like a character in a bad movie. Who did he think he was, Robert Mitchum? Richard Widmark? Some tough-guy dick out on a limb with another big case?

"You keep all these secrets inside you," Helen said now from the door between the bathroom and their bedroom.

"And just what secret is it you think you want to know?"

"Dad!" Jess called out from the living room. "Hurry up!"

Bartell stared at his wife for a moment before turning on the shower. "I've got to get to work."

She's suddenly so interested in bombs, he thought as the hot water stung his face, maybe he should tell her about the car bombing he'd worked a few years ago at an intersection downtown. He could describe the way the man's body fat was rendered into hot grease dripping from the dash and the headliner as it slowly congealed. And he could tell her how the next day, somebody called from an office on the sixth floor of a building bordering the intersection. Would the police send someone over, please, and pick up the finger that was outside on the window ledge? That would certainly help Helen grasp what had gone on inside the Cradle Creek helicopter. Tell her that, and she'd be heading over to Skelton's house with a mob and a rope.

Toweling himself off, Bartell wondered if anyone could understand the energy it took to live with all those stories and images while you mowed the lawn, washed the windows, painted the garage door, listened to your daughter talk about shopping, or slogged through a conversation about gardening and diets when you had dinner with friends who thought the police were both too powerful, and let criminals off too easily. Not the events themselves, but the burden of remembering them, which made you feel at once larger than life, and cheap. Because, rob those events of their context, and what do you have but sentimentality?

Applying deodorant, Bartell marveled at the concentration it took sometimes to get through the day. Not to continue exposing himself to his work. That part had proved to be frighteningly easy. Even exhilarating, which was worse. No, what wore you down was the effort required just to be ordinary, to know that sooner or later all terror was reduced to melodrama. Helen probably didn't realize it, but that was the one secret of his life that she really didn't want to know. He wondered if she understood how badly he wanted to be something besides a guy who lapsed into film-noir head games while he shaved? Sure, maybe it would be easy enough to share all this with Helen, but in the end that seemed a poor choice. As a result, whenever she started to carp at him about secrets, the last thing in the world that occurred to him was actually sharing part of that life with her. Instead, he found himself even more determined not to let on that he had any secrets at all.

Well, thanks to Henry Skelton, maybe Helen had at last gotten a glimpse of what it took to wade through all that bloody slush, all the while doing a perfect and legally acceptable job of reconstructing the past, and accurately predicting the future. Perhaps she was a step closer to understanding how it could all be turned into a collection of depraved jokes. Why do you balance the head of a decapitated man on his buttocks? So everybody can see what it looks like to kiss your ass good-bye.

Goddamn, Bartell thought, pulling on his boots. Jesus-fucking-Christ, he hissed deep down in his throat, angry now with himself for letting his mind lapse out of control. When Bartell fell into these moods, he got sick of himself in a hurry.

"Sonofa*bitch*," he muttered, threading his gun in its pancake holster onto his belt. Keep this up, and today was going to be a real ass-kicker.

Breezing into the living room, Bartell caught Jess around the shoulder and guided her toward the door. "Okay, okay, sweetie pie. Let's hit the road. I can't wait for you forever."

My God, Bartell thought as he and Jess dragged each other at a half-run toward the car, laughing. Damn, he loved this little girl. Why couldn't they turn around, run back into the house, and scoop up Helen, whom he also loved, and hold each other safe there inside the house forever?

When the detectives straggled back into the office after coffee, Bartell found a note on his desk from Vic Fanning, reminding him of the meeting later that morning at Merle Puhl's ranch. In the meantime, Fanning, Zillion, and the other pooh-bahs would be unavailable for consultation, since they were convening once again with Sheriff Riley Saulk across the street at the courthouse. For Fanning, Bartell mused, meetings were like sex. Even the worst was better than none at all.

After digging in at his desk, Bartell hefted a stack of manila folders from his file drawer and began shuffling through his caseload. His mind, though, was focused on how he might deal with the Skelton business. Once he'd gotten over being irritated at Helen's intrusion in his affairs—to say nothing of finding Skelton on his doorstep the night before—Bartell remained convinced that he'd already done everything necessary in that area of shithead research, and decided to stick with his assessment from last night: Skelton was nothing so much as a romantic crackpot.

Take all that suspicion of him on the Cradle Creek bombing, for instance. Cut through the bullshit, and what was there? Common sense, maybe, but that counts only when you apply it to evidence. When you thought about it, Skelton's story about witnessing the bombing was just stupid enough to be true. Why make up a lie that helps your cause, then not bother to tell it to anybody but your girlfriend, and swear her to secrecy in the bargain?

Still, there was the question of a destroyed helicopter, a working guy blown to pieces, and no answer for it. How much was Bartell willing to risk that he was right about Skelton? But, what could he do at this point, even if he was wrong?

The office phones were ringing like Notre-Dame announcing mass, and Linda Westhammer was telling anybody who happened to be listening about a guy she had who got his jollies licking the feet of the women he waited on in the shoe store where he worked. The guy claimed it made it easier to fit those tender little toes and heels into stiff, cruel new shoes. Everybody knew that, didn't they? What's customer service all about?

"Foreskin," Thomas Cassidy observed.

For once, even Westhammer was caught short. "I beg your pardon?"

"Foreskin. You know, circumcision."

"And that's why he licks women's feet while he's selling them shoes? Because his dick's clipped?" She looked across Billy Stokes. "What is this, some sort of guy thing?"

Stokes gave his head a violent shake. "Hey, don't take it out on me. I'm just an innocent bystander."

Cassidy sat back in his chair and gave Westhammer a smug, confident look. As a result of his writing career, Cassidy claimed to have done a lot of incidental reading as well, and felt he had a pretty good grasp, so to speak, of human sexuality. "Some men," he said, "spend a lifetime struggling to get over having been mutilated. Who knows how trauma like that might manifest itself."

Westhammer peered up at the ceiling. "Hello, Jesus, it's me, Linda. I know I promised last time I'd try harder to be good—"

"And some of us," Cassidy pressed ahead, "some of us even go so far as to be surgically restored—"

Westhammer threw out her arms, beseechingly. "—and I really meant it—"

"But, of course, now there are nonsurgical techniques. To make us whole again."

"—*please!*" Westhammer let her arms drop with a loud thud onto her desk. "Nonsurgical techniques. Well, that's good. Because I'll tell you, Cassidy, no man would want *me* down there with a knife."

"No," Cassidy said thoughtfully. "No, I don't believe he would."

"And what about you, Cassidy?" From the sound of Westhammer's voice, she wouldn't need a knife. She could do the job with her fingernails. "You got yourself *restored* yet? You gonna whip it out here and show it off?"

"Linda, please . . ." Cassidy shook his head, pursed his lips with distaste, and reached for the telephone.

Westhammer turned again to Bartell. "What about you, Ray?"

"To tell you the truth, Linda," Bartell said, "I feel cheap and dirty just being in the same room with this conversation."

A moment later, Cassidy was busy talking on the phone to his literary agent, and Westhammer had dropped off back into her work. Bartell made half a dozen phone calls himself, nursing along yet another nasty bar assault, this one about a week old. Everybody had been drunk when the fight went down, drunk, remembered nothing, didn't want the cops involved. Now they were all sober, remembered every detail, and how come the cops—how come Detective Bartell—didn't seem to care?

Between phone calls Bartell checked individually with the other detectives, who continued to come and go, asking if any of them had ever bumped into Henry Skelton. No. Never heard of him. There was a guy, Henry Felton, or was it Benny Shelton, something like that, who used to be good for a lot of burglaries . . . took a dump on somebody's kitchen table once, maybe he was related to this Skelton? Or could this be the same guy as Buckwheat Skelton? Remember him? That old dude who was always in Nails Hogan's card game across the alley at the Cloverleaf. No, couldn't be. Buckwheat Skelton was black. Always pissed off whenever you called him Buckwheat. That's why people called him goddammit-don't-call-me-Buckwheat Skelton.

No, sorry, no Henry Skelton.

Later that morning, as Bartell was getting ready to leave for his meeting with Zillion and the others at the Puhl ranch, Thomas Cassidy sauntered across the room, and slipped into the side chair at Bartell's desk.

"Got a second, Ray?"

Bartell had that, and not much more.

Cassidy scratched the side of his nose and glanced around the office, which was otherwise empty.

"This guy McWilliams? The actor?" Cassidy cleared his throat. "I didn't know you knew him."

"I don't."

"No, I know that, not exactly. Sure. But your old man the other day, that deal with the movie? He knows him, right? So it's like you *could* sort of know McWilliams. You understand?"

Bartell understood. "What's the pitch?"

Cassidy's laugh was sheepish. "Oh, no pitch. Not yet anyhow." He lifted a hand and moped a thick lock of sandy hair back off his forehead. "But I was thinking, hey, what the fuck. In the book biz, if you don't stick out your thumb, you never catch a ride. You know?"

Yes, Bartell knew. Normally brash to the point of being a pain in the ass, Cassidy really wasn't a bad guy, and his diffidence in the matter of asking a simple favor, an introduction, came as a surprise.

"I'll keep my ears open," Bartell said. "The chance to meet him comes my way, I'll let you know."

Driving out to Merle Puhl's ranch, Bartell couldn't shake the sense that Skelton was being straight about what he'd seen that night at Cradle Creek.

Okay, if not Henry Skelton setting that bomb, then who?

But there were too many possibilities, and they weren't confined to politics. Insurance scams. Bad debts. Disgruntled wife. Disgruntled girlfriend's husband. You might as well call dial-a-motive.

That left only Skelton.

Forget it. That case wasn't any of Bartell's business. The way things were shaping up, he was going to have all he could handle just keeping himself clean from any of the current fallout.

Puhl's ranch was about ten miles west of town, where the foothills trailed off into the floodplain of the Holt. Although the place was fairly out of the way, its location had become well known around town last year, when an article appeared in the *Free Independent* about Puhl's ostriches. Since then, the birds had attracted a lot of visitors, whom Puhl welcomed as long as they stayed outside the fences and away from the house and outbuildings.

As he followed the winding asphalt drive, which turned off the gravel county road about a mile from the house, Bartell kept on watching for a glimpse of the big, awkward birds. The fences paralleling the drive were unusually high, maybe over six feet, and he wondered if ostriches were big leapers. For that matter, how do you handle an ostrich at all? Would a man work them from horseback? God knows you couldn't throw a lariat around their necks, you'd pop their damned heads off. Maybe you could catch them up with a loop around a leg, same as you roped calves. But what do you do then? Those big old legs could probably kick you to pieces. And how do you identify individual birds? If you branded them, wouldn't all the feathers catch on fire? They didn't have ears to notch or tag, like a hog or sheep. And you couldn't tattoo them either, the way some people did with horses, because the damned things didn't have any lips.

No, there were some aspects of traditional ranch life that didn't seem especially adaptable to Merle Puhl's agricultural brainstorm. Bartell wondered what would happen if Brandon McWilliams ever got it into his head that raising ostriches would contribute to the salvation of Montana's natural environment. If Cash Bartell had reservations about wrangling buffalo, he was bound to go into orbit at the notion of cultivating large terrestrial birds from Africa. At least he would have until recently. Until he had his own Hollywood agent. Now, with the coming of that miraculous event, surely anything was possible.

Who knew, though? Maybe someone from the extension office already had a brochure citing the latest research on the agricultural compatibility of buffalo and ostriches. Could be. There was all kind of research these days. And if there wasn't such research, well, maybe there should be. Get a grant. Federal money. Hire some graduate students. Sure. When you thought about it, the whole history of Western civilization might come down to finding a way for ostriches and buffalo to live together out there on the range. And to hold back such an advancement of human knowledge because of something so crass as money—*money*, for Christ's sake—well, it was just downright unAmerican. Probably even against the First Amendment.

Just as he crested a small rise, Bartell caught sight in the rearview mirror of a black-and-white Sheriff's Department car. The car closed on him at a high rate of speed, and Bartell pulled over to the shoulder. The black-and-white skidded to a stop behind him, and Chester Boyles got out. As Bartell continued to watch in the mirror, Boyles swaggered up to his car, scuffing the heels of his black cowboy boots on the pavement as he finally came to a stop outside Bartell's window, where he stood, picking his teeth.

"Howdy," Boyles finally said without looking at Bartell. A corpulent little man with an appetite for melodrama, Boyles twirled the toothpick between his thumb and forefinger. The gold bars on the collar of his brown uniform shirt reminded Bartell that Boyles, despite his capacity for wrenching disaster out of harmony, was a lieutenant these days. "What's goin' on?" His tone, lazy yet somehow malignant, reminded Bartell that there were plenty of reasons not to like Boyles, even before he'd become a lieutenant.

"I didn't know there was a café out this way, Huck," Bartell said, needling Boyles about his well-known fondness for sour cream huckleberry pie.

Sweat glistened from the creases at the corners of Boyles's tiny brown eyes, eyes that were always alive with trouble.

"Asshole," Boyles said, dropping the toothpick onto the road, then taking a cigarette from the pack he kept stashed in his boot, where it wouldn't spoil the line of his uniform shirt. "I'm running the show securitywise out here. And you damn well know it, Bartell."

Bartell didn't know anything of the sort. Arguing the point with Boyles, though, would be a waste of time.

Boyles tapped the end of the cigarette against the crystal of his watch, an elaborate piece of timekeeping machinery, with maybe a hundred buttons and dials, which might have been made for a jet pilot secretly afraid his pecker was too small.

"Aren't you a little out of jurisdiction?" Boyles raked a kitchen match along the zipper on his fly and set fire to the cigarette.

"I'm the special liaison for maniac identification," Bartell said.

As he went on to explain his assignment to Boyles, Bartell was relieved that former presidents no longer had constant access to the nation's nuclear arsenal. Because one thing was sure. If Chester Boyles ever got within sight of the doomsday briefcase, he was bound to find a way to try it out.

Boyles blew a lungful of smoke at the match, then used the unburned end of the match to dig at the inside of his ear.

"I got a meeting at the house," Bartell said. "And I'm late."

"Yeah." Boyles studied a glob of yellow wax on the end of the matchstick, then turned up his nose and tossed the match aside. "Yeah. Puhl, and his boy Duckworth. And that hotshot Zillion from the Secret Service. Yeah. I gotta be at the same meeting. Kind of a cheesy bunch, you ask me. Except for Puhl. I figure I'll probably vote for him."

Bartell knew that if he listened to Chester Boyles for another thirty seconds—out here on the road without witnesses—he could be persuaded to kill him. He glanced at his watch and said they were already late.

"Suit yourself." Boyles stuck the cigarette between his teeth.

Bartell decided he should at least try to tend to business with Boyles. "How's it going on your end?"

The deputy pinched the cigarette between his thumb and middle finger and exhaled more smoke. "All saddled up. Except this guy Duckworth, he's all in a lather about some speck of naval jelly named Skelton. I guess maybe that's your department. Skelton?"

"So they tell me."

"Well, you better get him nailed down," Boyles said, sticking the cigarette between his teeth again, "or I will. Trust me, son, nobody's allowed to fuck up a Chester Boyles job."

No, Bartell thought, Chester could handle that all on his own.

Boyles strolled back to his car and followed Bartell on down the drive. The road ahead dipped behind a hill, and a moment later Bartell saw the house, a sprawling stone affair built into the hillside overlooking a meadow that bordered the Holt River. Near the river, the grass remained slick and green, then faded to tan along the rising slopes. The grounds adjacent to the house were landscaped with several tight, cultivated clusters of aspen trees, their golden leaves glinting in the afternoon sun. A neat barn and corral lay between the house and the river, and a new cedar building with adjacent pens sat just to the left of the drive not far from the house. Miles away across the valley, forested mountains rose in a jagged black line.

Bartell and Boyles parked on either side of a beige Oldsmobile sedan with Great Falls plates. A sparkling black 500-series BMW, licensed in New York, sat nearby. Just down the slope from the parking area, five or six ostriches gawked back at them, their heads lolling in random directions on the ends of their long, bald necks.

"Goofy-lookin' fuckers, eh?" Boyles said, nodding toward the birds, who now began to mill around as though they had understood Boyles's sentiment.

"I was at a rodeo once," Bartell said. "Long time ago. There was this traveling show with a bunch of ostriches. They hitched them up to sulkies and ran races."

"Jesus Christ," Boyles snorted. "How do you handicap a thing like that?"

By the time Bartell and Chester Boyles were halfway up the fieldstone walk, a woman had pulled open the sculpted door and now stood waiting for them.

"Not a bad piece," Boyles muttered out of the side of his mouth.

The woman was dressed in a snug red polo shirt, and tight jeans tucked into tall red cowboy boots. Pausing over the boots, Bartell noticed the distinctive welts—the places from which feathers had been plucked—that marked the boots as ostrich hide.

"Hello," the woman said, offering her hand to both men. "I'm Yolanda. Yolanda Huizer."

Chester pumped her arm. "Boyles, ma'am. Lieutenant Boyles."

Bartell smiled and said his name. She smiled back. Her grip was firm, her palm slightly calloused.

"Right," she said, a wisp of auburn hair brushing her smile in the breeze. "The other cop." Her tough hazel eyes flashed, and the shadows under her high, strong cheekbones seemed to fill with a kind of devilish warmth as she smiled. "The Henry Skelton cop."

"You know about Skelton?" Bartell said.

"Oh, everybody knows about Henry Skelton," Yolanda said. "He's the talk of the town in these parts."

"Putting your big production in jeopardy, I hear," Bartell said.

"Before that, even," Yolanda said. "Merle's good friends with that logging contractor. You know? The one who was leasing the helicopter Skelton blew up?"

"Nice ride," Boyles said, pointing to the BMW, which seemed to ripple in the sun like a big steel cat.

"That belongs to Kip," Yolanda said. "Kip Duckworth, Merle's campaign manager."

"I always knew politics was a lucrative line of work," Boyles said.

Yolanda shrugged. "Merle won't let him drive it on official campaign business. Says he's got to drive an American car. One with Montana plates. But Kip likes the Beamer. He's real proud of the electric windows. Claims they're great in traffic, because you can zip down the window on the passenger side and scream obscenities at the person in the slow lane, then zip it right back up before he spits at you."

Boyles shook his head and sniffed. "Hell, that's nothing. You can get power windows on a Chevrolet. We even got power windows in patrol cars these days."

"That's exactly what Merle told him," Yolanda said. "Come on. The boys are out back on the patio."

Yolanda Huizer led Bartell and Chester Boyles toward open French doors on the far side of a cozy room with a low ceiling and a cluster of large, deep chairs covered in dark leather.

"You must be Merle's . . . friend," Boyles said, letting his voice slide over the word *friend.*

"Personal secretary and driver," Yolanda said, then laughed, a sound that had all the steaming warmth of dry ice. "Not that it's any of your business."

To their right, a large stone fireplace and mantel filled the wall, and to the left, a long oak cabinet with glass doors was crammed with rifles and shotguns. The walls displayed an array of plaques and citations, along with four large western paintings. All of the paintings, each truly heroic and undoubtedly very expensive, depicted Indians in traditional outfits, staged in turbulent action scenes involving horses, sunsets, and dust.

Chapter 14

The patio was made of fieldstone that matched the front walk. Arnold Zillion and two other men sat in heavy teak chairs around a glass-topped table. Of the others, Bartell recognized only Merle Puhl, who seemed more bald in person than on TV, with large freckles, and pink scalp showing through what was left of his gray hair. Puhl had a W. C. Fields nose, and small ears with unusually heavy lobes. Gray stubble on his cheeks and chin sparkled like flecks of glass in the sun. He wore a dark green western shirt, and a braided leather bolo tie cinched up with a large silver-and-turquoise clasp.

The second man appeared to be in his early thirties, had carefully combed dishwater-blond hair. He wore expensive-looking tortoiseshell sunglasses and a crisp blue oxford-cloth shirt with an open button-down collar.

"Kip Duckworth?" Bartell said, looking at the younger man, who now stood, smoothed the pleats in his khaki slacks, and offered his hand. His fingers were long and articulate.

"Hello," Duckworth said. When he smiled, his teeth were large and perfect. Everything about him fit with the voice Bartell had heard on the phone the other morning.

"That's him," Merle Puhl said in a voice that was too loud, a voice Bartell had heard hundreds of times, first in automobile commercials, and lately in campaign spots. "Thirty years in politics, and Kip's the best right-hand man I've ever had."

"Good to meet you, son," Chester Boyles said, clapping Duckworth on the shoulder. Then Boyles nodded to Zillion, whom he had apparently already met. And to Puhl he said, "How's it hangin', Merle?"

"Not too bad, Chester." Despite his loud good humor, Puhl seemed to withdraw from Boyles's familiarity. "How's that new Suburban doing?"

"Okay, okay. I think they got her fixed last time in the shop."

Yolanda Huizer now stood at Puhl's shoulder, and the two of them laughed together, as though at some inside joke.

"I'm glad everyone could make it," Duckworth said, melting back into his chair. "We were just talking to Agent Zillion about—"

"Testicles. Talking to him about testicles," Puhl said, laughing again self-consciously. "Agent Zillion said he'd seen an ad for one of those testicle festival things they have around the state. So I had to educate him."

"Never cared for them myself," Bartell said. "We always just fed them to the dogs."

"Hah!" Boyles sputtered. "Terrible goddamn waste."

"They are something of a delicacy," Puhl added.

Perhaps the look on Arnold Zillion's face meant that he would much rather be playing tennis.

Despite Puhl's obvious fondness for Rocky Mountain oysters, Bartell hadn't noticed any cattle on the place. Perhaps the whole ranch had been given over to ostriches. Bartell looked across the table at Puhl. "I'm more curious about these birds. How many have you got anyhow?"

Puhl waved a thick hand in the air. "Oh, fifteen or twenty, maybe. It's a wonderful concept. There's the birds themselves, of course. Worth a lot of money. Then there's the eggs, which are big, and low cholesterol. And the hides. Every year we push exotic leather a little closer to the average fellow's price range."

"Time was," Chester Boyles said thoughtfully, "you could've sold the feathers to striptease dancers. But now, hell . . ." He gave Duckworth, the youngest man at the table, a knowing leer. "Now they all just jump around buck naked. No art to it at all."

Yolanda Huizer's smile could have cut a diamond. "Why, Lieutenant Boyles, you're an absolute cultural historian."

"Listen, boys," Puhl said, serious now. "This is Montana, and folks've gotta scratch out a living any way they can. Why, look at Anaconda. Closed down that smelter, and what was left? A toxic waste dump, and a town full of unemployed people with nothing to do but hang around waiting to get cancer. But were the good people of Anaconda defeated?"

Puhl paused here and looked from one to another of the three men.

"No, sir," Puhl said, pausing again as his conversation lapsed into the rhythm of a campaign speech. "People looked at all those acres contaminated with arsenic and heavy metals from a century of smelting copper, and what did they see? A wasteland? Not by a long shot. No, those people looked out there, and what they saw was a championship golf course. And then, by God, they went out, drummed up some federal money, and hired Jack Nicklaus himself to build it."

By now Puhl was out of breath and perspiring. Duckworth seemed impatient, yet polite, while Yolanda just looked bored. They'd clearly heard this riff before.

"Sounds to me," Chester Boyles said, "like there's only one drawback to raising ostriches." He glanced from Bartell to Zillion, and finally to Puhl, timing his punch line. "You never get to have all the neighbors in for a big testicle fry!"

"Chester," Puhl said, "I do believe you're a connoisseur of testicles." Boyles laughed harder than anybody. When the laughter died, Puhl looked up at Yolanda and patted her on the arm. "Honey, why don't you go hustle us up something to wash down the trail dust."

Yolanda sauntered off into the house.

"I tell you, it's not easy," Puhl said distractedly, watching Yolanda's jeans work as she walked away.

Boyles whistled softly. "Nope, I'd say it's plenty hard."

Puhl turned back to them abruptly, made a brief, uncomfortable squirm. "I meant running for the Senate."

Boyles chuckled. "That too."

Now Puhl was elaborately sincere. "I'm serious, Chester. Think about it. All these tree huggers with their trust funds, they act like nobody needs a regular old job. Animal rights people demand that we save every beast in creation, then turn around and not hunt them. Then what the hell's the point? And racism . . ." Puhl closed his eyes and shook his head.

"Racism," Boyles spat out. "Now, there's something I can tell you about. Jesus Christ, you can't even hardly arrest an Indian anymore. Not without a whole bunch of them raising hell."

"They don't like us, Chester," Puhl said.

"Imagine that," Bartell said.

Duckworth shook his head, patronizing them all. "At least you don't have a lot of blacks in Montana."

"True enough," Puhl said. "I mean, talk about racism—"

"Hey," Boyles said, "you ever hear what a colored girl says after her first sexual experience? Huh? Get off me, Dad, you're crushin' my cigarettes." Boyles giggled and nudged Bartell's arm with his elbow. "Not bad, eh?"

With this, Zillion chuckled nervously, while Merle Puhl glanced around, as though afraid that someone may have been eavesdropping in his own house. Feeling suddenly exhausted, Bartell took a deep breath, then exhaled slowly, letting his ribs settle heavily around his lungs.

Duckworth coughed gently, and adjusted his sunglasses. "Gentlemen, let's get down to business." He pulled off the sunglasses and slipped them into his shirt pocket. His eyes were startlingly blue, like a January sky.

Two matters were at hand, Duckworth started. General security at the house, and Henry Skelton. Since Bartell was concerned only with Skelton, Duckworth proposed that they address that situation first, then let Bartell be on his way.

Not wasting any more time, Merle Puhl smacked the table with the flat of his hand. "Eco-terrorist!"

Zillion squared his shoulders and clasped his hands on the table, looking at Puhl. "As I was saying before Bartell arrived, we deal with guys like Henry Skelton all the time. And by and large they don't amount to anything. If that weren't the case, every dignitary under Secret Service protection would be little more than a prisoner." Now Zillion's attention shifted to Duckworth. "I thought I explained that to you a couple of weeks ago."

Bartell was surprised to hear Zillion soft-pedaling the situation to Puhl and Duckworth. Could this be the same Arnold Zillion who had come asking the city police to call out the dogs on Skelton? Perhaps his subdued approach now was just a way of reassuring the client.

What caught Bartell's attention even more, though, was Zillion's last remark. *I thought I explained that to you a couple of weeks ago.* Now that Bartell thought about it, how had Skelton come into play at all? From the start he had assumed that Skelton was a big fish simply because Arnold Zillion had characterized him as such. Yet Zillion was far from being an expert on any sort of criminal underground in Montana, assuming even that such an underground existed. Skelton might be a bombing suspect, but who had dragged him out into the daylight in the context of the Puhl campaign?

"Let's be crystal clear on this, gentlemen," Duckworth said. He took the sunglasses back out of his shirt pocket and tapped them on the table for emphasis. "People like this Henry Skelton are a social cancer. Now, Merle Puhl is engaged in a high-stakes exercise over the future of Montana. Nobody expects you to protect him from the ordinary rough-and-tumble. That's not your job. But if this Skelton gets out of control"—Duckworth replaced his sunglasses, folded his arms—"if he becomes a *danger* . . . if he jeopardizes our rally with the former president . . . then somebody's going to take a fall." When Duckworth finished, his eyes were squarely on Bartell.

Zillion pursed his lips and shot Bartell a look. The look said that Zillion had heard this line more times than he cared to remember. As far as Bartell could recall, this was the first time Zillion had dropped his professional pose, tried to connect with him as one working stiff to another. Or perhaps that was just another aspect of the pose.

"Isn't he something?" Puhl said, clapping Duckworth on the shoulder.

Duckworth leaned forward, and an intensely reasonable air came over him. "Prudence tells me," he said, "that we should just cancel the former president's visit altogether—"

"Nobody needs to cancel anything," Zillion said curtly. "I told you that too. There is, however, something you all should be aware of. A new complication." With that, Zillion retrieved a leather notebook from under his chair. From the notebook he removed a small sheaf of papers, photocopies of a letter, which he handed out to each man seated at the table. Along with the others, Bartell read:

My dear sir:

As you are no doubt aware, within a very few days our community will play host to an actor from the world stage, a former president of the United States, a man of great eminence who now offers his support to Mr. Merle Puhl, candidate for the United States Senate.

Such a visit by the former president is certainly a feather in our local cap as well as a high tribute to Mr. Puhl. However, before we all climb on the Puhl bandwagon, isn't it important to look closely at some of the positions that Mr.

Puhl has taken, positions with which the former president has apparently aligned himself?

It is not my intention here to rehash these issues, all of which certainly amount to old grievances, for these are documented ad nauseam in our recent history. I do urge, though, that we all stop and listen, take careful stock of our leaders' actions behind their words, the whisper of deals drowned out by brass bands, the stench of greed smothered under red, white, and blue bunting, the promises drifting off into thin air on the tails of a million balloons. Simple, isn't it?

And who am I to be spouting off? No more than a citizen. A witness, if you will. And for my trouble I have been harassed no end by the government, including being identified as a criminal in the local press. But let this be clear: If I am going to be watched and studied, then I will watch and study in return. Remind the bastards every day that there is a man out here who does not approve, who *will not go away and does not care about the consequences.* My final advice to the cops is simple: If they are worried about my behavior, then they should be careful. Extremely careful. If they're that worried about the well-being of this little town, they could always try this: *Leave me alone!*

Now, as for Mr. Puhl and the former president, I have no illusions. Like everybody else, I'm just on a walk through life. And when you walk through life, sometimes you have to stop and clean off your shoes. Isn't that what you do whenever you step in a worthless piece of shit?

Sincerely,
Henry Skelton

Bartell set the letter aside and made a mental note that the letter bore no signature, that Skelton's name had been merely typed in at the end. Then he waited for the others to finish reading. That didn't take long, and neither did the reactions.

Merle Puhl floated his copy of the letter out onto the table and snorted. "And folks wonder why this state's on the ropes. This Skelton, I hear he's from California. Can you believe it? We have to take this shit from some fucking Californian."

Arnold Zillion's face betrayed a faint smile. "Almost poetic, isn't it?" Zillion said.

Duckworth shrugged. "At least he can write in complete sentences. That's more than I would have expected."

"How do we come to have this?" Bartell asked. And, he thought, how did such a letter fit at all, considering his meeting last night with Skelton?

Zillion consulted his notes. "Some woman named Monica Legrande," he said. Legrande was the city editor at the *Free Independent.* That morning, when she came to work, there was an envelope on her desk addressed to Editor. After reading the letter inside, Legrande recalled Henry Skelton's name from the stories last summer on the helicopter bombing. And since the letter mentioned Puhl and the former president, she decided it more rightly belonged with the cops than inside her newspaper, so she'd delivered it personally to Vic Fanning early that morning. Fanning had passed the letter along to Zillion during their meeting at the courthouse.

"Mailed from here in town?" Bartell asked. It was just like Fanning to direct the letter first to Zillion rather than to his own investigator assigned to the detail. Bartell had worked for Fanning long enough to know that the captain wasn't about to diminish any pop the letter might give him by disseminating it first to an underling.

Zillion shook his head. "Not mailed at all. Hand delivered. Somebody this morning found it wedged in the front door."

"There's no night staff at the paper?" Duckworth asked.

"According to Captain Fanning, just production and press people," Zillion, the out-of-towner, said, and Bartell backed him up. The building was closed after midnight, when the next day's edition was a wrap. And because the letter was delivered at the public entrance, a set of long glass doors facing Weaver Street, it wasn't found until people started showing up for work this morning. Legrande came in at seven-thirty, and by eight o'clock the letter was in Fanning's hands.

"And what does she intend to do with this?" Bartell asked. "Legrande?"

"I haven't talked to her myself," Zillion said. "But if she's like most press, I'm sure she figures that turning over the letter entitles her to some kind of payback."

"An official comment," Bartell said. "For a story."

Zillion nodded. "Probably. Just a question of what she'll settle for, and how long she'll hold off."

"Dammit," Duckworth stormed. "God*dammi*t, it galls me that

we could be forced into decisions by a fringe element like Skelton. That's what our whole campaign is about. Shaking ourselves free of the fringe element."

"I don't know," Bartell said, deciding now to commit himself. "Maybe you're jumping to conclusions. According to his girlfriend, Skelton's the kind of guy, you don't push him too hard, you won't have any trouble. And isn't that pretty much what the letter says too? Leave me alone. Stay away, and you've got no problems."

"I beg your pardon?" Duckworth said.

Puhl scowled and fingered the tuft of hair sprouting from his left ear. "How's that again, son? His *girlfriend* says?"

So Bartell told them about his visit to Gina Lozano the other day. He avoided, though, any hint that he'd met Skelton too. The wired-up crew there on Puhl's patio would be even less likely than Vic Fanning to understand how Bartell might come to have Henry Skelton for a houseguest. Without going into great detail, Bartell said he'd driven out to the house on River Flats the day before, looking for Skelton. Finding only Gina, he'd told her that Skelton should consider himself on notice, and that he should find it within himself to stop by Bartell's office.

"And did he show?" Zillion asked.

Bartell hesitated. "At my office?" Nothing he'd heard so far made him feel secure enough to open up his personal life to these people. And what did it matter? None of them were inclined to listen to anything optimistic about Skelton. Why risk anything?

If Zillion caught anything in Bartell's hesitation, he didn't let on. "That's right."

"No." Now that he'd committed himself to concealing his meeting with Skelton, what reason could he give for openly questioning the letter's origin?

"So that's it?" Duckworth said, apparently speaking for the group. "This guy's squeeze tells you he's not to worry about, and that's all there is to it. Is that right?"

Bartell nodded. "More or less." He studied first Zillion, then Duckworth, then Boyles. Back to Zillion. All three were impassive, dug in completely behind their professional faces. When Bartell spoke again, he wasn't talking to anybody in particular. "I miss something here?"

Now Puhl jumped in, sitting back in his chair, then clasping his hands behind his head. "Oh, no, no. Kip here, he just likes to worry. He doesn't have any vices, so he burns off all that extra energy by worrying." Puhl turned to Boyles as though Boyles could corroborate this. "Know what I mean?" Puhl said.

"I hear you, Merle," Boyles said, chewing on a fresh toothpick.

Duckworth, though, wasn't about to let it go. "I may worry, but that still doesn't answer the question. If I'm hearing Detective Bartell correctly, he seems to be telling us that a convicted felon and a known bomber isn't somebody we should worry about. I can't help wondering if you're responding to Skelton or to his girlfriend."

Bartell crushed an urge to tell Duckworth to stick to his speech writing and press releases. Interlopers in the cop trade were generally nothing but trouble. He gazed coolly at Duckworth, wondering if he was smooth enough to graduate into big-time politics, as Puhl seemed to believe, or just slick enough to mess up a one-car parade, maybe turn it into a funeral procession. Finally, Bartell batted his eyes slowly, almost indolently, at Duckworth. "Gina Lozano. Right. She says we should just leave him be. Like a snake, you know? You don't want to get bit, don't step on him."

"Like a snake," Boyles said, bobbing his head enthusiastically. "Right. You don't step on the sonofabitch, he'll let you alone."

"That's about it," Bartell said dryly, bewildered by what Boyles seemed to be able to pass off as a thought process.

Boyles, though, wasn't finished. "But we ain't talking about a rattlesnake here, are we, Bartell? You maybe didn't know this, but I was one of the first officers on the scene at that bombing last spring. Fact is, it was my coroner call, and I scraped the burned-up pieces of that boy in a body bag. So you'll have to excuse me if I feel some personal attachment to this thing. Who's to say, we buy into your measure of Skelton, I don't end up collecting up body parts again?"

"And the contractor who's running that timber sale," Puhl said, "also happens to be a friend of mine. Hell, I've sold that man trucks for twenty years." Puhl didn't claim that this relationship with the contractor entitled the man to any special treatment, anything outside the law. But it was clear that Puhl did believe the friendship should count for a little bit of something.

Duckworth appeared bewildered. "And you, Ray, you believe we should simply ignore this man Skelton."

"I didn't say that," Bartell said. "What I said—"

"What he said," Puhl brayed, "is leave us the hell alone, let the cops do their job. Not in so many words, but that's what it boils down to." He surveyed Bartell with those pugnacious let's-settle-on-a-price eyes. "Am I right?"

"More or less," Zillion said, jumping in with a conciliatory answer on Bartell's behalf. Zillion's manner told anyone concerned how much they—he and Bartell—appreciated smart people who knew when to let the professionals handle things.

"Good . . . good," Puhl said, glancing back into the house after Yolanda Huizer. "Listen, you boys can wrap this thing up." He stood and started into the house. "I'd better go see what's keepin' that gal."

Once Puhl was out of earshot, Duckworth sighed and shook his head. It dawned on Bartell that he was sitting in the heart of an enterprise that people would actually vote for in several weeks. At least he supposed Puhl would garner some votes. Bartell couldn't imagine a statewide election in which a candidate got no votes at all. None. Puhl, for instance, was certain to vote for himself. And Chester Boyles seemed to have made up his mind. Duckworth probably wasn't registered in Montana. That left Yolanda Huizer. Bartell wondered if her jobs with Merle Puhl included voting for the bum.

"So," Duckworth said, still not content to let the issue drop. "We do it your way because, essentially, there's no choice. Even before this," he went on, waving Skelton's letter at Bartell, "that would have been difficult. But now . . . now I find it hard to contemplate just *ignoring* him."

"The Secret Service doesn't ignore anything," Arnold Zillion said wearily. "Believe me, Mr. Duckworth, we have ways of dealing with guys like Henry Skelton. If I were you, I'd set my worries aside and just concentrate on your campaign."

"That's all well and good," Duckworth said, his voice measured, deceptively friendly. A voice that sounded like private schools and old money. "But I want this understood. We consider Henry Skelton to be a major threat. A *security* threat. Don't think for a minute that this is something I intend to let pass."

Bartell felt his stomach churn. Perhaps at this very moment Yolanda Huizer was inside zooming Merle Puhl's blood pressure toward a blow-out. Then none of this would be necessary. The former president could stay home. Puhl's heirs could sell off his idiotic birds. Sure, that was it. Henry Skelton could proceed in the quest for his *Wyakin*. Ray Bartell could return to the simple life of dealing with criminals. And Kip Duckworth could go screw himself.

"The letter. Right." Bartell fingered his copy and studied the end, where Skelton's name was typed but not signed. Trying his luck, Bartell pointed out to the others this lack of a signature.

"So what?" Duckworth said. "Maybe he's crazy. Maybe he's a genius and thinks this gives him some kind of deniability. Maybe he's both, a crazy genius who couldn't even tell you why he didn't sign the damned thing."

"Bullshit," Chester Boyles said, "I bet he just forgot. Did a bunch of dope, and got himself so fucked up he forgot to sign his name to his own letter. That's the way those people are."

"Signed, not signed," Zillion said wearily. "It doesn't really matter all that much. Captain Fanning is having the letter reviewed by a prosecutor. To see if there's any criminal charge that might apply. That's all that really counts right now. What your local prosecutor says."

Ah, so now they were actively searching for some way to bucket Skelton. When you thought about it, everybody—Skelton included—would probably be better off with Skelton in jail for the next week or so. An arrest right now might not be moral in the great celestial scheme of things, or even accurate. But it sure as hell would be safe and easy. And if Fanning could sell the pitch to a prosecutor, and the prosecutor could in turn slide it by a judge, it at least would be legal. Bartell felt like a candle flickering in the wind.

"What about federal charges," Duckworth wondered.

"We'll see," Zillion said. "But for right now, the local route's quicker."

That might be true, but Bartell suspected that if the letter were clearly a federal offense, Zillion would have snatched up Skelton like a big frog zinging a bug. Instead, here he sat, schmoozing with politicos.

To nobody in particular Bartell wondered aloud just how Henry Skelton had come to be such a big deal among the campaigners.

"Well," Duckworth said acidly, "I'll plead guilty if I must. I read about him in the newspaper."

"The helicopter," Bartell said, wondering why, if one of Puhl's friends owned the logging job where the bombing happened, nobody on the campaign seemed to have taken note of Skelton until Duckworth read about him in the paper. He decided that

Duckworth was probably just speaking for himself, claiming credit, the one trait all modern campaign managers seemed to have mastered.

Duckworth shrugged. "If the local police . . . if *you* can't keep tabs on dangerous people in your own community, well . . ." With no effort at all Duckworth had washed his hands of the whole business.

"Shoot the sonofabitch," Chester Boyles said.

"Oh?" Zillion said.

Boyles crossed his legs and hitched at his gun belt, trying to fit himself more comfortably into the chair. "Sure. Isn't that what it's all about? I mean, Duckworth here, he turns Zillion on to Skelton, then Zillion, he gets Ray detailed to take a look. Ray does that. And one way or another he gets the word to Skelton to keep out of the way. Am I right, Ray? You did make that clear to his sweet thing, didn't you, you're a good cop."

"Yes, Chester, I did do that."

Boyles went on: "So, then. You get yourself a bunch of cops with guns, and if this puke Skelton gets cute"—Boyles leaned forward, narrowed his eyes for emphasis—"then . . . you *put* the miserable fuck *down*. It's just that simple. Ain't that right, Zillion?"

Arnold Zillion allowed that Chester Boyles had summed things up pretty well.

"Goddamn right," Boyles said, patting his meaty hand against the big stainless-steel Smith & Wesson wheel gun on his right hip. "Guns. That's what she's all about. That's where the rubber meets the road. This's America, boys, don't ever kid yourself for a minute it ain't."

Much as Bartell hated to admit it, Boyles had fairly well summed up at least one aspect of contemporary society.

Duckworth, however, remained unconvinced. "That may sound perfectly logical, but talk's cheap. From what I know about the bombing—a bombing and a homicide, remember— I'm surprised Skelton isn't already locked up."

"That's not my business," Bartell said, trying not to sound defensive. "I was told to evaluate Skelton as a risk to your enterprise. That's what I'm doing. Anyway, after talking to the Lozano woman, I think it's a better than even chance he didn't do that bombing at all."

"And why is that?" Duckworth said.

"Because he claims he saw the guy who really did it." There, he had done it, given them a reason to question their entire assessment of Skelton.

Duckworth sat forward slightly. "You're kidding."

"Not hardly."

"And you believed it?"

"Like I said, I'm just telling you what she told me."

"What she told you." Duckworth sat back and surveyed Bartell as though he were an exhibit in biology class. "Gina what's-her-name gives you a piece of valuable information that's never been revealed to maybe a dozen other investigators, and right off the mark you buy into it. Well, you're quite the detective, aren't you, Ray?"

A tiny ringing sound started up in Bartell's ears as he felt the weight of the other men's interest bear down on him now. He looked to Zillion and Boyles for support, but decided he didn't want it. "I'm maybe not in the BMW class, but I manage to get through the day."

Duckworth chuckled. "Clever too. I notice you're careful not to argue that we should believe any of this."

Bartell stood up and looked down at Duckworth. He was about to start making anatomical suggestions to the campaign manager, when Zillion once again bailed him out.

"Maybe Skelton saw somebody, maybe he didn't," Zillion said. "And Bartell's right, that's not our concern. Not directly anyway. Our only job is to get through the rest of this week. That's it. Period. We don't have to save Western civilization."

Duckworth stood and put his hand on Bartell's shoulder. "I didn't mean to sound like a hard-ass," he said. "I . . . we value your input."

Bartell slipped his shoulder from under Duckworth's touch as though it carried something contagious. "It doesn't matter much to me one way or another. You don't like what I have to say this morning, the sun will still come up tomorrow." But the little speech was more style than substance, and Bartell knew it. If Duckworth set himself to the task, he could go a long way toward delivering Bartell's career to the trash heap.

Duckworth applied another dose of oil. "I'm sure you know your job. All of you. And everything will work out." Duckworth started back into the house now, clearly intending to lead Bartell out. "I've got some other things to go over with Agent Zillion and the lieutenant here. No need to tie up any more of your time, Detective . . . Ray."

For the first time, Bartell noticed that Duckworth was also outfitted in ostrich-skin boots. Gold colored. "Some kind of trademark?" he asked, pointing to the boots.

"Merle and his birds." Duckworth smirked. "You know, those idiotic rubberneck birds will eat anything lying around. Choke themselves to death on a rock or a bottle cap. Kind of reminds me of voters."

Chapter 15

"Don't take this wrong," Bartell said, "but do you people really think you have even a ghost of a chance in this election?" He and Duckworth were midway through the dark cavern of Puhl's would-be museum.

Duckworth, had he been less polished, might have been at least momentarily taken aback by such a blunt question from a low-rent public servant. Instead, he was coy. "With the electorate, you never know. We've got a fair amount of money." And now, for just the barest instant, like a whiff of rain on a summer breeze, he was even sly. "We've also got a plan."

Bartell wasn't sure about the money part. He'd encountered very little advertising on Puhl's behalf. But the election was still nearly a month off. Perhaps they were hoarding their resources for a big finish. He had no doubt, though, that Duckworth and Puhl were more than capable of brewing up a plan. How else could the former president have been lured into lending his presence to the enterprise? Politically speaking, Montana might not be the end of the earth, but it was sure as hell within sight of it.

"I know we're dragging bottom in all the polls," Duckworth said hastily. "But sometimes the polls are dog shit. And in this election, every time I read the latest one, I hear barking."

As they neared the foyer, Bartell became aware of a considerable commotion outside the front door. Voices. Laughter. Convoluted figures seen through the thick leaded-glass framing the front doors, moving disjointedly.

Duckworth noticed the hubbub too, and glanced at his watch.

"Ah, good," he breathed, satisfaction oozing out of him like sweat. He glanced at his watch again as though taking his bearings, and picked up the pace. "Right on time." Bartell was now clearly relegated to the status of old business.

"Wait till you check this out," Duckworth said over his shoulder. Reaching the door in a few long, quick strides, Duckworth now caught himself up there on the threshold and hesitated, hand on the latch, composing himself, a perfect study in self-admiration. A boy's parody of that greatest American hero of all, the winner.

Now Duckworth's moment of preparation was over, come and gone with the deft touch of breeze nicking the tips of a stand of lodgepole. With practiced nonchalance the campaign manager nudged the door open as if to say, Well, well, what have we here?

Of the fifteen or twenty people congregated outside Merle Puhl's front door, it's safe to say that not a single one was impressed by Kip Duckworth's entrance.

"Hold it . . . hold it . . . fuck!" Those were the first words Bartell heard as he followed Duckworth outside. Near as he could tell, the words came from a well-oiled young man in a safari jacket, who now twirled a microphone by its cord. "Who the fuck *are* these guys?" He was pointing at Duckworth and Bartell.

The bulk of the crowd was made up of several TV crews, and the objects of all that media attention were Merle Puhl and the tall man in a beaded and fringed buckskin jacket standing next to him. The man looked vaguely familiar in the way of old friends, long unseen, who have changed in those subtle ways that accrue over time and distort your memory of them. The addition of glasses, or glasses replaced by contact lenses. Hair gone slightly gray, perhaps, or gone altogether. A bit more flesh under the jaw, or if time and the surgeon have been kind, a bit less.

The man in the buckskin jacket. Yes. Definitely something about him. Ordinarily, Bartell might have suspected he'd arrested the guy sometime or another. But his clientele generally wasn't upscale enough to attract television interviews on the doorsteps of candidates for the United States Senate. No, Bartell's customers tended to run to men with hangovers who reeked of cigarettes and sour feet.

Well, whoever the guy was, Ray Bartell clearly accounted for no more than wasted space among that crowd. As he slipped along the margins of the tiny rabble, he heard Merle Puhl introduce Kip Duckworth to Brandon McWilliams.

Of course. Brandon McWilliams. The movie star. Unrecognized because his presence was so utterly unlikely.

"Brand," the actor said. When he smiled, his teeth were almost bright enough to make the crowd take a collective step back. "Everybody calls me Brand."

Brandon McWilliams. Brand. The world-famous celebrity. So much for haunting old friends. His hair looked carefully windblown and sun-bleached, and the crow's-feet framing his pale eyes gave McWilliams's otherwise smooth, youthful face the perfectly chorded composition of childish deviltry and stoic wisdom.

"Please," McWilliams said, his voice rich with humility, "I don't want to make a big thing out of this."

Yes, Bartell thought, and a liar too. Maybe the true mark of celebrities was that they could ladle on the gravy of their personalities in the presence of cynical people carrying guns—bodyguards, cops, Bartell himself—and always come away from the experience alive. Not just alive, but thriving. The very pulse of a culture on CPR.

And so the media herd, and the assorted handlers, went about the business of not making a big deal out of the fact that Brandon McWilliams, minor cinema deity, was climbing up on the bandwagon with Merle Puhl, authentic good old boy. God smiles, and celestial lights converge. Or was it the other way around?

After pausing for a moment at the fringe of all that drama, Bartell made his way to the edge of the flagstone patio, where he found Vic Fanning standing next to the van from KROZ, one of the three local TV stations. Looking cool and crisp in a dark blue suit, white shirt, and red and blue geometric tie, Fanning stood rocking slowly from the balls of his feet onto his heels and back. The captain held his hands clasped behind his back, and his eyes were hidden behind mirrored Ray-Bans. Whatever else you might say about him, Vic Fanning had excellent taste in sunglasses. Ask anybody.

"Quite a show," Bartell said, nodding back toward the door.

Fanning shrugged. The lenses in his sunglasses winked. "Twenty minutes."

Bartell was confused. "Say again?"

"Twenty minutes. You give these jackals twenty minutes, then ditch them, get down to brass tacks."

At that moment Bartell wondered how much Fanning truly understood public life. Based on what he'd seen of it so far, Bartell was convinced that these twenty minutes with jackals were the most precious commodity of all. Bartell didn't know what, if anything, Brandon McWilliams might believe in, and whether any of those beliefs might remotely coincide with Merle Puhl's plans for the Senate. One thing was sure, however. McWilliams could deliver the pack.

"What's the catch?" Bartell asked Fanning.

"McWilliams, you mean?"

"Right. Him and Puhl, you don't think that's kind of a reach?"

Fanning removed his sunglasses and folded them into the breast pocket of his jacket. "Does it really matter? One guy wants votes, the other wants to sell tickets. Put them together, chances are something from one will rub off on the other."

"All PR's good, long as they spell your name right. That it?"

"That's it."

Bartell should have known better than to underestimate Fanning's grasp of politics and celebrity, for the captain was himself the product of just such an equation. Back in the misty past, when Fanning was briefly a working detective with no supervisory rank, he'd quickly maneuvered himself into a jerry-built job as official spokesman for the police department. In the following months, his name was attached prominently to the department's every public success, while internally, he had the dexterity of a neurosurgeon when it came to personal damage control. In no time at all Fanning had managed to convince the chief that a lieutenant could be a much more effective spokesman, then successfully lobbied the mayor for funds to create the position. Once Fanning was promoted to captain of detectives, though, that lieutenancy had evaporated behind him, leaving a bunch of working cops to salivate over a promotion that had never been anything other than Vic Fanning's stairway to heaven.

"Anyway," Fanning went on, "Brand isn't such a bad guy." After that, his timing was impeccable, precisely long enough for Bartell to understand that a name had just been seriously dropped, but not so long that it was left to Bartell to pursue the comment. "When he stopped in at the office this morning," Fanning said casually, "I thought, Lord, do I really have time for this? You know—Hollywood, movie stars, all that nonsense. But then I thought, what the hell, he pays taxes, right? Just treat him like everybody else."

At that moment, if Bartell were bleeding to death, he would not have asked Fanning for pocket change to phone for an ambulance.

"Well, isn't that right?" Fanning heckled, clearly determined that Bartell was going to be a participant in this conversation.

"Whatever you say," Bartell said, supposing he should be flattered that a man of Fanning's stature felt the need to converse with him at all. Or perhaps Fanning, like all successful flacks, made it a rule never to pass up an opportunity to polish his routines. Any audience was better than none at all.

"Hmphh," Fanning grumped, then went on to elaborate on his encounter that morning with the actor. McWilliams had stopped in cold at the police station and asked to talk with somebody who was involved in the presidential security detail. That question led him to Fanning, whose antennae could have picked up those exquisite vibrations even if he'd been out of state at the time. It turned out that McWilliams would be taking part in the rally too, and wanted to clear up a few basic questions about the security. Nothing too technical, nothing that might have compromised the job.

"Just odds and ends," Fanning explained. "Will the Secret Service be involved? Would he need to use any of his own people? Standard VIP stuff. And then he tells me he's got a project in mind, a movie about politics, and would it be possible for somebody to, you know, give him a glimpse of just how the police fit into this kind of operation."

Somehow Fanning had found time in his busy schedule to be Brandon McWilliams's tour guide, the same as he would for any other taxpayer interested in making a major motion picture.

"Right now, in fact," Fanning said, his voice muted, as though he were disclosing a conspiracy, "Brand's with me." Fanning was already scheduled for a sit-down with Zillion and the others here at the ranch, and the campaign had also arranged for the photo op with McWilliams, which was now under way. It made perfect sense for McWilliams to accept a ride out to the ranch with Fanning. The miracle was that Fanning's arms hadn't been broken from the force of being twisted.

Fanning braced his hands on his hips and cocked his right toe behind his left heel. "You know," he said, that conspiratorial tone still slithering through his voice, "Brand says Montana's hot right now. The last good location. That's what he calls it. He says everybody's looking for a project to do in Montana. The last good location." Fanning savored the profundity of McWilliams's description.

"Poetic," Bartell said.

"I think so, yes," Fanning said. "If you ask me, Brand's a real visionary."

Bartell was ready to leave. More than ready. He said his good-byes to Fanning, who was no doubt relieved that his man was on his way back to doing some work. Or, at least to screwing off out of the public eye. Fanning was a notorious expert at dynamic inactivity—doing nothing, but doing it with style—and it always offended him to be in the presence of those who didn't know how to loaf properly.

As Bartell turned toward his car, however, he recalled the letter, allegedly from Skelton, that Arnold Zillion had produced at the recently concluded meeting on the patio. When he mentioned the letter to Fanning and inquired about the status of consultations with a prosecutor, Fanning scowled for an instant, then gave a slight start, jolted, perhaps, by the realization that he still appeared on the city's payroll under the heading of *police officer.*

"You remember," Bartell prodded. "The letter with Skelton's name on it. The one you apparently didn't think I needed to know about."

"Ah, yes," Fanning said, "the letter. Mike Sweeney has it now."

So it was Sweeney, the chief criminal deputy in the County Attorney's Office, who would measure out the intent behind that curious letter. While Sweeney was a fair, no-nonsense man in matters of the law, he was also a career prosecutor, and his disdain for all variety of misfits was an attitude he shared with most of the police. Sweeney prized his ability to calculate risks with a micrometer, and he was a well-traveled explorer of every back room in the county. Skelton might as well pack his toothbrush.

"Sweeney will let me know at nine o'clock tomorrow morning," Fanning said.

Bartell supposed that the delay was only to allow Sweeney to claim later on, if necessary, that he'd been thoughtful. And perhaps to confer in private with a judge before making any public filings, which would be necessary for an arrest warrant. Although Bartell remained unwilling to subscribe to the notion that the

entire local law enforcement community had migrated to kanga-
roo land, he also knew that Mike Sweeney wasn't in the habit of
applying for warrants unless he was confident that a judge would
come across with the necessary signature.

"What about a search warrant?" Bartell asked. "See what Skelton's got for a typewriter." If the machine that had typed, or
printed, the letter was found in Skelton's house, the case against
him could be a lock.

Fanning's shrug, and his blank stare into the middle distance,
put his answer in context. "And maybe we don't find any typewriter at all." No typewriter, no arrest. Skelton still out pounding
the pavement. Mike Sweeney might not be a saint, but he was
enough of a pragmatist to know that if you bent the law just far
enough, it would whip back on you.

"You get any more hot evidence," Bartell said, "you might
think about dropping me a line."

"And what's that supposed to mean?"

Bartell ignored Fanning's remark, and turned for his car. Halfway there, though, he caught sight of a man standing alone
against a fence, perhaps twenty, thirty yards downhill toward the
barn. The man seemed to be holding himself aloof from the
production at the front door. Not merely aloof, but completely
disinterested, for it looked as though the man was carrying on a
conversation with a pair of ostriches. Curious about the birds as
much as the man, Bartell wandered down to join him.

The man was in his late forties or early fifties. Burley, but obviously fit. Full-cut brown leather jacket. Black hair thinning on
top, graying in along the temples. Tan pants, with cargo pockets
along the outsides of the legs.

The two birds stood against the fence, their heads and perhaps
eighteen inches of neck extending through the woven wire. Both
ostriches stared intently at the man, but periodically glanced at
each other as though comparing notes by mental telepathy.

Jesus, Bartell thought. The whole scene was getting to him.
Endowing jumbo birds with psychic powers. What next?

"Howdy," the man said, still looking at the birds, who had
shifted their gaze to Bartell.

"They say anything worth listening to?" Bartell asked.

The man shrugged. "Not so you could tell. But at least you
don't have to put up with a lot of back talk out of them." At last
the man shifted his attention to Bartell. His face was hard and
gray, with a strong nose, sunken cheeks, and dark eyes that gave

Bartell a hasty once-over and left him feeling that once was enough. "More than I can say for most people around this place," the man said.

Bartell told the man his name, offered his hand, which the man took, and gave a single brisk shake.

"Ed Morley," the man said.

"I'm with the police department," Bartell offered.

"Good for you," Morley said.

"You part of the campaign?"

Morley shook his head. "Old friend of the family." His quick, frigid smile could give a Dale Carnegie instructor insomnia.

"Everybody needs a few of those," Bartell said. "Old friends, I mean," he added, spicing the remark just slightly with sarcasm, for Morley struck him as the kind of man who, if you didn't circle him, he would circle you.

Morley grunted. "Yeah. Good old Uncle Merle."

Bartell nodded toward Morley's feet, which were inside a pair of brown walking shoes. "I'm surprised Uncle Merle hasn't got you set up with a pair of those special ostrich boots he seems to pass out to everybody."

The two birds glanced at each other again. More telepathy? Imagining themselves one day accommodating Ed Morley's corns?

Morley reached inside his jacket, pulled out a cigarette, and balanced it between his lips. Then he fiddled in his pants pocket until he retrieved a lighter. Not one of those disposable butane jobs, but an old Zippo.

Morley thumbed open the lighter. Hours later, when Bartell remembered their encounter, he would laugh so hard that he could almost forget Morley's next remark.

"Cowboy boots," Morley said, steadily eyeing Bartell. Not hostility, but something beyond. "I can't stand fucking cowboy boots," he said, and Bartell knew immediately that Morley had observed that he was himself walking around in exactly such boots.

"I don't know," Morley said easily, striking the lighter, holding it inches from the tip of his cigarette. "It's just a thing with me."

The reflected flame danced in Morley's eyes, the closest thing to a sign of life Bartell had seen there. By now Morley's posturing had grown so outrageous, it was all Bartell could do to keep a straight face.

Once more the ostriches conferred. Did they, too, find this

goon outrageous? They must have, for in a flash one of them—
the taller one on the left—lunged forward, dipped his head, and
snatched the burning lighter deftly from Ed Morley's hand.

"Hey, goddamn!" Morley heaved himself after the bird, which
by now had retracted its head through the fence. Morley's arm
followed the bobbing head, and with a final burst he was able to
wrap the offender's nubile neck inside his large fist. But before
he could act further, the second bird struck, nailing the back of
Morley's hand, and his grip was lost.

For a moment the thieving ostrich seemed to look cross-eyed
at the two men, though Bartell wasn't sure if it was anatomically
possible for an ostrich to be cross-eyed. Then the bird gave his
head a rough toss, the muscles up and down his long neck
seemed to convulse from the effort of making such a swallow,
and when he cracked his beak, Bartell swore later, a tiny puff of
smoke came wafting out.

"Holy smoke," Bartell said, laughing now, unable to contain
himself an instant longer.

"What the fuck's that supposed to mean?" Morley snarled,
which Bartell took to mean that he, too, had seen the smoke.

"That's the dandiest action I've seen in a long time," Bartell
said.

"The fuck it is."

The second ostrich, the co-conspirator, flitted its head from
side to side, the way Elsa Lanchester had done as the bride of
Frankenstein.

"Tag-teamed by a couple of big old birds," Bartell said. "I'd
say that's quite a trick, pard."

"Asshole!" Morley hissed. He wasn't looking any longer at the
birds. Now his complete attention was on Bartell.

"I was you," Bartell said, "I'd make Uncle Merle buy me a new
lighter."

Morley took a deep breath, and Bartell sensed the effort he
needed to regain control of himself.

"Guess you're right," Morley said through his teeth. "Guess I'll
do just that." He turned away and walked with surprising light-
ness on down toward the barn. Without stopping, he said over
his shoulder, "See you around. Pard."

While Bartell might feel petty about it later on, he refused to
allow a man like Morley the last word. "And don't let him off the
hook with one of those cheapo grocery store lighters," Bartell

said to Morley's back. "You make Uncle Merle cough up the real McCoy. I was you, I'd even make him get it engraved."

And Ed Morley thought: *Every plan has some wiggle room in it. Somebody just managed to wiggle his way into mine.*

Back at the office, Bartell found Cash and Thomas Cassidy huddled at Cassidy's desk, with Cash playing Phineas T. Bluster to Cassidy's eternal Howdy Doody. In today's episode, though, Howdy was grim, and Phineas was almost apologetic.

"I can't believe he'd of done this to you on purpose," Cash said.

"Jesus Christ, Cash," Cassidy said. "You've got a lot to learn. You really do need representation."

Cassidy, it happened, had made good on his offer of lunch, and while Cash was busy trying to figure out what Caesar had to do with a salad, he'd told Cassidy what he knew about the story line of *Busted Heart II.* Something about the renegade young sheriff rescuing his reformed outlaw father from the old gang that's trying to intimidate the old man back into life on the run.

"That miserable sonofabitch," Cassidy steamed. "I had my agent send McWilliams that novel over a year ago."

Cash sat on the edge of Cassidy's desk and shook his head sadly. "I know Brand ain't no saint, Tommy. And I guess he probably is a sonofabitch too. But I'm telling you, he ain't a thief. Lord God, he's got so much money, he don't need to steal."

"That's not the point," Cassidy said. "Hollywood people don't steal because they *need* to. They do it because they *can.* They do it just to stay in practice. And then, goddammit, they think you should be flattered to have something they think's worth stealing."

"I thought," Bartell ventured, "this new movie was a western."

"Give me a break," Cassidy huffed. "You substitute horses for cars, dynamite for plastic explosives, and there's your goddamn western. I'm telling you, Ray, I wrote that fucking story. And I'll tell you something else. I'm calling my agent right fucking now." Not wasting further time on show business amateurs, Cassidy grabbed the phone and began pounding out numbers.

Now Cash shrugged, slid off the desk, and rambled over to his son's side of the office. "You know, this don't look much like a police station to me. You got any wanted posters around?"

Bartell was about to observe that he thought his father knew more about the insides of police stations than that, when Red Hanrahan came straggling in, looking as though he'd just returned from witnessing unspeakable carnage.

"Lawyers," Hanrahan growled.

"Yep, yep," Cash clucked, not missing a beat. "I shared a drunk tank once with a lawyer. Over in Lewistown, it was. Poor bastard kept mumbling something about habeas corpus. Putting on airs, that's how it is with lawyers. He looked like a regular old corpse to me."

"Right after this recess," Hanrahan went on, "we head into chambers. Now this lump of toe jam called a defense attorney is claiming his client's too irrational to continue with the trial. What the hell's that supposed to mean?"

Bartell thought about Skelton, and the cast of nuts he'd just left out at that walk-in clinic Merle Puhl called a ranch. "You're lucky, Red. At least you're dealing with a real criminal. Me, I'm still trying to find a scorecard."

"Sometimes," Cash said somberly, "I think we're all criminals, son. Most of us just haven't been caught yet."

Chapter 16

By dinnertime that night, the local airwaves were saturated with the Merle Puhl meets Brandon McWilliams story. Sound bites winnowed their way into the thousands of automobiles and pickups that clogged the streets of a town set up to accommodate roughly half the population that now coursed through the streets like so much steel and rubber sludge. Those vehicles hauled trendy new emigrants who believed that they had found nirvana, as well as old-time residents who were convinced that thanks to the newcomers, Rozette, Montana, had become just another suburb of hell. Indians had been making similar observations about all white people for centuries, but now that white people themselves were starting to feel the squeeze, by God, maybe it was time to do something.

"The working people of this great state," Merle Puhl intoned from TV sets all over town, "demand and deserve a decent standard of living . . . a decent home . . . decent job."

Who could argue with that? thought a Safeway clerk, stalled in the fourth cycle of a stoplight on his way home from a day of selling flavored bagels and designer water to elegant women who did their shopping dressed as flyfishermen. Or was that fisher*persons?*

"We've strayed too far from individual rights as well as responsibilities," pronounced Brandon McWilliams, standing arm in arm with Candidate Puhl.

It's the welfare cheats, huffed the wife of a carpenter as she buried a paring knife in the heart of a tomato before turning up the sound on the portable TV in her kitchen. The woman clung to two part-time jobs herself, while farming out the family's four kids to day care after school. Perhaps next week her husband would join the militia, and bury a machine gun in the back yard.

And the liberal environmentalists, steamed a heavy-equipment mechanic who stared at his dirt-creased hands and wondered why *he* wasn't born a trust-fund baby.

Real estate developers, they were the true enemy, nothing but a cluster of money-hungry antichrists. This clucked by a matron shuffling through her latest deck of lottery tickets.

When Gina Lozano watched the TV news that night, she told Henry Skelton that she and the other members of her ad hoc group—which included Helen Bartell, Gina would have Skelton know—were drafting a petition that would subject every proposed subdivision to a popular vote. Somebody had to stop the assault on open space, and if the politicians were too spineless to do it, then the people themselves would.

That was nice, Skelton said. Really nice. Special, even.

Later that night, Skelton hefted the rifle from the narrow white kitchen table. He smacked the bolt open with the heel of his hand, then slipped it clear of the action. He splashed solvent onto a small rag and began swabbing down the bolt. Once the polished sides of the long cylindrical bolt were clean, he twisted a corner of the damp rag around a toothpick and worked the rag into the recesses on the end of the bolt, where the extractor caught the head of the casing when you locked a round into the chamber. The solvent had a distinct tangy odor, like something sweet, an oddly pleasant complement to the red beans and sausage that Gina had simmered all afternoon.

So last night, he had done just what she'd asked. Gone to the cops, to Bartell. Opened himself up. Hadn't he sworn never to do that? But he'd done it. Done it for her. After she'd spilled her guts about what he'd seen, what he thought. Even what he believed. And now it turned out she'd told the cops who he was, *who he was.*

But was that enough?

Just before dinner, she'd gone after him again: *I'm sick of the cops coming around all the time, crashing in on my life just because they think you might be up to something again.* There it was, melody and harmony all packed into one sentence. Like she thought he enjoyed it. Maybe she was partly right. Maybe he did.

Skelton set the bolt aside, then freshened the solvent on the rag, picked up the rifle itself, and wiped down the barrel.

Late that afternoon, Skelton had decided to load up his gear and head back up to Cradle Creek, catch the remaining few days of decent weather before winter broke. Come back to town after the politicians folded their big tent.

Skelton held up the bolt to the light, admiring the spirals tooled into the bright steel.

No matter what the suits, or even Gina, might think, Henry Skelton wasn't about to start voting with bullets. They could keep an eye on him, and he would keep his own eyes on his own business. He could endure that. Just this once. For a little while longer. For Gina.

Skelton put the bolt aside, swung the end of the rifle barrel toward his head, then raised the butt up to the light and put the muzzle up to his eye. Flecks of dirt dotted the inside of the barrel near the muzzle while the lands and grooves wound back down toward the chamber in a bright twist. Skelton set the rifle on the table, then fit a clean patch into the slotted tip of the cleaning rod, dipped the patch in solvent, and began to swab the inside of the barrel.

Okay, admit it, Bartell seemed like an oddball, at least as far as cops went. So maybe it was true what he said last night. Maybe everybody was satisfied just to have a friendly little chat.

Skelton ran a series of dry, fresh patches through the barrel until the patches began to come out clean. And now he fed the bolt back into the action, locked it down, holding back the trigger so that the firing pin wouldn't cock.

Maybe last night was the end of it. Had there been any sign of the cops today? None, so far as Skelton could detect.

Bracing his elbows on the table, he leaned forward as he held the rifle to his shoulder and sighted out the kitchen window, toward the dark grove of cottonwoods along the river.

Maybe.

He heard Gina step into the door behind him.

"Henry?"

Skelton relaxed, lowered the rifle to the table. "The radio says we'll have snow by the weekend. Maybe sooner."

"Henry, please." She'd made no secret of her desire for him to stay in town, stay visible before God and the whole world until all of the political hocum due later in the week was finished.

Skelton buffed a dry rag, an old Oakland Raiders T-shirt,

against the wooden stock, cleaning off smudges of solvent. "But you couldn't tell it by the weather lately. Still almost as hot and dry as August up on the mountain. During the day anyhow. Nights are cold as hell at that altitude." He'd put off leaving until that night so that he and Gina could spend the day together. Why couldn't that be enough?

Skelton heard her footsteps, felt the floor shift as she approached him. Felt her hands on his shoulders, her fingers digging into the muscle.

"I can't go through this with you anymore, Henry." Unlike earlier, when they had done their shouting, her voice now was calm, straightforward, a singsong quality to it, her Spanish sounding through the way it did when she was exhausted. She might be telling a patient it was time for his medication.

Skelton closed his eyes. "Nobody's going through anything," he said softly. "There's nothing to go through. I told you that a dozen times."

"I want to believe it."

"Then believe it. Simple. Just relax, and let it happen."

A moment later, though, he could feel the tension through her fingers. Again he snapped open the bolt of the rifle.

Gina lowered her hands and walked around the table, stopping between Skelton and the window. For a moment she held her attention pointedly on the rifle, then turned away and stared out the window.

Skelton reached into his pants pocket and brought out the three 7-mm cartridges he'd removed earlier from the rifle. One by one he fit the cartridges into the magazine.

"You always think I've got some agenda," he said. "Isn't that what you call it?" With the last round loaded, Skelton closed the bolt on the empty chamber, once again holding the trigger back. "How many times I got to tell you, only bureaucrats and politicians have agendas."

"That's right, I forgot." When Gina turned to face him, her smile was tight, sweet as poison. "Excuse me. A quest. That's what would-be visionaries call their agenda, isn't it? A quest. And the difference has to do with purity of motives."

Skelton was sick of trying to explain himself to people, even to Gina. He turned the rifle aside. Then he reached for the black cordura case at his feet, slid the rifle into it, and zipped it closed.

Gina threw her arms out to her sides. "So I give up."

At that moment, Skelton could not meet her eyes. Standing, he took the rifle to the corner near the back door and set it on end against the wall near the rest of his gear, which he had cleaned and restocked earlier in the day. Still avoiding Gina, he looked around the small kitchen, looked at the small cluster of clean dishes stacked to dry on the counter beside the sink, at the strand of braided garlic that hung on the side of the freshly painted white cabinet above the stove. The walls were white too, along with the plain white table, and the chairs, only two of them. There was a large basket filled with apples and bananas on top of the refrigerator, where Skelton had moved it from the table while he cleaned the rifle. So clean and simple, all of it. Enough to break your heart.

Skelton went back to the table and started to pick up after his gun cleaning.

"Say something, Henry," Gina said. "Something that makes a little sense."

Skelton felt his eyes go heavy, the way they did at those moments when he was hung up between sadness and anger. Now, when he finally looked at Gina, the anger left him. Those blue eyes, so strange and lovely looking out from her strong, dark, Latina face, seemed to say that she could accept any answer if he could just tell her something, anything at all. Tonight her eyes appeared liquid, as though they might spill over at any moment. Whether from fear or rage, however, Skelton could not tell. Or maybe he was reading too much into her eyes. Maybe she was just pissed off, like any woman trying to deal with him would have every right to be.

"You'll think I'm crazy," Skelton said.

Gina's laugh was as rough-edged as a sharpened piece of chert. "No, Henry. I already think you're crazy. So look at it like this: What have you got to lose?"

Now Skelton laughed. "Fair enough."

When he was a kid, Skelton told her, he used to go to church. The whole family. Him, his sister, his parents. Grandparents. And regular too, not just Christmas and Easter.

"We were Methodists," he said.

Gina stared at him as though he might be from another planet. He realized that in all their years together, he had never talked to her about church. About his church anyway. Religion and God, sure, you couldn't get drunk with a woman and sleep with her for fifteen years and not talk about religion and God sometime along the way. He knew that she'd been raised a Catholic. She'd even shown him her first set of rosary beads, which she still kept in that little rosewood box tucked away in the back of her dresser. But he had never told her he was once a genuine card-carrying Methodist. In a way, he thought now, it did seem like being from another planet.

Anyway, once a year at the church he grew up in, they had this thing called Stewardship Sunday, a special day when the congregation rededicated themselves to taking proper care of God's gifts on earth.

"Where I grew up, see," Skelton said, "men fished and logged for a living, so God's gifts were salmon and trees. Those were the two things we promised God we'd take care of."

And now the salmon were vanishing because of overfishing, and silty streams caused by erosion from too many clear-cuts. And too many clear-cuts also meant that timber sales were getting harder and harder to come by. How long, Skelton wondered, before he might go back to northwest Washington and find nothing but ghost towns and mud? It was the government's fault, people said. Wasn't everything? And the environmentalists' too. Always somebody else's fault.

Skelton shrugged. "But we said we'd take care of it, didn't we? *We* did. We promised God."

"And you believed that shit?" Gina said. "I mean, you *still* believe it?"

It was lunacy, sure. Trouble was, it was just the kind of naive childishness that could get under a man's skin, eat on him for the rest of his life. He looked at Gina, getting that squirmy sensation inside, the kind a ten-year-old boy gets when he's tried to act like a man and not gotten it quite right. "So you're telling me you never feel like lighting a candle now and then?"

"Okay." She sighed and looked away. "Okay."

And now, over the months since he'd stumbled into that meadow among the Nez Perce graves in Cradle Creek, that old sense of stewardship had come back to him, taken another bite. Skelton realized he wasn't anywhere close to being a grand authority on Indians, the task he'd set for himself after first discovering the meadow. But he did know enough to understand that Indian tradition and religion didn't provide a ready-made justification for taking the world to pieces, and they didn't exactly have a lot in common with any notion of middle-class Methodist stewardship, not the way it was practiced. No, he wasn't too far gone to comprehend that.

Gina stepped around him and went to the sink, where she ran water and busied herself tidying up a sink and counter that were already spotless.

"So why the rifle?" Gina knew, too, that convicted felons could end up back in prison just for having a firearm.

What should he tell her? That the rifle was a necessary risk because of the bear? But he already knew he wouldn't shoot the bear. Did she really believe he was an assassin?

Was he?

Could he be?

"I guess," he said finally, "I carry it because *they* say I *can't.*" It sounded lame, but it was as close to the truth as anything.

"And what about the truck?" she pressed. "This crazy business of always hiding it? What kind of man is afraid to park outside his own home?"

"I never would've started that," he said, "except they kept coming around after Cradle Creek. I figured, they didn't see the truck here, they wouldn't stop."

"Then I suppose you do it for me. Hide the truck. So I won't be bothered."

"Whatever you say."

"And now you're planning to go back," she said. "Back to that goddamn mountain and your goddamn cave."

"Nobody told me to stay away." Not lately anyway. "Nobody official," he added, remembering his scrape with those two loggers the other morning.

"But you know what they'll think, they see you right back up there."

"They won't see me. Not this time."

"But do you have to leave tonight?"

"Yes."

"You won't even spend this night with me?"

"No." Bartell aside, for all Skelton knew, right now somebody was making plans to bust him, get him off the street. If that were the case, though, why had Bartell come to the house alone and given him a warning? But how could he trust Bartell? Who knew what any of them wanted? It made you dizzy, figuring the cops. If Skelton were in Bartell's shoes, he'd probably be thinking jail all the way.

"I'm sorry," Gina said. "For what I told him." Her eyes were completely downcast now, as though she finally understood that she had given him up. Because betrayal isn't found in what the words mean, it's what rests in your heart when you say them.

"You want me to leave Cradle Creek alone," Skelton said, "you might as well say you want me to be somebody else."

"Go on back up there, then." Her voice sounded rushed, nervous. "Just hide out till this whole thing's over." She started to say something else, but stopped short.

Was Gina part of it too?

Goddamn, maybe he really was crazy.

"Hide out," he said. Caustic. He watched as the words settled into her, like weather might settle into the sky. He started to tell her he was sorry too, but stopped. Sorry was for guys on their way to prison, guys who fucked up. Whatever his obsessions, Skelton was done with that. "You want me to be somebody else?"

"No."

He started toward her, wanting to wrap her into his arms, feel her face against his chest, smell the dark tangle of her hair. But Gina slipped past him and walked quickly back into the bedroom, her footsteps making tiny squeaks in the sagging floor. Skelton followed after her, but turned into the living room instead, where he sat down at the drafting table and tried to concentrate.

An hour later, Henry Skelton stood in the bedroom door and looked down at Gina, who lay sleeping under the black and green Roman stripe quilt that she had made while he was in Lompoc. They hadn't spoken since that last moment in the kitchen. Near her head, the window was open about six inches on the unseasonably warm night.

Skelton leaned against the doorjamb and folded his arms. In Lompoc, he would dream of the scent of her, then awaken and find himself at odd hours trying to recapture that sensation from amid the stink of disinfectant and cigarettes. And now she lay there, a pocket of heat under the quilt, which rose and fell almost imperceptibly as she breathed, snoring lightly. In a moment, she stirred and turned, hooking a bare foot and calf outside the edge of the quilt.

Skelton bowed his head, rubbed the tips of his middle fingers into the corners of his eyes at the bridge of his nose. He imagined Gina dressed in deerskin, sleeping under a buffalo robe, then shook his head and laughed under his breath. For all his manic preoccupation over the last year, he had never tripped into the delusion that diving headlong into a dying, alien culture was a solution for anything. No, beating drums around a bonfire with a bunch of New Age guys was nothing close to an answer. Maybe it was for some, but not for Henry Skelton. Skelton the lapsed Methodist. He wasn't even asking those kinds of questions. He looked up at Gina again, smiled, blew her a kiss before pulling the bedroom door softly closed.

In the kitchen, Skelton squatted, hooked his right arm through the shoulder strap of the large backpack, and hoisted the heavy load onto one shoulder. He picked up the rifle and fumbled his way quietly out the back door.

Just after dusk, Skelton had walked back through the woods along the river and retrieved his truck. Outside now, he heaved the pack into the back of the pickup. He propped the rifle on the seat, muzzle down on the floorboard alongside the gearshift. He started to slide into the truck after the rifle, but stopped.

After midnight, the ragged neighborhood was quiet. Behind his own house—his and Gina's—the veil of giant cottonwoods fanned out against the moonlit sky.

Smoke from the campfires would hang in those trees, a gray blur transformed into fog as the fires burned low during the night, and the temperature cooled up and down the river bottom. Sounds: small cry of a baby; dog growling at some rustle in the wild roses; horse scuffing against its hobble; a man and a woman grunting inside one of the shelters; the river and the wind blowing across the river through the cottonwoods.

What was it about the Nez Perce hunters in Cradle Creek? Skelton had grown up around Native people on the Olympic Peninsula. People from tribes such as the Quinault, Quileute, and Hoh. But at the time, he never thought of them as Native people, people with a culture of their own, which never let go. They were Indians. They lived on reservations in government housing, got into drunken skirmishes, kept to themselves. Indians didn't come once a year into the Methodist church and promise to be good stewards. They went to court and, claiming the rights of an ancient, ancestral culture, demanded to catch salmon without regulation. No matter how many breaks you gave such people, they just couldn't fit in. Go figure. Skelton might have a hard time now thinking about all this without feeling as though blood were oozing out of his heart, but he was also clear-eyed enough that he hadn't gone off into the Montana wilderness looking for ghosts. Was it his fault that the ghosts had found him?

Well, Skelton had never claimed to know everything. And at the moment, all he knew was that a cloud began to nudge at the three-quarter moon as though the earth were revolving out from under the sky. He knew that somewhere out there beyond the lights of town, a huge bear slept with his nose to the wind. He knew that this is a country where it's common to find the bleached and scattered bones of animals, and in such a country time is always short.

When Skelton pulled away from the house, fatigue seemed to mash in all around his body. He passed a milk truck. A night bird swooped through the headlights of his pickup. The rifle in its black case lolled over against his hip as the pickup fishtailed over the graveled street.

Everybody knew Henry Skelton had a plan. That cop Bartell knew it. The Secret Service knew it too. Even Gina. Okay, maybe it was reasonable for people to assume he did have a plan. He acted like a man who had something in mind. There was all that attention to detail. Like cleaning the rifle. Always tinkering with his other gear. Taking up residence in a cave. Witnessing a murder, then refusing to tell people what he'd seen.

Skelton turned onto a paved arterial, and picked up speed, heading into town.

All right, so up until a few hours ago, maybe he had been acting out a plan. Go back to the cave, watch, and wait. For what? The wind and the bear, bear and the wind?

But the wind blows all kinds of ways. And now his plan, or what had passed for a plan, was in serious disarray.

The light turned red at an intersection near a large bright Holiday station. It came to Skelton that the squat rectangular gas pumps arranged carefully around the black asphalt lot were a modern Stonehenge.

The light changed. He pulled ahead, the old pickup shuddering from a faulty clutch. Driving carefully just under the speed limit, he made good time through thin traffic and soon drew clear of town. Within half an hour, he felt the country close around him in the darkness, as the mountains necked down around the road at the valley's southern margin. Here, a heavy cloud bank had settled in, and ahead, Skelton saw the flash of strobe lights marking the passage of a power line. As he neared the power line, the clouds thickened, and soon it was as though all around him the sky throbbed.

Skelton swerved onto the shoulder and skidded the truck to a stop.

A plan. Christ almighty. If he had ever come into a plan beyond simply *being* Henry Skelton, he wished to hell he knew what it was. For a change, he decided, let the wind and the bear find him.

Back in town, Skelton left his pack in the truck when he stashed it but carried the rifle back to the house. It was well after midnight when he sat on the edge of the bed and touched Gina's hair, touched it tentatively, as you would the head of a jumpy cat. Gina turned silently and reached a bare arm out to him, took his wrist, kissed the back of his hand. And when she stirred, the scent of her gusted up from inside the quilt. It was that scent he had dreamed of all those nights in Lompoc.

"Henry?"

"Yes."

"I thought you were gone."

"I was."

"Come to bed, Henry. Please."

A warm breeze rippled through the window, brushing her hair. Skelton began to unlace his boots. He slipped out of his jeans, his heavy gray sweater, his shirt, and underwear.

"You think," she said, "this's all we've got left? Me asking you to please come to bed in the middle of the night?"

Skelton climbed under the covers. The chill from unwarmed sheets on his side of the bed sent a shiver through him. "I don't know." He stretched, raked the fingers of both hands through his beard. Stretched again. He yawned, and thought about how utterly stupid it would be not to share these few moments with her, then drift off to sleep. How much possibility is there in a man's life before he ends up a genuine ghost roaming mountains?

"You remember that time we drove all night over to Placerville?" he asked. "Then on up into the Sierras to Tahoe?"

He felt Gina nod against his cheek.

"And what I said about the mountains?" Parked in a turnout, watching all that steel and plastic slam by on the highway, he'd found himself rambling on through fatigue, the giant trees making lace of the dawn light flooding over gigantic granite domes that pressed against the sky, dwarfing everything below,

"You said it was like the landscape was eroded," Gina said. "From being stared at by too many people."

"Right." He cocked up a knee and tried to relax. "That's the way I felt when I heard from Bartell all the things you'd told him about me. Like the last little bit of me had been rubbed down to dust."

"I'm sorry."

How much of their conversation over the years had been salted with those two words, *I'm sorry.* "I know," he said.

"That's not what I wanted."

"I know it's not."

"I thought if he understood you the way I do, at least a little bit, then maybe he'd see you were really okay and everybody would leave us alone."

"Maybe they will," he said, not believing it.

Gina scooted closer, tucking the whole length of her body into his, and turned onto her right side, facing him. "Sometimes I hate it I can't let you go."

Skelton turned toward her. She threw her left leg over his hip. He kissed her. She tasted like sleep. "I know."

"We have each other," she said, "we have—"

"Shhh." He put his fingertips to her lips, and when he kissed her again, she ran her hand down the length of his spine, stopping to tug at the patch of hair that grew in the small of his back.

"Only thing I wanted up there," he said, "I wanted to feel that way you do when it's like the wind's blowing through you."

Gina put a hand on his shoulder, pushed gently, then rolled over on top of him. "There's all kind of wind, goddammit," she whispered. "All kinds."

When she rose up and the quilt fell away from her shoulders, he knew that things might be more difficult than he had imagined. Maybe even impossible.

Chapter 17

So he was a cop. That in itself was a neutral. Just another detail. But the fact that he turned out to be soft on Skelton, that made the whole thing problematic. At least, that was what the client thought.

The man left his truck, shouldered the duffel bag, and started uphill through the undeveloped meadow bordering the subdivision.

"What if this Bartell gets everybody to drop Skelton," the client said. "What do we do then?"

What we do, the man had advised, is we make sure nobody can back off.

The client hadn't liked the sound of that, but he hadn't exactly said to back off either. Thus, the man chose to interpret as a green light. He hadn't, though, gone so far as to discuss just exactly what that green light might entail. Clients were always that. clients. People without names. Essentially squeamish, or they wouldn't need to hire you in the first place. So once you formulate an initial plan and set it in motion, the less clients know, the less they can give up if things get dicey, which they sure as hell were now. Now that Skelton, through Bartell, claimed to have seen who'd done the helicopter job.

The grade was gentle through the meadow, but the man knew from his daylight reconnoiter that a wooded ravine separated the meadow from the band of houses enclosing the circle at the end of the cul-de-sac the cop lived on, and the cop's house was three lots down from the circle.

Once in the ravine, the man would stop and catch his wind

165

before moving between the houses. He could make good time now, but from the ravine on, he would move slowly, wary of dogs. Some dogs could put a hell of a bite on you, but the worst problem was the noise. A big, vicious, and quiet dog, you could always kill. But those little bastards, the ones that yipped and yapped, they were the ones that got people out of bed. If there were dogs at the end of the cul-de-sac, then he would be forced to withdraw, return to the base of the hill and risk walking up the street. He wouldn't risk driving up though. Vehicle descriptions and license plates got you identified, and you couldn't hide a pickup in the bushes between houses.

Skelton a witness. The stupid fuck. Still, if it was true, you had to admire a guy who'd rather stand up and take the hit himself than start ratting people off.

No. Skelton was still a stupid fuck. If he had any balls, or if he really knew anything worthwhile, he'd have come hunting.

And who was to say that Skelton really had claimed to be a witness. According to the client, they had only this cop Bartell's word for that, and after seeing their little powwow last night, for all the man knew, Skelton and Bartell had some kind of deal going on the side. Apparently, Bartell had neglected to mention that during the meeting at the ranch. And the man hadn't shared that little observation with the client either. Information is like trumps. You tell the client everything you're holding, sometimes he starts to worry you're holding too much.

And so now, without the client's knowledge, the man was taking business home on Detective Bartell. To discredit him, his advice to be patient, his witness theory. To bury Skelton. To make the stakes too high for anybody to get chickenshit and fold.

The moon was only a dim disc behind the advancing overcast, and as he climbed, he heard his breathing begin to whistle, felt an old surgery nag at his left knee. Stepped gingerly as his boots now and then caught on an exposed rock or a clump of grass.

Okay, the man had to admit that he held a certain affinity, left over from the old days, for cops. And as a general rule you always hated to take business home to a guy's family.

A yard light flickered through the trees as the man neared the edge of the ravine.

But somebody laughs at you . . . shames you . . . on account of some goddamn fucking bird *. . .*

The man glided now among the shadows of the ravine, which

was not wide, and not as deep as it had appeared from the street below.

. . . humiliates you . . . well, fuck him. *Things were personal now. All the more reason not to tell the client too much.*

The man stopped at the tree line, crouched, and peered into the backyard of the house just ahead. The yard wasn't fenced, and the light he'd seen earlier was from a neighboring house on farther around the circle. The stillness was broken only by gusts of wind drawing up the canyon. The wind would cover any noise from his own movements which, after decades of practice, tended to be utterly silent.

Again the man gathered up his bag, and, crouching low, took his first tentative step out from cover.

Bartell awoke sweating, the jagged noise of Michael Kinsley and John Sununu boring into him like a purple nail, and it came to him, no, dear God, please no, I'm in hell. And then he forced his eyes open into the flickering gray light, and he thought, thank Christ, it's only CNN.

Flipping the soggy pillow, Bartell took a deep breath and tried to tune out the din of America. He slid a leg over onto Helen's side of the bed. Found emptiness. He heard the toilet flush, and a moment later Helen slipped carefully back into bed. Pressed her hips into the small of his back. He began to turn, reach for her, listening for that little catch in her throat. Instead, he felt her breathing slow, then draw out in a long snore.

And now he was awake.

Listening to Kinsley and Sununu work themselves into a froth, Bartell began to wonder what the former president would have to say about current life and times in Montana. Vote for Puhl, that was certain. And what was Puhl saying? Open the gates and freshen up our bank accounts. Bartell was all for the bank account part, but he wasn't quite ready to hand the keys to all of Montana's gates over to the likes of Merle Puhl. Or anybody else, you thought about it. Bartell tried to keep track of public discourse as well as anybody—what kind of idiot tried to sleep to the music of Kinsley and Sununu?—and over the years it seemed like the whole show had come down to nothing more than the manipulation of hatred, fear, and blame. If he thought about it very long, it wouldn't be hard to throw in with Skelton.

Skelton?

No, not Skelton. Same tune, different rhythm. Me, listen to me. All noise.

After years of ranch life, the last thing in the world Bartell could believe in were the mushy illusions about nature, which, as far as he could tell, drove Skelton. If anything, the survival of human beings in the natural world depended on the judicious application of cruelty and waste. What animals, humans included, ever died without a dose of suffering and fear? Take an elk. Was a bullet through the heart and lungs any more awful than starvation and being eaten alive by coyotes? Even the most primitive shelter required animal skins and trees.

But some part of him kept whispering, *Wait, wait, what will we do when the last tree is gone, the last stream running brown with silt and cow shit? How long before you need permission from a committee of enlightened bureaucrats just to cut a load of firewood?*

Who are we? Where do we go from here?

What's it all about, Alfie?

Cosmic, cosmic, cosmic.

Rhymes with Gabriella Fosdick.

Are you well adjusted and harmonious? How nice. Holistically healed? Lovely. Let's all have a tofu feast. Judging from the look of things around town lately, there were three growth industries in Rozette: gourmet bistros, mental health professionals, and pawn shops. That left some pretty big gaps for people to fall through.

Now thoroughly unable to sleep, Bartell, in his mind, padded through the silent house, taking stock of those who, he believed, had somehow found themselves in his care. Helen, sleeping with her back arched against his side, snoring lightly, her feet now and then twitching as she perhaps runs through some dream she will not remember in the morning. Or will choose not to tell him.

Jess. Slumbering knot of teenage insecurities and hormones.

And Cash. Leathery old ex-drunk who'd been alone since his wife, Ray's mother, had made a Greyhound exit something like thirty years ago.

For a while, Lenore Bartell, Ray's mother, had come to earth down in Reno, and every Christmas her card managed to find him, though he never answered back. Lately, the postmark was Las Vegas. She dealt cards. Bartell pictured her as extravagantly yet perfectly made up, and flinty, flipping jacks and tens on hands held by tourists who should have known enough to stand with sixteen.

Cash again, whom Bartell now understood had been lonely for a long time before he was alone. Probably born lonely, like that country up and down the east front where he'd spent his life getting thrown and stomped by horses. The country where he'd raised his son, never making the slightest attempt to disguise the fact that a child, no matter how dutiful, was no sure remedy for a woman who hated your guts. Bartell wondered: Do dry drunks still dream themselves in the bag? Do their heads throb through sleep, and when they swallow, do they taste stale beer and puke? One way or another, the old man probably knew his dreams well enough to call them nightmares.

Bartell had always found his father repellent and alluring at the same time, like the pickled worm floating in a bottle of mescal. It was the alluring part that had sent him, along with Helen, on his annual trek out to Cash's place last Friday, tracking back through time and country, looking for a special moment and place, where he could rest. Now Bartell thought back, trying to use the memory like a lullaby.

The unpaved county road southeast of Cascade crossed over dark hills that leaned up into the Big Belt Mountains. About twenty-five miles from town, the road switched back along the side of an abrupt rise, then crossed on a narrow bridge over a steep draw. Below, a thin creek wove silver in the full moon and dusk through a stand of thick, pale willows. Then the road lifted again, and the pickup thudded across a cattle guard at the crest of a ridge, under a weathered sign that carried the name *Hillegoss* and half a dozen brands.

"Been thinking," Bartell had said, reaching across for Helen's hand. "Trying to imagine when this country was empty. Nearly empty, at least."

"It looks pretty empty to me now," Helen said. She grew up mostly in the East, hadn't come to Montana until her second year of high school, when her father took a civilian job with the Air Force in Great Falls. She didn't understand emptiness the way Bartell did.

"There's empty," he told her, "and then there's empty." He wondered how much his perception of the ranch country was affected by the infestation of subdivisions and five-acre ranchettes that seemed to have turned the Holt Valley around Rozette into one big tumor.

Three or four miles down the road from the gatepost, they rounded a bend and crossed another cattle guard, and then they were at the headquarters, a dozen buildings erected against the shelter of three hills. It was dark now, in the shade of the hills, and all the buildings were dark save for a few lights in the bunkhouse and the foreman's place. Both the bunkhouse and mechanic's shop were large cement-block buildings made to last. They were surrounded by a cluster of wooden sheds and barns. The foreman's place, a two-story white clapboard house, loomed under a scaffold of huge cottonwoods shedding bright leaves into gusts of wind sucked now and then over the lip of the hill rising in the near distance directly behind the house. A knot of raggedy pickups and cars were parked near the bunkhouse. The brake lights flashed on an old Ford outfit stopped next to a gas pump. Bartell pulled up behind it.

They said their howdies, first Helen, with whom Cash shook hands in a formal country manner, and then Ray, also the recipient of a handshake. The old man's long gray hair was watered back over his ears and pressed in place with a dark blue Scotch cap. He hadn't bothered with a razor for at least a week.

"Well," Cash said, "let's hit on outta here, somebody puts me to work."

They all got back into their trucks, and Bartell followed along behind the rusted-out Ford, first over a climbing road that gave way to a path, which eventually evolved into a set of parallel indentations in the grass, and finally disappeared altogether when they forded a shallow creek and pulled up at the edge of an alder grove. The alders were fully turned, and their bright yellow leaves flickered in the moonlight.

"Place's just through there," Cash said, pointing an ancient bullet-shaped flashlight toward the gently swaying wall of white-trunked alders. The three of them unloaded gear from Bartell's truck and started walking. "Used to be a road went all the way in," Cash explained, "but it grew up, place hasn't been used for ten years." A couple of months back, Cash had persuaded the foreman to let him move himself and some horses up to the remote cabin.

"You on the dodge again?" Bartell asked. The dodge, he meant, from the bottle. Over the years, Cash had been known to hide out in the mountains from booze.

But not this time.

Not yet a budding film star himself, Cash snarled, "Holly-wood."

They cleared the alders and came upon the camp. A canvas wall tent was set up next to the cabin, and about twenty yards on past the tent there was a large pole corral.

"I've never met a movie star," Helen said.

In the moonlight, Bartell could make out maybe a dozen horses in the corral.

"I myself," Cash said, drawing up at the cabin door, "have become an expert of sorts." He set down the bags he'd been carrying and winked at Helen. "Hell, I'm on a first-name basis with a genuine famous man." He shouldered open the rough door, then doused the flashlight, raked a match on the wall and set it first to a glass kerosene lamp, then a lantern. "Then again, famous men in this state are getting to be like fat ticks on a starved wolf."

The cabin was indeed small, just enough room for a narrow wood stove, a bunk, a rickety wooden table with two tippy-look-ing wooden chairs, and a rough cupboard full of canned goods. Hormel chili, Campbell's soup, Chef Boyardee spaghetti. The corner at the foot of the bunk was jammed with a mound of newspapers. Two kerosene lanterns sat on a narrow shelf near the stove.

"No dog?" Bartell asked.

"Gave up on 'em." Cash hoisted his bony hip onto a corner of the cold stove. "Ain't had a dog since that roan one. You remem-ber him."

Bartell nodded. "One with the brown eye, other eye half gold, half blue. Kept heeling your horse."

"That's the one. Horse finally kicked him in the brainpan, had to put him down last spring. Dog, not the horse. That was it for me 'n' dogs."

Cash handed over the lantern, along with a handful of kitchen matches, to Ray. "Gets light at seven. There's canned meat and bread and jam for breakfast, you're hungry. Coffee. I'll have the stove going." He said all this to Helen, since any fool would know it was a woman's job to fix food if you were lucky enough to have a woman available.

"Sorry we can't hunt," Cash said to his son.

Bartell shrugged. "I don't especially need to kill anything." Which was true. But it surprised him how much he resented a rich outsider like Brandon McWilliams having the power to tell him he couldn't.

"Sure," Cash said. Then he nodded them in the general direction of the cabin door, blinking his rheumy blue eyes several times before closing the door behind them. It was an odd sort of dismissal from a man who hadn't seen his only family for a year.

"Thanks," Bartell said to Helen after they were settled into their cots inside the wall tent.

"You're welcome," she said, sounding sleepy. "For what?"

"For not letting me live alone in a one-room cabin."

"You're the one responsible for that, not me."

She was wrong, but he was pleased she seemed to have so much confidence in his determination, for it was true, that without her he would be alone. Not just temporarily single, but alone. The way Cash had been alone since Bartell's mother ran off. That abandonment had left Cash prematurely old, a rambling drunk who would wonder aloud to his boy what had become of his wife, and then pretend the morning after—a whole lifetime of mornings after—not to remember. There wasn't a day went by that Bartell wasn't thankful for the attachment he and Helen shared. But there were also days when he hoped she never realized the power she had over him. The power to cast him loose in a world that was fundamentally a lonely and hostile place.

The cabin was a mile above sea level, and that night the temperature dropped to near freezing. The next day, though, it turned off warm, and the three of them went riding up into the mountains above the cabin. With altitude, the country opened in a green blur, which broke down into its own precise interior geometry, each component in its place, from the reaches of the tallest fir, down to the scrub of lichen that coated the dark volcanic rocks with a dull green-and-gold patina. Off to the east, the pastured hills were dry and brown, and pockets of golden alders marked the seam where foothills gave way to mountains.

"You remember those boys with the bear?" Bartell said. They were stopped to wind the horses. Just ahead, a high park blanketed the saddle between a steep, rocky pinnacle to the north and a lower, forested rise just south. "Up around Augusta?"

"Them boys with the ropes?" Cash scratched the stubble under his chin and chuckled. "Yeah, hell yeah." He looked at Helen to explain. "Tossed a rope on old mister bear. Caught old bear out on the flats, see, then roped him and drug him in three or four different directions at the same time. Drug him to death in pieces."

"I never saw anything like it," Bartell said. But of course he had, he'd seen plenty like it, and worse, and he always managed to end up laughing along with everybody else.

Helen wanted to know why anybody would do a thing like that, drag a bear to death, and all Cash could do was shrug and tell her they just did. "People're like that," he said. "Just get it in their head to do things, so they do 'em."

To the west, the country dropped steeply in a succession of rocky canyons, each too rugged to support much more than the odd clump of juniper. Huge cedars reached up toward them from the narrow bottom, and the updraft smelled brittle with dust, sage, and late-afternoon autumn heat.

"But Old Man Hillegoss," Cash said, perhaps sensing Helen's uneasiness, "he always ran a good outfit. Lotsa ranchers do. If the goddamn government'd just leave 'em alone."

Bartell knew that the goddamn government was one of Cash's favorite subjects. He was glad that the old man hadn't gone on to discuss the fact that his son was now an employee of that very same government. Like many country people, Cash had a deep and abiding respect for law and order, but not much use for cops and lawyers.

"This guy Merle Puhl," Bartell said, "he claims he's going to set things right." He didn't say anything about his pending assignment with the campaign.

Cash shifted his weight in the saddle and looked off to the east. "Every one of them greedy sonsofbitches says that, says he's gonna fix what the other greedy sonsofbitches bollixed up" —his eyes flicked briefly toward Helen—"excuse my French. We'll see." Then he nudged his horse on, saying that there was something Ray and Helen should see.

They rode a series of tight switchbacks down into a small canyon. Cash led, followed by Helen, with Bartell bringing up the rear. The horse felt good under Bartell, its gate a steady rhythm. But after just a couple of hours his ass was already beginning to get sore, and he found himself more and more standing in the stirrups.

Near the mouth of the canyon they came across an old homesteader's cabin built on the flat just under the peak of a wedge of grass pointing back up into the timber. Ahead, the canyon spilled out into miles of rolling hills and hidden coulees. The sky was huge and clear except for a gray smear of rain along the line of mountains hooking around to the south. Bartell shuddered under a chill, and flexed his shoulders inside his canvas jacket.

The cabin wasn't much larger than the one where Cash lived now. All the caulk was weathered out from between the logs, and the roof had collapsed into the single room. The circular skeleton of a corral lay overgrown in the grass near a thin stream.

Bartell couldn't begin to count the number of such places he'd come across while growing up on a dozen different ranches. What manner of people had settled here? How had they decided this was home? How many summers had they passed here, their skin getting tough and brown as jerky? And how many winters, with the wind full of teeth, and snow drifted to the roofline, hoping against all odds that a hundred and sixty measly acres would give them a toehold in this wild, terrible, beautiful country? How long had they endured not enough money and rain, too much madness and wind, before giving way to one of the larger outfits in the area? How many babies were buried in lost graves somewhere nearby?

Helen reined in and looked out across the hills. "Makes me feel like I need to catch my breath." The wind teased at her hair, and she squinted slightly against the sunlight reflecting off the far golden hills. "You can see almost all the way to Great Falls."

"Yep," Cash said. He found a canister of Skoal in his shirt pocket and tapped it against the heel of his hand before opening it to take a generous pinch.

"Back when Hillegoss had the place," Cash went on, "he let a couple of fellas from the university down in Missoula spend the summer poking around. Looking for old Indian camps. Tepee rings, old sweat lodges, and the like. Now, I ain't no fool, and I know white people did a lot of wrong things taking this country. But we got a history too, and this is part of it. Our history. People like us." He held out the Skoal to Bartell, who glanced at Helen before shaking him off.

"Ruins," Helen said.

Cash's laugh was a high cackle. "Ruins! Yep, I like that." He leaned off to the side and spit. "Ruins. Makes 'em sound important."

"You see this stuff all over the country," Bartell said.

"In a manner of speaking," Cash said, cackling again. "But

this here ruin, this is special. This here ruin is where Mr. Brandon McWilliams plans to make his new home."

Bartell frowned at Cash, puzzled.

"Yes, sir," Cash said, "I seen the plans myself. Down the foreman's house one day."

What McWilliams had in mind, Cash told them, was a sprawling stone-and-log affair laid out like a horseshoe around the contours of the canyon. And how did the ruined homestead fit into the play? Why, it was the centerpiece, son, the main attraction.

"See now," Cash went on, "the new house is gonna be built around the old. And this cabin and corral here, they're gonna be the main attraction in the courtyard."

As Cash explained it, the whole *Busted Heart* experience had left McWilliams deeply moved, to say nothing of rich, and now this homesteader's true life heartbreak was about to be part of a movie star's decor.

"And the creek," Cash said, pointing to the small stream threading out of the trees, "the plans call for rerouting the stream so's it runs right through part of the house, then past the front door of the cabin."

"Kind of a pioneer grotto," Helen said.

The way Cash explained it, McWilliams saw the project as a way of settling his debt to history. The architect called it *preserving the integrity of the view.*

"And bring back the buffalo," Cash snorted. "Three thousand head. It's the goddamnedest . . . excuse—"

"Your French is excused," Helen said.

"Anyhow," Cash went on, "McWilliams is hung up right now on how to dispose of, I'd say, six thousand head of livestock without involving a slaughterhouse. Something about keeping his *aura* in one piece." There was nothing even remotely revisionist about Cash Bartell.

Stepping safely from between the houses and into the street, the man did not pause to reflect on his good luck in not raising any dogs. Walking briskly, his breathing shallow, his feet distant and lighter than air moving across the pavement, he closed without hesitation the short distance between the circle and the cop's house. What he had to do next would take only a few moments of complete concentration, and then, once again, he would be gone.

Still unable to sleep, Bartell got up gently and wandered out into the living room, where he stood in the large window, his back to the front door, and stared down at the lights of town.

One time a long time ago, Bartell shot a golden eagle. He was what, eleven, twelve? Helping Cash push somebody's band of sheep into new pasture. Cash had spotted the eagle perched high in an old ponderosa pine. Eagles were hell on young sheep. Cash handed him the thirty-thirty and told him to try his luck.

Just as the eagle extended his huge wings and leaned ahead into the air, Bartell shot, knocking the bird back over the branch. The eagle thrashed for a moment, then fell down through the tree in a catastrophe of shrieking and feathers.

Ray started toward where the eagle had fallen, wanting to make sure it was dead. But his old man caught him by the arm.

"Leave him be," Cash said. "We got work to do. I seen eagles pick the meat off a lamb ain't even dead yet. You just leave the sonofabitch like he is, let him flop around and bite at himself for a while. Teach him a lesson."

Looking down at the sprawling lights, Bartell now felt wrenched away from the past. That left the job. Puhl and Skelton. It was in the cards, he supposed, that a man in Puhl's position would try to make political hay out of Skelton's kind. But there was some undercurrent in Puhl's approach to Skelton in particular that gave Bartell a nasty sense of dread. Nothing he could put his finger on. Not yet. But he knew he'd feel better about that whole business if he could figure it out.

A gust of wind tore through the linden tree growing near the deck, sending a spray of leaves across the lawn. The moon rode a cloud bank above Bride's Canyon, and if you looked hard, the shadows everywhere seemed to crawl. If a man believed in ghosts, this would be a good night to say his prayers.

Bartell was halfway back to the bedroom when the explosion happened. The living room flashed with a blast of light from outside, and the concussion nearly knocked him off his feet. He raced on into the bedroom, fumbled his gun from out of the nightstand.

Screamed at Helen to check on Jess.

Screamed something else.

Somehow, Bartell managed to avoid shredding his bare feet

on the shards of glass blown out of the living room window. When he finally eased open the front door and looked cautiously outside through the sights of his Beretta, he saw the twisted corpse of the police car smoldering in the driveway. With his bare toe he nudged the door wider and swung the Beretta from side to side, looking wildly for something to kill.

Chapter 18

Bartell got his wife and daughter dressed, ready to leave once the cops arrived. Helen was scared and determined, while Jess remained just plain scared, crying in one long, silent quiver. The two waited in Helen and Bartell's bedroom. Curtains drawn. Away from the broken glass and lingering smoke. In the dark.

Cash tromped back and forth between the bedroom and living room, waving an ancient Smith & Wesson .45 long Colt revolver, snarling about sonsofbitches, and not bothering to ask anybody's pardon for his French.

"Dirty sonsofbitches," the old man seethed. Dirty sonsofbitches, filthy sonsofbitches, rotten sonsofbitches. Cutthroat sonsofbitches. Every species of sonsofbitches imaginable.

Finally, Bartell was able to get his father stationed with a degree of semipermanence at the front door. Called 911. Stole a moment alone with Helen and Jess in the bedroom.

"They'll be talking to you," Bartell said to his wife with hurried deliberation. "Blieker, Woodruff, I don't know, somebody from work. Maybe the Secret Service."

Helen didn't say anything. She sat on the bed, hugging Jess.

"When Skelton and your friend came to the house last night?"

Helen's nod was eager. Too eager. "I know, I know. Oh, Jesus, I brought them here . . . brought all this to our home."

"Maybe you did, maybe you didn't. That's not the point."

"Not the point? Listen to yourself, Ray! That man Skelton tried to kill us!"

Yes, somebody had detonated a bomb outside their front door, and maybe it was Skelton, maybe it wasn't. Anyway, Bartell wasn't about to try that bit of rhetoric again. Why couldn't Helen understand that if the bomb were meant to kill them, they would be dead? Just this once, why couldn't she simply give herself up to the idea that maybe, just maybe, he was applying himself to chaos with some kind of method? After all his years on the job, how could he now, in this smoky tunnel of terror, explain the gummy labyrinth he slogged through day after day?

"Listen to me, Helen. Listen. Nobody knows that Skelton was here at the house last night."

"I don't understand."

"You have to trust me on this. Nobody at work knows about you and Gina."

"Don't!" She pushed him away and clung tighter to Jess, who pressed, mute and shivering, against her mother. "Just don't . . . do this . . . don't do this to me, Ray. Don't . . . handle me like you'd handle one of your criminals!"

When Jess tensed closer yet against Helen, Bartell felt old and shriveled, like a husk with dried-up parts rattling around inside. He reached out again to touch Helen's shoulder, but she drew back, not yet finished.

"No, Ray. No! Secrets, guarded conversations. Planning out every word you say to everybody about everything. I'm not like you, Ray, I can't do that. I can't think a dozen moves ahead before I open my mouth. My God, I don't even know enough about what's going on to make a plan."

Bartell started to say something more, but red and blue lights began flashing through the dark house, and Cash was hailing the cops from the front door.

Helen would tell them what she knew, what she believed, the truth as best she understood it. What kind of monster, in heaven's name, would expect someone he loved—who loved him—to do anything else? When he slumped onto the bed beside Helen, and this time was allowed to fold her and Jess into his arms, Bartell knew the answer: the kind of monster who would have to take Helen's directness into account when making his own plan.

Four hours later, Bartell sat alone behind a coffee cup in Vic Fanning's office. The same ordered and dandified office in which he'd been drawn into a scheme to make the world safe from Henry Skelton. Was that just three days before? A day that seemed like a lifetime ago, a more secure, sane time, when home was the place where work never followed you. Or, at least, followed you only inside your head. A lost, innocent era, before your wife and child ran shouting through the black reverberations of a bomb, and your crazy old man had to be restrained from firing shots wildly out into the neighborhood. Before you yourself were left crouching in your front door amid broken glass, half naked and sweating. Studying fire-rippled shadows for the next attack.

Bartell glanced at his watch. Seven forty-five. He'd just wrapped up making a taped statement for Woodruff and Blieker. A large part of the interview had centered around his coming clean about Helen's relationship with Gina Lozano, and his clandestine contact with Skelton. It had been stupid, certainly, to consider any other course. Even if he'd been able to bring Helen around, there was still Cash. And face it, the longer the story went untold, the steeper the tab once that account finally came due.

Both Woodruff and Blieker were concerned about what they considered to be Bartell's lies of omission, but neither had come straight out and accused him of any wrongdoing. In all likelihood they, and others, were doing that now, chasing after the different possibilities like cats leaping at grasshoppers in a field of weeds. Was Bartell a sympathizer, perhaps even a co-conspirator? Or simply naive and stupid? Might he even do the bomb himself? At his wife's instigation? If so, why? Or why not? And who's this old man, Cash? His father? Why does he show up at this particular time? Anybody ever heard of him being around before? No. Never. So why does he suddenly show up now? How can we check that out?

Does anybody really know Bartell? Is he one of us?

How do we *play* him?

Is he really one of us?

Nested there in Fanning's office, listening to footsteps on the floor overhead and to muffled voices outside the door, Bartell knew that the others were all asking these questions, the very ones he'd sought to avoid by keeping the details of his personal entanglement secret in the first place. They were the questions *he* would ask.

And once they finally pounced on a certain grasshopper, they would toy with it on through the days ahead, bat it from paw to paw, catching Bartell up now and then in jaws powerful enough to crush him either by design or simply by accident in the joy of the moment.

Helen, Jess, and Cash had been interviewed too, but Bartell didn't know the details of what they'd said. They'd all finished up a couple of hours before, and were now checked into a motel, snatched away before he'd had a chance to talk with them in detail. The Bartell house—front windows smashed, debris all over hell and gone—was still full of cops. Bartell imagined his coworkers standing around in his kitchen, shifting their weight from one foot to another while they picked their teeth and passed gas, and counted up on their fingers the hours of overtime they were nailing down.

Screw it. The house. Someday the house would be nothing more than a relic, same as all those log carcasses, like the one Cash had shown them last weekend over on the ranch. The house didn't matter. The people who lived in the house, the things they said and did, their dreams, those were all that counted. And right now all the people from Bartell's house were safe. But the dreams had been permanently jolted off course.

There was a short tap on the door, then Arnold Zillion slipped into the room. Zillion looked worn down, his eyes puffy, hair just slightly disheveled. Bartell had seen the Secret Service man briefly back up at the house, but they hadn't spoken. Now he was surprised to find himself relieved by Zillion's presence.

"Goddammit, Ray," Zillion said, "You caused me to cancel a tee time this morning." He glanced haphazardly at his watch.

Bartell laughed in spite of himself and motioned Zillion into a chair. "Why don't you just file a score anyway. Make up a lousy one, use it to pad your handicap. I'll even sign the card."

Zillion shared the laughter but quickly returned to his normal, solemn tone. "You okay?"

Bartell shrugged. "I'm fine. But I've got to tell you, Arnold, I am a little upset."

"Hey, that happens." Zillion pulled a face. "Some maniac blows up your car, rocks your house on its foundation. Terrorizes your wife and kid. No need to be a saint about that."

Briefly, Bartell wondered if Zillion was needling him, but decided he wasn't.

"I think they're all done with you here," Zillion went on. "You'll probably be going back to your family soon."

Bartell had been thinking about this, what he would do next, off and on all through the interview with Woodruff and Blieker. He'd talked privately for a quick moment with Helen and Jess before they left the station for the motel. Both were still scared, but Helen was at least as angry as he was. She might be a certified feel-good liberal, but getting on her bad side was not something Bartell would recommend to anybody. No, blowing up an automobile in the driveway of her dream house—even an automobile owned by the power elite—was certainly not the key to tapping into Helen's charitable nature. And while she'd once been upset that he was persecuting Gina Lozano's poor, harassed companion, Henry, right now Helen was carrying a Smith & Wesson .357 in her purse, and the last thing she'd said before leaving the station was that she and Jess would be fine, that he should tend to business.

"I'll probably be sticking around," Bartell said to Zillion. "If they let me."

When Zillion nodded without comment, more a gesture of resignation than anything, Bartell knew he'd been right, that the immediate future of Detective Bartell was on people's minds.

Now Bartell turned to Zillion. "Your people are probably pretty wired up about this thing. Considering the former president's coming to our lovely little town."

"Not anymore," Zillion said. "I made a call a couple of hours ago. Got some people out of bed. The visit's down the tubes."

"What about Puhl? Duckworth?" Bartell wondered. "You talk to them first?"

"They've got no say in it," Zillion said. "Not with a thing like this."

"So," Bartell said, "what happens next?"

Before Zillion could reply, Vic Fanning made his own entrance into the office, nodding curtly to Zillion, ignoring Bartell, and assuming the plush, rolling chair behind his desk. Despite the long night, Fanning didn't look any the worse for wear. The sleeves of his white shirt still bore the launderer's creases, and his red floral tie was snug as a noose under his chin. His eyes flickered back and forth around the room while he pursed his wiry lips.

At last Fanning coughed lightly into his fist, and when he settled back into his large chair, Bartell wondered viciously if his feet reached the floor.

"Now," Fanning announced, "everything's reduced to a manhunt."

This characterization of events apparently caught even Zillion off guard. The Secret Service man began to make a vague utterance about balancing suspicion and evidence—Bartell took this as a positive note—but the captain was not about to be distracted by rational thought. The way Fanning explained it, everyone had Henry Skelton all trussed up on the spit, and now they were just looking for the best way to light the fire. Were there any weak sisters left who could possibly think otherwise?

Bartell knew, however, that putting together a case against Skelton, or anyone, would demand considerably more than assumptions. "Anybody tried talking to Skelton yet?" he asked.

Talk to Skelton? Please.

"As far as I can tell," Fanning said, summing up his views on bleeding-heart law enforcement, "this man doesn't deserve the consideration of being listened to again. Isn't that what got us to this point, Bartell? *You* listened to *him?* I always thought it was supposed to be the other way around with assholes."

Right now, Fanning told Bartell, they were in the process of deciding on how to punch Skelton's ticket. Woodruff had sent Ike Skinner and Billy Stokes out to watch Skelton's house from a distance. They'd reported back that Skelton's truck wasn't visible, so right now nobody was exactly sure of his whereabouts.

Taking a swallow of coffee, Bartell was convinced that he was the best person to approach Skelton. If Skelton had made this move against Bartell, then Bartell might also be the most likely person to whom Skelton would respond now. On the other hand, if he wasn't the bomber, then Bartell could well be the only person Skelton would trust enough to talk. And talk was important. Physical evidence was vital, but its availability and meaning were always problematic. Just ask the people who'd investigated Cradle Creek. So, despite Fanning's hormonal response to asking for interviews, there was never any substitute for what a suspect had to say for himself, whether it be the truth or lies.

Besides, Bartell was far from convinced that Skelton was really the bomber. For one thing, it made no sense. He had to ask himself, though, what sense it made for anybody to come stalking his house.

Forget it. Whoever the bomber was, Bartell wanted him. Wanted him badly. Hunting people required tactics, and right now Bartell's most immediate tactic was simply staying on the job. If that required boarding the Skelton juggernaut, then what the hell. Though Skelton might be the wrong man, it seemed clear that the road to the truth at least passed his way. That made doing Skelton simply another tactic in the larger game.

But Fanning's inclination would be to scratch Bartell's involvement in the case, which made perfectly good sense. Never let a victim investigate his own crime. No objectivity. Too volatile. Bad business all the way around. Especially if you don't know which side the cop's on, because he's held back on you.

Finally, Bartell said, "Okay, if Skelton did it, and he wanted me dead, then I'd be dead." The same logic he'd applied earlier. Did he believe it himself?

"Maybe," Fanning said. "Or maybe you're just lucky. Who's to say the bomb wasn't supposed to go off when you got in the car this morning?"

"And who's to say," Zillion added, "that killing somebody was the goal?"

"Anybody know how it was detonated?" Bartell asked.

Fanning shook his head. "Not yet."

When Fanning didn't elaborate, Bartell pressed further. "Any help at all from the scene? The neighbors?"

This time, when Fanning stirred uneasily and made terse eye contact with Zillion, Bartell knew that something was up.

"We sent people door to door on your street," Fanning said, measuring his words. "With a photo of Skelton. A couple remembered seeing him talking to you the other night."

"Which I already told you about," Bartell said, preparing himself for the ax to fall.

A vein twitched momentarily across Fanning's left temple. "That's right. Told us this morning. Didn't tell us yesterday, when it might have counted for something." Now the tension began to squeeze out of Fanning. "And I've got to wonder, Bartell, we all do, we've got to wonder just exactly why it is you held that out on us."

"Then you've got several choices," Bartell said. Fanning obviously didn't trust him, so if he couldn't gain control of the conversation, he'd soon be out in the street. "You can push Mike Sweeney for the warrant over the letter—"

Fanning shot out a hand to stop him. "Just hang on, Bartell—"

"—at least that way you get him into custody."

"Ray!" Fanning's voice snapped through the small office like the noise of one of his countless practice rounds on the pistol range.

Bartell backed off. Babbling now would only signify failure.

"After the bomb at Cradle Creek," Bartell said, "Skelton's house and truck were searched. A dead end. And the components of that bomb were all generic, nothing that could be traced back to anyone. Another dead end. So unless somebody can place him around my house last night—not the night before, when we talked, but early this morning—unless you can do that, it's a tough case to make."

"For Christ's sake, Bartell," Fanning erupted, "it's obvious he's our man."

"But can we *prove* it?" Bartell said.

Proof? We don't need no stinking proof! At least not right now, we don't. Get Skelton in jail, that's what we need. Not that they were without choices, the first of which Fanning immediately advocated: Activate the SWAT team. Nothing subdues a guy like seeing the little red dot of a laser sight dancing around on his chest. And if that doesn't work, fill up his house with chemical agent, leave him hacking and wheezing, drooling snot all the way down to the ground.

Or, Bartell countered, maybe somebody could just call Skelton on the phone and ask him to drop by the office for a chat. Fanning was even less likely than Skelton to bite on this plan, but Bartell understood that if he was to have any say at all in the process under way, he had to start somewhere.

"Fuck that," Fanning said. "I told you, Skelton doesn't deserve that kind of consideration."

The only consideration that counted, Bartell thought, was the consideration involved in putting together a successful case. But why clutter up Fanning's mental process by scattering around the debris of logic?

Fine, then, if not the SWAT team and an outright assault, then why not continue to stake out Skelton's house while pressuring Mike Sweeney to speed up the arrest warrant in the *Free Independent* letter case. That would at least get Skelton off the street. That done, they could root around in the bombing case at their leisure.

"And search for the typewriter?" Bartell said, again raising the issue that Fanning had evaded the day before out at Puhl's ranch. "The evidence?" Evidence, evidence, evidence. Over and over, Bartell fingered the word through his mind, like beads on a rosary.

"I cannot believe this shit!" Fanning blurted out at last. He looked down at the table and massaged the back of his neck with both hands. "If I'd known things were going to get this fucked up, I'd have given this goddamned detail to someone else. And don't think for a minute that Puhl and his bunch haven't made the same point. When Duckworth called late yesterday, he said you even tried to sell them on the idea that Skelton was clean on that helicopter business. And all the time you're practically in bed with Skelton."

In a flash of paranoia, Bartell wondered if Fanning had somehow known all along about Helen's association with Gina, and suspected that he had deliberately taken a soft position on Skelton. Jesus, if that's what Fanning believed, how long would it be before he began to wonder if Bartell had blown up the car himself? Surely no rational person would believe that. But Fanning . . . once a thought like that began working on Fanning, it could spread like slow poison.

Bartell was scared to death of pursuing Fanning's last comment, but he couldn't let it pass either. "And what's that supposed to mean, Vic?"

"Watch your tone, Bartell." Fanning was clearly coiled, his voice an ominous buzz.

Too bad Helen wasn't there to hear what was going on. Then, by God, she'd understand what his constant angling was all about.

"Excuse me all to pieces. What's that supposed to mean, *Captain.*" The wrenched look on Fanning's face told Bartell that maybe he had gone too far. Mentally, he began to inventory his stock of uniforms, wondering how much stuff he'd have to buy to make the move back into uniform patrol.

As he had done the day before at Puhl's, Arnold Zillion chose the perfect moment to have his say in things. "I agree with Ray," Zillion said.

When Fanning started to object, Zillion cut him off. "I know there's a downside, but no matter how you look at it, Ray's still the logical person to take a run at Skelton." Zillion then went on to make his argument, using points that mirrored Bartell's own reasoning. When he was done, Fanning still wasn't sold, but at least he hadn't called for straitjackets and a bucket of Thorazine.

"Regardless of what some people may think about how Bartell has handled things so far," Fanning said to Zillion, "everything I know about human nature—cops' nature too—all that tells me

Bartell should be pulled. As a matter of fact, I don't know why we're even wasting our time having this discussion."

"Suit yourself," Zillion said, sounding matter-of-fact. "It's your city, your man, your call. Sometimes, though, you can go a long way with a little finesse."

"If I'm not mistaken," Fanning said, "finesse is what got us where we are now."

"So what?" Zillion said. "Look, Captain, you know as well as I do that eventually you're going to need something more on Skelton than"—Zillion's voice betrayed a rare hitch—"than common sense. Trying to talk to Skelton can't hurt you. And you've got a lot better chance of getting a statement from him if you don't start right out by throwing him in jail."

Fanning shrugged his agreement.

"Look," Zillion offered, "if the problem is you don't trust Bartell, then let me work with him. Put him under my thumb. I won't let him be exposed." And now Zillion pointed grimly at Bartell. "Or let him squirm around too much either."

There was a discreet tap on the door, and before Fanning could answer, the door swung open, and none other than Brandon McWilliams himself sauntered in. Bartell could have sworn he heard a gasp whisper through the small office.

"Captain," McWilliams said, offering his well-sculpted hand to Fanning. "I hustled on down as soon as I got your message."

Before either Bartell or Zillion had a chance to inquire, Fanning explained. "Once things settled down," he said, "I reached out to Brand and invited him down. We don't get this kind of excitement all the time, and I thought it was a good opportunity for him to see firsthand how a small police department responds to major crimes."

"Research," McWilliams offered self-consciously. Today McWilliams wore a bomber jacket made of supple black leather, black slacks, shiny black ropers, and a white silk shirt buttoned at the throat. He was crowned with a black baseball cap with a split red heart embroidered on the crown and gold scrambled eggs splayed across the bill. "I'm a real tyrant when it comes to authenticity. The captain here's been an ace in the hole in that department."

Fanning beamed with what could best be described as afterglow. Arnold Zillion, on the other hand, took the visiting eminence in stride. Once you've banged out eighteen holes with

Norman, Bartell decided, a mere movie star such as McWilliams must be just another warm body.

"I wonder," Bartell muttered to Zillion, "if he's going to toss us peanuts."

Zillion squirmed.

"What was that, Bartell," Fanning snapped.

"Bartell?" McWilliams said. "You must be Ray, then. Cash's boy."

"The very one," he said pleasantly, taking McWilliams's hand. Cash's *boy?* Bartell nodded toward Arnold Zillion. "And this is—"

"Right, right," McWilliams interrupted. "Agent Zillion. Sure. We met the other morning out at Merle's."

Zillion's acknowledgment was a perfunctory "Good morning."

"Cash has told me a lot about you, Ray," McWilliams went on. "And I understand you and your wife were over at the ranch a few days ago. He should have brought you by the house for drinks. Nothing like a G and T after a day on horseback."

"That would have been quite an experience," Bartell assured him. He was, however, thinking about having drinks with Cash.

"Well." Williams rubbed his hands together with relish. "Don't let me interrupt anything. I'll just mind my own business and soak it all up. This is a great experience for me, you know. I hang with a bunch of guys from LAPD . . . great guys . . . but watching you people is a real treat."

"There's a guy in the shop here you should meet," Bartell said, feeling wicked. "Cassidy. Thomas Cassidy. A writer." What the hell, why not test the waters on Cassidy's behalf. "Maybe you've heard of him?" A bait question if ever there was one.

McWilliams put a hand to the side of his face and glanced away. "Cassidy? No. No, can't say I have." Then he crossed the office and scooted a side chair into the corner behind Fanning. "Well, don't let me interrupt. Go ahead with your work. God, I just love this."

"Actually, Brand," Fanning said, "we were just breaking up."

"That's right," Bartell said, standing. He'd already had his house bombed. Why sit around with Fanning and add getting pimped by McWilliams to the list of insults?

Zillion followed suit. "My partner here," he said to McWilliams, "is a regular shark when it comes to sticking with the job."

"That's me, all right," Bartell said, throwing Zillion a smirk. "All eighteen holes, or none at all."

Both Fanning and McWilliams appeared perplexed.

"I don't get it," McWilliams said.

"No reason you should," Zillion countered.

"But," McWilliams said, insistent on having the last word, "it's dialogue that sounds like the real thing to me."

Chapter 19

"Do you vote?" Bartell said. He turned left out of the City Hall parking lot onto Ross Avenue, then stopped at the red light on Weaver. He and Arnold Zillion were on their way out to Skelton's place, where they would make a low-key stab at talking to Skelton.

"Excuse me?" Arnold Zillion said.

"You know, elections. In November. You go to a school or the courthouse, tell your name to some little old lady with blue hair—"

"Okay, I get it." Zillion was scribbling in his notebook. "This is some kind of gag, right?"

Skinner and Stokes remained in place on their surveillance and still reported no sign of Skelton or his truck. Sam Blieker was wrapping up the crime-scene work back at Bartell's house while Woodruff was organizing a more comprehensive search for Skelton. Fanning, meanwhile, would review the events of last night with Mike Sweeney, the prosecutor. That should buy at least a couple of hours, a chance to defuse Skelton. A chance to figure out who'd really attacked his home.

Off to the left, three young Indian men were draped over a parking meter in front of the Cloverleaf. Shards of newspaper swirled under a light breeze in the gutter at their feet.

Bartell resumed his kibitzing with Zillion. "No, I'm really curious. You vote?"

"You go to church?"

"Used to. And I still vote. Once in a while. When I get fed up."

By that standard, he should be scouting out an election every day.

The Indians were dressed in blue jeans, and run-down sneakers that looked like flat tires. Two wore their dark hair parted in the middle, with braids. The third had on a red-and-black Chicago Bulls cap, turned backward. One of the men with braids spotted Bartell looking at them, and pointed. Now all three returned his stare. Bartell glanced up at the light, which was still red.

"Okay," Zillion said, "you got me. Yeah, I voted. But only once."

Bartell turned back to the three Indians. Now they were laughing, pointing at his car. Bartell wondered if the three had developed a taste yet for cappuccino, which was quickly becoming the sacramental drink of western Montana. Cappuccino, designer water, and dark beer from micro-breweries. Just last week, Bartell had seen an old transient woman gumming a bottle of Evian water. The light changed, and he peeled away.

"Voted for LBJ," Zillion went on. "Figured Goldwater would have us in a war. Then I got drafted."

Bartell drove past a large auto supply business. Two parking lots. An old brick hotel—The Atlantis—that had been gutted, then remodeled into low income apartments. A lot of clients from Heartstone, the walk-in mental health center, lived in The Atlantis. Club Meds. That's what the cops called it. The brick façade was freshly acid-blasted, and a stylish maroon awning stretched along the front. The awning was flecked with pigeon shit.

"You think you'll vote for Merle Puhl?" Bartell asked.

"Ray," Zillion instructed, "a gentleman doesn't kiss and tell."

At Rankin, Bartell took a right and headed out onto the strip, which was lined with large discount stores, car lots, and suppliers of farm and ranch equipment.

"I guess you must get pretty jaded about politicians," Bartell said.

"Symbiotic," Zillion said. "Like those birds that pick bugs off the backs of rhinos. There are worse ways to make a living."

"Travel a lot?"

"Sometimes."

"Russia?"

"Once."

"Russia must have been tough. At least when the Soviets still had it."

Zillion shook his head. "Russia was a snap. Anybody who might give you trouble just disappeared. Communists and Fascists really know how to do dignitary protection."

"No problem a jail cell won't solve."

"Ten-four."

"Well," Bartell said, "in our own modest way, we've been trying." When Zillion didn't respond, Bartell decided to shift the subject, but not change it altogether. "You ever been assigned to a president?"

"Not full-time. But I drew a temporary detail to Reagan once. That was the trip to Russia. Oh, yeah, and I went on a fishing trip with Carter. Stood up on a hill above a river, carrying a machine gun, while Jimmy buffed up his flycasting."

"You get to fish a little too?"

Now Zillion deadpanned. "Hired help don't be doin' no fishin', boss. The fishing wasn't for shit anyhow. Zooming in on the helicopter tended to make the trout a bit shy."

The traffic was light, and Bartell made good time. As the businesses began to thin out, he turned left onto Mansfield Road, which led to the Holt River.

"By the way," Bartell said, "thanks for sticking up for me with Fanning."

"I did it only because I saw where you were heading, and it made sense." Zillion paused and cracked open his window. "I also know how police bureaucracies work. As far as I'm concerned, you handled Skelton okay. There were other ways, maybe, but yours was as good as any of them. You even tried to work things out so it didn't involve your wife. It's not your fault things went sour."

"Don't make it sound like I'm a saint, because I'm not."

"I know," Zillion said. "You tried to juggle everything out because you thought rubbing elbows with Ramrod would be a kick." Now Fanning spoke in a way that was almost fatherly, yet more weary and bemused than insulting. "Local cops always think that. Anyway, if Fanning put you on the shelf now, you'd be a long time getting right again around your department. Maybe never."

"So does that mean you've got your doubts about Skelton too? As the bomber?"

"I didn't say that."

At that point Bartell was simply glad to have Zillion halfway in his corner. No need to start preaching the gospel on Skelton. Besides, there was still the chance that Bartell was wrong.

Zillion, though, decided to toss him a bone. "But I did like what you said about evidence."

They crossed the Holt about half a mile ahead. The river, low this time of year, reflected the pale autumn sky. To the left, upstream, the bank was honeycombed with the abandoned pens outside Holt Prairie Meats, a sprawling slaughterhouse made of gray cinder blocks, with the peeling mural of red-and-white Hereford steer painted on the side facing the bridge. The pens had been abandoned under court order about five years earlier because runoff into the river was killing the fish for miles downstream. Nowadays, the cattle were trucked in from a new stockyard outside of town and killed immediately. In the grove of nearly bare cottonwoods along the river, perhaps thirty or forty crows dotted the spidery limbs, waiting for the odd scraps that inevitably found their way outside the slaughterhouse.

Just off the bridge, Bartell made a right, and they were in River Flats, Skelton's neighborhood. A short distance on, they came to the road that dead-ended at Skelton's house. Bartell stopped the car.

"Tell me," Zillion said, "what the Lozano woman had to say about just who Skelton is. Exactly."

Bartell tried to recall something Gina had told him, which might sum up Skelton. Finally, he said, "She thinks he's on a quest." Now, how could you ever explain the idea of a quest without having it come out like some sort of crackpot deal? "A spiritual quest. It's a Native American kind of thing."

"I didn't think Skelton was an Indian."

"He's not."

"And what's the object of this quest?"

Bartell shrugged. "Hell, I don't know. She didn't either. Stuff. He's on a quest for stuff."

It was about ten o'clock. Skinner and Stokes were parked at least a quarter of a mile away, and on a different street from the cul-de-sac that led to Skelton's place. If things turned ugly, Skinner and Stokes could call out the troops and storm in themselves, but that would take a while. Even if Bartell was right about Skelton not being the bomber—or even knew about the trouble at Bartell's house—there was still no telling how jumpy he might be. Back at the station, Bartell's original suggestion that they simply call Skelton on the phone and ask him to drop by again—a possibility that even Bartell had raised only as an entrée into a larger discussion—had been formally discarded. That angle, everyone agreed, was too detached to get a good read on what was happening inside Skelton's house.

"I figure," Zillion said casually, "we just start off like you did before. Real low-key, see where things go." Then his voice turned arch. "I think the narcs call it a knock and talk."

"A little knock and talk, eh?" Bartell decided that if Zillion could ridicule cop jargon, he was going to be forced to like the man.

Arnold Zillion remained deadpan. "I'm the Secret Service, Ray. Trust me, we've always got a plan."

Gina's blue Celica was parked in front of the house, but, true to the surveillance team's last report, there was still no sign of the green Ford pickup that was registered to Skelton. Bartell pulled his gray Dodge, a clone of the rubble now in his driveway, to a stop behind the Celica. By the time they got to the front step, Gina was waiting for them, standing solidly in the door. "What is it this time?" Voice tight as a millionaire's fist.

Bartell introduced Zillion and asked if Skelton was around.

Gina held her ground, gripping the edge of the door. "He's already talked to you," she said vaguely. "What is it you want now?"

Bartell took another step forward, stuck his hands into the hip pockets of his jeans, and leaned against the doorjamb. "It's no big deal, Gina." No big deal, he thought, we just want to toss your old man in the bucket. Trust us.

"No big deal," she said, mimicking him. "Like I don't listen to the news every morning. You still think he did that other bomb, and now you think he's done this one."

Okay, Bartell thought, grinning like an idiot, so we eliminate trust from our bag of tricks.

Skelton stood just inside the bedroom, listening. It was Gina who had spotted them, Bartell and the big guy in the suit, heading down the road toward their house in that conspicuously plain little car. While he was relieved that his habit of parking the truck well away from the house had finally paid off, Skelton now understood that he should not have returned to the house at all. And when Gina told him there'd been another bombing, a cop car for Christ's sake, he should have run right then. Run like hell. Except he knew they would be watching the house, waiting to take him down. He didn't know where they would wait, but he knew they were there. They were always there. Goddammit, he would have chanced anyway, except for her.

He heard Bartell: *Any idea when he'll be back?*

No, Gina said.

And so now here he was, cowering in the bedroom because she had asked him, pleaded with him, to swallow his anger and his pride and do nothing. Which he was doing. He tucked the rifle tighter against his right leg.

Nothing.

Where do you think he went?

I don't know, I'm not his keeper. I just live with him, you know?

He say anything? Before he left?

He said you were an asshole. Just like the rest . . .

. . . Okay . . .

. . . just another asshole. But that's what he always says about cops, so it was, like, no big deal.

No big deal. Hiding out in your own bedroom was no big deal. While somebody lied for you . . .

So like I said, what the fuck do you want?

You said you listen to the news. You're not stupid.

They said it was a cop car. That's all.

It was my car. Parked outside my house.

Skelton glanced around the room, which seemed to shrink and grow warmer as he stood waiting, listening, trying to squeeze every nuance out of Bartell's voice.

Bartell's car.

Bartell's house.

Now Bartell at his door.

Man, Skelton, when you're fucked, you're really fucked.

No, Skelton had not planned to come back at all. Not, at any rate, until the former president was safely in and out of town. He'd have hunkered down in his cave through the blizzard of the century, waiting for that. But after returning to Gina in the night, and lying cupped against her back through the first strings of sunlight, he felt disconnected for a time from his obsession with that perfect, threatened world outside of town, outside this world, this room, outside of Gina, felt safe and complete as he tucked himself closer against her, warmed himself on the heat of her neck against his cheek, settled into the sleepy rhythm of her breathing.

And now this disaster. He raised the rifle. Hugged it against his chest.

Gina was still talking: *I guess you think he did that too.*

And Bartell again: *What time did he leave?*

He was here all night. With me. If that's what you're getting at. He never left the house.

That's not exactly what I asked.

But it's what I'm telling you.

And lied for him again. The biggest lie of all, the lie that slammed the last door behind him. Now he was alone for real.

Skelton tried to imagine her making the quilt covering the bed, to imagine her working through those thousands of tiny stitches while he paced through endless days and nights in the joint. Near the foot of the bed, the closet door stood open. Gina's gown, thin white cotton, with lace around the neck and arms, hung from a hook on the back of the door. Skelton shifted his weight from one foot to another.

And then another man's voice, Bartell's partner. *Maybe you could let us take a look around.*

What?

You know. Search the house. Save us the trouble of getting a warrant.

Skelton continued to look at Gina's gown, to study the intricate loops and twirls of the lace. He stared intently into the folds of the gown as he listened, until at last he saw only a blur.

Zillion was smiling, the creases like a net of fracture lines at the corners of his eyes.

"You want to search my house?" Gina said. She was talking to Zillion. Now, when she spoke again to Bartell, her tone was different. Bewildered. "Search my house?" Scared.

"Well, yeah," Bartell said, suddenly afraid for her. Scared to death of the violence that he was now sure awaited her, awaited them all, in the house if she said yes. "That way, we'd know

Henry wasn't trying to hide anything from us. Makes perfect sense, you think about it. But you don't have to."

She inched her leg behind the door, blocking it. "I told you he isn't here."

Zillion put his hand over his mouth, coughed.

Watching Gina, the sunlight flashing through the dark ringlets of her hair framing her face, the defiance and fear shot all through her, Bartell wondered what kind of idiot Skelton must be, eating up his life in a quest for secret spirits, writing foolish diatribes about fools. He thought about his wife. Would Helen hold the world at bay on his behalf? Of course she would. This stupid bastard Skelton deserved every raw deal he got.

"Gina," Bartell said quietly, almost under his breath, "if he's here, you can just walk on out to the car with us. We won't say another word. Just follow us out to the car, and we'll get you out of here."

Skelton flattened his shoulders harder against the bedroom wall, feeling the muscles stretch across his chest. He closed his eyes and tried to hear the voices, the live human voices, above the ringing in his ears. Voices now nearly whispers.

Gina: *I said he's not here.*

And the other man: *Listen, honey.*

Listen, honey?

Skelton held his breath, and thumbed the safety on the rifle. Off. On. Off again. Surely they could hear his breathing, short and tough, as it echoed through the tiny house. What kind of man would allow her to stand between himself and this prick while he hid out in the bedroom? He started to laugh, a bitter, shameful laugh, and then he caught himself, compressed himself again into silence, and felt even more ashamed.

Bartell could sense that she was on the edge, but Zillion's hint of confrontation had pushed her back. He was about to interrupt, when Zillion surprised him again.

"I'm sorry," Zillion said. "I apologize for that. I've been up all night. I'm a little frustrated. Because what we're trying to get through to you is we're not convinced Henry's good for this thing. Get it? You think we'd be out here like this now if we were sold on that? You think Ray, of all people, would be here if he was sure Henry did this thing? You watch TV, right? You think all we'd do is come out here and *talk* if we thought that?"

Bartell tried to think of a closer for Zillion's routine, but held back when Gina slid her arm down along the doorjamb, and seemed to waver. A pleading look touched her face as faintly as the shadow of a flying bird touches the ground, and Bartell was thinking, yes, that's it, just nod, lean our way, step toward us, anything, we're so close. So goddamned close. Then Gina gathered herself and said: "Get a fucking warrant."

When the door slammed, the entire house reverberated up and down Skelton's spine.

"She's lying," Bartell said under his breath. The whole business smelled about as bad as three-day-old road kill. Walking back to the car, the back of his neck began to tingle as he wondered whether he or Zillion was in Skelton's cross hairs.

"Who cares?" Zillion said.

Bartell fished the keys from his pocket, then slid behind the wheel. Zillion slammed his own door, and seemed preoccupied with the scenery as Bartell turned around in Gina Lozano's driveway. Bartell took a pair of sunglasses from his shirt pocket and slipped them on.

Zillion pursed his lips, then shook his head. "His truck's gone. He's got an attitude like ground zero. He likes to spend his time outdoors." Zillion smiled with sweet sarcasm. "Maybe he really is just out recreating."

"But she won't let us in the house," Bartell said. The truth was, innocent people tend not to make you prove you've got an iron fist inside that velvet glove. "I'd say she's too scared."

Zillion's response surprised him. "She didn't have to. That was her right. Scared or not, I wouldn't have let us in that house either."

"You trying to tell me you admire people with principles?"

But Zillion wasn't going to dwell on it. "Find me one sometime, I'll let you know."

Standing at the edge of the living room window, Skelton watched the car glide off down the street. Brown, dry leaves fluttered over the gray gravel in the car's wake. Skelton looked over his shoulder at Gina. She stood in the corner near the bedroom door, her arms across her breasts, hands on each shoulder, hugging herself. It was the stance she took, he realized, when she was afraid he was about to blow.

"I told you everything," he said. "I always have."

"Okay," she said, almost a whisper.

"Then what is it?"

"When I went to bed, I thought you'd be gone."

Skelton remembered the hot tangle of them in bed, the slow, exhausted sleep afterward. "If you really believe—"

"You told me you were leaving, and I know you left. But just for a short time. You said you were going all the way back to the mountains, but instead, you come back here."

"I have to explain why I come home?"

"For an alibi? Was that it, Henry?"

"An alibi?" He took a step, two, three steps toward her, watched her brace herself. He stopped short, felt his pulse banging in his throat. He had never struck out at her, and now here she was, steeling herself to get bashed.

When she looked at him now and spoke, there was only rage in her. "You even hid your goddamn truck—"

"I always hide the truck."

"—and I had to lie for you."

"I know," he said softly. He started to point out that he had not asked her to lie, to protect him from the cops. But that would only add insult to an already impossible jumble of accusations, defenses, explanations. She had lied without being asked to because she loved him, and you don't rub somebody's face in a thing like that. Not ever. And now that one lie had contaminated all the true things that had ever passed between them. Her lies on his behalf, as far as she was concerned, had made everything about him a lie too.

"You sneak off in the middle of the night—something you never do—and then you sneak back home again." Gina wasn't arguing with him now. Under a great load of sadness, Skelton thought, she was simply trudging toward a destination that to her seemed obvious. Some things, once you put them into words, they start seeping out of your heart into your brain. Already, just thinking about what Gina's words meant, Skelton could feel the transformation race ahead. Everything about Gina—the arms with which she hugged herself, the distance in her voice, the tears that now tipped out of her eyes—all of it said she had finally come to believe he was completely out of his mind. This was the one thing in her he could not tolerate. It made him afraid.

Skelton struggled to remember that state of suspension that had overcome him just days ago, when he tried to dissolve himself into granite in the path of that great, shimmering beast. The bear in Cradle Creek. He inhaled slowly, letting air creep into his lungs.

"The other day," he said, "Monday, I guess it was, I saw a bear. A grizzly." He hoped that by telling Gina the story of the bear, he might somehow bring the bear back to life inside himself, find himself back inside that heart of recognition. And so he told her.

But it was gone.

And now Gina was gone too. "Henry," she said gently, her voice no more than a nudge. "Henry, you have to leave."

Chapter 20

"You could be down the road on this thing," Bartell said as he drove along the dirt street. "I mean, Ramrod's off, so this isn't really your gig anymore."

Zillion leaned his head against the headrest and closed his eyes. "Who knows," he said, sounding weary. "Maybe I just needed the exercise."

When Bartell got to the cross street, he hesitated, then turned left, toward the river, rather than back toward town.

"When in doubt," Zillion said idly, "kick back and wait."

"We go back to the station," Bartell said, "Fanning's just going to send me home." Skelton was his job, his and Zillion's, and truck or not, if his take on Gina was right, Skelton was holed up in the house. That meant that the next move was probably Vic Fanning's, and Bartell knew there was little chance he'd be included in any of Fanning's plans. So rather than head back to the station and expose himself to the captain's whims, he backed into a turnout next to a small weathered barn off the cross street, from where they had a passable, nearly unobstructed view of Skelton's house. He raised Stokes and Skinner on the radio and told them it was a no-go at the house.

"Too bad about Ramrod," Bartell said, making small talk with Zillion.

Zillion sniffed. "A regular American tragedy. Better watch out, Ray, your shoes'll get splattered by my tears."

"You were right, Arnold."

"You'll have to be more specific than that," Zillion drawled. "I'm always right."

"Big guys in dark suits talking into sleeve mikes. Got nothing at all to do with real life, but it would have been a whole lot of fun."

To their right, the dirt street disappeared into the dense sheath of cottonwoods and brush along the river, while to their left they could see down the street where Skelton would approach, in case they were wrong, and catch him heading back home in the green pickup. That part was troubling. The pickup. If Skelton was holed up in the house, where was the truck? Stashed someplace, probably. But the house sat out in the open, so they should be able to see him walk out. More likely, though, Skelton and Gina would soon climb into her blue Celica and make a break. If that happened, Bartell would alert Skinner and Stokes, and they would take Skelton down on the road. Briefly, he raised the other two detectives on the radio again and told them where he and Zillion were positioned.

Zillion dug a roll of Life Savers from his jacket pocket, popped one into his mouth, and passed the roll to Bartell. "Big Chief Ramrod, and Merle the Used Car Cowboy. Mother was right, I should have lived a cleaner life."

Bartell fiddled with the AM radio, found Patsy Cline on one of the country stations. Listening to that sorrowful voice, riding along on an undercurrent of honky-tonk piano and bass, he thought about cold beer and cigarettes with the boys after work, when he was still a kid ranching. He drummed his fingers on the steering wheel in time with the music. His hands felt soft.

"I remember the first time I saw TV," Bartell said.

"That right?"

"Me and my dad, we were checked into a motel over in Great Falls. Back in the late fifties. Wasn't much TV in Montana back in those days. Not out in the sticks anyway. And we lived in the sticks."

Zillion settled into a bored stake-out voice. "I can imagine."

Bartell remembered that Zillion lived in Great Falls. "You like Great Falls?"

"Not especially."

"Where you from? Originally?"

"Connecticut. Danbury."

Bartell had never been to Connecticut. Never been east of Minnesota, where he had gone once to visit some of Helen's family. "You miss it?"

"No. Too many hotels and airplanes between here and there. Know what I mean?"

The truth was, Bartell didn't know. Well, maybe he did. As he thought about that Great Falls motel, with its lumpy double bed, grainy black-and-white TV, and the cops bringing Cash in drunk after midnight, he tried to imagine what sort of connection that old memory could possibly have with the likes of Brandon Mc-Williams, the new baron of the plains. Could a man miss a place and still live in it at the same time? Maybe Bartell had tramped around in too many pickup trucks and sleeping bags since then, same as Zillion had seen too many hotels and airplanes between here and Danbury.

"You married?" Bartell asked finally.

"She went the way of Nixon. At about the same time."

"Resigned?"

"Impeached."

The barn, which sat on Bartell's side of the car at the edge of a five- or six-acre pasture, was enclosed within a triple-strand barbed wire fence. The fence angled around the notch that accommodated the turnout, giving access to the barn. In the over-grazed pasture on Zillion's side of the car, an old gray horse with black dapples clubbed his right front hoof at a mangled clump of knapweed.

"The world," Zillion said at last, "is full of bad, dangerous men." Now he turned to Bartell, his face almost quivering with steely concentration and resolve. "With only a handful of us true heros to keep the mean streets safe for women and children—" He paused for effect. "And snot-nosed politicians."

"They just pimped us on Skelton, didn't they?" Bartell said. "You had it pegged as garbage from the start."

Zillion sounded even more bored. "Duckworth, that kid running Puhl's campaign, he calls me two, three weeks ago. Worried about some terrorist maniac, he says, a lead pipe cinch in the political assassin department. Henry Skelton."

Zillion pursed his lips, sucking on the Life Saver as he squinted into the sun, which was dropping lower into the heavy cloud bank gathering in the mountains on the valley's western edge. Then he went on: "Fine, I say, I'll put him on my shopping list, thanks very much.

"But you don't get it, Duckworth says. This is Henry Skelton. *Henry Skelton.*

"Right, I say, now, who's—"

Bartell saw it all coming. "Who's Henry Skelton?"

"Exactly. Who's Henry Skelton. Far as I can tell, Skelton's just another ex-con needs a bath and a haircut and a job. But no, Duckworth, he has the goods on him."

Bartell thought back to the afternoon before, when he'd gone out to Puhl's ranch. "It was curious the other day. When I first met Yolanda Huizer—Puhl's squeeze?—she said the contractor on the Cradle Creek job was a buddy of Puhl's. But later on, Duckworth—"

"Right. Duckworth said he'd first learned about Skelton in the newspaper. You're wondering if that makes any sense."

"It doesn't," Bartell said. "Unless you've got a plan. Maybe somebody knew the story on Skelton before the first bombing."

"There you are, Ray."

"Then you don't think Skelton bombed the helicopter."

"Nobody can prove he did," Zillion said, "nobody can prove he didn't. All I know is the Puhl campaign had Skelton all signed, sealed, and delivered. Doesn't take J. Edgar Hoover to figure that out. And you can worry from now till breakfast about the why of it all, but so what? I'm still stuck. The Secret Service is stuck. Because Ramrod's on the horizon, and I've been given official notice of somebody who's conceivably a serious threat."

"You think about it like that," Bartell said, "it's probably best for the campaign if Skelton's still on the loose. Still out there lurking." If you want people to vote for you because they're angry and afraid, why settle for being abstract when you can deliver up an honest-to-God terrorist in the flesh?

"Put a wolf in a cage," Zillion said, "and what've you got? Just another big, smelly dog."

And now here they sat, a local cop and a genuine Secret Service Agent, validating a campaign issue for Merle Puhl, and his boy genius campaign manager. Bartell started to laugh.

Zillion scowled. "What's so goddamn funny?"

"Skelton. Skelton and us." Now Bartell turned serious. "We're the cops, right? We're supposed to defend freedom. Among other things anyhow. So how come one of the things we despise most is a guy like Skelton, a guy who really doesn't do much more than demand to be free?"

"Jesus Christ, Ray, freedom's got nothing to do with it." Zillion adjusted his collar. "Like you said, we're the cops. Freedom." Now he sounded indignant. *"Freedom?* That's the kind of thing people think about when they've got nothing better to do than jerk off. Guys like you and me, we're just the muscle behind what those people decide. The guys getting stroked."

"So I talk to Skelton," Bartell said, "figure he probably won't be a problem, and tell the boys on the campaign I don't think he's as big and bad as they believe." Bartell paused, considering the last twenty-four hours. "Tell them he's been put on notice, and now we should just let him slide. Tell them maybe he isn't even a mad bomber and a killer."

"More than that," Zillion said. "Could be he can identify the real bomber."

"Then a bomb goes off outside my house."

"That's right," Zillion said. "You figured that one out yet?"

Bartell reminded Zillion that he'd told Gina he thought Skelton was probably clean on the bombing last night. "You believe that?" he asked.

"It was a scam," Zillion said. "If it's true, so much the better." The same answer Bartell would have given.

"But if it is true, how do we get the dog off Skelton's heels and onto theirs?"

Zillion rolled down his window and crinkled his nose. "Whew. Smells like horse shit."

"Smells like home," Bartell said.

As always, the key remained with Skelton, only now they could be looking to open a different lock.

"You could have told me," Bartell said. "That you knew we were being used."

Zillion popped another Life Saver. "What for? You'd still be stuck too. Just like me. Anyway, you were already whistling that tune, even if you didn't have all the notes quite right."

"That's right," Bartell said. "But the list of people using me would have been one name shorter."

"Like you said," Zillion told him, "I'm still here, aren't I? That's the best I can do."

Skelton stopped short at the back door. Just minutes ago, watching from the front window, he had seen the detective's car turn left instead of right, then slip off the road near the barn, where Bartell and the other cop now waited. He tucked his right shoulder securely under the rifle sling and looked back at Gina.

She'd been watching the car along with him, and she knew what lay ahead too.

"Henry . . ."

"You told me to get out," he said.

"Not this way." She pointed at the rifle.

"I told you . . ." He raised an index finger, as though lecturing a child. "I will not go back to any fucking jail. Not for anything or anybody." Not even her.

"Then stay here—"

"Hide in the house."

"That's right, hide in the goddamn house, Jesus Christ, Henry. I'm sorry I said you had to go. Just stay here with me. You can stay with me forever."

The rifle suddenly felt unbearably heavy. His eyes locked onto hers, searched through them back into last night and on deeper into the years of holding fast to each other.

"If you leave now . . ." she said, measuring out the words as though they had been inside her for years, lying dormant until just this moment. But she could not go on.

The sling slipped on his shoulder, and at the same instant that he caught the rifle, it seemed to him that Gina leaned slightly toward the telephone on the wall next to the refrigerator. Without hesitation Skelton exploded across the kitchen, ripped the phone from the wall.

"Just . . ." he said, "just mind your own fucking business."

Without giving her any further chance to weaken him, he was out the back door, running across the flat behind the house, keeping the house between himself and the two cops watching from their car.

An irrigation ditch, drained now for winter, cut across the flat about fifty yards behind the house. Cradling the rifle against his chest when he got to the ditch, Skelton skidded down the bank, settled back against the rocks and the dried weeds, and caught his breath. The air was still, thick with dust and false autumn heat, while high above, rippled bands of stratus clouds streaked ahead, dragging weather along behind.

Get away.

The thought pounded through Skelton's head.

Get away.

Get the fuck away.

The back of his throat burned from the sprint across the open field. Had they seen him? No, they couldn't see him. Not possible.

And Gina? Goddammit, she would never have used that phone. He knew that. But now? All she had to do was walk out to their car and burn him.

Risking neither another moment's rest nor a peek above the rim of the ditch, Skelton rolled onto his belly, slung the rifle over his head, and scuttled fast as he could over the rocks, heading up the dry ditch toward the cover of the trees along the river.

A big dog stepped out of the barn, then lumbered around to Arnold Zillion's window. A huge, houndish dog with a basset's head but the wild coat, the tall, gangling body of an Irish wolf hound. Zillion seemed paralyzed by the sight.

And then this big, impossible kind of dog simply ambled on up to Zillion's window and stuck his head inside, eyeball to eyeball with Zillion. Given the comparative heights of a basset and an Irish wolfhound, Bartell marveled that such a dog as this could even be conceived.

"Isn't that amazing," Bartell said.

"What in the goddamned hell is this thing?" Zillion moaned.

"You've got a gun," Bartell said, "shoot it."

Zillion pressed himself deeper into the seat. "I just want to get back to some part of America," he said, "where you can get a decent cappuccino and biscotti. I got no use for mutant dogs."

The hound, with heavy flapping jowls, panted in deep primordial blasts, while a long, silvery rope of drool settled into Zillion's lap.

"Oh, God," Zillion wailed, staring down at his damp crotch. "Brooks Brothers."

"Think of it as a business expense," Bartell said. "Hell, maybe you can even bill the Puhl campaign, now it turns out we're doing this job for them."

Finally, Zillion regained his composure enough to crank up the window, forcing the beast to retract its head. The dog stared for a moment at Zillion, apparently as bewildered as the Secret Service man was disgusted. The dog sniffed at the glass, leaving a long, gooey smear before stretching, then trudging back into the barn.

"I was you," Bartell said, "I wouldn't use this experience for a

pickup line in bars." He looked at his watch. It was after noon.
Patsy Cline had long since given way to Randy Travis, then Tanya
Tucker, then George Strait. He switched the radio off. He was
getting hungry. And tired. Tired down into the core of his bones.
"How long you figure we should give this thing?" He was surprised that Fanning hadn't shown up yet with a warrant, the National Guard, and a black helicopter from the United Nations
thrown in for good measure.

Zillion pulled a white handkerchief from his hip pocket and
began mopping up his crotch.

In the trees, Skelton walks with cautious deliberation over
fallen cottonwood leaves and deer droppings along a well-worn
game trail. Now and then, the winding trail skirts the fringe of
the trees, where Skelton cuts away, holding to the deep cover of
the woods, moving with efficient speed, no sensation about him
save the need to get to his truck and get away. He begins to
cover the ground in a long, loping stride, until the dull green
pickup at last comes into view through the brush just ahead.

At the truck, Skelton leans over the hood to collect himself,
feels fear start to settle over him, then crowds it out with rage.

Get away.

Beyond reaching the truck, he has given no thought to how he
will proceed. The only way out is along the rough gravel road
past the two cops. They will stop him. Hell yes, they will. Have
to. No other choice, everybody committed now. They will try to
stop him.

Try.

Skelton looks at his hands, which now hold the rifle.

"That's it," Bartell said.

"I beg your pardon?"

"I'm calling it." For the last twenty minutes, Bartell had chafed
more and more at being played for a stooge by politicians.

Zillion shrugged. "Suit yourself. Maybe he's in the wind after
all. But what about Fanning?"

Bartell still didn't have a decent answer for that one. One way
or another, though, Fanning held all the cards. Maybe the best

Bartell could hope for was to walk away from things on his own initiative rather than mope around waiting to get canned. He had just started the car, and dropped it into gear, when Zillion threw out an urgent arm. "Hang on."

Off to the right, a green pickup bore down on them ahead of a rooster tail of dust.

"That lap. him?" Zillion said.

"Gotta be."

Bartell reached for the microphone to alert Stokes and Skinner, while at the same time he punched the engine, nosing the Dodge partway out into the road, hoping to stop the truck, yet leaving enough space for it to get by if the driver were truly determined.

But the green pickup had no stop in it, and Bartell had time to say no more than "Here he comes" before he threw the mike aside.

As the truck closed, rather than swerving away, using the escape Bartell had allowed, the driver—he saw in that last instant that it was Skelton, his face all hair and eyes and fury—wrenched the wheel around. Zillion flailed away after his gun, while Bartell desperately mashed the gas pedal again, trying to back out of the way. The tires broke traction, and in a chaos of dust and stinging gravel and noise, the pickup jammed broadside into Zillion's door, smashing Zillion's face flat against the window. Glass shattered. Blood sprayed all directions in a slow pink cloud.

Bartell felt as though the car had been knocked out from under him. His forehead caught the corner of the radio console as he plunged toward Zillion. He fought through the daze and scrambled for the door, groping wildly for the Beretta on his hip as he moved.

After the impact, Skelton backed up a short distance, then rammed the little Dodge again, this time at an angle, shoving it toward the edge of the road. He saw Bartell tumble out the driver's door, blood streaking down his face, gun in hand.

Bartell skidded in the loose gravel, began to bring the gun up toward Skelton, then fell back as the car, pushed ahead by the pickup, overtook him, slid over his legs, rear tire barely missing him, then stopped.

Now Skelton backed off, bailed out, rifle in hand.

Bartell could barely see, his eyes full of blood. He wiped a sleeve frantically across his eyes, then got to his knees and came up, gun first, over the trunk lid, where he found himself looking back into the scope of Skelton's rifle.

Skelton screamed: "Don't do it . . . don't!"

More blood drained into Bartell's eyes, and he couldn't see what he was about to shoot at.

Skelton screamed again. "I didn't want this, goddammit! None of it!"

Skelton held the rifle hard on Bartell, not sure why he was not killing him, why they were not killing each other. The gun was unsteady in Bartell's hand, and his head began to slump slowly onto the car.

And now Skelton said, "I just want to go away. That's all. Just go."

But Bartell was having none of it. It never entered his mind to tell Skelton to surrender, and he would have shot him seconds ago if only he could see through the hot red haze of his own blood.

He shot anyway, firing crazily until the slide locked back.

Skelton heard the shots, tiny and distant, felt the truck flinch as bullets slammed around him into sheet metal and glass. He dove on into the truck now, and as he began trying to drive, one round ripped through the top of his shoulder, near the base of his neck. Then another shattered the windshield, tore into his left hand on the wheel.

Skelton drove wildly around the car, looked back, and saw Bartell fumbling with a new magazine. He started to get out, finish it, when he heard a woman screaming. He looked back at the house, saw Gina running toward them.

Bartell jammed the magazine home with his free hand, then hit the slide release with the thumb of his gun hand. He fired two quick shots toward the truck while at the same time scrambling for fresh cover behind the car.

All Skelton heard this time were Gina's screams. He released his grip on the rifle and took off.

Ahead, Skelton saw the second cop car bearing down on him. His mind suddenly went clear and quiet, and he pressed the accelerator hard against the fire wall. The cop car didn't waver. Skelton's vision held steady, his truck crashing through the air, until in an instant he saw the two cops' eyes, big and white as goose eggs, just before the driver threw the car into a broadside skid angling off to the side of the road, and the truck blasted on by. Glancing in the mirror, Skelton saw through the dust the second cop car float into the ditch, jump the bank, and roll onto its side.

Finally, Skelton was free.

Chapter 21

First, there was that calm pit, where everything settles once the fight ends, followed by the radio call for help. And then the long wait, the repressed fear, the hope that the walls of that pit don't come slumping down and bury you. Help summoned, you keep on waiting.

Moments before, Bartell had watched as the car with Skinner and Stokes careened around Skelton's truck, then jumped the grader ditch and pitched ahead into a slow roll. He knew they could use help, but he had to tend to Arnold Zillion, who was out like a neon sign at daybreak, hacking and wheezing through the blood dribbling into the back of his throat. Bartell knew this was blood because at first touch Zillion hacked a clot onto the front of his shirt. Crouching next to Zillion on the front seat, Bartell tried to ease him away from the mess of broken window glass.

Bartell heard the back door break open behind him. Whirled around. It was the woman. Gina Lozano.

"I can help." She crawled in behind Zillion.

"You could've done that before," Bartell said, meaning she could have given them Skelton.

Gina ignored him. "We need something to hold his head."

Bartell, still groggy from the blow to his own head, made his way out of the car, found a gray wool blanket in the trunk, passed it inside to Gina, who fashioned it into a long, thick tube.

"Now," she said, "we move him just enough to get his face out of the glass.

Bartell crawled back into the front seat, helped her ease the blanket under Zillion's head, between his face and the window, then work the blanket into a crude collar, something to hold his head still in the event he convulsed. Then she slipped the fingers of her left hand under the blanket, feeling for a pulse.

"Fast, but not alarming." Voice distinct, professional. Fingers smeared with blood. "Breathing's steady."

"Sounds like hell," Bartell said. The noises coming from Zillion's throat reminded him of the terminal snores gurgling from some of the elk he had killed.

"Ugly breathing's better than no breathing at all." Gina settled back. Brushed the hair away from her eyes. Took a deep breath of her own, the forced professionalism slipping away.

"What about you?" Her face was smeared with Zillion's blood.

"I think I shot your goddamn boyfriend."

Her blue eyes did not waver. "You're sure?"

"I hope I did. Hope I shot him good," he said, immediately regretting this. Not because he'd told her the truth, but because of what that truth was.

Her cheeks began to twitch involuntarily. But she did not break down. And she never looked away.

Bartell daubed his fingers at the gash on his forehead, felt a loose triangular flap of skin. The cut stung, and when he flinched, he felt the drying blood crackle around his eyes. He reached to adjust the inside mirror so that he could see the cut, but changed his mind. For the first time, he noticed the jumble of radio traffic. He heard his call sign among voices as cops and dispatchers stepped all over each other. He found the microphone cord, retrieved the microphone itself.

Changed his mind.

When putting out the first call, he'd broadcast the description of Skelton, Skelton's truck, and his direction of travel. He'd told the world that shots were fired, that he was all right, but Arnold Zillion was not. That he didn't know about Skinner and Stokes, who never answered up on the radio. He'd ordered an ambulance. He had been calm and coherent. He remained calm now, and there was every reason to believe that he would momentarily be coherent again too.

"A lot of people are going to talk to you," he said to Gina.

"I know."

"You tell them the truth, you hear me?" None of the games he'd tried to play with Helen.

"I don't understand, why wouldn't—"

"Shut up and listen. Because—" He stopped short, studied her face, which was now screwed down with concentration as she bit into her lower lip.

"What?" she said softly. Her hair was a wild black fan.

"I'm banged up, and this guy here"—he nodded toward Zillion—"for all we know, he may die. Same with the two cops in that other car. And Skelton's shot. So there's going to be a whole line of people want a piece of you over this. Because you lied, see, you hid him out, and you maybe did it out of love or fear or God knows what, but none of that will matter."

"But can't you—"

"No. I can't. That's what I'm telling you." There were all kinds of understandable reasons why she had deceived him and Zillion. But from now on, everybody, the Secret Service, the FBI, local cops and prosecutors, even people who knew no more about the thing than what they learned on TV while nursing a six-pack, all of them would believe she was part of something. From now on out, any sort of explanation Bartell might offer on her behalf would amount to nothing. Everybody with a badge would measure Gina Lozano, and they would all, by experience, temperament, and necessity, be predisposed to assume the worst.

There were sirens now, and down the road Bartell saw two, three sets of red-and-blue overheads speeding their way. Urgently, he turned back to Gina. "You understand what I'm saying? This thing'll get picked clean by every cop you can imagine. You lie to any of them about anything, they'll pick you clean too."

"What about Helen?"

"Don't worry about her." If Gina had wanted to worry about Helen, Bartell thought, the time to start was the day before yesterday, when she'd still had the choice of not involving her friend at all.

Gina seemed puzzled at first, then suspicious. "And I suppose you're still trying to convince me you're different."

Bartell wasn't sure if he should be disappointed or angry. "Just do what I tell you, okay? And don't push it. I'm not sure why I don't reach back there and slap you silly." He was about to send her back to check on Skinner and Stokes, when he looked down toward their wreck and saw that both men were outside the car, pacing around and staring down at the overturned heap as though it held the answer to some kind of mystery.

Bartell rode the ambulance in with Arnold Zillion, who was unconscious most of the way. He was met at the hospital by Linda Westhammer and Thomas Cassidy, and he spent the next hour collecting seventeen stitches in his forehead while explaining to the other two detectives what had happened. At about two o'clock, Cassidy and Westhammer dropped Bartell off at the station on their way out to River Flats. For the next couple of hours, Bartell had the pleasure of laying out the story over and over for Vic Fanning, while Gina Lozano went through the drill with Woodruff and Blieker.

"Okay," Fanning said, apparently satisfied at last. Despite his insistence on hearing the details more times than Reggie Jackson used to read his own headlines, Fanning had been surprisingly uncritical. "I'm glad you're okay. And it looks like Zillion will make it too. Stokes and Skinner are banged up, but they're mostly at risk of having heart attacks from being so pissed off."

Fanning was pensive, paging through the notes he'd made on his yellow pad. Now his face shifted, and the tight skin across his narrow face looked momentarily like wrinkled gray paper. "I think that does it. Go home. Kick back. You're out of this for now."

"What about Skelton?"

"We'll get him."

Bartell knew that, of course. The machine was in full gear now, and this time there would be no mewling about evidence. Not even from that notorious stickler himself, Detective Bartell. Within their first hour out on River Flats, Cassidy and Westhammer had reported finding blood spatters on the road where Skelton had stopped the second time. Not much blood, but some. So Skelton was shot. Every cop on the street was looking for Skelton, and by tomorrow morning, with a federal agent assaulted, the FBI and Secret Service would be breathing down their collective neck. For all anyone knew, though, Bartell had shot Skelton bad enough he'd simply gone off someplace to die. Maybe dead already. If not, he already had a room booked at the county jail, a layover on the route to either the state pen at Deer Lodge, or some federal slam, depending on which set of prosecutors got their hooks in him first. No matter how you looked at it, Skelton was bought and paid for.

Despite the chaos of the day, people still hadn't forgotten about Merle Puhl. According to Fanning, Puhl was furious, apparently convinced that the whole debacle would cost him the election, as if he'd ever had an ice cube's chance in hell in the first place. Puhl's attitude probably wasn't helped by the fact that he was bottled up in his house under a heavy security detail commanded by that demented warrior himself, Chester Boyles. Maybe there was some justice after all.

"The sheriff wanted to send out Boyles and his crew last night, after the bomb," Fanning said. "But Puhl wasn't having any of it. It was that mess out there this morning that changed his mind."

What mess? Bartell wanted to know. It turned out that the mess Fanning was referring to was literal as well as figurative. When one of Puhl's hands was doing chores that morning, he'd come across the carcasses of half a dozen slaughtered ostriches.

"And I don't mean just slaughtered," Fanning said. "I mean, really fucking *slaughtered*. Decapitated. Guts strung out all over the place. Merle called me himself about it. Had me paged while I was in Mike Sweeney's office."

"And what did Sweeney say?"

This time, even Fanning found it within himself to lighten up. "He said bombing a city car in your driveway, terrorizing your wife and kid, was one thing. But murdering innocent birds, that was the goddamn limit."

And so now the list of crimes charged against Henry Skelton included ostrich murder. So much for Sweeney's renowned pragmatism. Well, that figured. Sweeney worked for a man who had to run for election too.

"It keeps nagging at me," Bartell said, "that we caused this to happen."

"*We?*"

"Us. The cops. The Secret Service." Bartell remembered again what Gina Lozano had told him the other day about Skelton. If you don't want him involved, don't push. And he thought about Skelton himself that night in the car. Big, wired-up guy, like a jolt of electricity with a beard. And finally, Zillion's own admission that Skelton had been thrown at them from the start as nothing more than the ante in a high-stakes political game. He was about to launch into his theory that Skelton had been railroaded since the time of the Cradle Creek bombing, but decided against it. If you're a missionary and you want to live to preach again, there are only so many sermons you can pitch at cannibals.

"Me," Bartell said finally. "I was the catalyst."

Fanning tensed. "That's ludicrous."

"Hang on—"

"If you're saying we've got some kind of exposure—this maniac Skelton's going to turn around and file a lawsuit . . ." Fanning drifted off into thought.

"That's not what I'm saying. For Christ's sake, Fanning, stop thinking like a goddamn policeman." What he meant was, stop thinking like a lawyer. Nobody could button up tighter than a cop who'd lapsed into a lawyer's frame of mind.

Fanning set the yellow pad aside and fiddled with the heavy gold ring, a graduation ring from the FBI National Academy, which he wore on the third finger of his left hand. Finally, he gripped his hands together on his desk, a high school principal's pose.

"Now," Fanning went on, "I don't know how hard you want to push this responsibility thing. But I do think you might want to work it all the way through before you go running off at the mouth." His words pounded through Bartell's head, leaving behind a ringing silence, the same silence Bartell had heard in the lull after the shooting. "You start talking about responsibility, Ray, that's a battle you're going to lose. Guaranteed."

Fanning was right. Regardless of the platitudes that flapped endlessly from the tongues of leaders, everyone knew that responsibility always took two forms. With success, it was a helium balloon soaring effortlessly up over the highest mountains. But when the operation failed, responsibility became shit, and shit, as they say, always rolls downhill. Sitting there in Vic Fanning's office, Bartell had no illusions about the fact that he was looking up, way, way up, at just about everybody.

Deciding not to waste any more time, Bartell got to his feet. To hell with Fanning. A guy with barely enough substance to stuff a shirt. Hardly a minute had gone by since the shooting when Bartell hadn't beat himself nearly senseless inside that hollowness that comes over you when you're scared, scared to death you fucked up and cost somebody big-time. He was finally sick to death of being played for a chump and mooning around about it. If you're going to get cosmic about Life's Big Questions, do it later with your horse. Or your dog. That's what they're there for. They won't give a rat's ass about your troubles, but at least they won't be bored. And they won't break it off in you for your trouble. But don't do it while you're still on the clock.

"I want to head out to Puhl's ranch," Bartell said. "Have a few words."

Fanning's grin was knowing, a one-of-the-boys kind of thing. "I don't think that's a good idea." He got up, too, and walked around the desk, dismissing Bartell in earnest.

Of course it wasn't a good idea. But Bartell was beginning to think that the only good idea he'd heard come out of this whole fiasco was Monday morning at coffee, when stupid Ike Skinner had threatened to badge his way up to the former president and give him a nice verbal whipping. Maybe Skinner would like to come on along to Puhl's outfit. Between the two of them, they could choke some politicians.

Fanning wrapped a hand, cold as a slab of meat, around Bartell's upper arm, and turned him toward the door. His back was starting to tighten up from having been bashed around during the crash, and the stitches in his forehead stung like crazy.

"I guess you don't have a car anymore," Fanning said with a dry laugh. "Two cars in less than twenty-four hours. Probably a record. Let's scare up somebody from patrol, get you a ride home."

Bartell said he'd rather call Helen, and walked back to his desk, leaving Fanning behind in the door to his office.

The bay was empty, since nearly all the other detectives were tied up with elements of what had now become the Skelton case. Bartell sat down at his desk and picked up the phone. He dialed his home out of habit, then remembered that Helen and Jess had checked into a motel. He was about to hang up, when Helen answered. He was surprised that she'd gone back there, then he remembered the piece she'd insisted on carrying, and felt almost sorry for Skelton—or whoever the bomber was— should he make a return visit to the Bartell homestead.

"I'm alive," he said.

"I heard that rumor," Helen said. There was a marked unit stationed at the end of their driveway, she told him, a handy precaution compliments of the PD. The officer, one of the department's numerous rookies, had come to the door and given her the news of the shooting. Helen would pick him up in fifteen minutes.

From a desk drawer, Bartell retrieved his new gun, another .40-

caliber Beretta automatic issued by the department, a piece identical to the one that Sam Blieker had seized from him as evidence after the shooting. He locked the slide back, then dropped the empty magazine into his free hand. From a box of ammunition in the same drawer, he thumbed ten rounds into the magazine, then fed the magazine into the well that opened in the base of the grip and tripped the slide release. The slide slammed closed, and he thumbed the decocking lever, dropping the hammer. Now he thumbed the same lever back into the *fire* position. Finally, he dropped the magazine free, replaced the round that was now in the chamber, then replaced the magazine and smacked it with the heel of his hand, locking it into place.

Ritual, he thought. Ritual of survival. And manhood? There he went, getting morose again without a horse or a dog to work it out on. Once again he recalled that winter night, when he'd looked down the barrel of another gun, brandished by another bucket of sewage with legs. He could still feel the aching cold, see the bad moonlight. Hear Paul Culp's shot, which had sent him down the long, spiraling chute that awaited anyone, he now believed, who was rescued. Culp had understood that spiral, and Bartell found himself missing Culp now more than at any time since Culp's own death. That long-ago shooting had taught Bartell all he needed to know about survival, and he wasn't about to waste the lesson now. He fit the gun into the holster on his hip and got on with things.

Bartell was about to leave, when he heard footsteps in the outer office, then Red Hanrahan rounded the partition, lugging his homicide file.

"How's it going?" Bartell asked.

Hanrahan set the file gingerly on his desk. "Guy pleaded out an hour ago."

"Lucky you," Bartell said. "Nice job."

"You'd think so," Hanrahan said. "Except Randy the Rope saw two weeks of ink evaporate before his very eyes, and now he's more pissed off than a tomcat in a dog kennel."

Just like good old Merle Puhl, Randy the Rope was running for election this year too. Was there anybody out there in the world who wasn't trying to slicker democracy?

Hanrahan swiped the fringe of his mustache away from the corners of his mouth. "You remember the other day, when I told you we were heading into chambers for that big harangue about the defendant being too irrational to continue with the trial?"

Bartell remembered, but only vaguely.

"Yeah," Hanrahan mused, "well, it so happened that wanting to come clean was the thing the guy's lawyer thought was irrational. Confession might be good for the soul, but it's tough as hell on billable hours."

"Your killer get a sweet deal?" Bartell asked.

"More or less. If you consider agreeing to life without parole sweet." Hanrahan jerked off his tie and snaked it onto the desk next to his file. "I thought for a minute Randy the Rope was going to toss Sweeney and me in jail for contempt just because we were in the neighborhood."

Bartell had forgotten that Mike Sweeney was also the prosecutor in Hanrahan's homicide.

"Everybody needs votes," Bartell said.

"Say what?"

"Never mind."

Now Hanrahan peeled off his jacket, a ragged wool houndstooth he'd worn for over a decade. The one he steadfastly refused to have cleaned despite the fact that everyone complained it reeked of autopsies.

Hanrahan flopped into his chair and yawned. "I heard all about your difficulties. When I was over in Sweeney's office this morning. You okay? Helen? The kid?"

"They're fine," Bartell said. "I'm more or less fine."

"You're alive?"

Bartell nodded.

"Still on the job?"

"I'm not sure that qualifies as okay."

"No. But that's beside the point." Hanrahan slumped deeper into his chair and clasped his hands behind his head. Moons of sweat darkened his pale blue shirt under his arms. "Feeling responsible?"

"If you're asking that, you must've heard the whole story."

"Fuck the story," Hanrahan said. "Anyway, I imagine you're the only one knows the whole story."

"Tell that to Fanning."

"Screw Fanning too. Guys like that don't make this place work. They can bitch things up, but they can't make them work. Guys like you and me, we make them work."

"Thanks for the vote of confidence. I'll put it on my résumé."

Hanrahan closed his eyes. His shaggy mustache riffled from his long, deep breaths as his broad chest rose and fell with the implacability of some great, shaggy beast. Finally, Hanrahan opened his eyes, and was once again moved to speak. "Don't start whining on me now, Ray. I didn't work my ass off getting you transferred in here just to listen to you bellyache."

For years, Bartell had heard rumors that it was Hanrahan's lobbying that had made good his transfer. Through it all, though, he'd never understood why Hanrahan had taken the trouble. And there it was again, that echo of fear. No, this time it was only the memory of the echo. "I've made a career," Bartell said now, "out of second-guessing myself."

"Nothing wrong with that," Hanrahan said. *"That's* part of why you're a good detective. You call it second-guessing, I call it keeping your mouth shut, taking care of business."

"Keep this up, you'll make me blush."

"And don't start dishing out bogus humility either. The thing I like about you, Ray, you know what it's like to do wrong."

"If you're talking about—"

"I'm not talking about anything in particular. Just a general statement. You know what it's like to do wrong. And the thing is, see, any man who doesn't know what it's like to be wrong can't ever be trusted when he knows he's right."

"Then how come things still turn to shit? Don't get me wrong, Red. I'm not feeling sorry for myself. Just asking a serious man a serious question."

Hanrahan chuckled. "Because we deal with assholes. And when you deal with assholes, you just naturally end up with shit. Get it, Ray . . . assholes . . . shit . . . it's a joke."

Bartell wasn't in the mood for jokes, but he was more grateful for Hanrahan's encouragement than Hanrahan probably wanted to hear. "Since you're dishing out wise counsel, Red, what would you advise for my present situation?"

"Like I said before." Once again Hanrahan closed his eyes, and he appeared to doze off. "Take care of business. And don't be sentimental about it."

"Amazing," Bartell said. "On top of being an excellent judge of character, the man's a mind reader too."

Outside, Bartell stood with his back against the red brick wall of the station, waiting for Helen. It was dusk, and the street lamps overhead were beginning to flicker on. The window of the chief's office was six or eight feet to his right. He couldn't see inside from where he stood, but he knew the chief was still on the job, because of the light spilling out onto the black asphalt. Now and then a marked unit moved around in the parking lot, the cops in uniform sometimes waving, sometimes stopping off for a few words, which Bartell barely heard, responding with quick shrugs, generic comments that he was okay, thanks for asking. A dose of weather had settled into the valley during the last couple of hours, sending an icy wind gusting between the station and the grimy back wall of the Cloverleaf. The wind felt good, as though it were blowing away the dust from behind his eyes.

To his left, the back door of the station swung open, and Gina Lozano stepped out. She stopped, surveyed the lot. Saw him watching her.

"All finished?" Bartell said.

Gina bunched her shoulders deeper into her blue windbreaker, and walked over to him. "Finished, all right."

He didn't know what Woodruff and Blieker had asked her, but he could imagine. What did Skelton say? And then what happened? Where would he go next? What would he do? Okay. Yeah. Un-huh. Okay, okay, okay. You're sure? You tell us. Okay? Cop questions, asked until everybody in the room was ready to scream.

"The trouble with talking to cops," he said, "we're all take and no give."

She made a curt face, shook her head. "Doesn't matter."

"I'm sorry about what I said. In the car."

She puzzled for a moment, then remembered. "Oh, about shooting Henry."

"Yeah."

"It's okay. I figured you didn't really mean it."

No, he meant it, every word of it. But since calming down, he'd grown sorry about saying it to her. "Sure."

"Maybe they'll catch him soon. Before . . ." Her voice trailed off in the wind, and she looked away. There were a lot of things that could happen before Skelton was run to ground, and it was hard to imagine that any of them were good.

"They probably will," he said, ignoring that he was part of *they*. "Any idea where he'd go?"

She shrugged. "The mountains, I guess."

"Cradle Creek? That cave?" He felt himself lapsing into a Q-and-A.

"Maybe. I don't know."

"You tell them that inside?"

She nodded.

"Anyplace else you can think of? Friends?"

Now she faced him again, guarded this time. Disappointed. "I told them everything. Told them the truth. Isn't that what you said I should do?"

"Sorry," he said. "Old habits . . ."

Helen's gray Taurus turned into the lot, and she pulled to a stop nearby. Helen started to get out, but Bartell motioned for her to hold on.

"You going back home now?" he said.

Gina's black hair, all tangled in the wind, kept blowing in her face. She didn't seem to notice. "I guess. I don't know. I think there's still maybe cops out there. Searching the place I told them it was okay this—" She stopped short, perhaps realizing what this permission to search her house might mean to Bartell of all people. "This time I told them it was okay. I mean, what the hell, you know, it's all lost now anyway. So I told them—"

"You don't have to explain." He took a couple of steps toward the car, then stopped. "You afraid to go back out there?"

"Maybe. A little bit, I guess. Yeah."

"Don't worry. It'll work out." He walked on around the car to the passenger door, where he stopped again. When he looked back this time, he noticed Vic Fanning inside the chief's office. Fanning, who was standing in front of the chief's desk, caught his eye. The chief himself was hidden behind the back of his tall brown leather chair. Fanning turned his attention back to his conversation with the chief.

Gina hadn't moved. She leaned against the brick wall, looking small and alone, her fists jammed into the pockets of her windbreaker.

Bartell said, "You got someplace else to go?"

"Everybody's got someplace. Right?"

"I mean, have you got someplace in the state of Montana to go?"

"I guess there are motels in this town, aren't there?"

"Get in the car," he said.

When Gina hesitated, Bartell grew impatient. "Don't stand

there and think about it. Just get in the car and let's all get out of here."

And without wasting another minute, she did. Inside the chief's office, Vic Fanning was staring out intently at them now, talking to the chief as he pointed out the window. The chief's big leather chair began to swing around, but before he came into view, Bartell ducked into the car and told Helen to hit the road. As they left the parking lot, Gina and Helen were subdued with each other, but obviously friends. Besides wildlife and trees, it appeared, they also shared an abiding fondness for fools.

Chapter 22

After the shooting, Skelton forced himself to drive within the law, and with care. Not that driving was all that easy. He bit back the pain in his hand, so hot and raw that the bullet hole in his shoulder was nearly unnoticeable. The steering wheel was slick with blood, and it was hard as hell to see through the spiderweb of the fractured windshield.

So he drove like an old man. Or a drunk. Willing the truck farther into the wooded foothills west of town, where he turned at last onto a dirt road and headed up into the mountains. About a mile ahead, the road steepened and narrowed sharply, traversing large, frequent clear-cuts, and forking at nearly every switchback. With each divergence Skelton took the rougher alternative, until the road finally disintegrated into nothing more than a trail through the brush under a dense stand of firs. Here, he stopped.

It was his own fault, all of it, the whole goddamn bloody mess. He knew that much. Knew it as well as he knew his own name.

He could have hung it up when he first saw Bartell's car there in the turn-out beside the barn.

Or he could have taken the shoulder and ditch, blown right on by when Bartell eased out onto the road. Bartell had given him that. All Skelton needed to do was take it.

Or, he could simply have stepped out of the bedroom and ended it all right there. Told the truth and taken his chances. Just like Gina said.

So what was this thing that burned deep in his belly and would not tolerate being pushed? This thing that burned even now through the nausea, swept along on a wave of pain cresting out of his hand?

For the first time, he forced himself to look at his left hand. The bleeding had stopped. He made a fist and felt the bones grating in the palm. And he realized, too, that the ring finger was nearly severed, held in place only by clotted blood and a few threads of mangled tissue.

Without an instant's hesitation, Skelton got a folding knife from his pocket, worked the blade open with his good hand, then braced his left hand on the head of the steering column and sliced through the remains of the finger, which dropped into his lap.

Skelton heard his own scream reverberate all through his body, but no sound escaped his throat. He set the knife carefully on the seat beside his leg, picked up the severed finger, and threw it wildly out the window into the brush. Then he fumbled quickly for the door handle, rolled out onto the ground on his knees, and puked.

At last, Skelton got to his feet. From the pack in the back of the truck, he took a T-shirt and bandanna, with which he fashioned a thick bandage around his hand. Then he found a down vest and a heavy sweater. It was getting dark, and cold, with splinters of rain mixed with snow on the gusting wind. When Skelton worked his upper body into the vest and sweater, fresh pain shot through his shoulder and met the pain rising from his hand in a scorching blast under his arm.

Goddammit, goddamn them all. He slumped against the truck, desperate for something to which he could lash himself and regain control.

He remembered Gina running from the house toward the disaster, Gina in bed the night before, Gina lying for him to the cops. Gina, when she pleaded with him the other night in the kitchen to explain. The California years, when she had stood by him through all manner of trouble.

Gina, who was gone.

His mind racing, Skelton tried to break through the glaze that surrounded that young life in Washington, a boy's life from which he had walked—no, run—a time of cold green mist, slate-colored sea meeting a sky like steel along a distant seam, which surely marked the edge of the earth.

But none of it took. Not this time, and maybe it never had. It was as though his life were nothing but one long chute, and for as long as anything mattered, the only thing slowing his run had been Gina. Now, without her, the speed of his fall was blinding.

Skelton closed his eyes, felt that chute of his own life drop away, saw himself racing through the air above Cradle Creek, the cold gray expanse of Red Wolf, huge and unspeakable, its icy glitter slowly fleshed into view through the broken clouds against a night sky choked with stars.

And the bear, knotted in fresh, perfect sleep for the coming winter, a dreamless sleep toward another spring, another first morning rested and hungry.

Here, Skelton's mind came to a stop. He took a deep breath, felt the pain in his hand and shoulder settle into some compartment of its own, which left the rest of him free to go on. He opened his eyes, straightened, breathed deeply again and again, amazed at the calm and clarity that now seeped through him, just as it had in that tiny fragment of day when he'd shot past the second cop car as though it weren't there at all.

The mist had turned completely to snow. Gingerly, Skelton stepped back to the door of the truck, where he got in, and slumped low in the seat. Watching the wet, heavy snow flutter through the bullet-shattered windshield, Skelton sat shivering. Here he'd spent months and miles trying to find a vision, and now, goddamn, if a vision hadn't found him. He gritted his teeth against the shivering, and tried to decide what to do next. He waited for it to get dark.

Chapter 23

Bartell stood in the shower, watching the water channel across his belly. His lower back and hips ached worse now from the crash, and he knew that by morning he'd feel tight and brittle as an elk hide thrown over the fence to dry. Tomorrow, he would have it out good with Fanning. The shower began to run cold. Tomorrow, he would . . .

Why kid himself? Five-thirty A.M., he would coax his seized-up body out of bed and make coffee. What was it Skelton had said? Take a shit, read the newspaper. Go to work. Drink some more coffee. Another notch toward payday, another payday toward retirement.

As Bartell was toweling himself off, Helen slipped into the bathroom, which adjoined their bedroom, and asked how he was doing. They hadn't had a chance to talk alone since the shooting.

"I'll make it," he said, then bent over to dry his feet, and sucked air as pain shot down his back and into his hips and hamstrings.

"Here, let me." Helen took the towel, then squatted down and began drying his feet. "I was scared to death when you called. Even more scared than after the bomb. I'm never scared when you go off to work, but I always am when you call me later, when something's happened. After it's all over. I guess that's crazy."

Bartell guessed it was too. But that's when being scared always got to people, after it was too late.

"I'm glad you asked her to come with us," Helen said.

"Gina? Yeah. You don't mind?"

Helen stood and draped the towel over his shoulder. "I'd have been disappointed if you hadn't asked her."

"You're okay," he said. After all the years of marital ups and downs, this seemed at the moment to be the greatest affirmation he could imagine.

Helen wrapped her arms around Bartell's neck and kissed him. He kissed her back, and as he stood there, flaccid, the thought lashed through his mind that this must be what middle age was like, get kissed in earnest while you're naked as a jaybird and nothing responds but an aching back and a deep sense of gratitude that somebody's bothering to kiss you at all.

When Helen left a moment later, Bartell dressed in old jeans and a well-worn blue chamois-cloth shirt.

All right, he told himself for the hundredth time, screw Fanning. Fanning. Skelton. Zillion. Puhl and Duckworth. Fuck them all. A man works for wages, doesn't mean he has to sleep all night in the barn. Wasn't that what Cash always used to say?

Out in the kitchen, Cash himself, along with Helen and Gina, was having a subdued conversation over coffee. The two women sat at the table, while Cash, like a gargoyle guarding a cathedral, stood next to the boarded-up window. Bartell helped himself to coffee and took a chair at the table.

"I was telling her about Jess," Helen said. Jess was spending the night with a friend. "I think she's afraid to be here, and to tell you the truth, I'm just as glad she's not here. But she's putting on a good front. Said she and her friend were working on a paper for school. Something about the current election."

"Ah, yes," Bartell said. He crossed his legs, trying to settle into the pain that now radiated down into his knees. "The miracle of democracy."

Helen's smile was bleak. She was far from an unsubtle woman. "That's the general idea, yes."

Bartell waved his cup in Cash's direction. "She must've forgotten we have this movie star wannabe in the house." Then he told Cash about meeting McWilliams earlier that morning in Fanning's office. Had he mentioned before that he'd also caught McWilliams's act out at the Puhl ranch? No. He must have filed that encounter under the heading of business. "Was that the other surprise you mentioned? McWilliams?"

His ardor from the day before now vanished, Cash merely blew across his coffee. "He's a deep pocket, that's all. No harm taking a dip, long as you don't drown."

Bartell studied Helen's face, the wide, thoughtful eyes pinched with concentration, thin lips that could seem at times to be the perfect instruments for measuring words. Or a kiss. The face of a woman confident enough to let things happen. Then he turned to Gina. "You're welcome here," he said. "This isn't a sympathy angle. Just a straight offer."

She nodded. "I know."

Bartell felt a curious bond with Gina, and wondered if she sensed it too. The bond was Skelton, of course, the man that she'd been compelled to love, and he'd been forced to shoot.

"And it's not guilt on my part," he said firmly. A heaviness settled over the room. Bartell could still hear the flat detachment in Fanning's voice when he'd ordered him home, still see the starched scorn on the captain's face as he looked out from the chief's office. It wasn't just Fanning who dragged at him. There was no escaping the bloat of Merle Puhl either, and Puhl's boy Duckworth, himself nothing more than a pissy dog at heel.

Bartell turned to Helen again. "Okay?"

Helen smiled. "It's been a long, bad day. While you were in the shower, I ordered pizza." She reached over and patted his forearm. "Pepperoni."

"Hog meat," Bartell said. "We should all be well adjusted in no time."

"And I'm buying," Cash threw in. "Hope you can stand to eat on Brandon McWilliams's money."

Gina stirred self-consciously, clearly not understanding their household code. "There's been something on my mind," she said. "Something I want you to do." Her attention now was fully on Bartell. "I want you to find Henry."

"I told you before, we'll find him."

"No," she said firmly. "You. I want *you* to find him."

Bartell tried to explain how the police worked when it came to locating serious fugitives, how everybody got involved and there was no telling the circumstances under which Skelton would turn up. He told her, too, about being pulled off the job by Fanning. "Out of all the cops in western Montana," Bartell said, "I'm probably the one who'll be allowed to do the least amount of looking."

"But you're the only one who knows him."

Bartell pointed out that this special knowledge didn't seem to have been worth much.

But Gina wasn't having any of it. "If somebody else finds him," she said, "they'll kill him."

"We're not murderers," Bartell said, hoping that in this case he was right.

"Maybe," she said, "maybe not. But the thing is, see, I know Henry, and he won't give them any choice."

"And you think it'll be different with me?" Bartell remembered not just the madness of the crash itself, but staring down the bore of Skelton's rifle, big as a hole in heaven. "I shot him, for Christ's sake. What makes you think he'd cut me any slack?"

"He respects you."

"Pardon me?"

"I've been through a lot with Henry," she said. "More, maybe, than you can imagine. He gets cranked at somebody, he doesn't make any great secret of it."

Bartell couldn't avoid sarcasm. "I guess that explains this afternoon."

"As a matter of fact, it does." Gina licked her lips, scowled down at the table for a moment, then lifted her face to Bartell again. "I saw what happened, remember? I saw the rifle. And I'm telling you, Ray, if Henry didn't have some feeling for you . . ." Her eyes laden with apology and regret, she looked fitfully at Helen as the words tailed off. Then, perhaps sensing his misgivings about recent events, she added, "Helen's been telling me about last night. I understand why they thought it was Henry. And I don't know, maybe it was. I don't know, but maybe. And I'm still not sure why it was you who came to the house this morning. Whatever the reason, I am glad it was you. Anybody else, things would have been a lot worse."

Bartell wasn't willing to speculate on exactly what *worse* might encompass at that point, but, in addition to feeling vindicated, he was grateful to her for letting him off the hook.

Helen let out a deep sigh, and when she sat back in her chair, the joints creaked. Around them all, the house, with nearly half its windows boarded up, grew more dim in the deepening twilight. Outside the wide, tall west window at Helen's back, the one overlooking the valley, all that remained of the daylight were yellow blotches among the gnarled clouds that were beginning to spill rain or snow over the mountaintops. As Bartell sat in the warmth of his home, letting himself settle into all that sky, it was as though the terror of his confrontation with Skelton began to seep out of his belly into his skin, and he quickly seared it off.

Bartell weighed the possibilities of succeeding at the task Gina sought from him. In old black-and-white movies, the man on the run is always quickly cornered. So simple. The traffic cop who spots his car. The unsuspecting woman in the crowded train station who looks up from the newspaper, finds herself face-to-face with the fugitive on the front page. The motel clerk reaching slyly for the phone. And the chase always ends ugly. More often than not, Bartell knew, bad guys just faded out of sight, became spooks who surfaced later in unexpected places as a result of pure luck—somebody's good, somebody's bad.

But there was something in Gina's request that might have more value than simply catching Skelton. Call it a chance. Call it absolution. A way to cut loose the strings that bound him to the likes of Fanning and Puhl. Bartell leaned his elbows on the table and frowned. "Gina, you said you thought he'd go back to that cave."

"That's right."

"But that has to be the one place where he'll know we'd look."

"It won't matter. Not to Henry. God, who knows, that might be the very reason he'd go there."

Bartell agreed, yet continued to press his professional skepticism. "But what's to say he won't just head on down the road?"

"He might. So what? I'm telling you, if he stays around here at all, then those mountains in Cradle Creek are the only place he'd go."

Bartell sipped his coffee. This whole business with Cradle Creek seemed pretty unbalanced, even for Skelton. Then he remembered what Gina had told him the other day about Skelton's quest for his *Wyakin,* and he asked her if the cave had something to do with that.

Gina nodded. "This afternoon he told me about a bear he saw up there. A grizzly."

"So you think this thing today will head him back onto his quest?"

Gina turned briefly to Helen, and smiled, as if in the belief that another woman would comprehend instinctively and immediately the follies of men. And to Helen she said, "Of course."

"I knew a Blackfeet healer once," Cash offered. "Up on the

high line. Edgar Kills Whiteman. Used to drag my butt over to his place once in a while after a bad week in town. Old Edgar, he'd talk to me about quests, all that hocus-pocus. I listened, but mostly I just wanted to sweat out the booze."

"And none of this," Bartell said, "has anything to do with politics?"

Gina clasped her hands behind her neck and stretched her shoulders. "Not for Henry, it doesn't." Years ago, she told them, when he got in trouble in San Francisco, then it was politics. All buzzwords and slogans. But part of the reason they'd moved to Montana, she believed, was Skelton's desire to get away from all that.

"One night," she went on, "he got to talking about wild animals. Especially predators. He said the fundamental difference between wild animals and humans is that something innate tells wild animals when they have enough. But people just keep hammering away, creating havoc until they're either exhausted or dead."

"Too bad," Cash said, disgusted, "he didn't apply that little lesson today."

Gina shrugged. "You're all alive."

Bartell found himself growing furious at the stupidity of it all. He was about to ask why he should care one way or another if Skelton ended up dead. But the answer, he knew, was to be found in his own sense of both complicity and justice, regardless of the degree to which his role may have been manipulated.

"And why," he asked Gina, "do you think we'll have to kill him? If he goes to Cradle Creek? I mean, some specific reason. Who's to say he won't come back for you?"

"Because this time I won't be there. He knows I'm through."

Bartell thought about this, imagining how he might feel if Helen one day closed the door on him forever. "Losing you means he's lost everything? That it?"

Gina didn't bother answering. And when Bartell saw Helen nod slowly, he knew he hadn't needed to waste the question.

"Last night in bed," Gina said, "he called that mountain a sacred place."

"And what's a sacred place?"

This time Helen, the assistant to Gabriella Fosdick, doctor of holistic well-being, answered. "Sometimes, it's a place you go to die."

And Cash said, "Amen."

Bartell was in the bedroom, fitting his gun onto his belt, when he heard the doorbell. He came out to find Helen paying the pizza guy. She seemed surprised to see that he had changed into heavy boots and had added a sweater. But it wasn't until he got his coat and gloves from the closet that she asked what was going on.

"A little errand," he said. He didn't bother to explain, and when Helen tried to press him further, it was Cash who shook her off.

It might be too late tonight to start hunting Skelton in the flesh, but it wasn't to late to start hunting the truth. The thought of Merle Puhl and company, politically sleek and smug out there on that goddamn ranch, with all those weird birds, had left Bartell with the urge to be, in Skelton's terms, extremely human.

Before heading out, Bartell wrapped a couple of slices of pizza in aluminum foil. What he had in mind was going to require a dose of pepperoni, bad karma and all, because now, after all the bombing and shooting, all the craziness and sneaking around after terrorists both manufactured and real, Bartell finally understood. If Helen was so interested in all his secrets, she'd probably get a real charge out of this one.

Chapter 24

As he drove, Skelton cradled his mangled left hand in his lap, bracing the wheel with his knee whenever he had to shift gears. Ahead, the snow streaked like white buckshot through the beam of the one headlight that still worked. The snow stung his face as it gusted through the blown-out windshield and froze in his beard. The blowing snow was perfect, Skelton thought, since it would give him cover, yet any tracks he might leave would soon be scoured clean by the wind.

So this was what it all came down to. No purpose, no plan. No noble crusade to save anything, not even himself. Just running through the night, through a winter storm, with nothing ahead save cold, blinding white.

Crazy.

That's what it was.

No, not crazy at all. Way the fuck past crazy. Crazy was when you couldn't find words for what drove the mania.

But that was still wrong. Crazy was when you had too many words, and he was past all the words now. Way past, off the edge. Driven sane, he figured, by the speed of his own free-fall.

Now there was only sensation. Pain. Cold. Fear.

Exhaustion.

More fear.

Speed.

And power.

Like the bear?

An animal smell there inside the truck. Smell of his own blood.

Skelton lifted his left hand to his mouth, sucked the taste of himself from the soaked bandage.

The bear.

Finally, Skelton came upon a turnoff, which led up the slope to the left, off the bare hillside into a stand of aspen trees. He checked the road ahead and behind, found it clear, then shifted into a low gear and eased up the turnoff until he was well into the trees, out of sight from the road.

Again Skelton considered the snow, hoping that what tracks he might leave would soon be obliterated. That part, though, the part about his tracks, didn't really mean all that much, not in the long run. Because it was just a matter of time before everybody came looking for him, looking even harder than now, and by then there wouldn't be any time left to worry about stealth. Stealth mattered only here, in the beginning.

Skelton bundled himself inside his clothes, got out, and pulled the rifle after him. Slinging the rifle over his good shoulder, he made his way down to the tree line, where he squatted behind a ragged thicket of wild roses, and for a while watched the long stretch of exposed road below.

Once satisfied that he could make it down the hill and across the road without encountering traffic, Skelton stepped free of cover and began to lope back through one of the truck tracks. Moments later, he was across the road, over the fence on the opposite side, safe in a crease among the gray, windswept hills rolling ahead toward the river. He paused a moment, panting not so much from the run as from the pain now ripping out of his hand and shoulder.

He forced the pain back, forced it with rage. Rage would always take you farther than pain.

Make the pain work, turn it into rage.

Skelton felt the air now, a cold knot in the bottom of his lungs.

Turn the rage into fuel for your legs.

Skelton flexed his toes, concentrated on the blessed fact that there was no pain there.

And then he began to walk.

Chapter 25

Politics, Bartell thought. The whole goddamn thing had started out as just another slick political move. Find yourself a heavy, then focus all of your fearful and righteous attention on him, and beat your breast about the enemy. Trot out some doddering has-been hero, a washed-up president, say, to quicken everybody's pulse. Wave the flag, show a little political leg. Maybe score a point or two in the polls. Maybe not. So what? It's only a game, and the world's full of players.

And if you don't have a convenient heavy? That's easy, just create one.

During the long drive through the snow out to Merle Puhl's ranch, Bartell had tried to plan what he would say. Yet, what if Puhl refused to see him? No, that was simply not a consideration. He was the police, right? Good businessmen and aspiring public servants always had time to make small talk with the police. All that buddy-buddy shit. And even more than that, like it or not, Bartell was a player. Next to Skelton, he was the most important player of all. If a badge and services rendered weren't enough to cover the price of admission, then goddammit, there was always the option of guns.

Coming upon the entrance to Puhl's ranch, Bartell saw a Sheriff's Department black-and-white parked at the edge of the road. Since he was driving his own pickup, Bartell rolled to a stop, lowered his window, and flashed his badge to the deputy, a young, sandy-haired man with a brushy cop mustache. In the years since Bartell had come off the road and into detectives,

237

the county had taken on a handful of new deputies whom he didn't know.

"Bartell," he said. "From the city. Chester out here?"

"*Lieutenant* Boyles?" The deputy smirked and rolled his eyes. "Yeah. He's down at the house. Sucking up, you know?" The kid was working on a fifteen-year attitude to go with his buffed-up new badge. He had the mannerisms, Bartell decided, but not the requisite aches and pains to make them come out right. The vocabulary, but not the *rhythm*.

"I'm going down to see him," Bartell said.

"Well, I'm not sure about that." The deputy straightened, his attitude abandoning him.

Bartell wasn't in any mood to waste time nursing a green cop along toward maturity. "Just get on the radio, tell him I'm coming in."

Without waiting for an answer, Bartell drove off.

The house and outbuildings sat in the eerie glow of floodlights shining through the shade of blowing snow. Bartell noticed a couple of black-and-whites parked down near the barn, and there were two more in the driveway. From inside the house a light burned from behind every curtained window that Bartell could see. He parked near the two sheriff's cars, and as he got out of his truck, Chester Boyles came out the front door of the house to meet him.

"What's up, son?" Boyles said. "Heard you had a long afternoon." He stuck out his chin, indicating the stitches on Bartell's forehead. Boyles had traded in his brown sheriff's uniform for a black A2 jacket and a set of black BDUs. The combination speaker/microphone from the walkie-talkie on his belt was clipped at the throat of his jacket. And along with packing his usual hardware, Boyles now carried a Heckler and Koch MP5 slung over his shoulder. The stubby black submachine gun looked deceptively casual. It was also equipped with a laser sight and a silencer.

Bartell shrugged. "Seems like it, yeah."

"Zillion too," Boyles said, lighting a cigarette. "Last I heard, he was still zoned out."

"He'll live." Bartell tried to decide if Boyles was blocking him from the door, or just out of habit trying to take up as much space as possible. He ducked his head between his shoulders against the blowing snow.

"So," Boyles said. He shrugged the MP5 aside, rested his right elbow on the butt of his revolver, which rode high on his black nylon gun belt. "What's on your mind?" Boyles squared himself to the house, and Bartell knew he wouldn't get by without an explanation of some sort. Abruptly, though, Boyles hunched up his own shoulders against the weather and said they should have enough sense to get their fool asses inside. He turned on his heel and started for the door.

"Is Puhl here?" Bartell said, following.

"Yeah. Him and Dickwad, Duckworth, whatever his name is. Them and that gal Yolanda, yeah. Out back taking a soak in the hot tub. Ed Morley was with them too, last time I checked."

"Morley?"

"Big guy," Boyles said. "Got a face like fifteen miles of bad road."

"Oh, right, the guy with the birds."

"Say what?"

"Nothing."

Inside, the house was both bright and still as a museum. The two men stopped in the foyer, Boyles standing with his back against the branches of a lush ficus tree that fanned out like a delicate web of leafy bones against the white wall.

"Nice piece," Bartell said, pointing to the MP5. Nothing made cops happier than the chance to trot out their exotic toys.

Boyles snorted. "No shit. Hey, check this out." He brought the gun to his hip and squeezed the grip switch mounted on the fore end, activating the laser sight. Slowly, Boyles swept the weapon across the front room, the tiny red dot from the laser passing along the walls, leather sofa, sales awards. "Kinda like the eye of God, eh?" Boyles said. Finally, he held the light steady on the painted portrait of an Indian man in feathered regalia. Trained the red light—and the silenced muzzle of the gun—squarely between the man's eyes.

"Custer'd of had a crate of these sonsofbitches . . ." Boyles said, ". . . gawd-damn . . ."

"These people," Bartell said, bringing Boyles back to earth, "they worried about Skelton?"

Boyles lowered the gun and pursed his lips. "Hell, I don't know. More like a celebration, you ask me. They're sloshin' around, knockin' down drinks. This whole thing with the former president—that being in the toilet, you know?—you'd think they'd be just a little bit pissed off."

"Maybe—" Bartell started to say.

"Well, *wouldn't* you?" Boyles interrupted, his voice rising to a squeal. "I know *I'm* pissed off, and it wasn't even my show." Ficus leaves rustled against his shoulders. "I was all set to get my picture taken with an authentic piece of American history."

Despite the fact that Boyles was a cretin, his observation tended to bear out what Bartell already believed. Why have the godfather of political finger-pointing come to town and point his well-worn appendage at the evils among us, when you can get just as much, maybe even more mileage out of being forced by a wild man to shut that visit down altogether? Do that, and you could claim that Skelton and his like had succeeded in strangling the whole damned republic.

Bartell, however, didn't want to dwell on this with Boyles, so he changed the subject. "Looks like you got a lot of guys on the job tonight."

"Six," Boyles said through a cloud of smoke, thinking. "Plus me. That makes seven."

"Yeah," Bartell said, feeling his brain go numb. "Seven. That's right."

Boyles took a long last drag on the cigarette, and then brushed aside the branches of the ficus and stubbed out the butt in the pot.

"That miserable old bastard," Boyles said, spitting out the last of the smoke. "Ate my ass out for smokin' in his house. Said I oughta go down to the barn if I was gonna smoke. Like I was one of them goofy birds. Fuck him. Seven. Yeah, seven guys. All of 'em packin' one of these." He gave the submachine gun an affectionate pat.

Bartell felt like grabbing Boyles by the coat and giving him a good shaking. Shake the stupidity out of him. Or maybe beat him over the head with his goddamn submachine gun.

As though reading Bartell's mind, Boyles patted the MP5 again. "Yep. All seven of us packin' one of these mongo heaters."

For an awkward moment Bartell waited for Boyles to take him on inside to Duckworth and Puhl. Or at least volunteer to go get somebody from the campaign to come out. Instead, Boyles launched into a long rant about Skelton.

"Goddamn worthless scum-drinking pile of dog shit," Boyles

railed, savoring every nuance of the rhythm that had eluded the uniformed kid in the car back down at the road. "Skelton and all those fucking out-of-state troublemakers like him. Gut-shoot 'em at the border, that's what I say."

Bartell listened with mounting impatience until the deputy finally ran out of steam.

"Anyhow," Boyles said, winding down, "you shot the commie sonofabitch. Nothing wrong with that, son." He clapped Bartell on the shoulder. "Not a fuckin' thing."

Bartell was about to come straight out and tell Boyles he was going inside to talk to Puhl and his handlers, when the two men were distracted by someone approaching them from farther back inside the house.

"Hey, Ed." Boyles beckoned Morley out into the foyer. "How's it hangin'? Ed, this here's—"

"We've met," Morley said curtly. He pulled up and stood with his hands in his pants pockets, eyeing Bartell. "Sorry about your house. And Zillion too. That's a pretty good gash you've got yourself," he added, nodding toward Bartell's stitches.

"Yeah," Boyles said. "Yeah, it is. Makes you look like goddamn Frankenstein."

"I'll live," Bartell said. "What about you boys? Having a long night out here?"

Morley was stoic. "I've had longer."

Boyles pounded Morley on the back. "Ed here's part of the campaign staff."

"Is that right," Bartell said, remembering that Morley had once characterized himself as a friend of the family. "What's your function?"

Morley's face briefly acquired more potholes as he forced a smile. "Odds and ends."

"Sneak out for another smoke, did you?" Boyles said conspiratorially.

"Don't mind if I do." Morley drew a pack of Camel straights from one pocket and a lighter from the other. Bracing the lighter between the thumb and middle finger of his right hand, he squeezed abruptly, snapping open the cap. Orange flame danced languidly before his face, and the cigarette hissed softly as he drew on it.

"Might as well join you," Boyles said, mouthing one of his own cigarettes, then jutting out his chin to share Morley's light.

"I see you got your Zippo replaced," Bartell said.

Now Morley's look turned indolent. "You might say that."

Bypassing Boyles, Bartell told Morley that he wanted to talk to Puhl and Duckworth.

"Sure," Morley said, "sure. They expecting you?"

"Not exactly."

Bartell heard the uncalculated edge in his voice. Trouble was, Morley and Boyles heard it too.

"Your boss know you're out here?" Boyles said.

"No."

"And you say these guys aren't expecting you?" Boyles jerked his thumb toward the interior of the house.

"No."

Boyles stroked his jaw, tugged at his lower lip. "You know, Ray, you got a look on you I don't quite like. You sure this is a good idea?"

Morley seemed content to let the two cops play things out.

Bartell was tired of dancing around. "Listen, Chester, I shot a man today on account of this bunch of humps out here. Now, don't you mess with me too." All the time, though, he was looking at Morley.

Understanding perfectly, Boyles now sidestepped away from Morley. "You got a problem with that, Ed?"

"No problem at all."

Morley motioned for Bartell to follow him, but when Bartell stepped off, Boyles held him up momentarily.

"What you wanna remember, Ray," he said, his voice hushed, "you don't wanna mark 'em up. No bruises or nothing. No missing teeth. You understand what I'm saying?"

Bartell got the message. He and Boyles followed Morley on through Puhl's momento-infested den, then turned down a short hallway. Along the way, Morley explained that the hot tub was in a glass solarium that opened off of Puhl's bedroom.

"Sitting out there in a big glass bubble," Boyles said. "No curtains or nothing. I tried to explain how that was a security problem big-time. But you know Merle."

"Merle's the man," Bartell said.

"You got it, Toyota," Boyles said. "I got people outside, sure, but how you gonna guarantee the safety of a guy won't listen to expert advice? But Ed here, he knows enough to stay back inside the house, right, Ed?"

"You know me, Chester," Morley said. "Cautious to the end."

At the door to Puhl's bedroom, Morley took Boyles by the arm and stopped. "I think the detective and I can handle things from here, Chester."

Boyles hesitated only briefly. "Listen, Ray," he said quietly, "do me this one more little favor, don't drown 'em in the hot tub."

Entering the solarium through French doors, Bartell realized that Boyles was right about the glass-bubble part. Yolanda Huizer and Puhl were immersed in a large tub, while Kip Duckworth, fully dressed, sat nearby in a wicker chair with his back to Bartell and Morley as they walked toward the tub, which was surrounded by a broad apron of ivory-colored tile. The apron itself was elevated perhaps twenty-four inches above a slate floor. Outside the glass wall Bartell saw the shadowed form of one of the deputies pause, then move on.

"Company calling," Morley said, hanging back.

"Ah, Detective Bartell," Puhl said, raising his arms from the water in a gesture of welcome. "Join us, please. We were just having a, ah, a staff meeting."

Bartell took a few steps deeper into the room and to his left, so that he could keep an eye on Morley without having to look over his shoulder.

The apron around the tub was decorated with a mosaic compass, inlaid figures topping each point: an eagle soared above the north, bighorn sheep and elk looked on from east and west respectively, a Chevrolet emblem anchored the south. Chlorinated froth gurgled into a fine mist that glistened on the dark hair pelting Merle Puhl's shoulders.

"I was just out for a drive on a snowy evening," Bartell said. "Thought I'd drop by, make sure everybody was okay."

"You're very sincere and well meaning," Puhl said, sounding as though he really meant it. "A great cop. The perfect police officer. Even if you are a lousy shot."

"My vision was a little clouded," Bartell said.

"It's always something," said Morley.

Bartell slowly unzipped his jacket. The frothing tub made the solarium feel like a swamp. "Everybody needs his deniability." He could get to the Beretta quicker with the jacket open. "Who knows though. I might be able to damage yours."

"And how, exactly, would you do that?" Duckworth said

calmly. "What would you tell people? That you made a mistake? That you hounded an innocent citizen, a man exercising his right to free speech, that you turned him into a criminal and then you shot him for his trouble? Is that what you're going to tell people?" Duckworth drained off his wine, then toyed the tip of a middle finger around the lip of the glass. "Somehow, I don't think so." The crystal goblet began to sing.

Bartell glared at Duckworth. "Who *are* you?" Then to Puhl: "One of your birds *hatch* this guy, or what?"

Puhl splashed a double handful of water on his face and snorted, then raked his fingers back over his skull. Heavy folds of skin the color of boiled shrimp lay slabbed over his shoulders, as though his flesh were nothing more than a garment.

"Thirteen," Bartell said. "That's how many caps I popped on Skelton this afternoon. You folks'd probably be happier than me if I was a better shot."

Puhl chuckled and splashed water on Yolanda Huizer, who ducked away, then splashed him back. Her pile of auburn hair bounced airily atop her head, while clinging in damp tendrils to her bare shoulders. In her current state, Yolanda could probably leave everyone breathless just by standing up.

"Thirteen," Puhl mused. "My, oh, my."

Duckworth took a sip of wine, then set the glass on the floor and toyed with something in his lap. "What a wonderful tool." He held up a remote telephone and gazed at it admiringly. "Reach out and touch the world." Duckworth dropped the phone back onto his lap and retrieved his glass. "Press conference tomorrow, nine A.M."

Now Duckworth chuckled, clearly all caught up in himself. "We can wring points out of this business till hell freezes over. The best thing Skelton could do for us now is not get caught until after the election."

"No." The voice, Morley's, came from the near the wall just inside the door, where he hung back in the shadows. "Best thing he could do would be to die. And if he's really doing favors, he should do it where nobody finds him. Never."

"That's enough," Puhl snapped, no sign now of the folksy used car dealer and ostrich entrepreneur.

"What about the letter?" Bartell asked.

Puhl's brushy eyebrows peaked. "Ah, yes, the letter. I hear Skelton called me a worthless piece of shit. But of course, I haven't seen the letter myself. Zillion left a copy with Kip, but I—"

"Now that you mention it," Bartell interrupted, "the phrase was applied to the former president. But you already know that, right?"

"I do?" Puhl's surprise was over-elaborate.

"Somebody called Merle that," Yolanda said, "nobody'd care. Probably wouldn't even notice."

A strained look came over Puhl's face, and Bartell realized that he was passing gas. Puhl fanned a meaty hand at the bursting bubbles, then made a different kind of face.

"Jesus Christ, Merle," Yolanda moaned, and scooted to the far side of the tub.

"You see, Ray," Puhl said, "the truth about Skelton doesn't really matter. Not to the public. To all those people out there with mortgages and car payments and credit cards and kids in jail, waiting to get into rehab . . . and a job they hold only by some skinny little thread . . . all those *scared* people . . . for them, somebody like Henry Skelton is whoever and whatever we say he is. And in this case we say he's a bomber and a terrorist. A killer."

"Simple as that," Bartell said.

Puhl nodded. "Afraid so. And unless I miss my guess, you proved the point today. A shootout with the cops. Jesus Christ, can you believe that? That guy's got better timing than George Burns."

"I feel kind of sorry for Skelton," Yolanda said. "You know?"

"Aw, baby . . ." Puhl leaned across and nibbled on Yolanda Huizer's ear. She made a noise that showed disgust, then groped him under the water. "Goddamn!" Puhl howled, grimacing as he jumped away. Water sloshed over the lip of the tub and onto the apron. Beached, Bartell thought. Like some big pale *thing* washed in on the tide.

"Those assholes," Puhl snarled. "After the way those East Coast pricks made me grovel just to get that old fart out here . . ."

"They knew you'd lose," Bartell said. "There was never any secret in the numbers. Why attach presidential prestige to some two-bit car salesman and bird farmer out in the boondocks?"

"Doesn't matter now, does it?" said Duckworth. "That's the way the game's played."

Bartell felt all his weight shifting forward onto the balls of his feet. He could barely tolerate listening further, yet he had to hear it all, every word. His teeth began to chatter. He clamped his jaw down hard, and the jittering moved down into his shoulders.

Henry Skelton, the man who would force his dangerous ideas on decent, hardworking folks, ruin their lives. Skelton, the imported Californian. The convicted terrorist who would commit political violence just to impose his perverted, elitist will on the public. Henry Skelton, Bartell now understood, was the most hated and useful person of all, the one who would never go along.

"It's still wrong," Yolanda said. "What you did to him. You three should be ashamed."

Bartell didn't know whether to be proud of her for what she said, or ashamed of himself for not having said it first. Or perhaps he should simply feel foolish and naive for himself and Yolanda both.

"Women," Puhl groused. "Always tea and sympathy. Till you go and try to unload one . . ."

"Well, well," Yolanda said, an edge in her voice now. "Merle Puhl. Turns out you're not only a political genius, but an absolute prophet of what happens next." The look she gave Puhl could have driven nails, and Bartell almost pitied him for what the next few weeks probably held in store. Almost.

The only part left unanswered was whether Puhl and company had ever intended that the former president's visit come off at all. Or was the whole exercise nothing more than a charade designed to end up at this very moment. If that were true, what did it say about the first bomb in Cradle Creek? About that miserable bastard blown limb from limb? Bartell remembered what Skelton had told him about that night. Okay, just who was Ed Morley?

"So, *Detective,*" Puhl said, "what's the real purpose of this little visit tonight? You want a job, maybe? For services rendered. What do you think, Kip, what kind of staff does a United States senator get to hire? Could we find a use for this man, Mr. Morley?"

Duckworth smirked. Ed Morley grunted.

Puhl closed his eyes and rested his great, glistening head against the back of the tub, reminding Bartell of Marlon Brando in some movie he'd seen once about Vietnam. Puhl settled deeper into the froth. *Acropolis Now.* That's what Ike Skinner called that movie one morning at coffee.

"Come on, Detective," Puhl goaded. "Let's hear it. Some jobs need a résumé, and some need evidence. I think you're a little short on both."

"I already got a job, thanks," Bartell said. "But I've got to tell you, Puhl, I always wanted to get a good look at a turd in a tub."

Chapter 26

Cold.

Skelton relaxed, felt his belly settle into the ground. Listened to the crackle of hair and beard, all marbleized with snow and sweat and steam.

No pain. Anesthesia of winter. And a blurred story playing itself out in the compressed silence of a rifle scope.

At first, seeing Bartell with Puhl and the others made no sense, and then the only kind of sense it made was bad. Fucking cop, slipping in alone at night. Not in a cop car, but a pickup truck. That made him part of it. All of it. From the start. What else was there to think? What else could it mean? Bartell. Another man, some yuppie puke. A woman. Puhl himself. And a fourth man, who was nearly concealed by a thick potted tree.

Together at the end, together at the start.

Every couple of minutes, a guard dressed in black passed outside the solarium, stopping often as not to size up the gal in the tub with Puhl. Between darkness, the storm, and that eyeful of woman, there wasn't a ghost of a chance any of the security crew would spot him.

Ghost of a chance. Appropriate. Ghosts—his own probably among them—waiting to be blasted free of their bodies, and wander off into the snow. Out here with him.

Question: Would glass deflect the rounds too much to risk head shots? A detail. That was all. The sort of mind game he used to play from his cave overlooking the helicopter.

No more games. What do you do with a lie? Deny it, or make it come true. Well, Skelton had chosen for keeps, so it was no longer a question of *what if.* Just *who first?* and *when?* with the *when* measured in heartbeats. Those parasites want the world to know what a real bad-ass Henry Skelton is, well, here goes.

He brought the cross hairs to bear on the center of Bartell's chest . . . drew in a deep breath . . . let it partway out . . .

"Let's talk about bombs," Bartell said.

"Bombs?" Puhl said idly. "I don't believe bombs are on the agenda." He turned to Yolanda. "You keeping notes, honey?"

When Bartell took a couple of quick steps toward the hot tub, Duckworth jumped out of his chair and stepped in his path.

"Easy, there, Detective," Duckworth drilled his right index finger into Bartell's sternum.

"Don't put your hands on me, slick." Bartell felt his voice tremble with rage. "You want to walk away from this thing—"

"I said, *easy* . . . ." Duckworth ground his finger harder into Bartell's chest.

Instantly, Bartell reached up with his left hand, grabbed Duckworth's finger, and jerked straight down, so that the finger, near breaking, bent back toward his wrist.

Mindful of Morley, Bartell risked a look back, hoping to warn him off. But Morley wasn't moving. He just laughed softly, entertained.

Duckworth screamed, but the scream was cut off abruptly when the heel of Bartell's right hand landed with full force on the point of his chin.

Duckworth, with blood streaming from both corners of his mouth, started to say something. Before he could speak, though, Bartell reefed again on his finger. Not much, but enough to remind him to keep his mouth shut. Then let the finger go.

Bartell slowly surveyed them all. "What a bunch of cocksuckers."

Though unsteady on his feet, Duckworth drew back a fist and gathered himself to throw a punch.

Bartell was done with the fight, but he wasn't ready to take a punch to prove it. "Idiot," he spat out, then smacked both palms against Duckworth's chest, giving him a heavy shove that sent him reeling back toward the hot tub, where the apron clipped his lower legs and sent him flailing backward into the tub itself. More water sloshed onto the apron, and there was a lot of shouting and swearing as Yolanda and Puhl scrambled to get out of the way of the falling Duckworth.

"Now," Bartell said. "Let's talk some more about bombs."

By the time Bartell sensed movement behind him, it was too late. Morley's shoulder caught him under his right arm, driving him after Duckworth.

And then nobody was still, none an obvious target.

The guy who jumped Bartell was quick and agile as a bad habit, driving him over the apron around the tub, half in, half out of the water. Then the man stood up and reached into his jacket.

Despite the snow, Skelton's vision was utterly clear. His own gunshot wounds momentarily nonexistent. He was part of the snow, inside the air itself.

The man standing over Bartell was the man he'd seen last spring. That night in the headlights near the helicopter.

The man's hand came out of his jacket holding a gun.

The man leaned, gun first, toward Bartell's head.

The shot sounded as though it came from someplace else, someplace far off and perfect.

Sandwiched between Yolanda Huizer, on his left, Puhl, on his right, and with Duckworth under him, Bartell felt the bulk of Ed Morley bearing down on the small of his back and tried to roll to his left to slip free. He sensed Yolanda begin to stand, and then through all the clamor he heard the small sound of breaking glass, followed by a slap, a grunt, and the full weight of Morley collapsing on top of him.

Bartell threw himself clear of Morley, squared himself on his hands and knees. By now Yolanda was standing, screaming.

"Get down! Down! Everybody—"

Now Duckworth got to his feet too, and Bartell drove toward him and Yolanda Huizer.

More breaking glass. Another slap.

Yolanda pitched backward and thumped against the edge of the tub just before she slipped under the water.

Chester Boyles's voice boomed from the door. "What the fuck—"

"Lights," Bartell shouted to him. "Chester, the lights."

In the endless moment before the solarium went dark, Bartell saw Yolanda's blank eyes staring back at him from under the water, bubbles tailing up from her mouth and nose while blood blossomed from the hole between her breasts.

During the scramble that followed, Kip Duckworth regained his balance and climbed over Bartell's back getting out of the tub. Puhl, naked and white as a maggot, flopped out onto the apron, then the slate floor, then scuttled on all fours after Duckworth into the bedroom.

Glass broke again, and a second bullet smacked into the side of the tub.

Frantically, Bartell leaned into the water, grabbed Yolanda Huizer under the arms, and dragged her after him down onto the floor. A fourth bullet broke glass, caught Yolanda high in her right thigh, sounding ugly, like a fist smacking meat, and uglier still because she gave no sign, not the slightest flinch or gasp, that she had been hit again.

Inside the bedroom, Chester Boyles and the three live men from the solarium lay for a moment, gasping, while Yolanda Huizer lay silent and still, no blood pulsing from either of her wounds. Dead. Bartell knew she was dead.

"I got an ambulance on the way," Chester Boyles said, indicating the radio clipped to his jacket. He was crouched in the doorway to the solarium, providing cover with the MP5. Cover from what though? Beyond the darkened solarium the winter storm went its own cold, indifferent way. And on the glass wall, fracture webs fanned out around four bullet holes, looking like the work of some maniacal spider.

The slick gray squares spread out before the man's eyes for as far as he could see, and when he breathed, the inside of his chest felt like crushed gravel. He knew what had happened, goddammit, he knew what had happened.

Just get a knee up under you . . .

The man blinked once, and when he opened his eyes, the farthest row of tiles disappeared, as though the horizon had somehow crept there into that small, steamy room. One, two, five, seven rows of tiles.

. . . just one knee, point it toward your chin and pull, like a baby . . .

The man brought all his concentration to bear on the nearest tile, the rounded edge of the nearest tile, and as he watched, the tile seemed to rise higher and higher from the black mortar that held it fast to the floor.

. . . first one knee, then two, then the elbows, and then the hands . . .

Four rows of tiles, and now the puddles on the tiles were big and deep as lakes.

. . . and then some rat bastard, some worthless douche-bag fuck . . .

The man coughed. Thick, red lakes.

. . . is going to pay . . .

The lump of gravel deep inside the man's chest shifted, then held fast.

. . . because

Skelton lay completely still now, watching, waiting to see if there was any indication they knew where he was. He felt his breathing grow shallow and fast, felt the sweat gathering inside his clothes.

He sucked air, long and slow, deep into his chest.

He did not move.

After the second shot the lights went out, and the others had been fired more at movement than at any clear target. What the hell, the target that mattered most, the motherfucker from Cradle Creek, he'd put him down first. That was what counted most, everything else just ice in the drink.

But why the fight with Bartell? The gun?

Fuck it, it didn't matter. You wallow around with the likes of Puhl, you make yourself worth killing.

There was a flurry of activity around the house, black-clad guards ducking quickly from shadow to shadow, searching for the threat. It was clear they had no idea where he lay hiding under the gathering snow.

But the woman, Christ, oh, Christ, in the stillness he could see her now, the image of her standing in the water. Could almost feel the deadfall of her after the second shot. She had made herself the next obvious target, and out of instinct Skelton had taken her.

Who was she? She was nobody.

Now she was nothing.

The snow gathered around him like dunes.

Without waiting for Boyles to protest, Bartell left him there in the bedroom with Puhl, Duckworth, and the two bodies. Running back through the house, he pulled his badge from his belt and clipped it to the front of his jacket, then drew his gun. Rather than going out the front, though, he left the house by way of the patio, where he'd first met Puhl and Duckworth just the day before.

Outside, he ducked around the side of the house, looking for somewhere from which he could see the hills rising outside the solarium, see some sign of the shooter. But the house itself was a limitation, an island of light out of which he could not see into the surrounding country. Off to his left he saw the low, dark form of an outbuilding, maybe thirty yards away. Crouching, he started to run through the slippery dark toward the shed.

"Freeze!" The voice, a cop voice, came from the shadows around the shed.

"It's me, Bartell!" he shouted back, skidding to an awkward stop in the snow, throwing his hands above his head. But not dropping the gun. "From the city!" Something caught his eye, and when he glanced down at his chest, he saw the tiny dot of red light frozen on his badge. His guts felt as though they had shriveled up to nothing.

"Chester told us you were out here," the deputy said. Bartell didn't recognize the voice. "Get your ass on over here to cover."

For several moments he saw no movement anywhere around the house. And then voices from somewhere out of sight. Shouts. Nothing, so far as he could tell, that was directed at him.

Satisfied now that he could safely move, Skelton scooted back from the crest of the rise, then rolled onto his hips and skidded down into the shallow coulee.

Getting to his feet, he took a moment to get his bearings, plot out in his head a route back to the truck.

And then he began to run. Run like hell.

Bartell dropped his hands and started on. Nearing the shed, he could now make out the deputy's form. He was about to ask if anybody had seen the shooter, when there was another burst of movement behind the deputy, deeper in the shadows.

The deputy whirled. "Hold it right there, asshole!"

The noise erupted again, a thumping sound that moved toward them.

"I said, *freeze,* goddammit!" the deputy shouted, and at the same instant the silenced MP5 bucked in his hands, made a breathy, chattering sound, like a deck of cards being shuffled, followed by the jingle of spent brass clattering off the shed onto the hardpack.

The noise continued, now a flapping sound. Cautiously, the deputy took his flashlight from his gun belt and aimed it toward the noise.

A cloud of feathers swirled in the air, and under the cloud an ostrich lay bloody and thrashing, its large bony feet spurring the ground.

"Jesus," the deputy hissed. "Jesus Christ. What's Chester gonna say?"

"Chester?" Bartell said. "I'll tell you your biggest problem with Chester. This time next week, he'll be telling everybody he shot the damned thing himself."

Chapter 27

He was on the highway south for a while, then oiled gravel, and finally decomposed granite, all the way wind pile-driving his face and chest through the smashed windshield, rifle bouncing against his thigh, the snow squall ending not far outside town, driving fast under the full moon, toward that shape, the long silver tube of the Chinook, the replacement helicopter. He picked up speed, drifting sideways through the turnoff, faster, fast as he could, until the pickup t-boned that ugly machine and everything—could it have been nothing but a dream?—came to a jolting stop.

Now, squatting on the ledge outside his cave, Skelton held his left hand up to the moon, studied the stump of his missing finger.

Vision of someone else's nightmare. There you had it. He lowered the hand slowly to his side and gazed out across the canyon, where pale moonlight lingered around the fringes of the trees, roll of mountainside, edges of shale and limestone outcrops. Instead of Nez Perce ghosts, though, or helicopters or bears or chain saws or cops, he found himself thinking about the ocean.

Remember it like this: a small boat, riding up onto the swells, then sliding back into troughs on black water, and a heavy line strung out from the stern, dragging a chunk of herring across the bottom hundreds of feet below. Sea off the Olympic Peninsula. A teenage boy alone, up to his eyeballs in big plans and hormones.

Peering over the gunwale while the boat drifted, the boy began to see shredded flesh rising on the current. Soon the water all around the boat was roiling with meaty debris. A whale, maybe, slashing through a school of fish down there in the cold.

Then the line went snug, as though he'd snagged bottom. Yet when he gave a tug, something tugged back. Solid, like the ocean itself. Bracing the end of the rod against his belly, he began the long grind of horsing the catch up a few inches, then quickly reeling the tip of the rod back toward the water, never allowing any slack. For nearly an hour it was as though he were coaxing a bucket of cement up from the bottom. The muscles in his back trembled and burned, while the hilt of the rod bore into his gut, and his lips tasted like salt. There was no run, no thrashing on the far end of the line. Just strong, relentless fight, until he finally saw it, the huge tan oval of the halibut, maybe two hundred pounds, fanning slowly toward him out of the darkness.

Holding the halibut suspended ten feet down, he fumbled for the gun in his coat pocket. A little .22 revolver. Because you have to shoot those big fish as soon as you can once they're alongside. Otherwise they'll snap the line at best, and maybe even swamp a small boat. That's what all the men said, and that's what he was ready for out there alone with himself on the glassy edge of the earth.

He held the gun between his knees, and once more began to nurse the fish closer, keeping the line tight.

Then the line went slack, throwing him off balance as the fish made a run. Not a run, but a charge, rolling the huge white slab of its belly against the boat. He fumbled for the gun. Dropped it overboard. Now the halibut flipped its tail against the gunwale, sounded, and the line snapped instantly, as though it had never existed at all, and the halibut was gone, the sea completely silent but for the noise of the boy's heart.

Another time, another vision. And nobody believed him. That was the first lesson. People never believe the monster that gets away.

But he could still hear that noise. The noise of his own heart.

Skelton thought about Bartell, whom he could have killed once, and didn't, and now may have left dead back at Puhl's house. Motive. A cop word, concept from the world of Bartell and those like him. What would they say, over their coffee and their beer, about Skelton's motive? How could they ever understand the motive of a man willing to kill for what, to them, might seem to be nothing?

Take that halibut years ago, dredged up inch by inch from some deep place, where it lay at once hidden and hunting in the muck, then going wild in the sunlight. What had been its motive other than to survive? Drag a man close enough to fear, you get the same thing. Get an animal. The kind of animal that leaves shredded meat in the water. Or does his best to cause death, then doesn't even stick around to discover whom he might have killed. And does not . . .

. . . care?

So what was this nothing that Skelton had been after? Had he found it? If so, what now? Hunched over in the cold, he felt fatigue settle into the core of his bones, a kind of symmetrical exhaustion, and outside the perimeter of that exhaustion, the horror of what he had done began to grind in on him.

There was a story around Montana about two guys, a man named Nichols and his son, who had gone off to live off the land in the wilderness of a country called Spanish Peaks. One day they kidnapped a young woman to live with them, then killed one of the men who'd come to rescue her. Skelton recalled a grim fascination with these two men, not as kidnappers and killers, but as people who had somehow conceived and executed a kind of lunatic freedom. So, was that what he'd done, turned his old life into a monster great enough to cast him free? Was that what he'd sought all along, the creation of manic, self-indulgent fear strong enough to drive him to a place where he didn't have the guts to go on his own? Not a wilderness of mountain and forest, but the wilderness of a man gone absolutely wild?

Skelton listened, as he had so often before, for the voices of the Nez Perce dead, wondering once again how long he could go before he could go no farther. This time his only answer was a ringing silence, the silence that comes only when even the dead have left you behind.

There was nothing more to say, even to think. Getting to his feet, he gritted his teeth against the pain as he shouldered his pack, then picked up the rifle and started off through the moonlight toward the giant gray dome, and thin air of Red Wolf, determined in his blood to make this moment last forever.

Chapter 28

Fury can be a kind of death sentence, and for Bartell the hours since the crash and shooting on River Flats had been nothing if not a long walk. In his bedroom, dressing for colder weather, Bartell remembered the looks on the faces of Fanning, Woodruff, and Blieker, when he'd tried to explain the truth of it all, a scheme that stretched all the way back to a lonely mountain night last spring. He might as well have been picking apart the Warren Commission Report for the benefit of Chief Justice Warren himself.

Forget it. Yolanda Huizer was taking, as the man said, the big sleep. Gazed back up at him from underwater, all the light draining from her lavender eyes as blood pulsed out of her chest in several bright, erratic gusts, spreading in a red cloud that remained connected to her by a thin scarlet root. In memory, that moment seemed to last forever, though the experience itself had taken no longer than the final involuntary spasms of Yolanda Huizer's circulatory system.

Ed Morley was no luckier, although to Bartell, this mattered less. The bloody streaks under Morley's legs were a record of his efforts to gain his feet and get to safety. Or, perhaps, to continue the fight. But the blood smears said his legs had finally accomplished no more than a dog's running through a dream.

Later on, when Bartell had come back inside after witnessing the slaughter of that giant bird, both Puhl and Duckworth, thank God, had managed to keep their mouths shut.

Step, by step, by step.

Not long after Bartell had arrived home, Cash rounded up a

pack of cigarettes, a jug of hot coffee, an old Hudson's Bay blanket, and his .45 long Colt, then proceeded to station himself on a chaise longue outside the downstairs door in back of the house, where he remained. His excuse was that he was guarding the house, though Bartell suspected that the real reason for picketing himself outside was that he was in the mood for a steady infusion of cigarettes, and Helen refused to allow him to smoke inside the house. Given the old man's mood and armament, any living creature venturing into the backyard would be well advised to tread lightly.

"I hate this," Helen said now from the bedroom door. He hadn't heard her come down the hall.

"Which part of it?" So many choices. Which would she tear into first?

"All of it," she said. "The phone calls, the racing around in the middle of the night. Brooding silence. Secrets. Guns."

"You mean the *man* thing." He shouldered past her through the door. Arriving home just after midnight, he'd managed only a few hours' sleep, not nearly enough to engage in this discussion.

"That's not fair," she said after him.

No, he thought, it's not. Fairness. Like a yardstick, people use it first to take your measure, then whack you upside the head. All depends on their mood at the moment.

"Those people . . ." she said, her voice tight as a bowstring. "Motherfuckers."

Bartell stopped, and stared at her. "Say what?"

"Motherfuckers," she said again. "That's what they are. Nothing but a bunch of motherfuckers."

"I called them cocksuckers," Bartell said.

"We're both right," she said.

How could he ever express how much he loved her?

Out in the living room, Gina sat in a small rocker near the large window overlooking the linden tree off the deck. As far as Bartell knew, she and Helen had been up all night. Earlier, when Bartell told Gina the story of what had happened at the ranch, she seemed to take it in stride, as if years ago she'd shoveled out a place in her life for just this sort of news and had been waiting patiently ever since for when the time came to fill it in. Now she met his look without hesitation. "Cradle Creek?"

Bartell nodded. "That seems to be what it comes down to." Based on Gina's statement, the police department and sheriff's office had put together a joint team to search Cradle Creek since late afternoon of the day before. The latest shootings at Puhl's only served to increase the urgency surrounding the operation. It would be first light in about an hour. Somebody had already contacted the boss of the logging site and told him to cancel work for the day, and the access road had been sealed by deputies since shortly after midnight. The plan was for the search team to enter the canyon under the cover of darkness, so the odds were that they would be in place at the helicopter site by the time Bartell got there.

"We can't just let him go," Bartell said. "You understand that."

"I know," Gina whispered.

"And if—"

"I know."

Finally, Helen came back into the living room, picking right up on where she'd left off. "I hate it, I guess, because there doesn't seem to be any other way."

"No," he said tersely, "there isn't." That's what the long walk was all about. Bartell hadn't told them that he wasn't part of the search team. His little social call out at Puhl's had left Vic Fanning less than overjoyed, and the captain's most recent edict to go home and cool his heels was propped up with the threat of a suspension. *Responsible prudence.* That's what Fanning wanted. Lovely. Bartell was to the point he could match the grind of Skelton's mania cog for cog.

"He only wanted to be left alone," Gina said.

"Don't we all," Bartell said. He didn't know if she meant to reproach him for pushing Skelton over the edge, to defend Skelton, or perhaps even to absolve herself of some kind of guilt by association. All he knew for sure was that he wasn't in any frame of mind to have the conversation that seemed to be on its way.

Gina stirred in the chair. "He cared about . . . I don't know, the earth, I guess."

"The earth," Bartell echoed. "So what is it, he thinks the *earth* shouldn't be anything but a pretty place for him to look at?"

"Ray . . ." Helen said, knowing him well enough to try to head him off.

Trouble was, most of what had remained of Bartell's self-control had been blasted to pieces a few hours ago in Puhl's solarium. So he did the one stupid thing that men have done since forever. He took it out on someone he loved. "I hate to break this to you, sweetheart," he said to Helen, "but most of the time feeling good about things—especially about yourself—just isn't part of the deal."

Helen, bless her, was never one to back away from frustration. "That's not—"

"I know." He held up his hand, shrinking back inside himself. "That's not fair. I'm sorry." He hoped that the unspoken codes between him and his wife were strong enough that she knew he understood his mistake. Not a mistake in what he believed, but in throwing it up to her under these circumstances.

"It's people like Puhl," Gina said. "The politicians."

"Puhl's no good," Bartell said, now completely exasperated. "So what? If Skelton wanted this world to be a clean and perfect place, he should have started with that part of it under his own feet."

Preferring to avoid any more unpleasantness, Bartell went to the door and collected his gear. A camouflage Gore-Tex parka, a knapsack jammed with food and cold-weather gear, and his scoped Browning .30—06 falling block. His walkie-talkie from work, programmed with all the local law enforcement channels, was already outside in the truck. Briefly, Bartell looked back at Helen, who nodded almost imperceptibly and followed him out to the pickup.

Outside, the marked unit was still in place. Bartell waved idly at the patrolman, then turned his attention back to Helen. She stood nearby, hugging herself in the cold, while he stowed his gear in the truck. Ready to leave at last, he pulled her close and kissed her. She kissed him back but kept her arms folded awkwardly under her breasts.

"You're not going to tell Cash you're leaving?" Helen asked.

"I'm afraid if I got close enough, I'd get shot." Anyway, he thought, if he told Cash what he had in mind, the old man would want to go along. Old grievances aside, Bartell knew his father had the heart and stomach for what lay ahead, but he doubted he still had the legs. "You tell him for me," he said. "After I'm gone. He won't shoot you. He's a country gentleman. He wouldn't shoot a woman without saying something first."

Bartell started to get into the truck, then hesitated. "I really am sorry," he said. "About what I said inside."

"Me too," she said.

"It sounded like I thought you were a fool."

"But I'm not."

"No. Not by a long shot." He kissed her again and she seemed to relax in his arms. "But I can't always be what you want."

"I know that too." When she looked up at him, her expression appeared more genuinely kind than any he'd ever seen before. "It doesn't matter."

He let her go and climbed into the truck.

"Be careful," Helen said. Her voice sounded as though she were making a wish.

Chapter 29

Bartell badged his way past the sheriff's roadblock, and as had happened the night before at Puhl's, the deputy didn't waste any time calling in ahead of him. When he got to the helicopter site maybe ten minutes later, Vic Fanning flagged him down before he got to the turnoff. Once Bartell pulled to a stop, Fanning sauntered up to the driver's window and braced his hands on his hips. Bartell cranked down his window to hear what the captain had to say.

"Are you crazy," Fanning said, "or just plain stupid?" Today his uniform was a near match for the one Chester Boyles wore the night before: crisp black BDUs, a black baseball cap with POLICE spelled across the front in silver letters, and a black A2 jacket. Silver captains bars flashed like magical bird droppings on the shoulders of the jacket, and his pants were bloused inside black spit-shined boots.

"I work for the government," Bartell said. "You figure it out."

Like Bartell, Fanning hadn't spent much time in bed lately. His face was drawn at the edges but slack in the spaces in between. Dark pouches sagged under his eyes while he chewed absently at his lower lip. The stubble around his mouth and chin was nearly white, and Bartell knew that if Fanning grew a beard, it would add fifteen years to his face.

Bartell smiled. "But this is recreation. Good for the soul."

In the daylight beginning to settle among the trees, Bartell could see the twin towers and the long, drooping rotors of the storied helicopter. Rather, he realized, the replacement helicopter. Beyond that, though, the site was shielded from view by thick underbrush. Although the high, thin air had plenty of bite, it had neither snowed nor rained yet in this part of the country, and above the trees, the bright tip of Red Wolf reflected the full force of the new day.

"Don't bullshit me, Ray. Right now I've got about as much need for you as for cancer. This stunt's going to cost you some days. Plenty of them." Despite the obvious tension on his face, Fanning's voice sounded unconcerned, almost soothing.

Bartell didn't really care what Fanning was up to. But he was a little tired, and it was a relief to have Fanning cut to the chase without a lot of his usual bluster.

"Today I'm just another taxpayer," Bartell said. "You guys having any luck?" He gave up an involuntary shudder against the morning chill and tried to rub the sleepy grit from his eyes. His and Arnold Zillion's Indian summer lark on the golf course was a long, long time ago.

Fanning shrugged. "They've cleared the site down here, and set up command post."

"A *command post*. Sounds like you're halfway to glory."

"Let's hope so," Fanning sniffed. "Anyway, they did it all without anybody getting shot. Folks were a little tense, what with Skelton turning himself into a sniper. But when you think about that poor fucking ostrich, I was pretty damned glad once all these deputies got done racing around with machine guns. And we know we're in the right place."

Bartell felt a tingle of anxiety. "Yeah?"

Fanning seemed genuinely pleased with the novelty of what they had found. "You ever see a helicopter get pretzeled by a pickup truck? Quite a few bullet holes in the truck too. Windshield shot out . . . blood inside the cab . . . yeah . . . but no Skelton."

"Mind if I take a look?"

"Not a good idea." Fanning frowned, officiousness now seeping back into him. "Some of these guys don't know you—there's been some talk."

"Talk?" Bartell had spent enough years with cops to know what was coming before Fanning said it. But he was genuinely surprised by what Fanning said next.

"I've told them there's nothing to it." Fanning sounded almost indignant. "But some of these deputies, they think it's kind of weird. I mean, you're the only man on the inside who's ever seen Skelton, let alone talk to him. Talk to him alone at your house without bothering to tell anybody until you're cornered into it. Then twice in the same day, the pair you—"

"We're not a *pair,* Vic."

"Okay, okay. The *separate entities* of you—how's that?"

"Better."

"Yeah. The two separate entities of you have a brush. Both times he gets away. And somebody gets fucked up."

Bartell swallowed his anger. "You mean somebody besides me."

"I didn't say I thought there was anything to it," Fanning said. "But it didn't help, you taking Skelton's girlfriend with you yesterday. Christ, right there under the chief's nose. Some people, they got it in their heads maybe you've got some responsibility for what's happened."

"I do," Bartell said. "I told you that. But not the way everybody seems to think."

"I know that too."

"Then how come, all through this thing, you never cut me any slack?"

"You force me to be the captain, Ray," Fanning said. "You force me into that all the goddamn time. I don't know why, but okay, fine, that's the way it is. You need to see yourself at odds with somebody in order to get your job done, then I figure that's the way I handle you. Usually, I don't have any problem with that. But I've also got a limit. Don't start pushing my buttons again. Not now."

"So maybe I should go jump off a cliff," Bartell said.

"That would help," Fanning deadpanned. "But I recommend against it. The way your luck's running, you wouldn't get killed . . . just paralyzed . . . Then everybody'd say you were nothing but a self-serving prick trying to make yourself look like a hero."

"Thanks a lot. You're about as reassuring as a travel agent in a leper colony."

"Don't bullshit yourself, Ray," Fanning went on, stern now, his lined face pinched and prim. He pointed to the gear stowed beside Bartell in the cab. "Now, you mind telling me what one of my boys is doing out here? Out of jurisdiction, and interfering in a law enforcement action?" Fanning, of course, knew the answer, but he was determined to make Bartell come clean with it.

Bartell shrugged his face with exaggerated nonchalance. "Like

I said, recreation. A little hike in the scenic northern Rockies. Who knows, maybe collect me a souvenir."

"That's what I was afraid of." For a moment Fanning stared at the ground, thinking. Then he peered up and down the road, as though afraid that somebody might overhear. "Like I said, we know he was here because his truck's here. Too bad they couldn't get the road sealed sooner."

On this, Bartell was fatalistic. A roadblock ahead of Skelton might have gotten them only some dead deputies.

"Right now," Fanning went on, "we've got two teams on the mountain. One cleared Skelton's cave about fifteen minutes ago. The other jumped off a couple of miles back down the road."

While the location of Skelton's cave was well known from the start, the planners from the sheriff's office had learned during the night that several months ago the pilot of the replacement helicopter had spotted where Skelton kept his truck stashed whenever he was in the area. Nobody believed Skelton would return to where he used to hide the truck, but that was as good a place as any to launch a team.

The plan was for both teams to sweep the bowl immediately surrounding the site, joining at some point above the command post. The chances were less than zero that Skelton remained in the search area, but there really wasn't a more logical place to start, and it was generally agreed that the command post staff and support people would rest easier if they knew the high ground overlooking their turf had been secured. Fanning said the operation would take most of the day. Tomorrow they would probably move higher onto Red Wolf.

"This goddamned nut," Fanning said. "Spends all his time creepy-crawling around the woods like he was on some kind of mission from God." Fanning stopped suddenly, cleared his throat, then turned his head aside and coughed deep in his chest, clearing his lungs. "Sorry. One thing I could never tolerate, it's a martyr." This last he added with a cautionary tone.

Until then, Bartell hadn't given any serious thought to how he planned to go about dragging Henry Skelton down off the mountain. He'd been in this country only once or twice, so Skelton clearly had an edge on him—and probably anybody else involved in the hunt—when it came to finding his way around Cradle Creek. At least, Bartell thought, he wouldn't be part of the organized search. The way he saw it, he had too much stake in things to be treated as just another grunt. Too much ego too, you got right down to it. Maybe being both late and suspect wasn't always a bad thing.

Bartell gazed up at the dome of Red Wolf and asked about the feds. Fanning told him that right now there were a pair of Forest Service investigators. By noon, six FBI SWAT out of Butte, Great Falls, Billings, and Missoula, would arrive. And HRT had been contacted. They'd be on the ground tonight. HRT was the FBI's Hostage Rescue Team, a highly specialized group out of Quantico, Virginia, that did nothing but train, and go out on down-and-dirty jobs like this one. The *hurt team,* people called it. With Zillion smashed to hell and the former president undoubtedly miffed about some butt-hole messing with his travel plans, odds were that even the EPA would be looking for a piece of this action.

"By tomorrow," Fanning said, "this place will be like something out of Desert Storm."

Looking past Fanning, Bartell noticed another black-clad figure heading their way. He thought at first it must be one of the deputies, but soon saw that it was Brandon McWilliams. All decked out like Fanning's twin, save for the absence of a gun belt.

"Or a movie set," Bartell said, nodding toward McWilliams.

"Yes," Fanning said absently, studying the approaching dignitary. "That too."

Again the captain took a moment to think, and in the space of silence that followed, Bartell understood that his boss was trying to come up with terms under which the two of them could go about their separate business.

"This road's pretty narrow," Fanning said hastily as McWilliams drew within earshot. "Runs on up maybe three miles to a meadow." Bartell could head on up there, find a safe place to turn around, where he wouldn't disturb the job.

Bartell understood. Fanning was shoveling on deniability like lime on a corpse, but it didn't matter. For by now it was clear that Bartell had been given license to do whatever he chose, and when the dust settled, Fanning would take whatever action was necessary to save himself.

Fanning exchanged brief pleasantries with McWilliams but wasn't inclined to speak further with Bartell. Motioning back toward the helicopter, he said to McWilliams, "I'll be back at the CP."

If McWilliams felt slighted, he didn't show it. "Quite an adventure," he said to Bartell.

"Well, I guess you look the part," Bartell said.

McWilliams gave the shoulders of his black A2 an exaggerated fluff. "Like I said, a tyrant for detail. Lucky for me, Vic scored a uniform that fit from one of the guys on your SWAT team."

"Backstory," Bartell said dryly.

McWilliams winked. "Sounds like you've been talking to your father. How's the old guy doing anyway?"

"He's fine." Bartell thought about Cash back at the house, all wired up on adrenaline and nicotine, trigger happy as a cattle rustler caught in a corral. "You ought to stop in and pay him a surprise visit."

"Maybe I will," McWilliams said, his attention now clearly drawn to the rifle hanging from the rack in the back window of Bartell's truck. "You going to be part of the search?"

"Not exactly." Bartell was about to give McWilliams the brush, when the devil whispered in his ear. "I'm just out for a little walk," Bartell said. "Maybe you'd like to come along. For the research."

McWilliams's face grew pinched. "A little walk? I'm not sure what that means." Although he was a lavishly successful actor, McWilliams lacked either the talent or the inclination—perhaps both—to mask his apprehension.

"It means," Bartell said, "just what you think it means."

McWilliams tugged at an ear, then looked furtively back toward the helicopter and the activity that now swarmed around it. "That's a generous offer," he said, once again in command of himself. "But I'm afraid it doesn't sound too productive. At least not for my purposes. I'd better stick around the command post. You know, where the action is."

With that, Bartell excused himself to be off on his own boring way.

Chapter 30

Skelton watched through his rifle scope as the lone pickup headed on up the canyon from the helicopter site.

They hunt you all the time. In town. In the wild. Maybe it was wild everyplace. Maybe wild was something you carried around inside, like bone marrow. You run because they chase, they chase because you run. Simple biology.

At first he'd been amused by the mob of cops combing the forest around his cave. More like a bunch of drivers than hunters. Would they resort to staking out bait? With the cops, who could tell? Soon, though, he'd tired of the game and moved off toward higher country.

What about the bear. Did the grizzly always run?

No.

More biology.

Where was the real hunter?

Who was the real hunter?

Where was Bartell? Because there was never any doubt.

The lone truck, what else?

Skelton considered a route with cover, which would take him to the head of the smaller side-canyon above the meadow roamed by Indian dead, through which Bartell would almost certainly climb. Settled now in his mind, oblivious of both the weight of his pack and the pain from his wounds, he loped ahead into the trees.

After sitting for a long time in the pickup, it was no easy chore for Bartell to work through the kinks from the car crash, the shooting, and the fatigue that tugged at him like quicksand. He stuck with it, though, climbing for nearly an hour before he stopped under the shade of a granite promontory. As he watched the breeze flit across the gold-colored meadow below, Bartell felt the cold working on his fingers and toes, his face and ears. The forested slope fell away steeply at his feet, and the air smelled clean and sharp. Crouching, he balanced the rifle across his lap and wedged himself into the rocks. High above the meadow, nearly level with Bartell's perch, a pair of ravens played tag on the wind.

Unlike most of the police, Bartell had accepted long ago that in its final resolution, any crime worth more than passing attention amounted at best to fifty percent facts, with the other fifty percent reserved for posturing and interpretation. Okay, so Merle Puhl was a criminal. Him and Skelton both. And Morley. All of them, except poor Yolanda Huizer. But Puhl was also a genuine candidate for the United States Senate, and Henry Skelton, for whatever demented reasons may have been jammed down his throat, had recently tried to blow his brains out. That's how the story would play. Didn't matter what was in Skelton's head when he actually pulled the trigger. Didn't matter what had set Skelton in motion. Because the same scarcity of evidence that had made Skelton a suspect in the Cradle Creek bombing would also continue to shield Puhl. The likely perpetrator himself, Ed Morley, was dead, and the one possible weak link, Yolanda Huizer, was lying in the morgue right alongside him. While Bartell might have enough to make a small stink, he had nothing on the order of proof, and taking his suspicions public would only generate lawsuits. More opportunity for Puhl to touch up the spin.

Incompetent cop.

Duplicitous cop.

Disgraced, unemployed ex-cop.

Simple progression, as predictable as high school physics.

For one precious instant Bartell felt as though he could curl up in his rocky niche and go to sleep. Sleep forever.

Forcing himself to stir his stiffening body, he fished a pair of binoculars from inside his parka and glassed the canyon. Nothing but rocks and trees. Not even a lousy deer. He closed his eyes, rested his head against the rocks. The view from this spot was too constricted. He should move. Had to move. But he wanted to rest. Not a good sign for a hunter. Especially if there was a chance somebody was hunting you back.

Maybe he'd be on one of those true-life cop shows. The kind where you tell your story while a bunch of actors stage it. Sure. He'd gain forty pounds, grow a mustache. Buy himself a polyester suit. *I arrived at the scene, and exited my pa-trol ve-hicle.* Everybody else in the world, they get out of the fucking car. But cops, no, cops, they fucking exit the fucking vehicle.

Action, a few minutes of good, clean action. That's what people wanted. A little slam-him-and-jam-him, and if the dirtbag resists, dish out a dose of bag-him-and-tag-him. Case closed. Who's buying the first round? But a guy choking down chili dogs and diet Pepsi—or sitting under a rock on a mountain, for that matter —a guy sweating things out while *nothing happens,* sorry, babe, it's *just not interesting.*

A good story needs tension. That's what he'd heard Thomas Cassidy, the cop-writer, say. According to Cassidy, tension is the car chase and resolution is the crash.

Tension is not shivering inside a cocoon of sweat on a subfreezing day.

Tension is not having eyes big and heavy as throbbing baseballs.

How could he ever get the noise of Arnold Zillion's bloody gurgle out of his ears? Rid his nose of the stench of Yolanda Huizer, naked and blue, relaxing into incontinence there in Merle Puhl's bedroom? What the fuck. Blood tells you life is going, and shit tells you it's gone.

Tension is not ragged concentration, not fear of past and future failures so tight it sucks your nuts up into your lungs like a pair of tumors.

Tension is not staring almost hypnotically down upon a crazy goddamn meadow, trying to imagine how some idiot had conjured up the ghosts of Indians.

Tension is not getting slowly to your feet, moving on step by cautious, boring step through the forest.

There. He was not tense. It was easy. One foot after the other. He might not be *interesting,* but at least he was on the move. At any second he might die from a high-velocity bullet slamming into his chest, turning his heart and lungs into hamburger. Death by inertia, though, was the one prospect he refused to endure.

Picking his way along a game trail up the back side of the outcrop under which he had rested, Bartell now caught another

glimpse of Red Wolf, a spectacular gray crag, against the cold
and cloudless sky. He pulled up for a moment and glanced back
down at the meadow. Something like a memory or a dream flickered just out of sight at the fringes of his mind. Then everything,
all of it, the whole works, crystallized. Fanning and the sheriff's
crew could block out and search the lower country from now till
hell froze over, and they'd never come away with anything more
than a hefty bill for the taxpayers. It might take a psychoanalyst
to understand the *why* of things, but the *what* was as obvious
and perfect as the ground on which Bartell now stood, and he
could sense that perfection as clearly as if it were part of his own
body. Spiritual geography, he thought.

No. Do not think.

Don't stagger off into analysis and romance.

Do not think.

Not *now*.

Without hesitating another instant, he cinched down the straps
on his knapsack and trudged up the slope. A few yards ahead he
heard a loud smack on the boulder near his head, and felt the
sting of tiny shrapnel against his the side of his face. He never
heard the shot at all.

"Ordinarily," the cop said, "I'd try to convince you this wasn't
the end of the world."

Skelton's chest felt heavy as he let the air draw in and out, the
wind playing through his insides. He held up his hand and
peered at Bartell as if the gap where the finger once wagged
were a gun site. "End of the world. What's that?"

The cop spit on the ground between his stocking feet. "I don't
know. Maybe it's today. Maybe it's always." His eyes were locked
into Skelton's, ignoring altogether the rifle that Skelton maintained pointed at his belly.

Philosopher. A philosopher cop. Low-rent version of the philosopher king? King of what?

"The woman was a mistake," Skelton said. He'd ordered Bartell to move away from his own rifle and pack, and then to remove his boots.

"I know," Bartell said.

"But not the other one."

"You mean the one you saw that night at Cradle Creek."

"So you figured it out."

"Most of it. But don't ask me what I'm going to do. I don't know."

Skelton studied the lead smudge where the bullet had struck near Bartell's head. A gray flower splayed across the black-and-white-speckled granite. He'd reached the midpoint of the draw ahead of Bartell, then lain in wait, catching sporadic glimpses of Bartell during the course of the climb up from the meadow. By the time he'd placed that shot near Bartell's head, the cop had been close enough to hit with a decently thrown rock.

"I don't care what you do," Skelton said. He and Bartell were now squatting, facing each other, with Skelton still strapped tightly inside his pack, which he used as a backrest.

"For a man who just wanted to be left alone," Bartell said, "you sure managed to get in everybody's way."

"Toss your boots over here," Skelton said.

Bartell complied, and the boots landed with a soft thud at Skelton's feet.

"The reasonable man," Skelton said. "Always the reasonable man. How come you let them send you up here to get killed?"

"Nobody sent me."

"Scared?"

No answer.

"Feel like the whole universe's crowding down on you? Like you're about to get busted in the head by a falling star?"

"I never had a *Wyakin*," Bartell said. "Guess I skipped school the day they passed out the guardian spirits."

"I was a Methodist."

Bartell scowled. "What?"

"Skip it."

Bartell felt the tension drain out of the muscles inside his face. Curiously, he wasn't afraid. And he wasn't angry either. In fact, if Skelton stopped talking long enough, Bartell might have dropped off to sleep. "Aren't you tired, Henry? I'm tired as hell." The coat over Skelton's left shoulder was blood-soaked.

Skelton started to laugh, then winced as the jostling of the pack streaked pain through his shoulder. "For a couple of guys who didn't want to do anything, we sure as Christ managed to get some miles on us."

"Look, you've killed one of the worst of the bunch. And Arnold Zillion—that guy in the car with me yesterday?—he'll be okay too. This thing here." Bartell gestured to the lead blossom on the nearby rock. "That's nothing but a calling card. I know that. Why don't the two of us just walk on back down to the road. Before we both pass out."

Was this nothing more, Bartell thought, than a replay of that night so many years ago, when his partner had "saved" him from another man with a gun? Which disturbed him more, Skelton in the flesh, or the thought of Skelton suddenly tumbling over dead thanks to another hidden savior? And why, after nearly a decade, must that question even haunt him at all?

"I might do that," Skelton said. The rifle, trained all this time with his good hand on Bartell, now felt heavy as the mountain itself. Skelton lowered the rifle, cradled it in the crook of his elbow. "Except for that woman. What was her name anyhow?"

"Yolanda. Yolanda Huizer."

"Damn." Skelton let his head settle back onto the top of the pack and closed his eyes. "God"—he let out a sigh—"damn," he whispered.

At that moment, when Skelton seemed almost comatose with grief, Bartell thought about trying to take him. Dismissed the prospect out of hand. The long trajectories of their lives had finally touched, not collided exactly, as he would have expected, but docked for a moment at a common outpost there in the shade of granite, fir, and gathering winter. It was as though he and Skelton had captured each other, and this marvelous shrinking wild country now contained them both.

"The woman," Skelton said. "Just so you understand I never intended that."

Intent, Bartell thought. Intent was a legal concept, and by now both he and Skelton were ages beyond legalities. "You know the last thing God says to you?" Bartell asked. "He says, 'Buddy, I don't give a shit what you claim you intended.'"

"That's about it," Skelton said.

Bartell was tired of word games. "If you're not going with me," he said, "then get on out of here." The other searchers had surely heard Skelton's shot. How long would it be before they sorted out the echoes and put it together with what Fanning would probably tell them about directing him to the meadow? "Go on, haul your sorry ass back into the trees."

Skelton straightened now and returned the rifle to bear on Bartell. "Why is it I'm the one holding a gun on you, but you're the one talking like he's letting me go?"

"Because you can walk every inch of this mountain, but you'll never walk off that woman last night. Let's just say I'll take particular satisfaction in letting you try it until your legs drop off."

Skelton shook his head and heaved himself to his feet. "Man, you really are an asshole."

"Thanks."

Stepping to Bartell's pack, Skelton knelt haltingly under his own load, opened the pack, and shook its contents out onto the ground. Among the gear he found Bartell's police walkie-talkie, which he held momentarily like a trophy.

Bartell thought at first that Skelton had sought out the radio for his own use in monitoring the search. Instead, the big man regained his full height, then dropped the radio onto the rocks and smashed it several times under the heel of his boot.

"You should have killed me yesterday," Skelton said. "Way back down there on the road by my house."

"God knows I tried."

Chapter 31

Bartell waited for twenty minutes before setting off up the draw after Skelton. It never occurred to him for even an instant that just because he was disarmed and bootless, he should return to the truck. And when, less than two hundred yards on, he saw his boots and rifle sitting prominently atop a boulder near the middle of a small park, he knew that Skelton had never entertained the notion either. That meant Skelton wanted him on the mountain too. No reason, as far as Bartell could understand. But since when had Skelton's motives ever made sense to anyone but himself?

For the next several hours Bartell's only concern was getting onto Red Wolf ahead of Skelton. He ran on fiery legs and sucked air into screaming lungs, all with no thought of anything save beating Skelton onto that mountain. Over downed trees, soft stretches of moss-covered scree, and at times nearly on all fours up talus slopes, above a grove of huge cedars, sometimes running all out until his body came to a screeching standstill. Anything he do could to keep one step ahead of the *why* of it all. He gave up all thought of concealing himself from Skelton, and also of glassing the mountain in search of him. For reasons that were as unintelligible as Skelton's, Bartell knew where he had to go, and his only concern was getting there.

Endure, he said to himself over and over. *Endure, endure, endure.*

It was nearly noon by the time Bartell made his way up the west face of Red Wolf. There he changed tactics, easing his way under the summit, moving a few feet at a time, always under cover, stopping frequently to scan the country below through the binoculars. At last he moved onto the east face at the edge of a steep boulder field overlooking all of Cradle Creek, and it was there that he perched himself. About three hundred yards below, near the tree line, a pocket of steam hung in the air above a hot spring. The area around the spring was the only place he couldn't see clearly. Even through the binoculars the view there was, at best, a green haze.

Now waiting became a different kind of chore. Waiting is when things gain on you. Another kind of endurance.

The altitude, Bartell figured, was probably just over ten thousand feet. About sixty-five hundred feet higher than Rozette, on the floor of the Holt Valley. The view reached for miles. Maybe two hundred miles. The mountain rose in a series of tiers, so most of the lower canyon was blocked from view. To the distant south and east, though, the world unfolded in a bright gold-and-green mosaic under a constant blue. Then swinging north, heavy clouds had begun to break above Rozette, exposing a landscape of perfect unbroken white from last night's fast, hard storm.

So where was Skelton?

Abruptly, Bartell lifted the binoculars again and scanned the ragged forest immediately below.

In custody already?

Dead? Bartell hadn't heard any shots.

No way of telling

How long do you wait? Forever?

Don't be stupid.

At least until dusk, though, now that he had his boots and his rifle back.

And what were the chances, then, that he'd bumble again into Skelton's gun site while climbing down off Red Wolf in the dark?

Bartell lowered the glasses and dug a sandwich from his knapsack. More then once he'd considered abandoning his perch to make a series of broad passes through the lower country, working his way back to the truck. Screw Skelton. Let somebody else find him. Let him wander off altogether. What was he going to do? Freeze to death during the coming winter? Become just another set of bones found years from now by hunters or berry pickers?

But that was just impatience talking. He chewed a mouthful of sandwich. Ham and cheese. Impatience and anxiety. The sandwich was good. Impatience plus anxiety equals stupid. And that's what giving up both cover and high ground amounted to, even if you're convinced the prey's not out to kill you. Stupid.

He took another bite of sandwich.

Too bad Merle Puhl and his boy Duckworth couldn't come up here. Maybe they'd learn something. What though? What kind of silly idealism did Bartell suppose might rub off on them out here in the country? Guys like Puhl and Duckworth, they're all about power, pissing on fire hydrants. Everything they touch, every word they speak, it's all just so much currency in an unending transaction involving power. Sure, the guy who gets the high ground first gets the chance to call his own shot and make it good. But Puhl already knew that by heart. Who says wilderness will teach you anything about what shot to call?

Mulling things over as he chewed the last of his sandwich, Bartell realized that all through this job he had given scarcely a moment's thought to the politics of the situation. From the first time he'd been briefed by Vic Fanning, until this very moment on the side of Red Wolf, he had done his job. Period. Maybe Zillion was right. The cops are nothing but muscle. Society's brain comes from somewhere else.

What about its conscience, then? There he went again, slogging into the mire of *why*.

Bartell was about to start through his knapsack for more food, when something below caught his eye. A flash of movement to the left of, and below, the hot spring.

Skelton.

Unconsciously, Bartell settled deeper into the rocks and brought the binoculars to his eyes.

With slow deliberation Skelton picked his way through the mangled trees, appearing to slump toward his left side as he walked. The rifle was slung on his right shoulder, and the large pack, blue, still rode high on his back. Once, twice, Skelton held up and glanced briefly back down the mountain. That was good. People on the run tend to guard their backs. As long as Skelton remained preoccupied with who might be on his heels, maybe he wouldn't pay much mind to what lay ahead.

Bartell made a quick scan of the tree line, and was about to lower the binoculars, when something else caught his eye. Not movement, really, but some kind of shape out of context in the margins of the swirling steam across the spring from Skelton. Something not quite right.

There. As Bartell watched, more awestruck than he would ever have imagined, a grizzly nosed its way up onto the last tier below the summit, working a leisurely course along the marsh.

He moved through gnarled spruce and junipers not far below where the mountain opened onto tundra. The glaring sunlight did little for the cold except harden it, drive it deep into joints that wanted nothing so much as a long rest. The ground underfoot was mottled with the browns and tans of bare earth and lichen-covered rocks. Like the back of a stony paw, Red Wolf punched through the tundra slope above, a bright gray slab against the indigo mat of the western sky.

Ahead, the slope folded gently into itself. A veil of steam rose above the trees, and the trees themselves glistened with hoarfrost. Closer to the steam, the underbrush thickened, then opened into a wide marsh, where the hot spring seeped out from underground. Near the center of the marsh, a warm pool was surrounded by thick, delicate ferns.

Tired with the season, he stepped tentatively into the glade, where it might be eternal summer. As he moved closer to the pool, the ground turned to mud, mud that was warm against his feet.

Then he was distracted by the rattle of brush, the wet, sucking noise of something moving through cover on the far side of the pool.

He opened his mouth, poised his face in the direction of the noise, and slowly drew in air through both his nose and mouth, trying to catch a scent. But all he could smell was the damp, sulfurous reek rising from the hot spring.

Now there was more noise, this time with movement, quick and determined. Acting on instinct alone, he tensed himself all the way down into the ground and got ready. Ready for noise and blood.

Very slowly, Bartell lowered himself out of view, exchanged the binoculars for the rifle. When he looked up again, finding first Skelton, then the bear, in the scope, he tried to imagine how things could possibly turn out well. So far as he could tell, neither Skelton nor the bear were aware of each other, or of him. By rights, the bear should long since have winded Skelton.

Killer or not, Skelton was still a man, and at least twice he had made a gift of life to Bartell. What true choice was there? Bartell wasn't sure he had enough gun to handle the bear at this distance, but if nothing else, a .30—06 slug, or at the very least the noise of the shot, should distract the bear from Skelton. Without hesitating, Bartell thumbed back the hammer on the Browning and leveled the cross hairs square on the tip of the bear's nose.

Jesus Christ, the bear was beautiful. The most beautiful sight, perhaps, Bartell had ever seen. All glistening there in the midday sun, an exquisite monster foraging ahead through the steam.

Bartell was about to shoot, when a bead of sweat seeped into his eye, blurring his vision. He turned his head away, dug at the eye with the heel of hand. Then, just as he found the bear again in the scope, the bear pivoted abruptly toward Skelton.

Bartell reflexively swung the rifle onto Skelton, half expecting to find that he had also drawn down on the bear.

Skelton had seen the bear now too, but he hadn't pulled the rifle off his shoulder. Instead, he kept on moving deeper into the marsh. As best Bartell could tell, he was in a staring contest with the grizzly.

And Bartell thought: I have a duty.

Abruptly, Skelton shrugged off both the rifle and the pack, letting them drop to the ground.

Bartell jerked the rifle back to the bear, looking for one quick, desperate shot.

The bear reared onto its hind legs, offering his heart to a shot.

Bartell's finger pressed against the trigger.

And that duty is?

Bartell's body told him the answer. At that moment it was as though another hand folded against his shooting hand, freezing it. And when he felt his hand and shoulders relax, the moment was gone.

Now Skelton charged headlong into the marsh, and almost instantly the bear was moving too, churning full tilt to meet Skelton.

Bartell checked himself a last, desperate time, and with more certainty than he had ever known, he let them go.

Both figures were soon lost in the steam. Later, Bartell would understand that there must have been snarling and screams, because surely neither Skelton nor the bear could have gone silently into that catastrophe. In truth, though, Bartell's memory was silent. A silence unblemished by even the rasping internal noises of his own body.

Holding tight the rifle, Bartell heaved himself over the lip of his hiding place and went scrambling down the boulder field toward the spring. He ran across the tundra to Skelton's gear, then pulled up, listening carefully. Through the scope he peered into the steam, but the bench containing the marsh dipped away abruptly, and he saw no sign of either Skelton or the bear. But there was no difficulty in spotting Skelton's tracks through the mud. Keeping the rifle shouldered, Bartell crept ahead into the steam.

One, two, three steps . . .

Nothing. No sound or movement.

. . . fifteen . . . . . .

Goddamn, what happened, where were they?

. . . twenty-eight . . . twenty nine . . .

He felt as though he might drown in the sulfurous steam. The mud was hot, soaking through his boots, sucking his feet deep into the mountain, making a deafening noise he was certain would draw the bear. All around, the trees, deformed by centuries of wind, seemed to reach out for him, clutch at him like ancient arms, through the bright cloud.

. . . thirty-four.

Now the mud was all churned up and splattered with blood. He saw the bear's tracks approaching from across the marsh.

The trail led downstream, over the rim of the bench. Bartell turned slowly to follow, and caught sight of something out of place, foreign, laying on a bed of kinnikinnick. Using touch rather than sight—he needed his eyes for the bear—he crouched down to examine it.

A hand.

Fuck an A, it was a hand, a fucking hand, a left hand with one finger missing. At rest there on kinnikinnick that glistened like green tears.

Bartell swallowed bile and fear, then set the hand aside and edged his way ahead, off the bench.

Once off the bench, he was on dry ground again, following a blood trail alongside the thin creek that drained the marsh. He'd gone maybe fifteen, twenty yards, when the steam lifted. He squatted on his heels and studied what lay ahead.

A thick finger of brush closed around the creek, then fanned out into heavier timber. The blood trail, rich and easy to follow, disappeared into the trees. There were bear tracks in the dirt and blood, but no tracks from a man.

Bartell moved on. He could still taste the sulfur, like rotten eggs. When he got to the edge of the trees, he stopped and studied again. It had been terrible moving through the marsh, and bad enough out in the open where he could see, and have at least a second or two to react. He did not want to follow the blood trail into heavy cover.

And then he saw it. A boot. Sticking out from behind a clump of junipers.

Bartell covered the distance to the boot in just a few steps. Thankfully, the boot was still attached to Skelton's foot, and the foot was still attached to the rest of Skelton, who lay on his belly, the remains of his left arm under him, and his mangled right arm sprawled out along his head. He nudged Skelton's hip with the toe of his boot. Nothing happened. And when he knelt and rolled the man over, he saw that nothing would ever happen for Henry Skelton again.

In addition to the missing hand, Skelton's belly and throat had been torn open, and there was no pulse from the throat. His eyes, both open, were flat and dry. At whatever instant the end had finally come, Skelton was looking dead square into it.

Bartell had seen plenty of dead people, enough that his interest in Skelton's body was soon purely clinical. But the tension of *finding* the sonofabitch, that was something else. Bartell felt his whole body slump. He settled onto his aching knees, took a moment to compose himself, then got to his feet and studied long and deep into the forest.

The next job was to get down off the mountain in one piece, then send a crew back up to collect the stiff and the assorted debris, a task he doubted could be done before dark. So Skelton's body might remain on the mountain overnight, a situation that could result in the bear coming back to feed. At first Bartell shrugged off the notion of Skelton being bear food. A guy decides to be an insane murderer, he forfeits a certain degree of dignity when it comes to how people think about his earthly remains.

Gina, on the other hand, was not an insane murderer. Briefly, Bartell flirted with the idea of trying to carry Skelton out himself. For Gina's sake.

Screw it. He might be a nice guy, relatively speaking, but not that nice. He also doubted that his body was up to the task.

Shouldering the rifle, Bartell fired off a round into the sky, then ejected the spent brass and dropped it onto Skelton's chest. An old hunter's trick, said to keep coyotes off the carcass of an elk or a deer. Something about the smell from the burned gunpowder. Hell, maybe it worked with humans and bears too. Couldn't hurt. And maybe the noise of the shot would spook the bear enough to keep him away from Bartell.

"So long, pard," Bartell said to the body of Henry Skelton. "Happy trails." Then he reloaded the rifle and started cautiously down the mountain.

Following the creek, he was less than a minute away from the body, when he heard something off to his right, a crackling at first like a whisper that became a full-blown crash in less time than it took to look. Already fully wired, he brought the rifle up without thinking, and by the time he saw it, the crash had grown into a cyclone of rippling silver fur, rage, and speed.

The rifle went off wild, and he took the bear full in the chest, felt something rip into his right thigh and shoulder before tumbling under the charge into the creek.

He lay very still. Head downstream, left cheek in the water. Warm water, seeping into his clothes. The water felt soothing. It was very quiet again. He concentrated on how good the water felt, how utterly simple and good. He did not move.

For a long time Bartell worked very hard at not moving. He concentrated briefly on the pain scorching through his leg and shoulder. He took control of the pain, and then set it aside, and listened to the water trickling around his body. He listened for other sounds too, but he didn't hear any. He smelled the sulfur in the water, and he wondered if that's what hell smelled like. Decided that it didn't. Couldn't. Nothing that warm and gentle could have anything to do with hell. Not today anyway. Finally, he lifted his head slowly and stared down at the water. A thread of blood, his blood, coursed through the stream, weaving over the rocks on the erratic current. There was absolutely no reason, no reason on God's earth, why he was not dead.

Winter

Chapter 32

Christmas. Christmas Eve, really. The damage done to Bartell by the bear had taken more time to heal than expected, and he'd been back on the job for only a couple of weeks. The truth was, he probably could have gone back soon after Thanksgiving, but couldn't see much point to it. The paychecks kept coming, courtesy of workmen's comp, and the cases would always be there. Finally, he'd given in to the inevitable, gotten a haircut one afternoon, and the next morning dressed himself up in a jacket and tie and hooked a ride downtown with Helen. Fanning seemed grudgingly pleased to have him back. The other detectives were more enthusiastic. They were tired of picking up the slack while he'd been gone. Linda Westhammer immediately asked him if he wouldn't like to take over one of her cases, some deal about a guy who claimed getting arrested for molesting his girlfriend's ten-year-old son interfered with the separation of church and state. Why not, Bartell told her.

Arnold Zillion was back on line in Great Falls, but the word was he already had his retirement papers in the mill. And Gina Lozano was still working at St. Francis. She and Helen had even met for lunch several times since that long, ugly week in October.

Helen, yes. Helen had been the best during the few days he'd spent in the hospital. And through the following weeks of convalescence, she'd been quite merciful in tempering her efforts to get him to have good, positive thoughts. So merciful, really, that he'd actually had one or two. For instance, none of Jess's close friends had been arrested yet. What could be a more positive thought than that?

The one thing, though, that did not generate any positive thoughts, was the election. Merle Puhl won. A landslide. He'd taken off in the polls the day after all the shooting, and gone through the roof once the public understood just what kind of scum Puhl had been forced to confront. For all Bartell knew, the honorable old senator himself even voted for Puhl.

Bartell had taken a stab at the truth, advancing his theory about the bombing both to his own bosses and to the federal investigators. Take Ed Morley, for instance. What did anybody know about Ed Morley? What people knew, Fanning said, was that Morley was the staff member of a candidate for the United States Senate, and he'd been murdered. What more did anybody need to know? Should they investigate Yolanda Huizer too? Was she a secret agent too?

Give it a rest, Bartell, you're on a fast track to the lunatic fringe. Heated advice from Vic Fanning.

And so now Ray Bartell was on his way home at the end of his second week back on the job. It was dark, and it was snowing. And it was almost Christmas. Heading up the long hill into Yellow Pine, he looked out at the bright holiday lights sparkling all up and down the canyon.

451—396.

Bartell scowled down at the radio.

Go ahead, a voice answered: 451 was Collie Proell, a twenty-year patrolman with an ex-wife, a new wife, and a new baby. Years ago, in what seemed another lifetime, Bartell and Proell worked the street together. They'd had coffee together the night Paul Culp shot George Rather.

Family disturbance, 1853 Lamont.

Christmas was the season for family disturbances. It was the season when people loved and hated each other in equal disproportion to the rest of the year, and poured enough booze down their throats to make sure everybody got the message.

10-4, Proell answered.

And then another voice: *Maybe daddy came home, found Santa munching his goodies.* One of the new guys, whose voice Bartell didn't recognize. Bartell was reminded of the deputy that night at the road into Puhl's house. More and more, it seemed, both the PD and the sheriff's office were hiring rookies who believed a cop needed black leather gloves just to write a traffic pinch.

Bartell switched off the radio.

Back around the middle of November, Bartell actually received a call from one of those true cop shows. A production assistant had read the Skelton story on the wire and wanted to know if Bartell was interested in having it done.

"A gig," Cassidy called it when he'd stopped by Bartell's house a few days after the woman called. Cassidy was in high spirits and wanted Bartell to know that he'd settled his grievance with Brandon McWilliams over the purloined plot. While McWilliams hadn't come clean on that deal, he had decided to develop the whole Skelton story and hired Cassidy to write the first draft of the screenplay.

"That's the good news," Cassidy said. The bad news was that McWilliams was going to play the Vic Fanning part, and Fanning himself was signed on as technical adviser. The working title was *Wild Man.* If Cassidy was at all embarrassed to be telling Bartell all this, he didn't let on.

"It's too bad those TV people won't take your story," he said.

"No car chase," Bartell said, remembering their earlier conversation while he concentrated very hard on not raving about Fanning. If McWilliams had once upon a time stolen an idea from Cassidy, what was the magnitude of Fanning's theft?

Cassidy laughed. "You got it, pal."

"But Skelton shot a couple of people. And I fired a whole bunch of shots at him. And somebody"—he said that pointedly —"somebody blew up a car right outside there in my driveway."

"Car chase."

"What about the crash with Zillion?"

Cassidy waved him off excitedly. "No, no, no. You don't understand, Ray. A car *crash* is not a car *chase.* And you may have fired enough shots to end a small war, even hit the sonofabitch . . . but you didn't put him *down.* And Skelton shooting people doesn't count, since nobody shot him back on the spot."

"What about the ostriches? Don't all those slaughtered ostriches count for something?"

"Maybe," Cassidy said, "if it was an endangered species. But *ostriches,* hell, they're practically farm animals these days. No. Sorry, but it all adds up to low production values." Cassidy pondered for a moment. "You tell those TV people what you think of our new senator-elect?" By then Bartell's views were no secret around the office.

"No. I'm not in the market to get sued."

"Forget it, then," Cassidy advised. "Sooner or later you'd start demanding to tell the whole truth, because that's the way you are. Who needs that kind of grief?"

It took Bartell fifteen seconds to understand that Cassidy was only partly right, several days later the TV woman called back, and said everyone at the network was completely sold on his story. And she was very gracious when he told her he'd decided to pass.

As far as the official version of what happened on Red Wolf, Bartell had reduced the essentials down to the barren phrases of a police report, leaving out his meeting with Skelton halfway up the mountain. He'd also left out the fact that he might have been able to save Skelton's life, but chose not to. Officially, Detective Ray Bartell had stumbled across the dismembered body of Henry Skelton, then been attacked by a bear—presumably the same bear that had killed Skelton—while heading back down the mountain for help. Those reports were now buried with the rest of the file, which included ballistic reports linking bullet jackets from the shooting at Puhl's to Skelton's rifle.

Now, rolling easily down the street to his house on Christmas Eve, Bartell followed a set of tire tracks through the new snow and was surprised to find that the tracks led to a shiny blue Range Rover that was parked in his driveway. For one insane moment Bartell wondered if his wife had won the lottery, and the Range Rover was his for Christmas.

No. A new Chevy pickup at best. And probably the small model. Millions or not, Helen would believe a Range Rover was too flashy to enhance his well-being. Something was up.

Looking through the window as he walked up to the door, Bartell saw his father sitting on a stool at the kitchen counter, laughing his head off as he looked back into the living room. And there was music too, Bob Wills and the Texas Playboys, lilting out of the stereo. Inside, he found Helen dancing with Brandon McWilliams himself.

"Oh," Helen said, breaking off in mid-spin when she saw her husband.

"Ray!" his old man said, rushing to meet him. "Ray! Goddammit, son, Merry Christmas."

Jess was sitting on the stone ledge at the edge of the fireplace, gazing up at McWilliams as though she wanted to run off and sin with him.

"Howdy," McWilliams said, stepping forward and offering his hand. He wore tight black jeans, a white western shirt with embroidered roses above the pockets, and black ostrich-skin boots. His silver belt buckle, big as a dinner plate, bore a large red heart cleaved in half.

McWilliams turned to the old man. "By golly, Cash, you were right. He's everything you said."

"I miss something?" Bartell said, by now completely bewildered.

"Ain't he though," Cash said, giggling again.

"He wants you to be in the new movie," Helen said, giggling herself.

Bartell eyed McWilliams. "The one you're doing with Cassidy and Fanning?"

McWilliams didn't miss a beat. "Casting's way down the road on that one."

"Busted Heart 2," Cash said.

"To play the sheriff's sidekick," Jess said.

Cops, Bartell thought. Everybody wants to talk about one, watch one, read about one, know one, study one, write about one. *Play* one. But not very many seriously want to *be* one. The thought made Bartell feel smug and arrogant. Fuck it. Now and then you're entitled. Half the time, not even the cops want to be cops. But that other half, that was what got under your skin.

"My good buddy Cash told me you were perfect," Brandon McWilliams said. "And I have to say the first time I met you, I said, baby, that old man is one hundred and ten percent right."

As he thought about this appraisal, Bartell didn't know whether to rejoice or burst into tears. He had experienced perfection firsthand on Red Wolf, and this development sure as hell wasn't perfect. But it wasn't bad either. Taking Helen in his arms, he two-stepped her across the living room.

"You remember," he whispered into Helen's ear, "that night in Polson? After we danced to fiddle music in the parking lot at the Ben Franklin?"

"Ray!" Helen gasped, throwing a cautionary glance at Jess. "You're absolutely wicked."

"It's a great part," McWilliams said. "You get to have me save your life."

Bartell twirled Helen under his arm, then caught her up and

kissed her. She was still smiling at him, when he said to McWilliams, "Maybe so. But what's it pay?"

And Helen whispered: "Not enough."

Late that night it began snowing heavily, and outside the bedroom window, the neighbors' flashing Christmas lights colored the snow like confetti. Bartell fished around under Helen's pillow for the remote control, found it, and punched mute, choking off some suit on CNN in mid-scream. He slipped his arm under Helen's shoulders and pulled her close so that her head lay on his chest.

"I have to tell you this."

"What—"

"No. Don't say anything. And don't look at me. Just be still and listen."

And then he told her. All of it, in a way he'd never opened up to her before. Every shade of what had transpired between himself, Skelton, and the bear on Red Wolf. As he spoke, he felt her breath deep and steady against his bare chest, felt the tickle of her eyelashes when she blinked, heard her sniffle.

"I want you to understand," Bartell told his wife, "he charged into that bear on purpose. And I let it happen. You hear me, Helen? *I let it all happen.*"

Helen stirred, and he was afraid she was drawing away from him. Instead, she rooted herself more deeply under his arm. "Even after he could have shot you, but he let you go instead. Let you live."

"That's right."

"But why did he do it?"

"With me, or the bear?"

"The bear."

"Because he knew he was wrong."

"And why didn't you stop it?"

"Because Skelton deserved it."

And so now Helen was the only other person who knew the whole story. As for everyone else, it was none of their business. Unless you counted the bear.

Once everybody was safely off the mountain, a pair of hunters from the Fish and Wildlife Service set about tracking that grizzly down to kill it. A problem bear, they said. But Bartell figured any bear that would kill Skelton and then take the trouble to leave him alive couldn't be all *that* much of a problem. It didn't matter though, since the bear turned out to be smart as well as a problem, and nobody had seen that bear since the moment when Bartell looked down its throat, figured he was dead, and prayed it would be over fast.

He thought again about that marvelous beast, that bear with a belly full of Henry Skelton, somewhere out there in the country, tucked away under snow, and knotted in sleep.

Yes. The bear.